Keep the
HOME FIRES
BURNING

First published in Great Britain in 2018 by

ZAFFRE PUBLISHING
80-81 Wimpole St, London W1G 9RE
www.zaffrebooks.co.uk

Map illustration by Robyn Neild

A CIP catalogue record for this book is
available from the British Library.

ISBN: 978-1-78576-360-1

also available as an ebook

1 3 5 7 9 10 8 6 4 2

Typeset by IDSUK (Data Connection) Ltd
Printed by Berryville Graphics

Zaffre Publishing is an imprint of Bonnier Zaffre,
a Bonnier Publishing company
www.bonnierzaffre.co.uk
www.bonnierpublishing.co.uk

Keep the
HOME FIRES
BURNING

S. Block

ZAFFRE

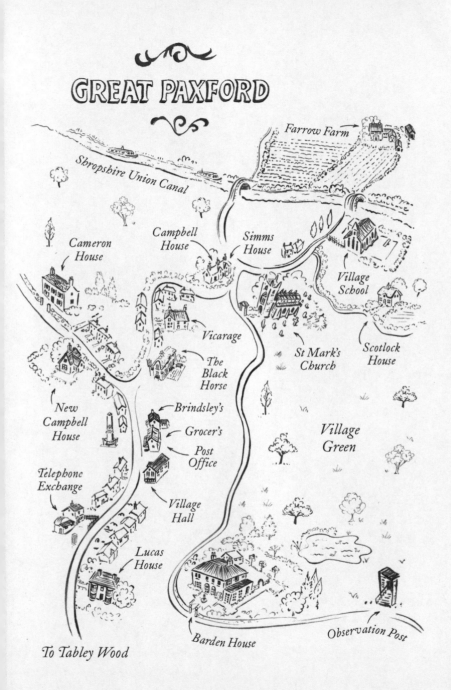

For Kerryn and Jess, without whom this book would simply not exist

Prologue

PAT SIMMS STOOD BEFORE a scene of such outlandish devastation that she couldn't move. The harsh Cheshire wind drove icy drops of rain into her face and eyes at an acute angle, forcing Pat to wipe it away with her hands to get a clear sight of what lay before her. Having run from the village as fast as she could manage in her best dress and shoes, she was struggling for breath. For a few moments she believed that perhaps it was the lack of oxygen that caused her to hallucinate the vision in front of her.

A Spitfire was sticking out of a house in her village.

As she gasped for breath, Pat thought it so ridiculous it couldn't possibly be real. She *must* be imagining it – the tableau as a whole, but also its details. Smoke rising from the wreckage. The silhouette of a pilot in the cockpit, slouched against the closed canopy, splashed with red. The intact tail and broken wings. Even the smell of aviation fuel.

Is it possible to hallucinate a smell?

To prove she was imagining it all, Pat looked behind her to confirm there was no trace of where this phantom plane had come from. She then reasoned that if the Spitfire had come from the sky there would *be* no trace. To her left she noticed the fresh damage to the church she had been sitting in just hours earlier. Then behind the church, Pat saw the shattered chimney stacks smashed from another rooftop, reduced to bricks and dust on the wet ground.

I can't be imagining all of this.

She was getting her breath back. This was real.

She turned back to the scene that had stopped her in her tracks. Only a sight as incongruous as this could have done that. Only something so utterly extraordinary would have over-ridden her mission to seek out her lover before it was too late.

Pat stared at the Spitfire and realised it had crushed the house it was embedded in. It looked like a huge bird lying in a brick nest. Pat looked around for someone to call out to, then recalled that the entire village was celebrating the wedding in the village hall, from where she'd just run.

And then Pat heard it.

From beneath the doomed Spitfire.

From beneath the fresh rubble.

A newborn baby's cry, struggling into the air through the gaps between the smashed, fuel-soaked masonry.

Plaintive, outraged, and despairing.

Calling out to its mother to save its life, wherever she might be.

PART ONE

Spitfire Down!

PART ONE

Chapter 1

Two weeks earlier

OVERLOOKED BY ITS fourteenth-century church at one end, and by Cholmondeley Castle at the other, attached to the outside world by a single thin road and the slender ribbon of the Shropshire Union canal, Great Paxford had quietly minded its own business at the intersection of three Cheshire hills for over six hundred years.

Nothing came into the village that wasn't seen by most of its inhabitants. Nothing of note took place that wasn't heard by most as it happened, or told to the rest within the hour. Privacy within such a small, rural community was almost impossible. Gossip and secrets were commodities, exchanged and bartered day and night, the transactions part of the tight social fabric.

Though the Great War had left deep scars on individual minds and families of Great Paxford, in subsequent years its citizens had fallen into the understandable habit of taking one another for granted. Prior to the declaration of a second world war just twenty-one years after the first, there would always be tomorrow to drop round for a chinwag, resolve a dispute, or do a good turn. But from 11.15 a.m. on 3 September 1939, anyone owed an apology for something, or who might benefit from a favour or a rebuke, could be killed by a bomb in the night. Every book read, every meal enjoyed, every cup of tea either drunk in haste or lingered over with a friend, every walk in the countryside, every moment of lovemaking, every breath and heartbeat might be your last. Every German bomb and bullet had someone's name on it. War made life more fragile, and each lived moment more intense.

Before war's outbreak, the regulars at the Black Horse barely registered the voices of their wives, sisters and daughters singing 'Jerusalem' at the start of yet another monthly meeting of the village's Women's Institute. At 7 p.m. on the first Thursday of every month, their voices rose as one from Great Paxford's small village hall, to the general indifference of the men a hundred yards up the road in the pub. But since the onset of war, on those Thursday evenings, the men had started to wander out onto the road with their pints, and stand in the soft moonlight to listen to their women sing with a distinct edge of defiance about their newly endangered green and pleasant land.

The meeting on this Thursday evening in October 1940 was particularly important. Outside the village hall, crows in the trees that surrounded Great Paxford were settling for the night under a cloudless sky. Inside the hall, members of the WI sat back into their seats after the last notes of 'Jerusalem' signalled the start of the evening proper. The women sat shoulder to shoulder in silence, facing the executive committee on the raised platform before them. The hall was charged with nervous excitement, for tonight was to see the return of their elected Chair, Frances Barden, to lead the branch for the first time since her husband had been killed in a rather horrific car accident just five months earlier. Joyce Cameron, the previous Chair, had been asked to helm the branch while Frances had stepped down to grieve, and sort out her husband's considerable and complicated affairs.

Joyce was a small, well-dressed, intelligent woman with a natty taste in expensive hats that invariably sported a pheasant's feather. Her face was soft and round, her skin smooth and pale, untroubled by the elements. Her expression could switch from benign to venomous in an instant. After moving to Great Paxford from Oxford with her solicitor husband some years earlier, Joyce had led a comfortable life of relative leisure, busying herself on local committees and organisations. While her husband became a local magistrate, and joined the local Rotary and golf clubs, Joyce had immersed herself in the WI, had become a governor of the local school, and involved herself in several small local charitable organisations that gave assistance to the rural poor. In each organisation, Joyce earned a reputation as an effective scourge, frequently asking questions no one else dared ask, often bullying others to get her way.

'Thank you, ladies. Settle down, please.' Joyce's voice was clipped and authoritative. When she asked for quiet she got it.

Joyce's beady eyes looked over the members, gauging the mood in the hall. She wondered if it hadn't been a mistake to have held back from trying to take over as Chair on a permanent basis, while Frances had been mourning for her husband. Joyce's younger self wouldn't have hesitated. Joyce had always been one-tenth demagogue – probably two-tenths, perhaps three. She instinctively knew which levers to pull to get her way on most issues. Where others may have hesitated, Joyce never lacked the steel to drive home an advantageous hand. She not only had the stomach for Machiavellian wrangling, she possessed the liver and kidneys too. Her younger self would have seized back control within a month, 'in the best interests of the branch'.

But Joyce was no longer that woman. Having left the village with husband Douglas ten months earlier for a safer environment along the north-west coast at Heysham near Morecambe, 'beyond the interest of the Luftwaffe', as Douglas had put it, Joyce had reappeared in the village just a month and a half later. It hadn't taken Great Paxfordians long to notice the change in her. It was as if the time away had been an ordeal that had knocked her sideways. Indeed, the month away had been the most difficult of Joyce's life. During that period, she'd finally admitted that her marriage had been sterile for many years. Moving to Heysham had been Douglas's decision, and Joyce's loathing of life on the coast came upon her almost immediately. If it wasn't the wind it was the rain. If it wasn't the rain it was the salt on the air, or the lack of people like her, or the smell of fish everywhere, or the impenetrable grey sea stretching beyond the horizon, intensifying Joyce's sense that her life had become becalmed, and deepening her conviction that she no longer wanted to be Douglas's consort, wheeled out at social events to help him drum up business for his legal practice. If she didn't act decisively she felt this existence would claim her sanity. So she'd packed her suitcase and returned to Great Paxford, alone.

'Douglas,' she told those who asked, with a tone of fatigue in her voice, 'has long-standing ambitions to become a Conservative member of parliament, and is remaining in the north-west to pursue that. I wish him every success, but for myself . . . I want to see out the war among my *friends*, at *home*, in *Great Paxford*.'

Joyce concluded her potted explanation with a tired smile that said: *That is all I shall say on the matter.*

While Alison Scotlock considered Joyce's explanation characteristically grandiose, her fellow WI members weren't so certain about the change. Sarah Collingborne, the vicar's wife, was more charitable, believing the swiftly returned Joyce did *appear* to be less self-confident, less spiky, more subdued, even a little vulnerable.

Joyce looked down at the rows of women seated in front of her. Great Paxford's village hall wasn't large, but it always looked bigger than it was on WI nights, when it was full of local women. On those evenings, the old, whitewashed wooden walls and cobwebbed, gabled ceiling could barely contain their energy. Joyce could see the excitement in the women's eyes, and knew it wasn't for her. With a smile of resignation, she swallowed her inclination to speak, and turned to Frances. With a subtle nod of concession, Joyce ceded the chair of the branch committee back to the elected Chair and sat down behind the trestle table.

Frances was a dignified, educated, elegantly dressed woman in her early fifties, known to the women of Great Paxford as a woman of integrity and passion, given to acts of extreme kindness, but also extremely short on patience – a quality her sister

Sarah described as 'my sister's Achilles heel'. Frances tried to hide her uncharacteristic nerves with a broad, confident smile as she stood to address the women in front of her.

'Before anything else, I should like to thank Mrs Cameron for helming the branch so competently in my absence.'

Frances turned to Joyce and began to applaud her. Immediately, the membership followed suit. Given that she had been a competent but never an exciting branch Chair, the applause for Joyce was appreciative but not what anyone might call *enthusiastic* – managing to express a level of gratitude one might offer someone who turned down the heat on a pan before its contents boiled over. Joyce nevertheless accepted the expression of thanks with a graceful nod of the head. She was about to take advantage of the moment to say a few words, but as soon as she opened her mouth to speak, the applause abruptly stopped, and the moment immediately passed. Joyce closed her mouth and turned, with the others, to Frances.

Frances cleared her throat and took a deep breath. Every face beamed at her, bathing her in goodwill. It was entirely in character that Frances had prepared for this moment by drafting many possible speeches in recent days. She had abandoned them all on Sarah's advice to 'just speak from the heart'. Frances looked along the ranks of friendly faces, eager to hear from her after months away. She felt pleased to be back, yet carried an anxiety that with everything she had gone through in the aftermath of Peter's death she might have lost her capacity to lead. *I'm not the woman I was. Do I remain the woman the branch needs me to be?*

'It is so wonderful to be back. To see you all. To hear that hymn sung from the bottom of your hearts once again. With each day of war that passes, it grows in poignancy.'

She saw the women nod in solemn agreement. Frances clasped her hands in front of her, pressing the palms into one another, urging herself on.

'So much has changed since I last looked at you from this platform. I've lost my husband . . .'

She stopped for a moment. Every heart in the hall skipped a beat as the women wondered if Frances was yet ready to come back to them. Frances took a deep breath.

'I have taken in a child evacuee. While you . . . you are all so different too, in so many ways . . .'

Pat Simms, the WI's efficient, watchful and diligent Branch Secretary, sat on the platform behind Frances and reflected on what was different about herself since Frances last addressed them. *Nearly everything*, she concluded. *Because of Marek*. Pat smiled to herself as she recalled making love with the Czech soldier in her bed at home. She remembered the calm, reassuring look in Marek's eyes as they made love, the feel of his soft hands electrifying her skin. Though they were last together over two weeks ago, the intensity of the memory left Pat feeling it could have been that afternoon. She felt not one drop of remorse about the affair she was having.

Where her husband Bob had used Pat for his own satisfaction over the course of their thirteen-year marriage, Marek had been a tender and generous lover.

Where Bob existed in a state of perpetual anger and discontent, Marek had always been calm and effortlessly at ease with himself.

Where Bob's words towards Pat were patronising, dismissive, and stripped of affection, Marek's were always warm and elevating.

Where Bob was occasionally brutal towards Pat, Marek – well, when she had looked at his face in the concealing long grass outside the village, Pat had never felt more protected or more valued.

'I love you,' she had said tentatively for the first time, not knowing how he might respond. He had looked at her directly, his gaze only intensifying. Early in their relationship Pat had realised Marek never wasted words, or said anything he didn't mean.

'And I you,' Marek had replied, his English beautifully correct. It sent a pulse of relief and reassurance and love coursing through her. Before she could speak again Marek kissed her.

From then on, whenever Marek told Pat he loved her, she'd smile and reply, 'And I you' in his accent. Until Marek had come into her life Pat had long forgotten what it was to properly kiss and be kissed, to hold and be properly held. Marek told Pat that he and his men would soon be mobilised, though they had no fixed date. For security reasons, it would come at short notice.

Though they knew Marek's time in the region was going to be limited, his imminent departure had crept up on them. Pat couldn't bear to think of life without Marek.

Life without him means life only with Bob. I can't bear the thought of it. How can I go back to that now?

The prospect left Pat feeling sick, even at the WI, among friends. Determined not to think about it, Pat focused her attention on Frances.

'The war has bitten into each of us,' Frances continued. 'Whether we win or lose, the changes we will experience individually, as families, as a community, are likely to be irreversible.'

The women looked at Frances intently. For this moment in this hall in this village, she was their leader every bit as much as Churchill was the country's, and her words tonight struck a chord every bit as much as his when he addressed the nation.

Frances's mind went suddenly blank. Her mouth became dry as her confidence drained away.

What am I doing? What nonsense am I talking? Who am I to lecture these women? My loss was an accident. It could have happened at any time. It had nothing to do with the war. I sound like a fraud, I'm sure of it. They can sense I'm making this up as I go along. How could they not?

Frances looked at the front two rows of friendly faces looking expectantly at her, and tried to draw strength from them to continue.

Sarah looked at Frances and nodded encouragingly. Frances could almost hear Sarah's voice saying: *You can do this. Keep going. Joyce isn't what the branch needs now. The branch needs you, Frances, and you need the branch . . .*

Next to Sarah was Steph Farrow, who had come straight from her farm, and had offered so much no-nonsense fortitude to the Institute since her hesitant first meeting nearly a year ago. She now looked up at Frances, willing her to continue.

You're why I joined. Joyce has been . . . all right. But if you hadn't come back I'd probably've left. You made the WI somewhere I feel I belong. And not just me . . .

And then there was Teresa Fenchurch, soon to marry the wing commander from the RAF station at Tabley Wood. A strikingly handsome woman in her late twenties, with brown hair and brown eyes that were constantly alive to everything around her, she smiled encouragingly at Frances, as she might to a child in her classroom who had been doing very well giving a presentation, but who had suddenly lost their nerve.

Frances gathered herself to continue, but caught sight of Alison Scotlock, hidden away towards the rear of the hall. Frances almost wished Alison hadn't come to the meeting, their friendship had recently ruptured over the dramatic and ignoble closure of Frances's factory. An intensely private individual with fair hair and startlingly blue eyes, Alison was a match for anyone behind closed doors, but in public she always avoided confrontation where possible.

Not wishing to be distracted by Alison, Frances continued, 'Our village has been the victim of two stray bombs since the start of the war, with no loss of life. Though by God we've come close! One might argue that thus far, Great Paxford has got off lucky.'

Frances paused to allow the suggestion to sink in. The women were nodding in agreement. She could push on with her theme of the branch's evolution to meet the changing demands war placed on them.

'Be under no illusion, ladies. That luck could run out at any time.'

The women now looked at Frances with an intensity she hadn't seen before. They waited to hear what solutions she might offer to the current situation.

'Over the past few months our nation has come closer to invasion than at any time for centuries. But for our stupendously courageous pilots we would almost certainly be living under German occupation, and this meeting would not be taking place. Great Paxford is well and truly *in* this war now. We see this every day in menfolk who are absent. In rationing. In the blackout. In turning every garden into a vegetable patch. In the way we take gas masks everywhere as a matter of course. The way we regard taking shelter during air raids as a nuisance as much as a necessity. *Our* resolve as individuals and as members of the Women's Institute is being – *and will be* – tested like never before. Many of you remember the Great War. It was a terrible time, wasn't it?'

Many in the hall nodded in silence or looked down at their shoes, remembering loved ones lost, recalling the particular horrors of war that none present believed they would see repeated in their lifetimes.

'A terrible, terrible time. In that conflict, the fighting was "over there". Not now. What has become abundantly clear *this time* is that our village and every village, town and city of England is being dragged onto Hitler's battlefield. That is why I am calling on you this evening to look into yourselves and ask what more can you do. So that we may pool our resources like never before, and become far, far greater than the sum of our parts.'

Frances looked at the women's faces and suddenly felt entirely at ease. She felt her old confidence and strength grow from their belief in her. Words were flowing easily. She instinctively knew how to pace her speech. How to pitch each word without seeming to strain for effect. Her breathing was calm and relaxed. This is what she did better than anyone in Great Paxford. It was for this quality that these women had almost unanimously voted for her: *leadership*.

'Some of you might be asking, what can I do when our own army, navy and air force are doing all they can and only just holding the line? Well, when I look around this hall, I see that – *as always* – we can do *rather a lot.'*

The women smiled. Where Joyce used to focus on *not* over-stretching themselves, consolidation, and playing it safe, Frances spoke of going beyond expectations and testing limitations.

'Ladies, my dear, dear friends, if ever there was a time for *not* playing safe, it is now.'

Her voice grew in warmth and confidence with every sentence. She raised herself an inch taller and lifted her chin as she continued.

Miriam Brindsley, approaching the ninth month of pregnancy, had felt her unborn child kick during the early parts of Frances's address. Whenever she felt a kick Miriam wondered if it was in response to something going on outside. A voice or sound causing a physical spasm of fear, or delight. As Frances developed the theme of her speech, Miriam had little choice but to wonder about the timing of bringing new life into the world.

Who would do it intentionally? We've been extraordinarily lucky with David. Almost lost him to the war, but for the grace of God. But who can say what kind of world will be left for this one to live in if Hitler tries again to invade, and succeeds? Doesn't bear thinking about. But . . . how can I not?

She wondered if she was mixing her anxiety about the war with her anxiety about unexpectedly becoming a mother again, seventeen years after her first. She rested her palms protectively over her bump and refocused on Frances on the platform. She remembered Frances had recently taken in a young relative of Peter's, and took some strength from the deed.

If Frances can become a mother of sorts in her fifties, why not me again in my late thirties?

So effective was Frances's speech that even Erica Campbell was focused on what she was saying. Erica had only come out reluctantly, after her husband, Will, had suffered a racking coughing fit during supper that left him gasping for breath. Despite that, he had insisted she come for an evening of respite from his 'killjoy' – her husband's nickname for the mass of cancer he envisaged skulking in the humid chambers of his lungs.

Despite that, Erica hadn't wanted to come. They had lived with his diagnosis for over a year, and he had entered a period of reprieve following radiation treatment in Manchester. He wanted her to have as normal a life as possible under the circumstances. So, despite his coughing fit at supper, Erica had reluctantly left the house, leaving Will in the care of their youngest daughter, Laura.

None understood Frances's talk of war and sacrifice better than Erica. Her eldest daughter, Kate, had lost her husband just a month after their wedding, while Laura had become embroiled with a married RAF officer some months after that, enduring public disgrace when his wife had petitioned for divorce. Together with Will's illness, going to battle on so many fronts had left Erica feeling that she was enduring twice as much war as everyone else. Yet she felt energised by Frances's speech, leaning forward to catch each word.

Don't imagine yourself so special, Erica. Fate hasn't singled you out.

'While I've been away from public life these past few months, I've nevertheless given great thought to how our WI might proceed in the days ahead. To begin with, we can do our very best to prepare ourselves as a social organisation to help others in our village who may find themselves in sudden need. I thought we might do that by establishing an emergency committee that is able to mobilise swiftly to tackle immediate crises that befall the unfortunate. I am also aware that many of us have struggled with the WI's pacifist philosophy – especially those with menfolk fighting, or preparing to fight.'

Frances knew this was a difficult subject to raise. So many women in the branch wanted to cleave to the WI's constitutional pacifism at all costs, while others felt it was foolish, if not ideologically myopic, during wartime. But effective leadership meant not backing away from impassioned debate.

'I have often found myself asking, "How can helping on the home front not *also* be helping our boys on the front line – and consequently, the war effort?" Anything we may do to help our chaps feel better, warmer, more comforted is likely to help them endure the privations of battle – which can only make them more effective soldiers. Of course, whatever we tell ourselves, the reality is that working to keep the home front intact and helping the war effort go hand in hand, even if we and the wider organisation wouldn't wish it to. We knit gloves for our mariners and submariners. Socks and balaclavas for our soldiers. We send food parcels and write letters to the "friendless soldiers" who have no one else to write to them, keeping up their morale. And for what purpose? So they will fight more effectively for *our* survival. *Of course* providing these small comforts for our boys is helping the war effort. And yet we are told we may raise money for ambulances at home for those injured by war, but not for tanks or planes to help bring hostilities to an end sooner rather than later. It is this aspect of the WI's pacifism that feels confusing. What seems morally crystal clear in peacetime seems terribly muddled during war. This is what war does. It muddies everything. It will continue to challenge our moral compass the longer it continues. Just as the country cannot become complacent about the prospect of a renewed attempt at a German invasion, we women of the Women's Institute cannot be complacent about easily giving up long-held beliefs simply because it would be expedient to do so. Wrestling with our consciences is not a sign of weakness. On the contrary, it is a sign that we live in extraordinarily difficult times. To easily succumb to that which simply makes us feel better is the weak path to take. While I'm Chair that is a path this WI will never go down. Instead we will focus on doing all we can to keep life in Great Paxford constant while our men are away at war. We will do whatever's necessary to maintain the home front, whether it be preserving fruit or fundraising for ambulances.'

The women broke into a rousing round of applause. This was precisely what they wanted from Frances. They might not all agree with her, but they also knew she wouldn't ever try to bully them into agreeing with whatever her own view might be.

Frances waited for them to fall quiet and began to outline suggestions for campaigns and activities she'd been thinking about during her absence. With every suggestion the women's smiles grew broader and their eyes shone brighter. They began to feel newly empowered, and started to envisage what they might do in the days to come.

Frances could feel her heart beat faster. Ideas for organising and mobilising the WI in the following weeks flowed from her, and the members were quick to respond with suggestions and amendments of their own. The institute had trundled along under Joyce's caretaker leadership in a solid but underwhelming manner, and most had forgotten how it felt to be inspired. Frances, too, had forgotten the exhilaration she felt when she saw the galvanising effect her words had on other women – hands shooting up to offer points, women turning to their neighbours to quickly debate an issue. As she'd struggled to bear the weight of Peter's death and all its ramifications, there had been moments when she believed she might never again leave her house. But here she was, standing before the WI, leading from the front.

Joyce could feel the excitement ripple through the hall. With a little sadness she recognised that this was something she had never managed to elicit, and wondered if Frances was simply more suited to being Chair than she was.

Or is it just that she is the right woman for the current time? She certainly has an impressive capacity for coming up with all sorts of initiatives, and that's what's needed, most definitely. I entirely concede that. But when the war ends all these programmes and drives might feel exhausting, and Frances too aggressive. In normal times she never stood against me for the Chair, perhaps recognising I was the right woman for then. And might be again. But however you look at it, she does seem to be the right woman for now. I would be terribly daunted by what she is proposing. She seems to come alive with it. And is able to bring the members alive too. An invaluable quality. I shall certainly do my best to support her in whatever way I can.

When Frances came to the end of her address, Joyce was first to her feet to trigger a standing ovation. The old Joyce would have viewed Frances with envy as the hall resounded with thrilled and thunderous applause. But now she clapped harder than anyone. When Frances turned to Joyce to mouth, 'Was that all right?' Joyce smiled and mouthed back, 'Bravo, Mrs Barden. Bravo . . .' And wholeheartedly meant it.

Cometh the hour, cometh the women . . .

Chapter 2

SMALL AND STILL, forty-two but looking eight years older, Pat Simms sat at the table in the smart, floral-print dress made for her by the village seamstress. Pat had pinned up her hair in her customary style for an occasion, and had even applied a little make-up. She looked around the small kitchen where she spent most of her waking hours. The drab walls and floor were spotless, as were the shelves and cupboards. The criss-cross blast tape on the small window above the chipped sink was so neat that it seemed to Pat to be mildly decorative. In this rare moment in which her husband was neither hammering away at his typewriter nor demanding she make him tea or a sandwich while he worked, Pat felt calm. Every plate, bowl, knife, fork, spoon, pan, utensil and cloth lay where Pat had meticulously cleaned and placed them. They had to be. After thirteen years of marriage Bob still carried out spot checks, and would happily make Pat's life miserable if he found anything he could construe as 'below an acceptable standard'.

Knowing there was nothing for Bob to find fault with, Pat relaxed into the moment, the soft scent of her perfume making her think of her lover, Marek, who never forgot to comment how much he liked it when they met in secret. The Czech army captain had knocked into Pat as she'd made her way home from a shift at the telephone exchange. He'd been breaking up a brawl between two of his men and some locals outside Great Paxford's pub. Pat had fallen, and Marek – Captain Novotny, as he'd introduced himself – was so apologetic that Pat had to ask him to stop. At the time, she hadn't much noticed him. Owing to Bob's temper, Pat had learned how to absorb and digest physical pain that resulted from violence, and get on with things. Moments after being knocked to the ground, she had got back on her feet and walked stiffly home.

It was only when Marek had knocked on the door with wild flowers and a further apology that Pat had really taken his measure. He was tall, like Bob. Slightly more thickset. His features were not unlike Bob's, but less pointed, his forehead less furrowed, the corners of his eyes more generously scored with laughter lines, his expression open, and curious. Where Bob's eyes were furious black holes from which no lightness escaped, Marek's were pale blue, like two drops of recently thawed ice. They observed Pat with wry interest. He smiled as he watched her find a vase, and seemed in no hurry to leave once his flowers were in water. Marek had no idea how panicked Pat was that someone might see a strange man at her front door with a bouquet of flowers, however modest.

Are you thinking about me as much as I'm thinking about you, my love? When can I see you next? I have to see you. This silence is killing me.

Pat remembered being attracted to Marek from that first meeting. She had walked him back to the Czech camp at

Cholmondeley Castle, showing him a short cut. They talked easily, and by the time they arrived at the camp gate Marek asked if he could see Pat again. She had every reason to say no, but somehow said yes. And as she'd bidden him goodbye Pat had held out her hand for Marek to shake, and he'd gently kissed it. Pat had walked home wondering if she had imagined what had just happened. She'd sat at the kitchen table for the rest of the evening thinking it over, pausing on details, trying to work out if she had dreamt the whole thing. But she could smell Marek's cologne on her hand and she knew their meeting had been real.

Their relationship had quickly blossomed after their first walk. Though they'd had to conduct their affair with an even greater degree of secrecy in the weeks following Bob's return from reporting on the Battle of Dunkirk, knowing Marek was just five miles up the road made life with Bob bearable. Just. They left regular, secret notes for one another in the village churchyard, in which they arranged to meet in remote areas of the surrounding countryside, away from village eyes alert for any 'dirt' that could be converted into gossip or scandal. Secrecy, subterfuge and an intense passion for one another became the hallmarks of their association. Pat had felt like a spy operating behind enemy lines. One slip and disaster would result, destroying her reputation. The pressure was constant, but worth every moment.

'Pat?'

Despite leaning on the walking stick he'd been given by the hospital, Bob stood tall and striking in the dark suit he wore for special occasions – marriages, like Teresa's today, but also funerals, meetings with his London publisher, or with the editor of the local paper for whom Bob grudgingly reported on local events that he lauded in print and mocked in private. Bob considered the parochial work of a rural reporter beneath a man of his talent, and there was some truth to that. But since he had failed to follow up on the modest success of his first novel they'd needed every penny he could earn even to afford their small house on the outskirts of Great Paxford, which was all but tacked onto the Campbells' much larger house and surgery. Furnishings and decor were kept to a functional minimum, according to Bob's taste, which meant no pictures, ornaments or the memorable knick-knacks most people accumulate through life. Pat was allowed one small mirror in the bedroom. When it became cracked during an argument three years ago, Bob refused to replace it. The only books allowed on the few shelves that lined the dark walls were Bob's. Any books Pat read were collected every second Tuesday of the month from the mobile library, read by her, and then exchanged a month later.

Bob stood in the doorway staring at Pat, who clearly hadn't heard him. His hair lay Brylcreemed against his scalp, drawing attention to his gaunt, bony face. He'd trimmed the moustache he'd brought back from Dunkirk into a precise line across his upper lip. Pat thought it made him resemble an older, less striking version of the author George Orwell, who she had once met before her marriage to Bob, when she was a trainee editor at a London publishing house.

'Pat!'

The sharpness in his voice cut through Pat's reverie, and she turned in the chair to face him.

'Sorry, Bob. I was thinking about the wedding.'

Pat had long since learned to dissemble and keep her inner life secret from her husband, and her affair with Marek had forced her to draw on all her powers of duplicity and self-control.

Bob held out his tie. 'I can't do this.'

Nerves damaged in an artillery blast on the French coast now made fiddly tasks difficult. Pat crossed to him. Avoiding eye contact, she patiently threaded the tie through Bob's starched collar, her fingers working delicately, careful not to yank either end of the tie or pull its knot too tight. As she worked she felt Bob's breath on her face – a bitter blend of stale tobacco and coffee that made her gag.

Bob watched Pat intently, twisting his mouth into a thin smile of appreciation. 'You smell nice,' he said.

Pat didn't look at him. She was always more unsettled by Bob when he tried to be pleasant.

'I found an old bottle of something at the back of my dressing table. Nearly empty.' And then, wondering if this was what he meant, 'You don't think I've used too much?'

'I like it when you make an effort,' he said. 'Should do it more often.'

Why would I want to do that? The very last thing I want is you pawing at me.

Pat couldn't recall the last time she'd enjoyed Bob's touch, and had long since come to dread a compliment as it was usually an overture to mechanical sex in which she parted her legs and locked her eyes onto a point on the bedroom ceiling until Bob had finished his mercifully brief thrusting below. After finishing, Bob would lie on top of Pat for a few moments, regaining his breath. He'd then roll off without looking at her and go downstairs to wash himself, as if he couldn't bear to carry any trace of her any longer than he had to. He never asked if she enjoyed sex. Either Bob no longer noticed or no longer cared that his wife had received no pleasure from it for years.

With Marek it was the opposite. The first time they'd had sex almost two months ago in the bedroom upstairs, Pat had immediately understood they were truly making *love*, with and *for* one another. Marek's tenderness had unlocked Pat both physically and emotionally. She'd willingly offered herself to him that first time, and every time since. Because their moments together were so precious to her, Pat went to inordinate lengths to protect them. If Bob were to find out about their affair, the consequences would be catastrophic. Pat knew what he was capable of. Flashes of violence, certainly. But worse than kicks and punches, Bob had a grip on her self-confidence that he could tighten and tighten until Pat felt increasingly insignificant, incapable and, finally, utterly imprisoned within his will.

Pat finished tying Bob's tie and took a step back to look at her husband, hoping Marek was at that precise moment writing a new message to leave under the piece of old slate on top of the oldest headstone in the churchyard. She knew Marek and his men were preparing for mobilisation within the next two weeks, and was desperate to discuss their future.

I'll check before the wedding service. No – better to look immediately after the wedding, before everyone leaves the church, while Bob is limping out. I'll make an excuse and look then.

She could feel her heart race as she tried to will her longing into reality. The possibility of finding a note made her head swirl with excitement.

Pat suddenly became aware of Bob's voice.

'. . . they can think what they like. But when my novel's published, this shitty little village is going to sit up and take notice. You'll see.'

Bob had been talking for a while and she'd missed his opening salvo. Pat chose a reliable retort.

'No more than you deserve,' she said. He nodded agreement.

Bob seldom required an authentic response from her these days, especially about his new book – a fictionalised account of his experience following the British Expeditionary Force out of France. Pat had read the first draft and found it hard going. Not because it wasn't a page-turner, or reasonably well written – Bob's craftsmanship meant it was both. But because its journalist-hero was clearly Bob's heroic version of himself, which Pat had found revoltingly dishonest.

'I don't know why I'm expected to come to this bloody wedding. She's your friend, not mine.'

'It's expected.'

'Problem with this village all over. Everyone does what's expected. No one does anything out of the ordinary.'

'That's what makes it such a nice place to live, Bob.'

'Only if you lack any imagination.'

She glanced at the small clock on the wall.

I'd prefer it if you didn't come. It would certainly make looking for a letter from Marek easier. In fact, I'd be happy if we never left the house together again.

'Anyway. You look very smart, Bob,' she said blankly, trying not to antagonise him further. 'We should be on our way . . .'

Pat carefully pushed past him into the hall to collect her coat.

Bob looked at her and a flicker of a smile played across his mouth before it disappeared. He took a deep breath, and then another. Keeping his emotions in check. Biding his time. He looked at his watch. Not long now . . .

Chapter 3

WALKING UP THE hill towards the church, the trim, elegantly dressed woman in her mid-fifties tried to curb her natural disposition towards briskness and kept to the pace of the smartly dressed eight-year-old boy at her side. The strong wind buffeted them both as they passed by the hedgerow. His hand was like a small ball of warm putty in hers.

To a stranger they looked like any other mother and son, yet just a few months earlier Frances Barden had been entirely unaware of little Noah's existence. As the product of a ten-year, secret relationship between her husband, Peter, and his company accountant, Helen, Noah's existence had been kept from Frances. When her husband and his lover had been killed in a car accident just outside the village, events had spiralled from that moment to this at a speed that left Frances gasping.

She looked down at the boy.

How is it I've ended up playing mother to their child and not to my own? Have I taken you in to help you, Noah, or myself? Are the feelings I'm experiencing 'maternal' or 'pity'?

After putting Noah to bed and reading him a story, Frances spent most evenings in the drawing room with a glass of whisky, trying to make sense of everything that had happened in the last eight months. Peter often told her she thought too much, a criticism that irritated her immensely. Is it ever possible to think *too much*? Would he have accused a man of the same?

Noah looked up at Frances. His dark eyes were the colour and shape of Peter's. They often fooled her into believing she might hear Peter's voice when he spoke. But it was always the voice of a small boy.

'What plane does he fly?'

Frances knew Noah was talking about Teresa's fiancé. Noah had been obsessed by the prospect of seeing a real wing commander ever since she told him he would accompany her to the wedding.

'I'm not sure. Hurricanes, I think.'

His eyes widened, the name instantly exciting him, as it now excited all English boys his age.

'Don't hold me to that, Noah. I may have that wrong. Aeroplanes aren't my strong suit.'

'Has he shot down any Germans?' He looked at her intently.

Frances sensed where this was going. 'I really couldn't say.'

'But has he killed people?'

During the Great War, Frances had seen that most boys had a weakness for picturebook glory, which no one seemed to discourage. Stupidly, in her opinion.

'I'm sure Wing Commander Lucas would be only too happy to discuss how many Germans he's killed with an eight-year-old boy who *really* shouldn't be thinking about such awful things. Though perhaps *not* on the day he's getting married.'

Noah looked a little disappointed, but accepted the point.

Frances started to think about her own wedding day, then stopped when she remembered Helen – her husband's mistress – had been a guest.

She always struck me as a clever woman, but unambitious. Whereas I couldn't stop pushing at everything. Was Helen his respite from me? Stop this . . . Peter had betrayed her terribly. There was no justification for it. *No justification. But should I not look for some explanation?*

The road got steeper and a silence grew between her and Noah. Frances could see the tall trees surrounding the church at the top of the hill hurling their branches around in the wind, as crows rode the turbulence. Outside the church, congregants gathered in their finest, holding down hats and skirts.

Frances couldn't think how to break the silence.

Peter would point out something amusing or interesting along the way. Or make a silly joke that would leave Noah in stitches.

Frances smiled at the memory of Peter readily making a fool of himself to elicit uncontrolled giggling from children.

Having learned the full extent of his betrayal, Frances had determined to never think well of Peter again. Yet she found trying to sustain a form of hatred towards him utterly exhausting. It had threatened to drive her mad.

Thank God for Sarah.

Frances could see her sister standing outside the church up ahead with two other women.

Thank God for you, my darling sister. You saved my life.

In the terrible weeks after Peter's funeral, Sarah had pressed the argument that rather than loving Helen *instead of* Frances, Peter had loved Helen *in addition to* Frances. Then, even the idea of sharing Peter's affections with another woman had torn Frances apart. Yet the more she considered the proposition, the more Frances wanted it to be true. Over many months, as the pain of Peter's violent death had settled into grief, Frances had slowly absorbed Sarah's reasoning. The alternative was to believe Peter had spent every moment with Frances wishing she were Helen. That would have been too much to bear. Besides, it didn't match what she felt to be true: that she and Peter loved one another. Their life was, as he'd told her one evening after returning from a concert in Liverpool, 'an utter blast'. Frances used to make him laugh until he cried.

You can't do that to someone who'd rather you didn't exist.

Peter had betrayed her in an extraordinary fashion, but one could argue that the inordinate lengths he went to in order to conceal his double life were an expression of his desire to protect Frances; which was, in turn, an illustration of his love for her.

As they drew nearer to the church Frances glanced down at the top of Noah's head.

'None of what happened is his fault,' Sarah had said.

How could it be? I've lost my husband but he's lost his mother and father – in many ways he's bearing up better than I am.

By the time Noah's grandparents – Helen's parents – had come to beg Frances to shelter Noah from the Luftwaffe's bombardment of Liverpool, her anger had given way to an intense curiosity to see what of Peter the child might possess.

33

Beyond that, he wasn't her responsibility, and it made little difference when she was told that Peter would have wanted Noah brought to a place of safety. Frances had felt no sense of duty towards the boy, and resented the emotional black-mail she believed Noah's grandfather was trying to exert. And yet there was something about the way Noah had looked at her through the window of the taxi when he'd arrived at the house. She'd seen the same expression on her own face in the bathroom mirror in the weeks following Peter's death. A loss of confidence around the eyes. A fearfulness about the future.

In that moment, Frances realised Noah was a fellow traveller in loss, grief and sheer bewilderment. Before the boy had got out of the taxi, Frances had resolved to take him in. Leading Noah into the house, she'd recalled a remark Sarah had once made in response to the child of one of her husband's recently deceased parishioners, sent to live with a relative they'd never met before.

'Children just need love,' Sarah had said. 'It doesn't always matter from whom.'

Frances watched Noah look around as they approached the church; everything seemed to interest him, just as it had Peter. His questions were pointed, not general, just like Peter's. He listened to the answers and remembered them, and expressed affection at unexpected moments, taking Frances's hand to stroke, or kissing her cheek, just like Peter.

Noah is Peter's son. I am Peter's wife. Noah is therefore my . . . ? What are we to one another? I wonder.

Frances squeezed his little hand with a pulse of affection, prompting Noah to look up and smile at her.

'Remind me, Noah. Have you ever been to a wedding before?'

'No. Never been asked to one,' he said, in all seriousness.

Frances laughed. She waved at her sister, who Frances could now see was standing with Erica Campbell and Joyce Cameron outside the church. They smiled and waved back.

'I think you'll enjoy it immensely.'

'Why?'

'It's where people are at their *most* happy. Not just the man and woman getting married. *Everyone . . .*'

'Were you at *your* most happy at your wedding?'

Frances glanced at the darkening autumn clouds overhead.

'Absolutely.' The thought of it raised a lump in her throat. 'We should hurry, Noah. Before the rain starts . . .'

Chapter 4

GREAT PAXFORD'S SIX-HUNDRED-YEAR-OLD church wasn't simply *full* for Teresa's wedding to Wing Commander Lucas, its pews were packed with villagers, and the choir stalls of carved oak were bursting with children ready to sing their hearts out for their beloved teacher. Everyone was smiling and excited as they settled to the Flower Duet from *Lakmé*, sung by two beautifully voiced leading lights from the local operatic society. Even the figures painted onto the medieval stone screen of the chapel seemed to be looking upon the event with a benevolent air, and the life-size monuments of ancient knights lining the walls seemed less morbid today, lending the occasion a sense of unabashed pageantry. The enthusiasm among the congregants wasn't merely a reflection of the village's need to let off steam amidst the daily chaos of war, it was in large part a testament to how popular Teresa had become during her brief time at the village school.

The womenfolk debated how beautiful Teresa looked in her white wedding gown, trimmed with Irish lace, and were almost as impressed by the tall figure of the wing commander in his crisp blue uniform and cap. The menfolk were perhaps less struck by the couple's sartorial details, but nevertheless admired Teresa and Nick for their determination to pursue the course of their relationship in spite of world events. For everyone present, whether loved ones were at home or fighting overseas in whereabouts unknown, *this* marriage at *this* moment was a timely restatement of the truest adage known to mankind: life goes on.

Alison Scotlock sat stiffly on the front pew, where Teresa had asked her to sit with her family during the wedding service. It was a compliment to be asked to sit with Teresa's parents and older brother, but since childhood Alison had disliked sitting at the front of anything. A reserved, watchful individual, being 'on view' left her feeling exposed. In her first year at school, Alison had been the cleverest child in class by some distance. Her teacher made her sit at the front, using Alison to correctly answer questions other children got wrong. It was only a matter of time before the boys turned against her, swiftly followed by the girls. Being a clever girl, Alison discovered at the age of eight, was a burden best hidden.

Before Teresa had arrived in her life Alison felt most at ease sitting behind her desk, tucked into the corner of the front room, out of view of anyone passing by the window. There, she could lose herself in clients' business accounts for hours, quietly plying her trade as a bookkeeper.

When Alison had suggested to Teresa that she would feel more comfortable in the middle of the congregation, or even at the back, Teresa had refused.

'You took me into your home when I first came to Great Paxford. Became my closest friend. Helped me fit into village life. You've no idea how much seeing you at the front will help me get through the ceremony.'

'When the day arrives,' Alison had replied, 'you'll fly through it. You'll see.'

'Whether I fly or crawl through it, knowing you're at the front will make it immeasurably more possible.'

Alison had come to greatly value their friendship, so had dropped her request for anonymity.

The congregation fell silent as Teresa was followed up the aisle by two nervous bridesmaids from her class clutching small bouquets of marigolds. Nick turned to watch his bride approach, and couldn't suppress a smile of unadulterated joy, discreetly wiping the beginnings of a tear from his eye before it spilled over. As Teresa moved next to Nick the expressions on the faces of the congregation were unanimous – they were looking upon a truly golden couple.

As Teresa and Nick were led through their wedding vows by the stand-in vicar, Alison felt a small ball of dread turn slowly over in the pit of her stomach. Despite reservations about taking in the young teacher when Teresa had first arrived, a profound comradeship had been swiftly forged between them. With Teresa now gone, Alison's small cottage suddenly felt cavernous. With only her dog, Boris, for company, the prospect of returning to her old seclusion caused Alison to pull her shawl around her shoulders.

Had she still been going into the Barden factory on a daily basis, Alison might not have felt this so strongly. But with the factory closed following an investigation over substandard parachute silk, there was little but daily necessities to take her out of the cottage. Indeed, the blame Frances levelled at Alison for inadvertently introducing a crooked silk supplier to the factory forced her to remain inside her cottage most of the time. She even altered the times she took Boris for a walk, bringing the morning walk forward and pushing the evening walk back an hour to minimise the number of people they might encounter.

Alison glanced around. She knew Teresa's pupils had quickly found their new teacher warm, kind, funny, clever, strict, but rigorously fair. Their parents followed suit, as did members of the Women's Institute, which Alison had suggested Teresa join to quickly get herself known around the village.

Alison watched as the Reverend James gave Teresa and Nick his blessing, then turned to Sarah in the row behind.

'You can *see* how much Nick loves her,' she whispered. 'His *eyes*.'

Sarah nodded. She had been thinking how much more relaxed and enjoyable her husband, Adam, would have made the service than this dour replacement. Adam's services were compassionate, interesting, and not without entertainment value. He believed people should attend church because they actively enjoyed the experience, but he neither insisted nor expected others to share his faith. How could he, when his own wife couldn't?

Now, without Adam at its heart, the church's dark corners and high ceiling amplified Sarah's fears for Adam's well-being following his capture at Dunkirk. She had no idea where he was being held by the Germans, or when she would see him again. Or *if*. This last thought usually struck her precisely two seconds after waking most mornings, and followed her all day, draining the colour out of everything. She knew he was too wise to deliberately antagonise his captors into treating him harshly. But she also knew he was too compassionate to avoid conflict with them if it meant securing better treatment for the young men in his pastoral care. In combat and in capture, Adam saw himself as their father figure.

Not knowing how he's getting on is just crippling. I can deal with almost anything but this damned uncertainty!

A shuffling from the back of the church caused Sarah to turn round. She saw Miriam Brindsley, heavily pregnant, ushered towards the door as quietly as possible by her husband, Bryn, Erica Campbell and her husband, Will, the doctor. Others towards the rear of the church watched Miriam leave with her escorts. Sarah sensed Adam's hand on her shoulder, prompting a dutiful urge to follow them out with an offer to help. Sarah then saw something that rendered such an offer unnecessary – Joyce Cameron, bustling along her pew in hot pursuit . . .

Chapter 5

WILL, ERICA AND BRYN carefully steered Miriam along the church path, through the gate, down the small set of steps and onto the road. They were aiming for the surgery at the Campbell house, just across from the church. Erica was holding her own and Miriam's hat, reasoning that no one needed to wear their best hat while giving birth, or assisting.

The clouds overhead had thickened since everyone had filed into church for the service. They carpeted the sky, pumped and fluffed up by the strong wind that whipped across Cheshire from the Atlantic. The leaves in the trees shimmered and rustled as the autumn air rushed through, pulling weaker leaves off branches to briefly dance on the air before dropping to the ground.

'No need to rush her,' Will cautioned. 'The baby's waited nine months, it can wait a few minutes more.'

Miriam winced as she walked across the wide road junction separating the church and the surgery. They were walking slowly, and were halfway across, but she didn't know if she could make it all the way.

'I'm not so sure!'

Bryn gripped her arm. 'Try not to talk, love.'

'Talking's fine, Bryn. It's *moving* I'm having trouble with!'

Erica glanced nervously at Will. His cancer meant physical exertion was to be avoided, but she resisted the urge to step in and take his place on Miriam's left. She knew his state of health was in part down to his state of mind. Helping him feel strong and capable was part of his therapy.

Joyce Cameron burst out of the church and hurried down the path, pressing her hat onto her head against the rising wind. Joyce was used to being at the heart of any major event in the village and it left her convinced that without her supervision most things would almost certainly go awry. This conviction now extended to the imminent birth of Miriam's baby, despite the presence of a fully qualified and highly experienced doctor, and Erica, an equally highly experienced pharmacist and assistant to her husband.

Joyce caught up with the birthing party halfway across the road, and fought to catch her breath.

'If I go on ahead, Dr Campbell . . . is there anything I can get ready?'

Will glanced at his wife. 'Erica, why don't you take Mrs Cameron and set up.'

Erica nodded. 'You have to do *exactly* as I say, Joyce – *without question.*'

Joyce nodded. 'But of course.'

Miriam caught Erica's eye and smiled at Joyce's tone of mild indignation that she might be anything but completely obedient.

'Come on, then . . .'

Erica led Joyce towards the house to get the surgery ready, as Will and Bryn continued to assist Miriam. She winced again and stopped, suddenly gripping Bryn's hand so tightly he could feel the bones grind against one another.

'Contraction?'

'No, Bryn, small piece of grit in my shoe – *what do you bloody think*?!'

Will glanced at Bryn. 'Best not to talk.'

'I've tried telling her, Doc.'

'Not Miriam, Bryn. You.'

'Just get me across the road, Bryn. And tell me how much you love me every step of the way, because the way this is shaping up I'm going to need to hear that as often as you can get the words out!'

Bryn strengthened his grip around his wife's waist, gently ushered her forward, and whispered in her ear, 'I adore you so much at this moment I genuinely don't have the words.'

He kissed her on the side of her head. A smile flashed across Miriam's face and vanished in a spasm of pain. She focused on the Campbell house ahead.

'Not far now,' said Bryn.

'Maybe not for you, boyo. Journey of a lifetime for me and this one.'

'Everything's going to be fine, Miriam.'

Miriam looked at Dr Campbell. His expression of calm reassurance gave her instant and complete confidence in what was about to happen to her and her baby. With her two escorts on either side, she took a deep breath and set sail towards the surgery, just thirty yards away . . .

Chapter 6

A THICK SHOWER OF confetti enveloped the newlyweds as they emerged from the church door, publicly man and wife for the very first time. Before most of the confetti could land, the wind grabbed it and sent a swirling blizzard of colour into everyone's faces. This distraction gave Pat the perfect opportunity to slip out of the church and scurry along the west wall towards the churchyard's oldest gravestone. Pretending to be overcome by the occasion, she'd told Bob she needed a little air. This suited Bob down to the ground, as it meant he needn't be dragged outside to pretend to celebrate the marriage of a couple he barely knew. He could sit out 'all that nonsense' in peace and quiet, without being buffeted by the cold wind outside.

Arriving at the lichen-encrusted gravestone Pat immediately saw there was no message from Marek. She felt a paroxysm of disappointment, but quickly tried to fathom what might have turned Marek from an ardent, regular correspondent into a man who seemed to have forgotten her over the course of a week. Her head was pounding. *Is it something I've done . . . written . . . or said?*

She knew Marek was busy training his men in preparation for remobilisation; perhaps he was too tired to make the effort to communicate? It did require a walk to and from the castle. Perhaps he was waiting until he had definite news to impart? Pat couldn't help but develop this thought. *What if he's deliberately putting some distance between us – getting me used to the idea that it's over?* She knew he'd been concerned about how she'd be left feeling if anything happened to him when he returned to action. Was this his way of releasing her from those feelings, should that happen?

A cheer from the church entrance made Pat turn and see the bride and groom walk through a guard of honour created by men from Nick's RAF station. The austere figure of Bob stood apart from the celebrants. He wasn't watching them. He was watching Pat with an intensity that made her freeze with fear.

How long has he been watching me? Did he see? What did he see? There was nothing to see. I needed some air. That's all you need to say. Calm down. He saw nothing. Smile.

Pat smiled at Bob and blinked as the first drops of rain splashed onto her face . . .

Chapter 7

By the time Great Paxford's newest husband and wife took to the floor for the first dance, the colourful bunting outside the village hall was starting to take a beating from the wind and rain.

Inside, everyone's attention was on the self-consciously sunny couple moving elegantly to the swing music from the band onstage. Nick's colleagues raised their beer jugs and brayed approval as their boss sashayed elegantly past with his new wife, calling out, 'Lucky sod!' to him, and to Teresa, 'It's not too late to change your mind!' To which Nick quietly whispered in her ear, 'Actually, it is.'

Teresa took it all in good spirit. Teachers are performers by nature, and she played the role of blushing bride to perfection, holding Nick close, nuzzling her cheek against the cloth of his uniform, looking deeply into his eyes, giving every impression to those watching of being the happiest woman in the world. It wasn't solely an impression. She *did* feel happier than she'd felt for a long while. She was well and truly married. The deed had been done. It was time to move on from months of self-doubt and anxiety and go forward with her life. Yet small flickers of doubt still flared in her mind.

Teresa regularly told the children at school that *practice makes perfect*. As the reality of spending the rest of her life with Nick yawned before her, Teresa couldn't help but wonder how many years of practice it would require before she'd be able to perfectly pass herself off as 'a respectable married woman'. She smiled more intensely, and gripped Nick's arm more firmly. *This is who I am now. This is what I am.*

Dancing past the smiling faces of a community that had taken her at face value, Teresa was unable to avoid the irony that her sanctuary had become a form of prison, in which her security was guaranteed only as long as she played according to its social mores. *I have to do this. This is what women like me have to do. Nick is a wonderful man. Never forget that. Nick is a wonderful, wonderful man.*

Teresa repeated it in her head like a mantra as they continued to dance, past Alison, who was watching her from a table, smiling with delight at what she perceived to be Teresa's newfound contentment. And she repeated it as she passed Annie, who was not smiling, but looking at Teresa impassively over a glass of white wine.

Annie had been with the Air Transport Auxiliary for six months, and had become a staunch friend of Nick's while transporting planes for the RAF to and from Tabley Wood for use in theatre against the Luftwaffe. She had first noticed Teresa at a welcome dance for Marek's Czech contingent, and hadn't been able to take her eyes off her the entire afternoon. The same had happened the next time their paths had crossed, and on occasions since.

For her part, Teresa had noticed Annie watching her, and had been unnerved by the fascination she'd felt towards the remarkably self-possessed young pilot. Teresa hadn't felt able to discuss her developing attraction towards Annie with Alison. But as her relationship with Nick became more serious, Teresa's anxiety about her feelings for Annie manifested itself as 'marriage jitters'. Alison told her these were perfectly natural and should be ignored, advice Teresa had tried to follow whole-heartedly. But now, as she danced around the hall with her husband, Teresa recalled the evening she'd found herself briefly alone with Annie at Tabley Wood. Annie had been urgent and direct, warning Teresa against marrying Nick unless she was certain it was the right thing to do.

'Women like us can't be conventionally happy,' Annie said. 'You know this.'

'What on earth are you talking about?' Teresa replied. 'Women like *what*?'

Annie had smiled. 'You know what. Not the marrying kind.'

Teresa recalled watching Annie walk away, as a chill started at the top of her neck and rapidly travelled the length of her spine.

Annie caught Teresa's eye as Nick waltzed her past. They didn't smile at one another, but held each other's gaze. Annie winked at Teresa and Teresa felt the blood drain from her face. She glanced at Nick to see if he'd seen, but he was too busy grinning like the cat who'd got not just some of the cream but all of it, as more colleagues on the periphery of the floor raised their glasses as they danced past. He grasped Teresa's waist firmly and danced them towards a crowd of couples keen to cut loose. Teresa breathed a sigh of relief and put her mouth close to Nick's ear.

'I love you so much,' she whispered.

'You'd better,' he replied, and kissed her, to a rousing cheer from the guests.

Annie watched Teresa disappear into the swirling bodies of men and women, and sipped slowly at her glass of wine.

Chapter 8

SARAH SAT WITH FRANCES, who was trying to weigh up how much cake Noah could consume against how much was good for him. The boy was feeding himself adroitly with both hands without losing a crumb and Frances was sure it would end in tears, almost certainly at the bottom of a bucket.

Sarah had sat in church watching Nick declare his commitment to Teresa, and had listened to Reverend James portentously consecrate the significance of a Christian union. Adam had no time for public 'piety by the yard', as he called it. He would have discussed the challenges of married life with Nick and Teresa in private, weeks before the big day.

The ache of Adam's absence usually hit Sarah hardest in company. It was now compounded by the understanding that her close friendship with Nick would never be what it once was. Their relationship had begun when Nick was billeted to the vicarage, and Sarah had become his de facto landlady. Later, with Adam's enforced absence, Sarah's friendship with Nick had grown deeper. She'd come to rely on him to bump her out of her dark moods with a sense of humour that disparaged her ill-judged attempts at gardening as 'indiscriminate murder', and found her atheism as someone married to a vicar by turns curious and amusing. She recalled the day Nick left to take up residence at the RAF station. There had been a moment – just a moment – when their relationship might have taken a more dangerous turn, but Sarah had snuffed out the possibility, and Nick had respected her decision.

Watching the Reverend James officiate had made Sarah miss Adam more than ever.

He is my life.

She wanted to slip away and curl up in bed and think only of *her* husband. But as the wife of Great Paxford's vicar, she knew public expectation condemned her to be one of the last to leave.

Duty calls – smile!

She sighed and aligned her facial muscles into her well-practised smile, and looked around the hall. Adam loved these men and women to a degree that often shocked her.

He would have adored this. He would have pulled me onto the floor and made me dance the war away, and I would have loved it. He's the only man I've ever met who could do that.

Sarah watched Nick and Teresa shake everyone's hands and accept hugs and pats on the shoulder and slaps on the back. They looked as happy as it was possible to be.

Neither of you have any real idea what love is. Not yet. Not until it's tested.

Sarah brought forth in her mind her favourite image of Adam's face and charged her glass to the ridiculously happy couple as they wheeled past a third time. She took a slug of wine. And then another . . .

Chapter 9

Pat sat with Bob at a table in the corner and watched Teresa and Nick slowly work their way around the hall, thanking everyone individually for coming to the celebration. They seemed immeasurably happy. Pat recalled without pleasure that she had once done the round of guests at her own wedding thirteen years ago. Running through the memory felt like watching another woman and man in another lifetime. Bob had recently published his first novel to some acclaim. He had been confident and optimistic about their future. They'd felt the world lay at their feet. But he'd proved unable to deliver on that early promise.

The acrid smoke from Bob's roll-up snaked across the air between them and wrapped itself around her face, stinging her eyes.

'Not crying, Patricia?' Bob's voice was mocking. 'Big girl like you.'

'It's just the smoke from your cigarette,' she flatly replied.

Pat turned away from Bob and watched the party, smiling briefly at Steph Farrow, who was enduring a dance with her son,

Stanley. Steph winced as Little Stan trod on her toes with every other step. She mouthed 'Help me!' at Pat as they galumphed past, out of time with the music.

'Oh . . .' Bob said. 'Only my smoke.' And then, quietly, with an edge, 'Nothing to do with this, then?'

Pat turned to see Bob place a piece of folded foolscap on the table between them. Every muscle in her body instantly froze. The folded paper was the type issued to the Czechs for their letters home – the type on which Marek always wrote to her. Pat wanted to snatch it up and devour its contents, but had to invoke every drop of self-control to calmly ask, 'What's that?'

Bob smirked. 'I thought you'd do better than that, Patricia. I really did. I mean, really. That's truly pathetic, even by your standards.'

'I'm sorry, Bob. I really don't know what you're talking about.'

Pat had decided a long time ago that if Bob wanted her to break then he was going to have to break her himself – she wouldn't do his dirty work for him.

'Found it this morning. In your usual place in the church-yard. Very sweet. Almost moving. It's not very well written, of course, even accounting for the fact it's his second lan-guage, but what can you expect from those people?'

Pat's mouth was bone dry, her tongue sticking to the roof of her mouth. She felt as if she was falling into a dark, bottomless pit. *He knows. How does he know? Since when?* The questions were like hands reaching out to grab at anything that might stop or at least slow her descent. Pat felt her heart stop in her chest for several moments, and then start to race alarmingly.

'What do you mean, you found it this morning?'

The blood was pounding in her head as she struggled to form coherent thoughts. The words she needed to combat Bob were beyond reach, their passage from brain to tongue strangled by rising fear. Bob looked at Pat, his face contorted into a sneer.

'Where did I find it? You know where I found it. On your grave.'

Bob's words were deliberately ambiguous. He was a writer – he chose them carefully to entertain his readers, and to terrorise his wife.

Suddenly, the pressure building within Pat's skull forced a single thought of complete clarity into her consciousness.

Stop wasting time with this. It doesn't matter. Find Marek. Get up and go. Now. Leave!

Bob's eyes narrowed in victory. He'd never been a gracious winner, always relishing his moments of triumph over her. Pat instantly recognised his expression, but refused to be its object for another moment.

I hate you. I can't quantify how much I absolutely loathe everything about you. And now I'm going to leave you.

'I suspected something at the Czech dance. And when I regained the ability to walk – which was long before you thought I did – I followed you and watched you whoring after him. I followed you a second time and watched you leave a note in the churchyard. I check every morning when I go for the paper. I don't know which I look forward to reading more.'

Pat's eyes flicked down to Marek's message. She was desperate to know what it said. As Bob well knew.

'You can read it if you want. But why don't I save you the bother? In brief, your Czech bastard is being mobilised with his men at fifteen hundred hours. Today. That's three o'clock to you and me.'

Pat glanced across at the clock on the wall of the hall.

It's twenty to three. Twenty minutes . . .

Bob smiled gleefully at his wife, and nodded.

'He so wanted to see you before he left.'

'How dare you read my private letters,' said Pat. 'You had no right.'

'You're *my* wife. *Mine*. Not his. I feed and clothe you. Put shoes on your feet. I give your life meaning. I have *every* right, yes?'

Pat tried to summon the energy to stand up and walk out of the hall, but her legs felt like stone.

'How can you do this now? *Here?*'

Bob smiled and took a deep drag on his cigarette, blowing the nauseating smoke back into Pat's face. She stared at him, her eyes blazing with pure hatred.

'If there was a knife on this table I would cut that sneer off your face. I would hang for you, Bob. Willingly.'

Knowing Pat wanted to annihilate him in that moment made Bob's sneer deepen with sadistic delight.

'So much in life is about timing, Patricia. Choosing one's moment. I do believe the moment has come for you to choose yours . . .'

Chapter 10

Pat's focus on the road ahead was so absolute that she failed to register the soft whoosh of a stricken Spitfire, engine shot to pieces, glide low over the wet roofs of Great Paxford in the direction of the now empty church. Had she looked up Pat would have seen thick, oily smoke streaming from the plane's choking exhaust stacks. She might even have caught a glimpse of the helpless young pilot inside the jammed cockpit canopy, screaming for his mother.

She continued to run towards Cholmondeley Castle in the driving rain, deaf and blind to anything that wasn't connected to finding Marek before he was shipped out of the area. A quarter of a mile to Pat's left, the crippled aircraft continued to sink inexorably lower. Its left wing obliterated a chimney stack in a spray of rubble, before the rudderless, powerless machine ricocheted off the west transept of the church and disappeared from view with a soft crump. The noise it made upon landing made Pat turn in its direction, but what had caused it was out of view. Pat puzzled on it for a moment, then continued. Her mind was focused on one thing – finding Marek before he was gone for ever from her life.

Pat hadn't run since childhood, and even then never as fast as she was running now, propelled by a dread that she might already be too late. The heavy rain drenched the shape from her dress, and her lungs struggled to suck in sufficient air to keep her legs moving. A blister was forming on her right foot, but she didn't slow. The first image of Bob after his return from Dunkirk flashed into her head – lying on his side in a hospital bed. She'd felt a pulse of loathing for the familiar curve of his spine beneath the sheet. The nurse had smiled at her, touching her arm as she passed. 'Lucky him, Mrs Simms. Lucky you.' But Pat's blood had chilled as she'd watched Bob sleep. *Why did you have to survive? Of all men, why you?*

Fuelled by an incandescent fury with Bob, and an absolute determination not to let him prevent her from seeing Marek, Pat ran against the harsh Cheshire weather that seemed determined to push her back down the hill. She continued on, failing to register the fresh litter of Spitfire-smashed bricks and tiles across the graveyard where the wedding party had applauded the happy couple just two hours earlier. She ran onto the road towards Cholmondeley Castle, where Marek and the Czech contingent had been stationed for the past four months.

But the instant she turned the corner she stopped dead.

The scene before Pat overwhelmed her senses. Just thirty yards ahead a Spitfire was sticking out of the front of a house, wreathed in a cloud of smoke and dust. Both its wings had snapped on landing, making the plane look like a model that had been dropped by a careless child. The pilot lay slumped against the inside of the cracked canopy, as if stealing a few moments' rest before his next sortie. A slick of oil and fuel had started to gather under the Spitfire's tail, oozing into the road towards Pat. Smoke was starting to rise from the debris. The front of the house had disintegrated, pushed into the rest of the property by the force of impact.

Pat stood transfixed by the extraordinary scene. Then a baby started to cry close by. She scanned the immediate vicinity for the child, but could see no sign of one. Nor of anyone else. Pat's brain, so flooded with adrenaline, and so focused on finding Marek, now struggled to process a sight so bizarre. It matched nothing in her experience, and the incongruity of standing before a house in the village with a Spitfire embedded in it proved so utterly astonishing that she failed to recognise that the house was the Campbells' – which meant the house next door was her own.

The sound of shouting some way behind punched through her numbing bewilderment, causing Pat to turn round and see what seemed to be the entire population of Great Paxford running along the road, calling Pat's name, yelling at her to get away.

'Pat! Get back! Get back! For Christ's sake, woman – *move away!*'

The baby's cry suddenly bubbled up from beneath the rubble, before sputtering into silence.

The villagers of Great Paxford were now almost upon Pat, yelling at her to move away. But Pat stood her ground and turned to face them, shouting 'Baby!' as loudly as she possibly could.

Chapter 11

'M^{IM?}'

In pitch darkness a man's voice struggled to speak.

'Mim?'

She thought she recognised the accent from somewhere. And then again.

'Mim?'

The accent was Welsh. Her brain worked slowly, its customary speed dulled by a blow to the side of the head. Erica only knew one Welshman: Bryn Brindsley.

She tried to move, but a great weight pressed her slender body into the floor. She could flex her fingers and toes but nothing else. Her eyes were gritty with dust trapped under the lids, but she was unable to lift so much as a finger to clear them.

'Miriam?' Bryn called weakly.

Erica tried to sit up and immediately cracked her forehead against a thick slab of masonry an inch above her, and sank back to the floor. *I'm in my coffin. This is my coffin. I'm not quite dead yet, but this is where I'm going to die.*

'Miriam? Is that you, love?'

Erica opened her mouth to speak and felt grit fall from her top lip onto her tongue.

'Bryn . . .'

Erica heard a faint scrabbling to her right as Bryn tried to turn towards her in the darkness.

'*Miriam?!*' The hope in Bryn's voice raised it an octave.

Erica's head was pounding, her thoughts swirling into one another, impossible to separate. She tried to focus on something other than the pain in her head.

'It's Erica . . .' she eventually managed.

She waited for a response but only heard herself breathing.

'Bryn . . . I can't move.'

'Where's Miriam?'

She spoke slowly. 'Bryn . . . where are we?'

'Miriam? If you can hear me, please, love—'

Erica's voice sharpened. 'Bryn – where *are* we?' She shifted her position slightly to redistribute the pain caused by something sticking into her lower back, between two vertebrae.

'Your house.'

'*My* house?'

'Mim, if you can hear me, say something. Make a noise. Mim, *please* . . .'

Erica tried to make sense of how they could possibly be in *her* house. *Her* house had a surgery, a pharmacy, a sitting room, a dining room, a kitchen, three bedrooms and a bathroom. *Her* house was a light-filled family home for Will and her two daughters. *Her* house smelled of baking, and soap, and medical disinfectant, and Will's pipe tobacco. Wherever they were now was the opposite of that. No light whatsoever, and the air carried a dreadful stench of brick dust and gasoline.

Bryn started to sob quietly where he lay.

'Bryn. What happened?'

But before he could answer, Bryn's low sob mutated into the quiet grizzling of a baby. *A baby? How is that possible? Bryn's a grown man.*

Erica listened for several moments before realising the grizzling wasn't coming from where Bryn lay, but from her left.

Erica tried to orientate her head to the baby crying as best she could, twisting her neck. She listened as the grizzle wound up into a full-throated wail, the way an air-raid siren starts with a low whine and works itself into an almighty howl to alert everyone for miles. The baby was now wailing at the very top of its lungs. The piercing noise had the effect of clearing Erica's head, allowing submerged fragments of recent memory to bob into her consciousness. *The wedding. Miriam brought from the church into the house by me, Bryn and . . . Joyce Cameron. Yes. Miriam's waters breaking. Yes. Will leading her into the surgery. Will and Erica delivering the child, her hands slimy with vernix . . .*

'Mim?! Can you hear that?! Our baby! Mim?!' Bryn called to his wife to respond.

But there was no response. The pitch and volume of the baby's cry increased as it recognised Bryn's voice as its father's, heard every day from inside the womb.

'Mim . . .'

Bryn's voice was weaker. He was a big man, and his breath struggled as his functioning lung fought to retain sufficient air to keep him conscious, while the other wheezed uselessly inside his chest, punctured by a rib that had fractured when the Campbell house caved in on him.

The baby fell quiet.

Gasoline fumes had started to dull Erica's senses once more. Words were hard to come by. Coherent thought even harder. It was now or never. She took a deep breath and opened her mouth, hoping the sound that emerged would penetrate the darkness and connect.

'Will?' she said in a whisper that she could barely hear herself. And waited for him to respond.

Chapter 12

A CORPORAL FROM NICK'S guard of honour was the first to reach Pat. He grabbed her by the arm and pulled her away from the immediate vicinity of the smouldering wreck of the Spitfire, and the smashed house it had impaled. The rain was dampening flames among the debris, but there was no way of knowing what was slowly coming to the boil within the fuselage, or beneath the broken wings. The corporal pulled Pat into the grounds of the church.

'Stay right back!' he yelled into her face, and ran back across the road.

Pat watched as he joined his colleagues, who were staring at the plane, assessing the risk of explosion and fire against their determination to get the pilot out.

'Miriam's baby!' Pat shouted, now completely understanding the full extent of the situation. The corporal turned.

'She's just given birth! In the house. It's stopped crying now, but I definitely heard it.'

Nick arrived at the scene out of breath, the rest of the village not far behind. Without stopping, he eased his six-foot-plus frame effortlessly over bricks and timber to reach the Spitfire's cockpit. He wiped dust and earth from the glass with the sleeve of his uniform and peered inside. A thick red smear of fresh blood coated the inside of the canopy. The pilot slouched almost casually against the side of the cockpit. He had seen dead pilots before, but never so soon after death, when mortality was at its most apparent, wounds wet and vivid, skin still pink and youthful.

Nick glanced down at the young man's gloved hands, similar to his own flying mitts. The pilot's bloody fingers gripped a small black-and-white photograph of his mother and father, similar in type to the one Nick kept of his parents when he'd flown sorties. Nick looked at the young man's face, pulped and split open, and saw his own broken face projected onto the pilot's. He wondered how his parents would take the news of his death. How Teresa would respond to becoming a widow on her wedding day. Over time he had made his peace with his own mortality. But he suddenly realised he had no clue as to how those who loved him might react.

The corporal climbed over to Nick and gestured towards Pat in the churchyard.

'Sir, that woman claims to've heard a baby crying just before we arrived.'

'A baby?'

'Yes, sir.'

'By itself?'

'I don't know, sir. She's in a bit of a state so she could've imagined it.'

'Where?'

'Inside.'

'Inside the house?'

'I think so.'

'Get any residual fuel out of this thing before what's left catches and blows.'

The corporal nodded and headed off to search among the rubble for something suitable to rupture the Spitfire's fuel tank.

'Something wooden, Corporal – no sparks!'

'Nick?!'

He recognised Teresa's voice immediately and turned to see his new wife standing in front of a growing crowd of villagers, breathtaking in her wedding dress, despite the rain. Nick looked at the anxious faces of the villagers surrounding his bride.

'A baby has been heard crying from under the rubble!' he shouted.

A murmur of dread rippled through the crowd. Someone said, 'Miriam,' and others nodded. Someone else said they'd seen her slip out of the wedding service with Bryn, Dr Campbell and Erica, and Joyce Cameron. More nodding. Someone replied that none of the above had been seen at the wedding reception.

From her position in the church grounds, Pat watched as Nick quickly organised the search to find the baby and those buried with it. The police and fire brigade arrived in a strident jangle of bells, and then an ambulance. She looked at her own house and saw that it was clearly badly damaged. A thought flashed into her mind.

Where's Bob?

She felt a brief glow of hope rise in her stomach at the possibility that he'd been at home when the Spitfire struck, but it vanished as she remembered he had been with her at the reception, that it was he who had caused her to run through these streets.

'Step away!'

The senior fire officer commanded the crowd as his men began to hose the plane with water to drown any possibility of fire. Once that was completed, firemen and RAF personnel swarmed over the rubble, tossing bricks and timber behind them as they began to dig into the remains for what lay beneath.

'Quick as you can, boys!' called Nick. 'Stop as soon as you think you've seen or heard anything!'

Spencer Wilson and two other firemen smashed open the Spitfire's jammed canopy and carefully lifted out the dead pilot.

Everyone but the search party stopped for the few moments it took to place the limp body on a stretcher, cover the dead boy and put him inside the ambulance.

The silence was broken by Laura Campbell's pounding footsteps as she ran from the direction of the Observation Post, from where she'd watched the stricken Spitfire's fatal descent through her field glasses. She wanted to run onto the mound of rubble and start digging with her hands, but women from the WI held her back.

'They're working as fast as humanly possible, Laura,' said Frances gently. 'And I've absolutely no doubt they will find your parents. *Alive*.'

Laura stood with the women, tears streaming down her face.

Pat watched another figure slowly make his way up the hill and along the road towards the scene. Bob, leaning heavily on his stick, making no effort to join her. He looked over at their devastated house without a trace of alarm, or even upset. Pat knew that he was already thinking of the insurance money.

For what he'd engineered that afternoon, Pat wanted to walk over to Bob and drive his walking stick through his heart. He looked at Pat and smiled.

He thinks he's won.

Reaching the perimeter of the crowd of watching villagers, Bob took out a cigarette and matches.

'Are you an imbecile?' shouted one of the firemen. 'Do you not understand the situation?'

'Sorry. Wasn't thinking,' Bob said apologetically, and put away the matches and cigarette.

Suddenly, a shout rose from one of the searchers. Laura recognised the area from where the cry had risen – her father's surgery. The girl's heart sank like a stone as she let out a sob of anguish for her parent's well-being.

Pat looked again at Bob, watching Laura with calm fascination, almost certainly ingesting her pain to use later in his work.

Disgusting parasite. Feasting. It's all just grist to you.

Held back by a line of policemen, the villagers of Great Paxford inched closer. Nick and his men carefully pulled a dusty form from the rubble with low, urgent words.

Each man, woman and child held their breath as they waited to see who had been exhumed, and whether they were alive or dead.

Chapter 13

JUST UNDER A MONTH after a Spitfire had destroyed her old house, Erica stood in the new surgery of her new home on the west side of Great Paxford. The dimensions of the new surgery and of everything in the house were smaller than in the old, and Erica had found it initially hard to adjust in the weeks following the crash. She likened the experience to having her life taken out of an airy box and then squashed into a much smaller one. Sometimes she felt herself bending as she entered a room, though there was really no need. Despite this acclimatisation, Erica had been profoundly moved by the extent to which the women from the WI had left no stone unturned in their determination to help her source a new home, and furnish it.

Within two days of the Spitfire hitting the Campbell and Simms houses, Frances had convened an emergency general meeting of the WI, and its members had coalesced into the same well-oiled machine that had saved Steph Farrow's crop earlier that summer. The hall had been packed and solemn as they'd discussed what needed to be done for the survivors of what had been the worst accident the village had suffered in either war or peacetime. That all who had been buried had been pulled out just about alive had led Frances to suggest the calamitous event be henceforth dubbed 'The Miracle of Great Paxford'. At the time it didn't seem hyperbolic. The injuries to those trapped had included broken bones, severe concussion, substantial bruising and blood loss, and irritation of the lungs caused by substantial smoke inhalation. The WI members were tasked to relocate the Campbells by finding and furnishing a suitable, vacant property in the village as a new home that could accommodate a surgery; and with rehousing Pat and Bob. Erica recalled the masterful way Frances had enjoined the members to the task.

'Ladies, this is a test. Yes, we can fundraise for a good cause. We can write letters to lonely soldiers, knit socks and gloves for them in cold and wet climes. We can preserve fruit until the cows come home, and we can even help local farmers to bring their cows home if they are short-handed. But the shocking event that's happened here in our own village is a test of how we take care of our own. Because the Campbells have lost everything. Their home and every stick of furniture within it. Every cup, saucer and item of clothing. The Simms are virtually in the same boat. That the Spitfire crashed and a young pilot lost his life is a tragedy. That no one else died is a miracle. I'm calling for a second miracle now. I want nothing less than to see how quickly Great Paxford's Women's Institute can put these two families back on their feet. New places to live. New furnishings. Clothes. Some of it we will find in donations. Some we might have to fundraise for. Where the plane crashed was random. What happened to Erica and Pat could have happened to any one of us. They are our sisters. They do not need our sympathy. They need our *support*. Let us show them what that really means.'

The members broke into applause. Not the kind of applause reserved for a guest speaker. Nor the kind of outburst that follows a piece of oratory designed to elicit it. But emphatic, spontaneous, ongoing applause to reflect the commitment and motivation of those applauding. It was nothing short of Great Paxford WI's equivalent of a call to arms. The members immediately subdivided into four small committees: a rehousing committee led by Sarah Collingborne; a re-furnishing committee led by Alison Scotlock; a re-clothing committee led by Claire Wilson; and a health and welfare committee led by Frances herself, to monitor and act upon any health and welfare needs of those caught up in the Spitfire crash, including preparing and delivering meals to those in recovery, delivering prescriptions and simply visiting victims on a regular basis to make sure they had everything they needed. As Sarah said towards the end of the meeting, 'Medical care can help heal their bodies; we can help heal their souls.' The members had nodded in unison.

The branch members were true to their word. Within one week a new house was sourced for the Campbells, and it was arranged for the Simms to move in with Joyce, giving Pat and Bob a place to live while it was determined if their damaged house could be made habitable, and giving Joyce company, which she missed, and; for Pat, someone to help her recover from the after-effects of the crash.

Erica looked around the surgery at all the new and unfamiliar objects and medical instruments. She coughed as a consequence of inhaling too much fuel vapour beneath the rubble, and winced with pain due to her still-healing, fractured ribs. It didn't feel like home. Will remained in hospital so the house hadn't yet acquired the lingering odour from his pipe. Only when his smoke was able to drift between rooms and flavour the air would it feel like their home again. Not all the sourced furniture was to her taste, but needs must. She smiled broadly and thanked the person profusely whenever a new piece was brought over. None of it matched but she didn't care one iota. Gradually, it was becoming a home she could bring Will back to from the hospital, as soon as he could be discharged.

Dr Myra Rosen appeared beside Erica. Still in her twenties, she was short, round-faced, with two eyes like blackcurrants pushed deep into her pale face, a small, naturally red mouth, dark black hair tied up in a bun, and possessed a stocky frame that could only be described as 'crammed' into a shapeless grey suit. She wore no make-up and no jewellery. Her eyebrows seemed almost permanently arched in mild disappointment with everything she saw, and everyone she encountered. She gave the impression that life was not currently living up to her expectations, and certainly seemed unimpressed by the second-hand medical equipment Erica had managed to beg and borrow. Erica greatly resented Dr Rosen's barely masked disdain, but with Will incapacitated for the time being, a locum GP had been needed in very short order. Possibly even one who gave every impression of being too good for the position.

Dr Rosen had initially declined to accept Erica's invitation for interview, but a second telegram informed Erica that she had changed her mind, owing to 'unforeseen circumstances' (which

Erica had taken to be another job falling through). When she received Dr Rosen's telegram to say she would be attending the interview after all, Erica had rushed round calling in favours to give the surgery the semblance of a functioning medical practice so the incoming doctor could visualise herself *in situ*. Frances had sent over Peter's old desk and office chair. Other surgeries in the area had sent spare medical equipment. Erica thought it all looked convincing enough under the circumstances.

Dr Rosen's small black eyes came to rest on the desk and chair by the window.

'It's all rather tired, isn't it, Mrs Campbell?'

'Well . . . it's modelled on Will's old surgery. All the furniture and equipment has been donated by patients and local colleagues.'

Dr Rosen buttoned up her jacket against a chill.

'Does the desk need to be in front of the window like that?'

'Dr Campbell always has his desk in front of the window.'

'I can't imagine patients very much enjoy sitting facing their doctor with the sun shining directly into their eyes.'

Erica's favourable impression of Dr Rosen from her curriculum vitae was starting to evaporate.

Such impertinence. How dare you question where Will has his desk, or what his patients may or may not prefer? I should march you to the front door and push you out into the street, Oxford degree or not.

'We've had no complaints.' Erica tried to smile as she spoke, but it was a struggle to engage with this charmless young woman. She made a mental note to have another look at the applications of some of the lesser qualified applicants for the surgery's locum position. Though none had Dr Rosen's stellar credentials, they might possess other useful qualities, such as grace, tact and humour.

'Are you surprised no one's complained?' asked Dr Rosen. 'He's their *doctor*. Venerable. Venerated. This is *his* surgery. Hallowed. *Holy*. One doesn't go into a church and ask the vicar to move the font, even if it should be relocated.'

'I suppose not.'

Dr Rosen looked at the desk doubtfully. Erica looked equally doubtfully at Dr Rosen.

'It should be easy enough to move,' the young woman said.

Touch that desk and I shall swing for you!

Erica opened her mouth to speak and closed it almost immediately.

Try and stay calm, Erica. She's one applicant among many who will soon apply. Though no one with her experience has yet applied, their letters of application are no doubt already in the post. Patience. Put her remarks down to the arrogance of youth. Or the arrogance of Londoners. It doesn't matter which. Our patients require a doctor brimming with confidence not arrogance. A seasoned, confident *practitioner is just around the corner. I'm sure of it.*

Erica told herself what she wanted to hear. But she was too honest to wholeheartedly believe it.

'I'll certainly give your suggestion some thought,' Erica said.

'I would if I were you,' Dr Rosen replied. She finished looking over the rest of the surgery. 'Are you any clearer about the precise length of the contract on offer?'

Yes. Zero days. There will be no contract for you. Goodbye.

'I'm trying to resolve that question as we speak,' Erica said. 'I need to know as soon as possible.'

I'll be writing to you as soon as you leave, don't worry. My rejection will be brief and to the point.

'I understand, of course,' Erica said. 'But the current situation is a little . . . *challenging*.'

Erica felt the urge to go further and grab this arrogant young doctor by the lapels and shout into her face, 'Have you the slightest idea what we're going through, you self-centred *child*?' Instead, though with great effort, she held back.

Dr Rosen looked at Erica, her dark, characterful eyebrows rising half an inch with mild indignation.

'I do have other offers, Mrs Campbell.'

You're bluffing, otherwise you wouldn't be here. No one your age would be here if they could genuinely be somewhere else.

'I need to be able to weigh up the elements.'

'Elements?'

'Length of contract. Fees. Time off. Accommodation. I need to be able to compare and contrast all those with other offers under consideration in order to make the correct decision.'

'Of course.'

Erica wanted to tell this Dr Rosen that she didn't take kindly to being strong-armed in negotiation. Furthermore, if she continued down this track, Erica would be forced to butt heads with her, and when Erica butted heads there was generally only ever one winner, as her daughters Kate and Laura would testify. Erica fixed a smile on her face.

'I *should* be in a position to tell you everything you need to know by the end of the week.'

'Thank you, Mrs Campbell. May I have a look round the rest of the house?'

You can do a jig round it for all I care.

'By all means.'

Dr Rosen nodded and walked out of the surgery.

Alone in the surgery, Erica felt her anger slowly subside.

You're being overemotional, and you can't afford to be. We need someone to take over the surgery until Will recovers, and whether you like the fact or not, this is the only properly qualified doctor who has yet applied. There may be others. Equally, there may not. You cannot let your emotions to get the better of you and cloud your judgement. Does it matter how you feel about her so long as the patients take to her? Most doctors have a personal and a professional persona. You're seeing the personal, but she can't surely be the same with her patients or else she'd end up in hospital herself on a regular basis. Go the extra mile, Erica. Try and see another side. Assuming she has one.

Erica thought about inviting Dr Rosen to stay for a bite of supper. Perhaps a less formal situation might give her better insight into the abrasive young doctor. But she was due to visit Will later at the hospital. Laura was doing a shift at the local Observation Post, and Erica planned to spend her time alone preparing for her visit to Will. He might become conscious, even for a minute, and she needed to be able to project that she was coping in his absence. Supper might be off the table but maybe she could persuade Dr Rosen to stay at the Black Horse tonight and spend more time with her tomorrow. At their expense, of course. More outlay, but it might be worth the investment. That is, if Dr Rosen could be persuaded.

Erica listened to Dr Rosen stomp up the stairs to look at the first floor, where she would – if she accepted the position – be living. The thought of having her under their roof made Erica shudder.

I don't have the energy to argue over every tiny detail of what we do here. I simply need someone who will slip in, seamlessly.

Erica looked at Will's desk. A final shaft of afternoon sunlight streamed through the window and cut across the desk and the patients' chair. Erica glanced behind her, crossed to the chair and sat down, facing Will's chair. The sunlight hit her full in the face, causing her to wince and turn away. The desk and chairs would have to be moved.

Chapter 14

Miriam's bruises from the crash were starting to fade and the cuts and wounds she received were disappearing into scars. She stared into the brown eyes of her new daughter. The whites of Miriam's eyes had filled with blood by the time she was pulled from the rubble, but they had now cleared, and she gazed down at her girl with wide eyes of clear blue and white. Vivian stared back at her mother, examining every speck and contour of Miriam's face, as if each detail held great personal meaning for her.

'They can call it the Miracle of Great Paxford if they want. But you're my very own miracle,' Miriam whispered.

She held Vivian in the crook of her left arm in the warm bathwater and gently bobbed her from side to side, then up and down. *My little miracle girl.* Vivian maintained eye contact as her mother moved her through the water. She frowned slightly, as if asking herself a question that only scrutinising Miriam's face with even greater intensity could answer.

'Now there's lovely. My two favourite women in the world.'

Miriam glanced up and saw Bryn standing in the sitting-room doorway, leaning on a walking stick with his good arm, the other held in a white sling across the chest of his butcher's apron. The bruising across his face was faded now, like Miriam's, but still visible around his eyes and jaw, especially when he smiled. The doctors hadn't been able to tell them which of Bryn's injuries from the Spitfire crash would leave a permanent scar or impairment. It could be all or none.

'Supper won't be long,' she said. 'Soon as I've bathed her and put her down.'

'No hurry, love. We're just cleaning down.'

Miriam turned back to Vivian and beamed at her.

'How is she?' Bryn asked.

'Still perfect.' She turned and looked at Bryn. 'We're going to survive this war, Bryn. This family. The Brindsleys. You, me, Vivian and David. All of us. I know it.'

'Let's hope so . . .'

'No "hope" to it. I *know*.'

'What makes you so certain?'

'Her. The fact she survived all that. The fact *we* survived with her, to take care of her.'

'Just.'

'Doesn't matter. We came through it. It's God, providence, fate – whatever you want to call it. We were all *meant* to survive.'

'We were certainly very fortunate.'

Miriam looked at Bryn.

'You're not listening, Bryn. "Fortunate" doesn't come into it. It was *meant*. Just as David returning from the sea was *meant*.'

In Miriam's determination to see only 'good omens' around her family, that her son had returned with terrible burns from a fire on his ship as it went down was forgotten. To be more accurate, it was omitted from the narrative she was starting to protectively spin around them. That David was alive and home was all that mattered.

Bryn looked at his wife and daughter for a moment.

'What are you saying, Mim? That we've been . . . picked out?'

'Why not?'

'For special treatment?' Bryn tried to hide his scepticism but knew he hadn't entirely succeeded.

'If you like.'

'But why us?'

'I don't know.'

Bryn looked at Miriam and his brand-new daughter and found it difficult to disagree that they had indeed been exceptionally, perhaps even extraordinarily, fortunate. But hadn't the Campbells and Joyce Cameron also survived? Bryn knew his wife well enough not to push the point now. This would be better discussed in bed, with the light out, holding on to one another.

Bryn looked at Mim bathing their glistening baby daughter. He recalled the complete darkness in which he had been buried beneath the Campbell house, wishing then, above all else, that he could have been holding on to his wife. But she had been in the surgery when the plane struck, giving birth to their precious daughter, while he had been in the hall, anxiously waiting. And as he'd lay pinned beneath a slab of masonry, he'd begun to feel that Miriam might as well have been at the other end of the earth. He had fallen unconscious by the time the rescuers had managed to open small shafts of light onto the entombed casualties, and eventually drag them out one by one. Bryn had heard many times that each person was pulled out to cheers and applause from the entire village, who had gathered to watch, with collective bated breath.

Miriam didn't notice Bryn slip out of the room. She was too busy looking down at the pristine infant, pulled from the rubble of the Campbells' house *without a graze*. Vivian softly gurgled.

'I know a miracle when I see one, don't I?' Miriam said gently. 'I saw it with David. And I'm looking at another one now, aren't I, my love?'

Vivian looked back at her mother with a serious, steadfast gaze that brought tears to Miriam's eyes.

'We've been blessed. I know it.'

Chapter 15

By late October, three weeks after the Spitfire had crashed into the Campbell house, the trees had dropped all but the most resolute of their foliage, and by late afternoon the Farrow tractor spewed up a brown spray of dead leaves as it chugged home along the narrow lane. Bone-tired from her day in the field, Steph Farrow held on to the steering wheel, slouched against her sixteen-year-old son, Little Stan, and basked in the waning warmth of the white autumn sun. Steph struggled to keep her eyes open, and more or less steered from memory, relying on the tractor's wheels bumping against the verge to correct their course. This was her favourite time of day, when her mind was too fuzzy with fatigue to think about anything more demanding than a bath, supper, then collapsing in front of a warm fire to work through what they had to do tomorrow, and finally, spending a few moments thinking of her husband, Stanley, away with his regiment, preparing to fight.

'Ma! Look out!'

Little Stan's cry made Steph sit bolt upright. Six figures were coming round the corner right at them. Steph wrenched the steering wheel hard to the left and managed to steer the old tractor around the group without crashing into the hedgerow, bringing it to a stop. She twisted in the seat to look at who she'd so narrowly missed. The group continued along the lane as if nothing had happened. Steph looked at their backs.

Those clothes. Their hats, coats and shoes. The bundles they're carrying. The way they walk. City folk. But why here?

'You wanna watch where you're going, pal!' Little Stan shouted after them. 'It's not a bloody pavement!'

One of the men in the group turned, raised his trilby apologetically, and called back, 'Sorry!' before continuing with the others. Steph looked at Little Stan, his puzzled expression matching hers. They each turned back to look at the group, shuffling up the lane.

'Who are they?' he asked.

'I . . . don't know,' Steph replied.

'Where do they come from?'

'I don't know that either, but I'm guessing they are city folk.'

She wished he'd stop asking questions to which she didn't know the answers. All she did know was she felt a strange sense of alarm. Not that the man had been directly threatening in any way, but his presence in *her* countryside surrounding *her* village felt like a form of trespass, only with no form of redress.

'Why are they here?'

'I don't know, Stan.'

'Because of the war?'

'Let's just get home, shall we?'

Though they'd seen them in photographs and newsreels, the man in the trilby possessed the first black face either Steph or Little Stan had ever seen in the flesh. She released the brake and pressed her foot hard on the accelerator, wanting to get home as quickly as possible.

As the tractor moved off, Steph glanced nervously behind her at the receding figures, and reminded herself to load the shotgun after supper.

Chapter 16

TERESA THOUGHT THAT what she was looking at *should* pass for an acceptable-looking stew, but wasn't completely convinced. She poked at it with a wooden spoon to see if mixing it up would make it look more enticing. It didn't. If anything it made it look *less* appetising as it forced the pieces of meat to sink beneath the surface of what she optimistically thought of as 'the sauce'. As a wedding gift, Alison had filled a school exercise book with recipes for Teresa to try on Nick, with the words '*nil desperandum*' encouragingly inscribed on the front cover. Teresa had followed the recipe for 'stew' to the letter, give or take a couple of 'clever short cuts'. Though looking at it now in its near-finished state, she wasn't altogether sure she was looking at what an experienced cook would recognise as 'stew'.

It's stew-ish. Nick might not exactly lap up the final product but he'll give it a go and he can't fault my effort. I never claimed to be a good cook. In fact, I specifically warned him on several occasions against marrying me on the basis that I'm terrible at it.

'Caveat emptor,' *I said, many times. So if he doesn't like it, he's only himself to blame.*

'Something smells good!'

Teresa turned to see Nick hanging up his overcoat in the hall. She'd been so engrossed in trying to decide if her cooking could be passed off as 'dinner' that she hadn't heard his car pull up, or Nick enter the house.

'I've seen bombardiers staring into their bombsights with less absorption than you're looking into that pan.'

'I'm determined to cook something you can keep down. I've been at it since I got back from school. What do you think?'

Nick crossed to the stove, placed his arms firmly around Teresa's waist and looked at her with mock sincerity.

'I'll enjoy every mouthful of whatever you make.'

'Don't make that sound like a dare because I'll win without trying.'

'I've never been a husband before. You've never been a wife. This is new for both of us. Don't put pressure on yourself. I have the stomach of an ox.'

'That's not quite as encouraging as you think it is.'

Nick leaned forward and kissed her, in part because he wanted to and in part because he wanted to nip Teresa's self-criticism about her cooking in the bud. It didn't bother him nearly as much as it bothered her, largely because he usually took the precaution of having something in the officers' mess before returning home for supper. It allowed him to nourish himself properly until Teresa either got the hang of cooking, or gave up and allowed him to do more of it when he was able. Unlike her, Nick found cooking a relaxing antidote to the grinding stress of his job.

'How was school?' he asked.

'Two more girls asked when I'm going to have a baby.'

'And what did you say?'

'I said, all in good time.'

She kissed him. She loved him. *I do love this man very much. So why must Annie's face appear in my mind's eye every time I kiss him?*

'I saw a few more of them on the way back from Tabley Wood . . .'

'Them?'

'A whole family of blacks making camp in a field just two miles outside the village.'

'From where?'

'I assume Liverpool. I mean, you would know better than I would.'

'You'd know as soon as you heard them speak.'

'I would. After all, it was one of the first things that drew me to you.'

She smiled. 'Not sure your mother was as taken with my voice as you were.'

Teresa had always been unapologetic about her rich, knotty Liverpudlian accent, especially with snobs from the south who affected disdain for anything except RP English. With Nick's parents she turned it up a notch, to his quiet amusement.

'It isn't just blacks coming into the countryside,' she said.

'Not at all. There have been reports of Londoners leaving the city at night to escape the Blitz. Returning the next morning for work. Liverpool is taking a terrible pasting at the moment, so it makes sense that something similar would happen.'

'I sometimes feel I should be there.'

'You didn't cut and run when the going got tough. You established a life here before the war.'

'Only just before. Is that what you think *they're* doing – cutting and running?'

One of the characteristics Nick most admired about Teresa was her impulse to come to the defence of people under any form of attack. He had learned quickly to tread carefully whenever he heard her voice harden. It meant she was preparing to strike, having first lured him into an admission of intolerance or prejudice.

'I don't. But I've heard it remarked in the mess.'

'Going to a shelter or leaving the area – I don't see the difference. They both amount to not wanting to be blown to pieces, don't they?'

'Yes, my darling. They do.'

'As long as they're not causing any trouble it's no one else's business, if you ask me.'

'I agree.'

Teresa looked at Nick's kind, dog-tired face. He had dark rings under his eyes from lack of sleep, and premature wrinkles were beginning to amass at the corners of his eyes from the sapping concern he carried round the clock for the young men under his command. Teresa wanted Nick to come home and completely forget about the RAF station, but knew it was impossible. She wanted home to be a respite. A sanctuary, as Great Paxford had initially been for her.

'You don't have to eat the stew if you don't want to. I won't be offended.'

'I want to.'

'But if it was a choice between this and a ham sandwich – where no cooking is required – which would you rather?'

Nick hesitated for a moment too long for a woman as sharp as her. Teresa nodded resolutely.

'Ham sandwich it is.'

'Can't wait. I'm sure it will be *marvellous*.'

Nick smiled and gently kissed her, then went upstairs to change out of his uniform. Teresa listened to him moving around overhead as she prepared his sandwich. As she did so she thought back to her wedding day with Nick – a memorable one for all the wrong reasons. She had wondered if the Spitfire crashing into the house of Great Paxford's most happily married couple just hours after her marriage to Nick had been an omen or, worse, retribution against what might be perceived as her mockery of one of Catholicism's sacred institutions. She'd stood on the periphery of the onlookers with growing dread, as Nick and his men dug into the rubble, and carefully disinterred the buried casualties. As they pulled Joyce Cameron, then Bryn, then Miriam out alive, Teresa became convinced that Erica and Will would be drawn dead from the debris as her own, unique punishment. But when Erica was pulled out still breathing, and then Will, and finally the newborn child, Teresa all but broke down with relief. That night, she had held Nick tightly in her arms as he made love to her. When he fell asleep, exhausted from his exertions at the Campbell house and in bed, Teresa lay awake in the dark. She now believed the crash might not have been a punishment, but a brutal warning to take matrimony seriously or suffer the consequences. If God could flick a Spitfire from the sky to teach her a lesson, think what could be unleashed as a *full* expression of His anger. She had pulled the covers up, and resolved to do her best to make the marriage work. She had taken Nick's unconscious head in her hands and gently stroked his soft hair, kissing him tenderly, showing God what a good wife she could be.

She'd worked hard at their new life together in the weeks since, throwing herself into domesticity with a fervour that left her shattered by evening. It was difficult to teach in addition to completing all her chores, but she just about managed. Gradually, Teresa began to convince herself she could survive this.

She finished making Nick's sandwich and looked at it sitting on the plate, perfectly square, the ham visible from all angles, slices of tomato peeking out, and just the right amount of butter and mustard.

If this doesn't tell You how seriously I'm taking this, I don't know what will.

As she looked at her work she thought one corner of the sandwich rose higher than the others. She laid her palm flat on the bread and pressed it back into shape, squashing the tomato and ham into conformity. She removed her hand and looked again. The corner was as flat as the others.

Better.

She turned to prepare a cup of tea for Nick, and failed to notice the errant corner slowly rise and return to its previous, awkward prominence. As Teresa filled the kettle, Nick came into the kitchen, crossed to the table, picked up the sandwich and took a large bite.

'Mmmm . . . lovely . . .' he said, chewing vigorously. 'Just the ticket . . .'

Chapter 17

ALISON LOOKED OUT of her kitchen window across the grassland at the end of her garden, towards a forest half a mile away, from where a few trails of smoke rose into the grey, darkening, autumnal sky. While walking Boris in the late afternoon, Alison, like Nick, had seen outsiders making little camps for themselves within the copses that lined the roads and lanes. From the snatched fragments of the strangers' conversation she could divine they were from Liverpool and the Wirral. She understood why they were here, fleeing the nightly bombing, but she disliked anything that threatened the equilibrium of her life, and against her better nature felt their presence as unwelcome as any uninvited intrusion. She wondered if she felt that more strongly at the moment, following the fiasco at the Barden factory.

The day the Ministry of War closed the factory, Alison's relationship with Frances broke down completely when Frances – ignorant of the full extent of what had taken place in the factory – told Alison she held her personally responsible for switching to a parachute silk supplier who turned out to be a crooked profiteer. When the Spitfire had crashed into the Campbell house, Alison had stood within the gawping crowd, transfixed by the silhouette of the dead young pilot in the cockpit. While others were silently praying for the survival of those buried, Alison wondered whether the pilot would have been saved even if he had managed to bail out. Or would he have plummeted to the ground, staring up in horror at a defective Barden canopy that had failed to inflate and decelerate his descent.

Though Frances hadn't made the scandal widely known, Alison nevertheless felt the taint of shame upon her, and retreated into herself, putting the world at arm's length. She shopped during hours she knew most of the other women of the village did not. She walked Boris at hours other dog walkers seemed to avoid, keeping to less popular paths and back lanes.

Why did the world always find a way of creeping back in? Out of nowhere, strangers were in the vicinity, encroaching on the fringes of her life. As much as she wanted to ignore them, she couldn't.

Tonight the weather is fine enough and they're in the forest. But what about tomorrow when it's raining and the temperature drops? How long before there's a knock at my door, seeking shelter from the elements? What do I say then? Come in? Go home? Or do I ignore the knock and hope they go away?

Alison drew the curtain across the window, rechecked the bolts across her front door, and sat at the kitchen table with her meagre supper.

She looked down at the chop and mashed swede and potato on the plate. One of the constants of her life was that whenever she ate, no matter what he'd already eaten himself, Boris would always sit up in his bed and look at her expectantly. Alison had learned enough about canine psychology over the years not to encourage his sense of entitlement where her food was concerned. She knew he was primed to want it as well as his own, but didn't want to encourage his greed. She gave him treats on a random basis so that his expression would always be one of polite enquiry, never that of the beggar.

Alison looked across the floor and, sure enough, Boris was sitting up in his bed looking at her. His patience and his constancy made her feel a surge of affection for her companion. She picked up her knife and fork, slowly cut a portion from her meat ration and placed it in Boris's bowl along with his biscuits. She had tried to secure offcuts unsuitable for human consumption from Brindsley's, but David had told her they were hard to come by in rural areas now all their meat came from wholesale distribution centres, and inedible elements went direct to manufacturers.

If Teresa still lived at the cottage she would have prohibited Alison from giving half her ration to her dog. Alison could clearly hear the teacher's voice scolding her.

'Are you crackers?! He doesn't need it, Alison. *You* do.'

Alison looked guiltily at the slice of meat in the bowl and thought about taking it out.

But he does need it. He's an old man.

She picked up the bowl and put it on the floor before she could change her mind, and watched Boris look over, lift himself unsteadily from his basket, and amble to the bowl. He was an elderly dog, and yet his eating speed had never withered with age – he still ate like a pig. Within moments the meat and biscuits were gone, and Boris, exhausted by the effort of his jaws and throat to consume his food so fast, staggered back to his bed and flopped back down with a small sigh, as if relieved to have dispensed with the labour of eating for another day.

Alison picked up her own plate, carried it to the table and sat down. She looked at the clock on the mantelpiece and felt the empty evening stretch out in front of her like a daily challenge of endurance. She braced herself to get through the hours ahead and reach her bed without feeling lower than she currently did.

One day this business with Frances will pass, and everything can be as it was.

She cut off a piece of potato and put it into her mouth. As she chewed she reviewed her own fortitude in the face of difficulty. From her late twenties, since her husband George's death at the end of the Great War, Alison had trained herself to be able to tolerate her own company. As a young widow, if anyone questioned how much time she spent alone, she would routinely dispel their concerns by expressing an active preference for solitude. The reality was that solitude had been forced upon her, as it had been forced upon every war widow without children to fall back on for love, company and distraction. That had been the case right up until Teresa had come to lodge with her. But Teresa had come and gone.

Without me, would she have gone at all? All 'that' talk. All her doubts about marriage. Secrets are a part of life. We learn to bury them, the same as we learn everything else required to fit in. No one in the village knows George and I were never actually married. That his wife wouldn't divorce him. We lived as man and wife so everyone believed we were. I taught Teresa the importance of appearing like every other couple in Great Paxford. Without me she would have succumbed to her fears, and missed out on a wonderful marriage to a wonderful man. Isn't she happy now?

Alison turned and looked at Boris, now curled up and lightly snoring. She smiled.

'We're fine, aren't we, boy?' she said quietly. The loneliness she feared would come back following Teresa's departure had swiftly taken up residence. Alison had been surprised how quickly she had re-embraced it, like a bad habit.

What choice do I have? Get on with it.

She briefly wondered what Teresa might be doing now, at home with Nick. Eating supper together. Reading together. Listening to the wireless. Going for walks. As indeed she and George used to during the only days she could recall when she had experienced true happiness.

Alison looked down at her plate and calculated how long she could stretch out her modest supper.

An hour might be a stretch. Perhaps not. An hour and it will be dark. Then bed.

Chapter 18

JOYCE SAT IN HER armchair with her eyes closed, listening to the rattle of Bob's typewriter. Once it had been established that the Simms were not going to be able to return to their house, Joyce had offered to house Pat and Bob in her home while they sorted out a new place to live. This made sense to Joyce in three ways.

First, it meant she would have live-in company in the form of Pat, to help with daily chores as Joyce recovered from her injuries from the crash.

Second, it meant she was able to bask in the 'celebrity' of Great Paxford's bestselling author. The fact that Bob had only previously published one novel, and it wasn't a bestseller by any stretch of the imagination (including his own, though he frequently referred to the two positive reviews it had garnered in the national press, in which Bob had been respectively described as 'promising' and 'very promising'), didn't bother Joyce in the least. To her, Bob was an *artist*, someone able to spin entire worlds from his own imagination and transpose them to paper. To be able to sit quietly in the same room as he engaged in the creative process all but made Joyce a midwife to his creative output.

And third, Joyce relished the prospect of company to take the edge off being by herself. Before the Spitfire crash she had got on with the task of living alone but it had been far from easy. She was no longer young, and now in constant pain down her left side as a consequence of the crash, which had also left her anxious. She found herself stressed by any alien sound, either in or outside the house, as if it heralded a new disaster.

For their part, the Simms seemed only too grateful to have somewhere to live while alternative arrangements were made. Pat had embraced the idea quicker than Bob, believing the presence of Joyce in their living space might blunt his bullying for a while and grant her some safety from Bob's spite over Marek, as well as affording her some breathing space to come to terms with Marek's departure. Bob had eventually been typically grandiose in accepting Joyce's offer.

'It would be an honour, Mrs Cameron. After all, aren't the people of London suffering *far* more extreme privations than mere cohabitation? We must all come together like never before.'

Bob sometimes had a habit of speaking as if giving a speech. It was a common habit of a lot of people – mainly men, it had to be said – who liked to hear the sound of their own voice above all others. The reality was that Bob would pay less rent to Joyce than his old mortgage payments, so the prospect of moving in with her in the short term had been financially attractive.

The typewriter stopped and Bob ripped the paper from the roll and scrunched it up in disgust. Joyce opened her eyes at the interrupted creative flow and looked over at him.

'I feel exceedingly privileged to have a front-row seat at the creative coalface, Mr Simms. Not many get to see it.'

Bob stared miserably at the keyboard, from which he was currently unable to elicit anything worthwhile. He sighed and swallowed a little rising bile.

'With good reason, Mrs Cameron. The "creative coalface" is exceedingly dull. Like a real coalface – a backbreaking place to work, dark and gloomy, affording only occasional glimpses of useful material.'

'Such a fascinating process!'

'For you perhaps. I have to sit here hour after hour, hammering away. It's *bloody* soul-destroying much of the time.'

Bob hoped his use of the word 'bloody' would shock Joyce into silence for a few moments, allowing him time to gather his thoughts and try another tack with the article he was trying to write. Joyce merely considered it 'artistically salty', and thought nothing more of it.

That Bob had an unasked-for audience who possessed no understanding of his need for complete silence wasn't helping him work, to say the least. But this was Joyce's house and if she wanted to sit in her room while he typed at her table while seated on her chair, he was in no position to say no. He threaded a fresh piece of paper into the typewriter's roller and prepared to recommence. At that moment Pat entered.

'Supper's ready.'

In fact, supper had been ready twenty minutes ago but Pat's attention had been taken by an article in the paper in which a social research organisation called 'Mass Observation' invited members of the public to write down and send in anonymous accounts of their lives, like a kind of diary. When she'd first read the idea Pat had immediately thought no one would want to read a diary written by her. But after some reflection she started to change her mind.

Why shouldn't people know the truth? What it's like to live with Bob? What it's like to live with Bob under Mrs Cameron's roof? Having to play happy families. Having to pretend every moment that I'm proud of him and feel privileged to be his wife. How it's killing me to be part of an excruciating charade with my husband in front of this silly woman, while the man I love is out there somewhere, training to fight. Or fighting. Alive or dead, I have no idea.

Bob had fought in the Great War and was too old to fight now. Pat thought it distasteful that he had made the evacuation from Dunkirk the subject of his new novel. It was too soon. He had no distance from the event, and therefore no historical perspective on it. All Bob could do was cynically exploit the raw material for a racy thriller for the pulp end of the market.

To make a killing from killing.

She didn't want to think of Bob any more and momentarily closed her eyes and imagined Marek's hands stroking her hair and face.

Bob looked up at Pat through his round glasses, his face pinched into its resting scowl.

'I'll just have a sandwich.'

'But I've made supper. You knew I was making it.'

'I need to get on, *yes*? I'll *have* a sandwich.'

'Why do you *have* to be like this?' Pat's voice was low and terse, to avoid Joyce overhearing.

'I think you'll find I'm not being like anything – except perfectly reasonable. I need fuel to work. The *right* fuel, according to my need. And what I need at this moment is a sandwich.'

Pat looked at Bob and imagined picking a sandwich off a plate, stuffing it into his mouth, packing his nostrils with it and squashing it into his eyes until his face turned blue and he started to choke.

Joyce beckoned her over.

'Help me up, please, Mrs Simms. My left arm is not yet at full strength.'

Pat crossed to Joyce's armchair and helped her to her feet. Joyce brought her face close to Pat's.

'Such a privilege to watch your husband work!' she whispered loudly.

'The privilege is ours, Mrs Cameron,' Bob replied. 'To be allowed to stay here while we sort everything out.'

'It is my absolute pleasure, Mr Simms. You really have no idea.'

Pat held out her arm for Joyce to take, and helped her towards the door to the kitchen. As she passed Bob she turned to him.

'I've been asked to do a shift at the telephone exchange this evening.'

'So?'

His attention remained focused on the blank page in front of him.

'You don't mind?'

'Of course he doesn't – he has his work to do, and *me* to keep him company.'

Joyce had no idea of the minefield she was stepping into, nor that her company was the very last thing Bob wanted. Bob turned and looked at the two women.

'Why should I mind? It's not as if you're going off to meet a handsome soldier for a sordid, secret assignation. Is it?'

Pat stared at him, shocked by his audacity in front of Joyce. Joyce also looked at Bob, wide-eyed. Bob smiled, enjoying the panic he knew he was making Pat feel. Joyce laughed nervously.

'Such a vivid imagination, Mr Simms! How *ever* do you come up with such things?'

Bob looked at Pat, his smile dropping.

'It's a knack.'

Pat stared at him.

If I could poison you, I would. If I could burn this house down around you, I would. If I could pick up that typewriter and smash it into your head, I would. If . . .

The word seemed to roll around the inside of Pat's head like a silver ball on a roulette wheel, looking for a meaningful place to stop.

If I could do something, I would.

'Enjoy yourself.'

Bob grinned and turned back to his work.

Doing this in front of Joyce is more fun for you.

Pat closed her eyes and swayed a little on her feet, allowing the urge to scream her hatred at Bob to rise and subside. She felt Joyce's small hand grip her arm and give it a little tug.

'Come along, Patricia. Let's get *the great writer* a sandwich to feed his wonderful ideas.'

Joyce gently led Pat from the room and closed the door behind them.

'It's such a responsibility, isn't it?' she said gleefully. 'Keeping an artist properly fed and watered. Very exciting! Let's see what we have for him, shall we?'

Joyce slowly made her way along the passage and into the kitchen. Pat watched the old woman totter along, newly unsteady on her feet. She wanted to scream the truths of her life at Joyce until she was hoarse. Instead, she repeatedly banged the back of her head against the hall wall until it started to hurt.

'Come along, Patricia!' called Joyce, from the kitchen.

With Bob to her left and Joyce on her right, Pat felt like a lamb on a cattle grid for whom neither backwards nor forwards movement would bring a positive outcome. Only Marek could come and lift her to safety, but the war had taken him before they could agree on a plan for the future, or say their goodbyes. Bob had seen to that.

'Patricia!' Joyce's voice was more insistent.

Pat would have preferred to have stayed in the hall for ever, neither Bob's slave nor Joyce's dogsbody. It wasn't an option. For the moment she must oscillate between the two.

Pat sighed, and started to walk towards the kitchen, where she would prepare Bob's damned sandwich. She consoled herself by thinking of all the ingredients she would like to include, and smiled at the extent and inventiveness of her own imagination.

Chapter 19

Frances watched as Noah unhurriedly pushed an unwanted dumpling to the furthest side of his plate.

'There are plenty of people who would be grateful for that,' she said, trying not to sound harsh.

He looked up at her sternly.

'Why don't we send it to them?'

Frances smiled. In his navy-blue pyjamas and dressing gown Noah seemed like a tiny man.

She considered it demeaning to enter into this kind of debate with an eight-year-old, and kept her counsel.

'Why don't you just eat it, and then you can have a piece of jam roly-poly?'

'I don't want jam roly-poly.'

'Do you know what it is?'

'No. But it sounds stupid.'

'I think it sounds fun.'

'I don't.'

'It's suet sponge—'

'Don't like that.'

Frances was sure he didn't know what she was talking about, and decided to persevere to get to the sweet stuff.

'It has lots of jam in it too.'

'I don't like jam,' he said, determined not to allow his dark mood to be bought off so easily.

'That isn't true, Noah. I've seen you eat jam on toast almost every morning for breakfast.'

In the weeks since she had taken Noah into her home, she had used the same considerable powers of persuasion on Noah to get him to go along with her wishes as she had used at the WI to defeat Joyce in the election for branch Chair. Her method was to establish what she wanted him to do, then explain why it would benefit him, and conclude by explaining how it would ultimately benefit everyone in the long run.

Noah looked at her with his customary, determined expression. She could see he was thinking, working through his list of responses for his next answer. Noah blinked, deciding to preserve his integrity by bailing out of the debate altogether.

'I don't care,' he said.

Frances was stumped. Her legendary powers of persuasion were dependent on the willingness of those she was trying to persuade to be open to persuasion. In three brief words Noah signalled he was not. He looked down, avoiding all eye contact. Frances could see his small cheeks were rosy with indignation. It was the first time Noah had rejected her in some form, and Frances felt all at sea. She couldn't force him to eat against his will. All she had was persuasion, and if he proved resistant then she wasn't sure what else she had in her arsenal to get the child to do as she asked.

The housemaid, Claire, came in to clear their plates. Claire had been Joyce Cameron's housemaid until Joyce had discovered Claire had voted for Frances over her for the presidency of the WI. Claire was twenty, and had a more relaxed way with Noah than Frances did. Noah plainly responded to it. Where Frances tried to affect a maternal air, Claire was simply the little boy's 'friend'. They played together whenever Claire finished her shift. Claire's husband, Spencer Wilson, Great Paxford's postman and part-time fireman, played cricket with Noah on the Bardens' extensive lawn in the afternoon. Without this young couple around, Frances would have struggled far more with the child. Claire had a deep well of patience to draw upon with Noah that Frances struggled to locate within herself, and an ability to understand what was going on in his head at any given moment. Frances knew Noah had a crush on Claire, and thought he might find it difficult to be defiant in front of her.

'Just eat the dumpling, there's a good boy. Come on. Don't cut off your nose to spite your face, Noah. Big day tomorrow. You'll need all your energy.'

Frances had gone to great lengths to prepare Noah for his imminent departure to boarding school. It wasn't – as Peter had intended – to Peter's alma mater a tremendous distance away, but a school somewhat closer to Great Paxford, just north of Warrington. Frances had given the matter a great deal of thought, and discussed it with Sarah.

'Is that a good idea?' Sarah had asked. 'Taking him in only to send him away again?'

'I'm not "sending him away", Sarah. I'm sending him to boarding school, as his father would have done had he been alive. And not too far at all.'

'It might not seem that way to the child. Away is away to a little boy.'

Both Sarah and Frances had been sent to boarding school by their mother. Frances had loved it. Sarah had loathed it.

'It might seem to Noah that after a short period you've decided you don't actually like him, and are packing him off as a result.'

'Nonsense!'

When cornered by anything she disagreed with, Frances often resorted to denying the legitimacy of her opponent's argument.

'I have gone to great lengths to explain to Noah that he is going to boarding school because that's what Peter would have wanted. Because it will be in his best interest.'

Sarah had sighed, trying to muster all her patience.

'Yes, *I* can see that. Of course. But *Noah* might not be able to. Being *eight*.'

Frances had told Sarah to her face that she was talking rubbish, but later that day sent Claire to reiterate to Noah that he was being sent to boarding school to accede to his father's wishes, not because Frances didn't want him in the house. Claire had returned convinced Noah understood.

Though Frances had taken to playing the role of Noah's 'mother' as well as could have been expected under the circumstances, it was possibly too much to expect it to continue in perpetuity without hitting the buffers from time to time. On occasion, Frances had found it difficult to respond when Noah became confident enough in her company to be good-naturedly defiant, and barked at the child a little like her mother used to bark at her when she'd been displeased.

'Now that is quite enough of that, young man!' she would say, her voice tightening enough to squeeze out all of its warm tones. Noah would look down, and stand still for a few seconds. He clearly didn't like to be chastised, and Frances felt a twinge of shame from the act. She knew it amounted to throwing her weight around, but she could think of nothing better that would bring the same desired effect. She genuinely thought sending Noah to a boarding school whose staff were expert in raising children would lift a lot of pressure from both Noah and Frances, allowing their relationship to develop away from daily niggles.

It was only now, on the eve of his departure, that Frances realised how much she was likely to miss him. Having insinuated himself into her life, the boy had insinuated himself into her house, and finally, undeniably, into her affections. He was clever and funny. He was the best of Peter in character and appearance. To begin with it hadn't been easy for Frances to be around him at all, as the boy proved a constant reminder of Peter's grand betrayal. But in a short time, Noah had started to assert himself in his own right. When she woke up each morning Frances found herself looking forward to seeing him. When he kissed her goodnight at the end of each day, she knew she'd miss him a little until the next morning.

She heard a sniff, looked up and saw a tear running down Claire's cheek as she collected Noah's plate and uneaten dumpling.

'Is everything all right, Claire?' Frances asked, concerned.

Claire glanced over at Noah and nodded, and hurried out with the plates. She and Spencer had talked of having children of their own one day, and she couldn't understand the reasoning behind sending a child like Noah away to school. She had wanted to say as much to Frances, but Spencer told her not to in no uncertain terms.

'It's what posh people do,' Spencer had told her. 'It's just what they do. They think it builds character. Maybe it does, of a certain kind. Maybe that's how they stay posh. But say nothing to Mrs Barden. However kind she has been to you, never forget she's your employer. Which means there are lines you can't cross. Don't make the mistake of thinking you can.'

Claire did as Spencer advised, but it was a struggle.

Frances looked at the little boy across the table and felt a lump rise in her throat. *This is for his own good. It's not good for a boy his age to spend so much time in the company of women, however kind and well-intentioned. He needs the space to be himself with his peers, away from here. He's a child. He needs to be with other children.*

Noah looked at her.

'Jam roly-poly . . .' he said tentatively.

'What about it?' Frances replied, sensing a softening in his position.

'I didn't eat the dumpling. So does that mean I can't have a bit?'

On any other day Frances would have insisted Noah finish his main course to 'earn' dessert. But this was the night before he was going away from her, and for both their sakes she didn't want them to part on bad terms.

'On any other night I would say "no pudding", Noah. Food is scarce, and I wouldn't put anything on your plate you can't eat – like that dumpling. That's how it will be at your new school too. Do you understand?'

He nodded solemnly.

'If you don't eat your main course at school they definitely won't give you pudding.'

Frances didn't know if this was strictly true, but she accurately calculated Noah didn't know it *wasn't*.

'But on this one occasion, even though you *haven't* finished your main course, you can have pudding if you want.'

Noah looked at Frances for several moments and then got down from his seat, walked round the table, crossed to Frances and wrapped his small arms around her and held her tightly. It was the first time he had been this spontaneously affectionate towards her. Frances had seen him hug Claire in the garden and around the house and had felt small pangs of envy at the sight of the little boy becoming overwhelmed with affection towards her housemaid.

Frances now gratefully kissed the top of his head and thought her heart was about to explode. She blew out her cheeks softly to contain her emotions.

'I'll miss you,' she said almost inaudibly, managing not to cry. She'd felt upset on occasions when Peter had to leave on business trips, but Peter had known exactly where he was going, what he was going to be doing there, and when he was coming home again. Noah knew none of these things.

I'm hurling him into the complete unknown and simply hoping for the best. He has no idea about any of it.

'I don't want to go. I want to stay here with you and Claire and Spencer.'

His voice was small and helpless. Though his words hadn't been framed in a way that asked Frances to change her mind, it nevertheless sounded to Frances as if he was begging her to stop the inexorable process she had set in motion. She squeezed her eyes closed and took a moment before speaking.

This is what Peter wanted. Peter knew him for years. I've known him for little more than a few weeks. Even his grandparents approve of this. This is no time to be sentimental. Keeping him here might make me feel better in the short term but would be to Noah's detriment in the long. This isn't about my well-being but his. If he were my own flesh and blood I would be doing the same.

Frances took a deep breath and composed herself.

'Your father knew going away to boarding school would be the very best thing you could do. He went to one himself, remember? As did I. To a different one, of course. But we had a wonderful time. You will too. I promise. Sometimes we need to do things we don't want to do because they will make our lives so much better in the future. I don't expect you to understand that now. But you will. I promise you, within days you will be writing me wonderful letters about all your exploits with the other boys.'

Out of the corner of her eye, Frances was aware that Claire had returned and was standing in the doorway. Though her eyes were markedly red from crying, Claire had brought herself under control.

'May I bring Noah some jam roly-poly, Mrs Barden?'

Frances nodded.

'Yes, Claire. Thank you.'

Claire wiped her eyes before she could start crying again, and hurried back to the kitchen. Noah's grip tightened around Frances.

'You really will have such fun with the other boys, Noah. I can't begin to tell you.'

Noah held on to Frances.

Frances hung on to the hope she was right.

Chapter 20

ERICA SAT BESIDE Will's bed in the hospital ward. She held his hand, watching him breathe slowly. Even under sedation, Will's chest moved up and down in a seemingly haphazard movement. Of the six people trapped by the impact of the Spitfire, Will had taken the brunt and was the most seriously injured. He was also the last to be found and rescued, which meant he'd ingested more dust and fumes than any of the others.

In fact, Will wasn't *quite* the last to be found and rescued. After Erica, Miriam, Bryn and Joyce had been dug out and taken to hospital, the crowd of villagers had gathered round the last remaining area where the rescuers were searching. By a simple process of elimination, everyone knew the last person to be found would be Dr Will Campbell, though a whisper quickly circulated that he would almost certainly be found dead after being buried for so long. When the last chunks of masonry were carefully lifted away, Will was finally revealed, curled in the fetal position. When he was gently turned over to be lifted out, his rescuers discovered Miriam's newborn baby lying securely cradled in a second womb made of Will's arms and chest. She was all but unscathed, and started crying the moment sunlight penetrated her eyelids and sparked her retinas into life. Somehow, in the seconds between the Spitfire crashing into the house and the house collapsing on top of them, Will must have snatched the newborn and rolled onto his front, selflessly using his back and legs to shield her from the full impact.

Erica watched her husband's chest shakily rise and fall, and squeezed his hand a little. His hand didn't squeeze back. The words of Dr Rosen floated into her mind.

'How long is the contract likely to be?'

Erica had told the young doctor the situation would be resolved as soon as possible. In her gut, she knew the situation had already been resolved. Will had been suffering from lung cancer for eighteen months, and despite seeming to be in remission when the plane hit, was nevertheless frail. Erica struggled to see him ever returning to work.

Why didn't you say as much to her? Why haven't you admitted it to the girls? What are you waiting for? It's ridiculously impractical.

She had been tempted to say something about it to Laura as her daughter made a Thermos of tea for her evening shift at the Observer Corps, but had decided against it. She hadn't wanted her to sit in the cramped post with little to do but dwell on her father's health.

'Mrs Campbell?'

Erica recognised the soft voice of Dr Mitchell and turned. Will's doctor was approaching sixty, spry, with slim hands that moved elegantly to complement his speech, which was immediately calming, as if nothing he could witness in the field of medicine would ever shock or surprise him, or was in any way out of the ordinary. He had the most natural bedside manner she had ever seen. Even better than Will's, and Will's empathy towards his patients was well known. On several occasions, Erica had heard Dr Mitchell say to relatives of other patients on the ward, 'Life happens to us all' – his kindly formulation for saying death is a fact of life relatives of the sick must start to embrace. On another occasion Erica had heard Dr Mitchell asked what advice he might give to the young about growing old. Dr Mitchell had smiled, and said, 'Get used to the idea. It's coming.'

Erica stood and faced Will's physician.

'May I have a word, my dear?' he said.

The temperature of the ward was high yet his words sent the iciest chill along the entire length of Erica's spine. She could tell when a doctor was preparing the ground for bad news. The question was, how bad was it? Erica struggled to retain her composure. She felt her hands begin to shake and clasped one in the other to stop it. Some part of her mind thought if she acted calm and unconcerned then Dr Mitchell wouldn't dare give her terrible news. She looked into his patient brown eyes.

'Of course.'

Dr Mitchell glanced at Will and then looked back at Erica.

'Outside?' he suggested softly.

They left the ward and sat in the small rose garden at the back of the cottage hospital. Erica was the first to speak.

'Is he dying?' she asked, signalling that she simply wanted the truth, and that Dr Mitchell wasn't to try to manage her expectations in any way.

Dr Mitchell nevertheless considered her question for a few moments, choosing his words carefully. There was a rhythm to these conversations, and he felt safer keeping to it.

'Mrs Campbell, as you know, we have no cure for lung cancer. It was gaining ground some time before his diagnosis.'

Erica had no desire to argue with Will's doctor, yet felt compelled to put up a fight for her husband's prognosis – it was the closest she could get to fighting for his actual life.

Hadn't he been selected for a special programme of radiation therapy in Manchester? Hadn't that made a significant difference?

'But the X-ray treatment in Manchester apparently reduced the size of his tumour quite significantly.'

Dr Mitchell nodded. 'But it hasn't eradicated it. Will inhaled a great deal of dust and all manner of potentially toxic particles when the house collapsed on top of you all. This material has penetrated deep into his lungs, which is why his breathing remains as laboured as it is. I know you all suffered the same. But he was buried longer than anyone else. And coupled with his pre-existing condition, for Will the consequences are far more serious.' He paused for a moment and placed a calming hand lightly on top of her own.

'Erica, I'm speaking in complete honesty now. As one medical professional to another.'

Erica nodded and braced herself.

'I know you retain a hope that Will might eventually recover enough to return to work. It's perfectly understandable, given how well he seems to have been the last few months. But I have a responsibility to be *completely* honest with you. It is time for us to embrace the fact that Will's life as a working GP has come to an end.'

Erica looked into Dr Mitchell's eyes. She saw how painful this was for him. It was what made him such a good doctor. She appreciated his use of '*we*' in 'we must embrace the fact'. He smiled gently at her.

'Life, I'm afraid, happens to us all.'

*   *   *

The next morning, Erica sat at the breakfast table with her chin resting on her clenched fists, deep in thought, and yawned until her jaw ached. She slowly closed her mouth and sighed. She suddenly began to cough, her slight frame repeatedly convulsing as her lungs fought to expel the irritant that had made its presence felt. Though the Spitfire had crashed weeks earlier, everyone trapped under the masonry had since been coughing up dust and God knows what else.

The cough eventually subsided and Erica sat in silence once more, catching her breath. The toast she had made twenty minutes earlier lay untouched and cold on the plate in front of her. The tea she had poured from the pot sat unsipped in the teacup, no longer steaming. She had omitted to put on any moisturiser or make-up, and the skin on her face felt thin and dry. Though she had stopped crying at some point during the night, the whites of her eyes retained the pinkish glow of distress behind her glasses.

Since Will had been diagnosed with lung cancer they had both known there would be a moment when the time he had left would switch from the probable to the reasonably certain – from years to months to weeks. Yet it nevertheless had taken her by surprise when she'd heard the news from Dr Mitchell.

'Life, I'm afraid, happens to us all.'

Erica repeated the phrase over and over in her mind, before the sound of the front door opening and closing in the hall outside brought her back into the present. She quickly wiped her eyes and looked up, trying to smile a millisecond before Laura entered, a little crumpled and tired from her night shift with the Observation Post.

'You're home earlier than I was expecting,' Erica said, trying to sound as if she had just got up herself and was looking forward to the day ahead – neither of which was true.

Laura picked up a piece of cold, dry toast and scraped a thin layer of hard butter across its rough surface.

'The east coast is quiet, so Brian said we may as well go home. The next shift will be in position before anything gets anywhere near us – if anything is even on its way over, which Brian doubted. He has it on authority from someone at the Ministry that the Luftwaffe took such a hammering over the summer they can't risk daylight raids for the time being. I thought I'd have a quick bath and then go up to the hospital.'

'You don't need to sleep first?'

Laura shook her head. 'Do you want to come with?'

'I can't. I'm showing Dr Rosen around the village. I'll go later.'

Laura looked a little puzzled.

'Dr Rosen? I thought you couldn't wait to see the back of her?'

Erica had told Laura as much when Dr Rosen had returned to her room at the Black Horse prior to catching the train south this morning. But following her conversation with Dr Mitchell last night everything had changed. Erica had left a note for Dr Rosen with the landlord at the Black Horse to ask if she might stay in Great Paxford for a day or two longer.

'I think there's more to her than she puts across in a first meeting.'

Laura munched on the toast and started to eye a second piece.

'Are you actually considering that woman for the locum position?'

Erica looked at her youngest daughter. She had grown so much in so many ways in recent months. Her affair with a married RAF officer had forced maturity upon Laura sooner than any parent would have wanted. Yet she had emerged from the scandal scarred but stronger, with an enhanced sense of perspective about the world and her place in it.

Erica calculated Laura would be able to accept that Will's injuries from the crash meant he would never return to work. And that consequently, overnight, they were no longer looking for a locum to replace him at the surgery but a *permanent* replacement. But Erica had no way of predicting how Laura would respond when she realised – as Erica was sure she would – that if Will was now too ill to ever work again, it wouldn't be long before he would die. How to convey to Laura that her father's life was entering its final stage had kept Erica awake all night. She looked at Laura chewing toast and thought she looked like a little girl again. Erica decided to tackle the matter one step at a time.

'Dr Mitchell made a point of coming to see me at the hospital last night.'

Laura stopped chewing, looked up at her mother, and waited for her to continue. Erica took a deep breath and drove on.

'Your father's condition isn't . . . well . . . Dr Mitchell said it isn't improving.'

Laura swallowed the toast she'd been eating, and then calmly said, 'I see.'

'Whatever he ingested in the accident has reversed any remission he seemed to be enjoying from the radiation treatment.'

'Reversed?'

Erica nodded.

'How severely?'

'Dr Mitchell thinks it's very severe indeed.'

Laura swallowed – not toast, but her own dread at how her mother might answer her next question.

'Will he get well enough to work again?'

Erica looked at Laura for a moment as she weighed the difference between telling Laura everything Dr Mitchell had told her, or keeping some of it back for another time when she felt more able to deal with the possible outcome. She slowly shook her head.

'On my last visit I did wonder,' Laura said quietly.

'I'm going to give Dr Rosen a tour of the village and then ask if she might consider a permanent appointment.'

'So soon?'

'She might be the only qualified applicant we receive for the post. I can't afford to lose her if she is willing to take it. With a probationary period, of course.'

'Sounds sensible in principle. But if you don't actually *like* her—'

'I'm not suggesting she's the easiest person in the world. Doctors can be quite arrogant at the best of times, and God knows she's no slouch in that department. But she's extremely well qualified, from one of the best medical schools in the country, and has excellent references. I can't afford to look a gift horse in the mouth, Laura.'

'There's a thin line between arrogance and rudeness.'

'I'm hoping it's a London veneer that will soon rub off. I'm going to spend time with her this morning to see how she is with people she'd be looking after.'

Laura looked at Erica matter-of-factly.

'You've clearly made up your mind.'

'I'm afraid it's been made up for me. For all of us.'

Erica had an almost uncontrollable urge to deliver the third and final piece of information, and unburden herself of everything she knew so that she and Laura were not held apart by a secret. But as much as she wanted to, she couldn't steal the last shred of hope her daughter might be harbouring for Will, however redundant it would be. Laura finished the toast and stood up.

'I'm going to have a bath.'

Erica watched Laura cross to the door, where she hesitated and turned back to her mother.

'He hasn't got long, has he?'

Erica felt her deep love for her daughter suddenly surge in her chest. Laura had made the final connection herself.

'No, darling,' she said, determined to hold her feelings in check. 'Dr Mitchell doesn't think he has long at all.'

Laura looked at her mother blankly for several moments, then crossed back to her and held her tightly in her arms.

'Thank you for being honest with me . . .'

Erica clasped her youngest daughter. When Laura lifted her head her eyes were wet with tears.

'We knew this would come . . .'

Erica nodded and stroked Laura's hand.

'Just . . . not so soon,' Laura said.

'No, my love. Not so soon.'

Laura took several deep breaths and wiped her eyes.

'I'll go and see him later.'

Erica nodded.

'He'd like that.'

'When will you tell Kate?'

'I'll write to her this evening.'

Laura nodded and kissed the top of her mother's head.

'I don't envy you having to write that.'

'You've made it slightly easier, darling. Go and have your bath.'

Laura kissed Erica again and left the room. As soon as she heard Laura go upstairs into her bedroom and close the door, Erica covered her face with her hands and began to sob inconsolably.

I can't live without you . . .

Chapter 21

Whatever the size of queue she was anticipating when she went to pick up a copy of *The Times*, Joyce was determined to be at its head. She didn't usually take *The Times*, preferring the more digestible *Daily Express*, the self-proclaimed 'greatest newspaper in the world'. But this edition of *The Times* was *special*. This edition of *The Times* contained the first instalment of the serialisation of Bob Simms's new novel. When she arrived at the newsagent Joyce was surprised to see that, in fact, there was no queue at all. Great Paxfordians *were* buying *The Times*, as they did on any other day of publication, there just wasn't any need to actively form a queue for a copy.

Joyce felt a pang of disappointment for Bob, and a marginally smaller pang of guilt for having spent the previous evening assuring him the village would turn out in force to secure their copy of the paper. In truth, the disappointment she felt for Bob was also in part for herself. She had hoped to bask in Bob's glory in front of other villagers. Joyce hoped they would be green with envy that she was sharing her house with a famous author, and might even offer a gentle ripple of applause as she walked along the high street holding *The Times* aloft, with Bob's serialisation within. Her craving for a similar level of status that she had previously derived from being the wife of the village solicitor hadn't gone away, even if her desire to live with Douglas had. She thought Bob's presence under her roof might rekindle it. After all, it takes a special kind of person to understand the whims and needs of a creative genius. She – Joyce Cameron – wanted to be regarded as precisely such a person. After this morning she realised she might have to wait a while longer for reflected glory, and the evidence it would herald that her status in the village had been resurrected.

Clutching the paper as she trotted home, Joyce resolved to fib to Bob about the size of the queue to save his blushes, and to admonish her fellow villagers when she got the chance for their lack of support for her gifted lodger. As she walked up the garden path to her front door, she could hear through the downstairs parlour window the sound of Bob already typing. She could barely contain her enthusiasm, calling out, 'Mr Simms! Mr Simms! I have it, Mr Simms!' Joyce burst into the house and into the front room, waving *The Times* aloft with such glee that Bob thought for a moment she must be bringing news of the end of the war.

'I have it, Mr Simms! The first instalment of your novel!'

Bob looked at Joyce and slowly removed his glasses. Bearing in mind the sales of his first book, Bob had never been a successful novelist. Nevertheless, he had encountered a few members of the public at low-key public events who expected him to behave in the manner expected of a man of letters. The role involved taking all criticism on the chin with a wry smile, and uttering sentences in the form of epigrams that usually sounded cleverer than they were. As Joyce stood before him, he recognised she was hoping for Bob-the-author to speak, not Bob-the-tenant.

'Well, well. What a nice surprise,' he said. Understatement was his customary response to public attention. It had the twin benefits of making Bob appear modest while quietly encouraging whoever was bothering him to go away. Joyce failed to take the hint.

'There was quite a queue for copies,' she lied.

'May I see?'

'Of course!'

Joyce gave Bob the paper and he flicked through the pages to where his work was displayed and furrowed his brow in a 'writerly fashion' – as he knew Joyce hoped he would. He was aware he was performing for her benefit, but playing up to her adulation helped keep his and Pat's rent at a peppercorn level during their stay. Joyce had initially asked for no rent at all, so chuffed was she to be playing landlady to Great Paxford's greatest living author (and wife). But Bob had insisted they pay their way, so Joyce accepted a nominal rent, to cover food.

Joyce gazed at Bob reading his own words in the country's most revered organ.

'You must be so excited, Mr Simms.'

Bob looked up and smiled benevolently, as if his work were published in *The Times* every week.

'It's just part and parcel of being published, Mrs Cameron. All a bit of a game, really. Marketing. You know . . .'

He knew she didn't know, but also knew that just leaving the word 'marketing' hanging in the air would create the effect of seeming above the concerns of Mammon.

'You really are shockingly modest, Mr Simms.'

Bob looked up at Joyce and smiled modestly.

'Not at all,' he said, even more faux-modestly. 'I just have a gift – or is it a curse? – for seeing things for what they really are. Any post?'

Bob asked Joyce this question every morning, establishing in her mind that all post addressed to himself or Pat should be offered directly to Bob. It was his way of intercepting any correspondence from Marek Novotny intended for his wife. Having ruined Marek's departure from the village for Pat, this ensured any remaining connection between them could be permanently severed.

'No post today, Mr Simms,' she replied.

Joyce came out of the front parlour to make Bob a celebratory pot of tea as Pat started to sweep down the stairs.

'I've finished upstairs,' she said.

Since Joyce had taken them in, Bob had insisted Pat act as a glorified housekeeper for the duration of their stay. This wasn't to thank Joyce for her kindness in sheltering them, but to offset a portion of their rent by paying it *in kind*. Pat had tried to argue against the idea of being turned into Joyce Cameron's skivvy, but Bob's logic was ruthlessly cold.

'You'd be doing the same for me at home, wouldn't you?' And then for good measure, 'We're not here on holiday.'

Pat knew she was being punished for her affair with Marek. Offering Pat to keep house for Joyce was his version of hard labour. It also kept Pat within sight and earshot. With Marek departed from the area with the rest of the Czech troops there was no reason to do so. But it amused Bob to treat her as a woman who might commit adultery with any man if she were let out of his sight.

Joyce looked at Pat sweeping the stairs.

'The serialisation of your husband's novel has started.'

Pat continued to sweep.

'Has it?'

'You don't sound very excited.'

Please, Mrs Cameron, it's bad enough I have to live with Bob. It's a hundred times worse I have to live with him under your roof, pretending to be happily married. I feign so much in your presence, every minute of the day. Please don't force me to feign interest in his published dross.

'Of course, I'm pleased for Bob if it means more people will read his book.'

'Success of this order doesn't knock on everyone's door, Mrs Simms. This is a significant moment in both your lives.'

'Perhaps more Bob's than mine.'

'Not at all. As the wife of a successful man you share in his success. You helped him do it, without question. People in the village will change the way they perceive you.'

'I do hope not.' Pat couldn't think of anything she'd like less.

'This is your moment to shine, Patricia! Enjoy it!'

Joyce hurried away from the bottom of the stairs towards the kitchen to make tea, leaving Pat standing halfway down, the sound of Bob pounding away at his typewriter hammering in her ears. She would give up any share in Bob's 'success' to spend a minute more with Marek. Or just to know he was still alive.

I don't think I can do this much longer. It feels like I'm watching my life die in front of my eyes.

Chapter 22

TERESA CYCLED TOWARDS the RAF station at Tabley Wood wondering if she was, in fact, doing the right thing. Nick had forgotten the packed lunch she had made for him that morning and Teresa had initially considered it an oversight on his part. He was, after all, a tremendously busy man with the weight of an RAF station on his shoulders, and all the young lives it contained. Who could fault him for forgetting a packet of sandwiches and two apples picked from a tree in their garden?

Teresa had initially thought nothing of it and continued to prepare for school. But a nagging thought had insinuated its way to the forefront of her mind.

What if Nick has deliberately left his packed lunch because he doesn't want it?

Teresa didn't mind in the slightest if Nick *didn't* like her sandwiches. What niggled was the worry that Nick didn't feel able to tell her that he didn't.

What would that say about their marriage? What would it say about her prowess as a 'wife'?

Teresa had just finished packing her school bag when another thought struck her.

What if this was a test? What if Nick deliberately left the sandwiches to see what she'd do?

Teresa couldn't help wondering if this was the sort of thing newly married men did: set their new wives little trials of love, loyalty and devotion to assess who exactly they had hitched their lives to. Teresa certainly didn't feel compelled to do the same to Nick, but then, she wasn't a man. Also, she had very little experience of being in a relationship with one, from which to make an informed judgement. She wondered if Nick was sitting in his office right now, waiting to see if Teresa would dutifully bring him the sandwiches. If she did: tick. If she didn't: a black mark.

What if he suspects I'm not like other married women?

Teresa suddenly felt deeply anxious. She had no other way to gauge whether she was successfully playing the role of a dutiful wife than by Nick's attitude towards her. He *seemed* happy enough, but what if he was masking some deeper concern? Had she ever given anything away? They had settled into living together easily enough. The sex they had was enjoyable under the circumstances, though Teresa could do with a bit less of it. Nevertheless, she threw herself into it. Was very passionate, and voluble. Yet what if there was something about the way she made love with Nick that gave away the fact that she would rather be in bed with another woman? Would Nick say anything? Was his leaving his packed lunch a sign that he cared less about hurting Teresa's feelings than he would have weeks ago? It felt to Teresa that the honeymoon period that people spoke of was over.

As she approached the barrier at Tabley Wood's entrance, Teresa recognised the sentry as one of Nick's men who had attended their wedding. She hoped she wouldn't have to fish her ID card out of her bag, and squeezed the brakes long enough for him to get a good look at her. He recognised her instantly, and raised the gate to let her through.

'Morning, Mrs Lucas!'

Teresa almost looked over her shoulder to see who he was addressing, before realising he was referring to her by her still unfamiliar married name.

'I'll be very quick! He's forgotten his packed lunch!' she freely offered, as she cycled through.

Why did I tell him that? He doesn't need to know. Now I've made Nick – his boss – seem absentminded. I'd be a terrible spy.

She entered the station, cycling across the quad towards Nick's squat, single-storey office block. She dismounted and set the bike against the wall.

'Teresa?'

Teresa froze and momentarily stopped breathing. She turned and found herself face to face with Annie.

'How nice to see you, Annie. Nick didn't say you were coming up this way.'

'Orders change all the time. We don't always know until the last minute where planes will be needed.'

Annie smiled. Her long, fair hair was tied in a loose bun on top of her head. Her cheeks were tanned where sunlight had caught the skin below her flying goggles. Her forearms were nut brown from extended exposure to the sun at altitude. She stood with her hands tucked casually into her coverall pockets. Tall and slim and always with the same expression of wry amusement, she seemed unlike any woman Teresa had ever met. Always perfectly composed. Never hesitant, or caught off guard for the right thing to say at any moment. Always clever without ever sounding superior. Always effortlessly comfortable in her own skin. *Breeding*. Teresa had always hated the term, but what Annie had was *good breeding*.

As much as Teresa resented it, she felt intimidated by Annie. She knew this was ridiculous in a grown woman who could instantly silence a classroom of thirty rowdy children with the raise of an eyebrow. Teresa knew it had nothing to do with logic and everything to do with social class. Growing up in the class Annie had, had enabled her to learn to fly a plane, which was as likely for someone from Teresa's background as learning to ride an elephant in Assam, or sailing a yacht into the marina at Monaco. Not that Annie flaunted her background. She didn't have to. It infused every single thing about her, causing Annie to be what Teresa thought of as 'wholly herself'. Ironically, the only other person Teresa had met who fitted the same description was Nick. That Annie had not ended up marrying Nick, and Teresa had, only confirmed Teresa's belief that Annie was 'wholly herself', while she was not.

Teresa suspected that Annie's preference for women excluded any sexual attraction towards men. Teresa had never seen her so much as glance at a man with interest, and her attraction to Nick was purely platonic. Teresa had always lacked the confidence to be wholly herself. It meant that for some time after they had first met, Teresa wasn't sure whether what she felt for Annie was because she liked her, or because she wanted to be her.

'I just rode over on my way to school because his nibs left his lunch behind.'

'I can take it into him, if you want?'

Annie extended an arm, her hand already open, as if the question was already settled. Teresa had no choice but to agree.

'Would you mind? I'm pushing it to get to school on time as it is.'

She took Nick's packet of sandwiches and the two apples from her bag and placed them in Annie's hand.

'Aside from forgetting his lunch from time to time, how are you finding married life with Nick?'

'I didn't forget Nick's lunch. I made Nick's lunch. Nick forgot it.'

Teresa had been irritated by the implication that she had been somehow misfiring as Nick's wife, and then felt immediately more irritated with herself for seeming so sensitive about it. She knew why she felt this way. It was because she knew Annie believed Teresa was only pretending to be Nick's wife.

'Sorry,' Annie said with genuine sincerity. 'My mistake.'

'I'm finding married life wonderful.'

'That's . . . *wonderful*.'

'Yes.'

Teresa couldn't think of anything else to say, and felt momentarily compelled to start listing all the 'wonderful' things she loved about married life, but the sheer charade of her life with Nick overwhelmed all else, so she said nothing.

'I've never seen Nick happier,' Annie said. 'Which is a tremendous testament to you, given his work pressures.'

Teresa couldn't tell if Annie was being sarcastic. She didn't sound sarcastic, but Teresa had encountered women of Annie's class before who were sarcastic without ever sounding it. It was another product of breeding.

'I'm doing my best,' Teresa said.

'Whatever it is, it's working!'

'I'm glad.' Teresa looked at Annie for a few moments. 'Thanks for taking in his lunch.'

'No problem.'

'Very kind of you.'

'Not at all.'

Teresa realised she had no idea how to bring this chance meeting to a close except by suddenly jumping on her bike and cycling away as fast as she could.

'I would have gone in and we would have started a conversation and I'd be late, and—'

Annie stepped forward and kissed Teresa on the cheek, silencing her instantly. She stepped back and looked at Teresa with her clear blue eyes. Teresa felt her heart pound in her chest like a little kettle drum, and looked at Annie's face.

Even the way you blink – unhurried, wholly yourself.

Annie smiled, as if she had just read Teresa's mind.

'Go.'

Teresa nodded, mounted her bike and cycled away. As she pedalled, she felt compelled to turn back to see if Annie was looking at her. But she was also conscious of not wanting to look as if she was looking to see if Annie was looking at her.

Stop being so bloody adolescent and keep riding.

When she reached the gate Teresa squeezed the brakes to give the sentry time to raise the barrier. But instead of squeezing the brakes just enough to glide through without stopping, Teresa squeezed them a little too hard, forcing the bike to stop, requiring her to put a foot on the floor. It gave her just enough reason to casually glance over her shoulder towards Nick's office block, and see Annie still standing where Teresa had left her. There was no question about it. Annie was watching her. Teresa's heart leapt a little in her chest.

'Have a good day, Mrs Lucas,' the sentry said.

'Thank you, Pilot Officer,' she replied, smiling. 'I shall.'

Teresa put her foot on the pedal and cycled away at speed. She wanted to look back once more, but forced herself not to. Instead, she pressed harder on the pedals, doubling her speed in her panic to get away from the RAF station.

Keep away from her. You're married. Keep away . . .

Chapter 23

THE TAXI TO TAKE Noah to his new boarding school stood patiently on the gravel drive of the Barden house. The driver leaned against his door and enjoyed a quiet smoke while he waited for the party he was conveying to come out of the house.

Inside, Frances stood at the bottom of the staircase in the large, wood-panelled hall of her house and listened to the sound of Noah sobbing upstairs. Between Noah's sobs, Frances could hear Claire's and Spencer's voices, though not what they were actually saying to try to calm the child. Their tone was clearly soothing and encouraging. Frances had wanted to go up and try to help Claire and Spencer comfort the boy but Sarah, who was standing beside her, suggested she leave the young couple to it.

'If anyone can get him downstairs in a fit state to leave,' Sarah had said, 'it's them.'

Frances hadn't been offended by the remark. It was true. Since Noah had come to live with Frances they had certainly grown closer, but she nevertheless lacked that carefree spark he so readily responded to in both Claire and Spencer, and which drew him closer to them than to her.

It's almost certainly their age. They're young. On the cusp of having children themselves. He's far closer to them in age than he is to me. It's perfectly understandable. And it isn't as if he never comes to me for affection and reassurance, because he does. Or that he doesn't like my company, because I know he does.

Frances had often heard Noah and Claire, or Noah and Spencer, laughing uncontrollably together in another part of the house, or in the large garden where they played nearly every day. When she first heard them she had felt jealous, but had quickly realised that having a whale of a time with Claire and Spencer needn't mean Noah had a subdued, sombre time with her. He simply had a different sort of time. It was perfectly natural. Frances marvelled at how adept Noah was at fitting in perfectly with the different personalities and moods of the adults he lived and mixed with. It was a very 'Peter' characteristic.

'Like a little diplomat,' Frances had said to Sarah.

Sarah worried it might mean Noah would struggle to assert himself at boarding school, forgoing establishing his own personality as he attempted to fit in with stronger personalities around him. She had raised this as an argument for Noah perhaps not going to boarding school at all, but remaining in Great Paxford and attending the village school. Both Claire and Spencer agreed with Sarah's concern and her suggestion that Noah might not leave, but Frances had dismissed the idea.

'The independence will do him the world of good,' she had said. 'He'll find his own level.'

The sound of Noah crying upstairs made such optimism seem unfounded. Claire had tried another tack to persuade Frances not to send him away. She had decided to address Frances towards the end of the evening, when she'd had a couple of Scotch and waters. Frances remembered it clearly.

'I know it's not really my place to speak about this, Mrs Barden, but you've asked Spencer and me to help look after him and we've done our best and have become very close to him in quite a short time.'

She had paused to allow Frances to tell her to be quiet and send her out of the room, as was her right as Claire's employer. But the Scotch had done its work and Frances was reflective enough to hear Claire out.

'You've done wonders with him, Claire. Whether at the WI or at the house, you must feel free to speak your mind.'

Claire had decided not to gild the lily and spoke from both her head and her heart.

'Well, given how much Noah's been moved from pillar to post the last few months, do you really think yet another move to live with yet another set of people is the best thing for him?'

Frances had looked at Claire for a few moments, considering her question. It was one she had asked herself a number of times.

'Whatever you or I might think about the issue, my dear, this is what Peter wanted for him. We have become Noah's custodians, yes. But I feel an obligation to follow what Peter would have done with him had he remained alive.'

And that had been the end of the conversation.

Hiding behind my dead, philandering husband is an utter disgrace. I should be ashamed of myself. Why can't I admit the truth?

I'm sending him away because I'm scared of getting too close to him. Boarding school isn't for his sake, it's for mine. Coward, Frances. Admit it.

Frances and Sarah looked up towards the landing when Noah stopped crying.

'They've done it,' Sarah said quietly.

Neither she nor Frances looked happy. Both sisters felt complicit in an episode in which a child's will had been, if not entirely broken, then at best twisted to accommodate a decision with which neither felt comfortable.

Coward, Frances.

'I'll go and tell the taxi driver we won't be long.'

'Thank you.'

Sarah was glad to assume a task that would take her out of the house for a few moments. It would mean she wouldn't have to watch a red-eyed, wet-faced Noah being led downstairs by Claire and Spencer doing their utmost to put a gloss on a mistake.

Frances watched Sarah go, then looked up the stairs and waited for Noah to appear. She could hear Claire's low murmuring becoming more coherent as they approached the stairs on the upstairs landing.

'. . . you'll be running around with the other boys in no time, you'll see.'

And then Spencer.

'Two days. Three tops. That's how long it'll take before you've forgotten us completely.'

Finally, Noah appeared at the top of the stairs and looked down at Frances. She thought he had the look of someone who had been betrayed and who had become resigned to both the betrayal and its dire consequences. Though her heart broke to see such emotions plainly visible in his expression, Frances thought the kindest thing was to see this through.

He's made peace with it. Don't mess him around. That would be crueller. Let him go and get on with it now. Spencer is right. In three days he will be as happy as Larry and will have forgotten all about us. This is for the best.

She hoped it wasn't simply a lie one tells others to console oneself.

Claire and Spencer led Noah carefully down the stairs towards Frances. When they reached the bottom stair she said, 'Ready?' Noah looked at her with his red, glistening eyes and nodded meekly. Frances glanced at Claire and saw she was using all her willpower not to cry. Spencer wasn't finding this at all easy either. Frances felt a wave of regret build in her abdomen and rise into her chest and throat. To stop herself from telling Noah to go back upstairs and unpack she put her arms around him and held him tightly. His little body felt hot in her arms and he smelled of soap. He didn't move, simply stood as if paralysed, refusing to hug her back as he normally would. This was his judgement on her decision.

'I'll miss you,' she whispered.

Frances imagined this is what her mother must have felt when she had said goodbye to her and Sarah when they were girls. It was little consolation that she had never felt as sad when leaving as a child as she did saying goodbye to Noah now.

Noah said nothing. Resistance broken, he simply stood waiting for the process of transferral from house to school to begin.

Five minutes later, Noah was gone. Frances and Sarah had dutifully waved off the taxi containing Noah and Claire and

Spencer, who had offered to escort him to his new school and help settle him in. Frances had wanted to go but couldn't trust herself to see the job through without completely falling apart. Besides, she knew Spencer and Claire would make a better job of amusing him into relaxing and looking forward to reaching the school. Even so, Frances had never felt such gut-wrenching sadness as when she watched the taxi chug up the drive and turn into the road. Once they had all disappeared completely from view, Sarah made her excuses and went home, clearly upset.

Frances walked slowly back to the front door and returned inside the house. The air was silent and still. She walked into the drawing room and calmly poured herself a large Scotch and water. She took it over to the cream sofa, sat in the middle and took a sizeable, numbing gulp. She felt confused. On the one hand she agreed with Peter's decision to send Noah away to school. It's what would have happened to any children they might have had together. They had agreed as much long before it became apparent they were unable to conceive. On the other hand, she wanted Noah in the house, near her. She knew it was selfish, but there it was. She wanted to be surrounded by his laughter and chatter and cheek. She wanted to learn what he thought about things, and answer all his questions about whatever he didn't understand. But . . . this *was* what Peter wanted. Her mind clung on to this single consoling thought as a ship-wrecked sailor clings on to a rock.

Frances sipped at her Scotch and wondered what Noah was doing now, in the taxi. Laughing at one of Spencer's silly knock-knock jokes, perhaps.

Knock-knock. Who's there? A broken pencil. A broken pencil who? Never mind – it's pointless.

Frances took another gulp of Scotch and let out a long sigh.

Knock-knock. Who's there? Etch. Etch who? Bless you!

Frances remembered how easy it was to make Noah giggle and smiled.

Will you remember me in a week, Noah? Yes. Will you remember me in a month? Yes. Knock-knock. Who's there?

Frances stared at the opposite wall. Tears pricked her eyes as she suddenly realised her greatest fear.

What if he forgets me altogether?

Sitting in the armchair, Frances made a conscious effort to bring Noah's face to the forefront of her mind so as to concentrate on every feature, and imprint his visage in her memory.

I should have had a photograph taken of him.

He had seemed so small walking hand in hand with Claire and Spencer towards the taxi, diminishing with every step away from her. When the taxi drove away, all Frances and Sarah could see were his eyes peering back at her over the back seat, and his forehead, and the small top of his head – as if he were vanishing before them. They had waved, but he hadn't waved back.

She lifted the tumbler to her lips for another numbing slug of Scotch, but nothing poured into her mouth. She reached for the whisky decanter to refill her glass but it too was empty. She looked at the gin decanter. It was half full but it was too early for gin.

She sighed and sat back. She thought of everything that lay ahead for Noah now she had placed him beyond the Luftwaffe's reach. New things to learn. New sports to play. New friendships to make. Last night she had sat on his bed and had told him these were all opportunities that would enrich his life.

But with Noah gone, Frances suddenly viewed them as obstacles, hurdles, tripwires and traps the world placed before the unwary, which only the most robust children could successfully negotiate. She had only known Noah here, in the protected surroundings of her house and care. Out there, he was alone. Her eyes widened as if seeing a glaring truth for the first time, and her mouth dropped open as if to speak it. But no words came. There was no one to speak them to.

Oh God, what have I done?

PART TWO

A Woman's Work . . .

Chapter 24

'Mrs Barden . . .'

Dr Derek Nelms, MA (Oxon), the headmaster of Noah's boarding school, already sounded defensive, and the conversation was only two words in. It would not have mattered what time of day Frances telephoned, Nelms's tone became immediately wary the moment his secretary informed him Mrs Barden was on the line.

'Good morning, Headmaster. How are you today?'

Frances knew he didn't look forward to her telephone calls but it didn't deter her from making them. Her priority was Noah, and how he was getting along. Was he happy? Was he making new friends? Was he coping with the workload? Could she speak to him? To which Dr Nelms's responses were: 'Yes', 'Yes', Yes', and 'I think that would be a little destabilising at this moment in time.' That she called every day was the issue.

'I am feeling well, thank you for asking, Mrs Barden. As is young Noah.'

Frances could tell he was trying to pre-empt her enquiries. She didn't appreciate being 'managed' at the best of times by men who saw her as an irritant, least of all by one who barely concealed his growing antipathy to her calls.

'I'm very glad to hear it, Headmaster. Could you be a little more specific?'

Was that a sigh? Is the man now openly sighing down the telephone at me? Is he trying to be confrontational?

'How specific would you like me to be, Mrs Barden? For example, would you like me to itemise what Noah ate at breakfast this morning? Or—'

Frances didn't appreciate his tone.

'There's really no need to be facetious, Headmaster. I am simply a concerned parent telephoning to make sure the child for whom I am responsible is not unhappy. It would help us both if you would treat me with a little less annoyance, and a little more respect.'

There was silence on the other end of the line while Dr Nelms ran through his options. He had run through them before on several occasions, but none of them had worked out as he might have wanted. Being indulgent merely encouraged Frances to keep calling. Being brusque merely got her gander up.

'I'm not trying to be facetious, Mrs Barden,' he said, trying to sound emollient.

'If that's true, you're not trying very hard.'

'It is just that, as I have explained several times since Noah began at the school, you call far more frequently than the parent of any other child. Consequently—'

'Could that be because I care more about my child than they do about theirs?'

Frances knew this was unlikely to be the case, but she regarded 'care' and 'anxious' as interchangeable.

'I don't think that would be a fair assessment, Mrs Barden. And I suspect, neither do you.'

Frances didn't want to have an argument. She never wanted to have arguments with all sorts of people she eventually had arguments with; it was simply her nature to be more challenging of other people's positions than they were used to. It put them on the defensive, and an argument would inevitably ensue.

'I don't wish to be confrontational—'

There was a sudden snort at the other end of the line. Like the sound of someone choking on their tea, perhaps.

'Is everything all right, Headmaster?' Frances asked.

'Everything is fine, Mrs Barden. A piece of biscuit went down the wrong way, that's all. Do continue. You were telling me how non-confrontational you wish to be.'

Frances caught the faintly mocking tone in his voice and decided a different strategy was called for. All she wanted was to be taken seriously as Noah's guardian, and receive the information she requested, without editorial comment from Dr Nelms.

'Dr Nelms, I know I am a great deal older than many of the parents who leave their children in your charge. And I am a widow, which means I perhaps lack the advantage of other couples, in that I have no one at home who can assuage my anxieties about Noah when they spring up. I suppose I am – to some extent – using you in this regard. If you find that onerous I apologise.'

Frances could hear a clock ticking in the background.

'It isn't you I find onerous, Mrs Barden. You are evidently a highly intelligent, delightful woman. But the frequency of your calls is – if I may be frank – becoming counterproductive. Because—'

'I understand that,' Frances interrupted.

'It doesn't help that you scarcely allow me to respond to one point before you jump in with something else.'

Frances felt chastened.

'I do apologise. Please, finish whatever it was you were saying before we get back to the subject of Noah's well-being.'

That probably sounds more antagonistic than I want to sound. But I don't care any more. Let the man waffle on if he must. I won't be diverted.

'Your daily calls, Mrs Barden, are entirely unnecessary. And, if I am completely honest, they eat away into time I need to be spending on other issues.'

'Is that so, Headmaster? Such as?'

'The school is home to many boys whose fathers are away, fighting. Some of those boys mask their anxieties admirably and try and get on with life here. Others are not so adept, and need a lot more consideration. Only yesterday one little chap in the fourth form learned that his father had perished in the Atlantic, protecting a food convoy targeted by a German U-boat patrol. The boy was distraught, as you can imagine. His mother was too . . .'

Dr Nelms's voice trailed off for a few moments. Clearly, the episode had affected them all. Frances felt awful. She waited for the headmaster to speak, but he did not.

'I'm so sorry,' she said, softening her tone. 'I didn't realise.'

'There is no reason why you should. Under any other circumstances I would try and respond to your concerns as they present themselves, but with a lot of our younger housemasters gone off to the Forces—'

He broke off at this point. Frances wondered what was happening.

'Headmaster?'

When he came back on the line, his voice was less assured than it had been a moment ago.

'It isn't only boys we have here, Mrs Barden. Since the outbreak of war we have lost three outstanding members of staff in the fight against the Luftwaffe. Again, I don't wish to minimise your concerns over Noah, but that has had a tremendous effect on the morale of my remaining staff. These brave young men were much admired by their colleagues when they signed up, and loved by the pupils . . . '

Frances felt sick with remorse.

'I'm so sorry, Dr Nelms.'

'I really didn't want to get into this with you. But—'

'I left you with no choice.'

'Well—'

'I'm so sorry, I interrupted you again.'

The line went quiet.

You're such an idiot. Let the man speak.

'We have a great amount to deal with on a day-to-day basis – let's just leave it at that.'

Frances nodded, sympathising greatly with everything the headmaster was telling her. When she next spoke, her voice was soft, almost pleading for him to help her deal with her own personal crisis of confidence about having sent Noah away.

'But I can't just leave it, Headmaster, can I? How can we find a happy medium with my concern for Noah?'

'Can we agree that I will telephone you directly if there is any cause to? And if I have had no cause to, why don't we arrange a round-up conversation at the end of each week, if only to completely set your mind at rest?'

Frances could be horribly stubborn when she wanted to be. Yet terribly understanding when the mood struck her. She finally realised that calling every day was, indeed, counterproductive.

'I'm willing to try that, certainly.'

'Thank you, Mrs Barden. I cannot begin to tell you how much of a weight off my mind that is.'

It was the sincerest Frances had heard him sound since she had begun to telephone daily.

'But he's fine at the moment?'

'He's flourishing, Mrs Barden.'

'Thank you. I'm so sorry to hear about your three members of staff, Dr Nelms.'

'Many schools are suffering similarly. Each death feels like one of our walls has fallen down.'

Frances ended the call. She put down the receiver and stood looking at the telephone.

She had wanted to ask if she might have a minute or two with Noah on the telephone, but Dr Nelms had explained how disjointing it could be at a time when he was transferring some of his attachment from home to school. He assured her that she would be very pleased with how much progress Noah had made when she next saw him at half-term. As she walked away from the telephone Frances wondered if she would have made similar progress, or would she still regret sending him away?

Chapter 25

Erica watched with some trepidation as Dr Rosen examined Miriam's new baby in the Brindsleys' comfortably appointed front parlour. Photographs of the Brindsleys' son, David, and of their unexpected new daughter, Vivian, and of David holding Vivian, sat proudly on the mantelpiece between two silver candlesticks. Watercolour prints of the bridge at Llangollen, and a view of Snowdonia from Betws-y-Coed, hung on adjacent walls, leaving visitors in no doubt about the origins of the Brindsley clan.

Though Dr Rosen looked dressed for the part in smart, sober clothes that suggested their wearer spent more time thinking about healthcare than fashion, Erica was matched in her concerns about her doctoring abilities by Miriam, who watched the young GP like a hawk. Erica had asked Miriam if she would help her assessment of Dr Rosen 'in the field' by allowing her to examine Vivian. Though she hadn't gone into the full implications of Dr Mitchell's prognosis on Will's declining health, Erica had explained that Will would be unable to return to work 'for the moment' and she was therefore having to consider Dr Rosen as a locum.

'Vivian's gorgeous,' Erica whispered to Miriam, so as not to disrupt Dr Rosen's concentration. 'Such a lovely temperament.'

'We're very blessed,' Miriam whispered back. 'How long is it likely to be until Will returns to the surgery?'

It was a question Erica couldn't answer. She knew the answer was 'never', but she also knew that in having to give it she would reveal to Miriam what Will had asked her to keep from everyone: his cancer. This request dated back to the time when Will's diagnosis had first come through. Then, Will had begged Erica to keep it secret to prevent it unduly affecting the lives of their daughters, Kate and Laura, until they absolutely had to be told. Within a few months, Will's illness had become impossible to keep from the girls. Erica had returned home one afternoon to find them on either side of their father as he sat in his chair in the front room, hugging him, red-eyed and wet-faced. He had told them in her absence. He hadn't intended to, he explained later that evening, but the moment had come upon him in a rush, and he felt he had no choice. Erica had felt a pang of anger that Will hadn't discussed such an important moment with her first, but it passed swiftly.

After all, wasn't it his illness to speak about, as he pleased? I have to trust his judgement. If he felt it was the right time to tell the girls, then – in his mind – it was. Perhaps, in the back of his mind, he felt it might be easier to tell them without me. To spare me having to go through the revelation a second time.

'We're not sure how long we'll need someone to cover Will,' Erica replied to Miriam's question. 'The full extent of his injuries is still being determined.'

At that moment, Vivian began to cry in Dr Rosen's hands. Miriam instinctively held her own hands out to take her, but Dr Rosen kept Vivian out of reach.

'We really don't want to reinforce this behaviour,' she said.

Miriam frowned.

'What do you mean, "behaviour"?'

Erica watched with interest. This was precisely the kind of interaction between Dr Rosen and Will's patients that she had wanted to assess.

'Contemporary thinking recommends new mothers refrain from excessive reassurance when neonates cry for attention.'

'She's not "crying for attention". She's crying for her mother. And by the way, I'm not a "new" mother. I have a boy of seventeen.'

Dr Rosen stood firm, holding on to Vivian.

'I disagree, Mrs Brindsley. Vivian is crying for nothing else but your attention.'

'Furthermore,' said Miriam archly, 'Vivian isn't "a neonate" – she's *my daughter*.'

Possibly picking up on the distressed tone in her mother's voice, Vivian started to cry louder.

'With all due respect, Mrs Brindsley, I do understand your instinctive response is to offer reassurance to your child. But current thinking is quite firm that molly-coddling her will do neither of you any favours in the long run.'

'Why don't you let me be the judge of that, Doctor?'

Erica had never seen a patient directly challenge a doctor before, and decided it was her cue to intervene before the situation turned unpleasant.

'Dr Rosen—' was all she managed to utter before Miriam continued.

'I think I know what's best for my child, don't you?'

Dr Rosen was considerably younger than Erica and Miriam, but what she lacked in years she made up for in a self-confidence derived from being up to date in both medical theory and practice. She looked at Miriam squarely, refusing to give ground.

'That's a common misconception, Mrs Brindsley. In my experience, giving birth to and keeping a child alive does not inevitably mean a new mother is in full possession of the knowledge to adequately take care of the entirety of her child's physical and emotional well-being.'

Erica felt a sudden rush of adrenaline, knowing Dr Rosen might get away with a comment like this with some patients, but not with Miriam Brindsley – a woman the rest of the village knew could single-handedly hold off a horde of invading Nazis with a gutting knife for a solid half-hour. However, instead of lunging for Dr Rosen with a cry of outrage, as Erica anticipated, Miriam was perfectly restrained.

'You are speaking from your experience *as a doctor*, Dr Rosen. I am speaking from mine as a mother.'

'I understand what you mean, Mrs Brindsley. But I don't subscribe to the idea that one has to have had children to appreciate what's in their best interest.'

Despite her lack of tact, Erica could not help but be impressed by Dr Rosen's fearlessness. She had seen Will occasionally wilt in the face of the deep ignorance of a parent concerning the treatment of their young children, and he understood all too well the preponderance of 'traditional cures' in rural communities for a vast range of ailments, some of which he admitted had some scientific basis, but many more of which he dismissed out of hand as 'simply lunatic'. Here was Will's replacement, standing up for her scientific understanding to one of the strongest women Great Paxford had to offer. Erica couldn't help but admire her for this. Despite this, she felt Miriam was reaching the breaking point of her contained civility.

Still the young doctor persisted in going toe-to-toe with the butcher's wife.

Have I told her Miriam is the butcher's wife? I thought I had. Perhaps I'd better mention it again, in case Dr Rosen thinks she's up against a wallflower, or someone who couldn't literally skin her alive with one hand while washing a floor with the other.

'Contemporary thinking—'

'Is my daughter fit and healthy – yes or no?' Miriam's tone suggested that any negotiation between the two women was at an end.

Dr Rosen paused for a moment, finally assessing the situation.

'Yes, Mrs Brindsley. Very healthy indeed.'

'Thank you, Doctor,' said Miriam. 'That is all the "contemporary thinking" I need to hear this morning. Good day.'

With that, Miriam took Vivian back. Dr Rosen glanced at Erica, who was looking on with some amusement, and set her jaw.

'Mrs Brindsley—'

'As an experienced mother to a *new* doctor, I said "good day".'

Erica decided it was time to intervene.

'Dr Rosen . . . why don't you wait outside?'

Erica's expression told Dr Rosen that this was less a suggestion and more an instruction. To Erica's relief, Dr Rosen decided discretion would be the better part of valour in this instance.

'Very well, Mrs Campbell. Good day, Mrs Brindsley.'

Dr Rosen packed her doctor's bag and left. Erica turned to Miriam, who was now gently rocking Vivian in her arms.

'What do you think, Mim?' Erica asked about Dr Rosen's performance.

'Not fit to lace Will's shoes.'

Erica couldn't disagree more, and knew Will would concur. Dr Rosen might have shown a lack of finesse in her handling of Miriam, but in standing behind her medical training and up-to-date reading she had performed the duty the village would come to expect from her. She wasn't in medicine to be liked, but to help people. That was her priority. In time, the village would grow to like her for that.

Erica found Dr Rosen waiting for her in the high street, watching villagers stroll by, enjoying the winter sunshine.

'I thought you handled that very well, Myra,' said Erica.

'Are they all like her?' she asked.

'In what way, exactly?'

'Argumentative. Stuck in the past. Unwilling to engage with the latest developments.'

Erica smiled.

'This is a small, rural community. Most of the people walking past us now were born on their own kitchen tables, by methods passed down the generations.'

'Parochial, you mean.'

'No, Dr Rosen,' Erica reasoned patiently, 'I don't mean *parochial*. They have developed their ways in the absence of anything else. But that doesn't mean they are resolutely stuck in the past. In my experience, most can be convinced by calm explanation about what is now understood.'

'She wasn't.'

'Then perhaps you need to learn to be more persuasive. They are good people. The salt of the earth.'

Erica looked at Dr Rosen to see what effect her words might be having. As she considered what Erica said, Dr Rosen's expression softened. Her black eyes blinked a little more, the nostrils of her sharp nose flared a little, as if trying to take in more air with which to help calm herself down. The tension in her jaw relaxed. Her whole mien seemed less austere, and a little more open. Erica wanted Dr Rosen to like their patients because she wanted her to stay and run the surgery, and how would she do that if she didn't like the people she was going to be treating? Yet any appearance of desperation on Erica's part would undermine her negotiating position.

'You just have to get to know them,' Erica said.

The young woman smiled. 'And they need to get to know me.'

Erica smiled with relief.

Yes! She understands!

'Precisely,' Erica said, barely able to contain her delight.

'I'm not the easiest person in the world,' Dr Rosen continued. 'My father has called me "quite impossible" on many occasions. But he knows I always mean well, even if it doesn't always come out in quite the way it should. Creating a caring persona is something I need to learn.'

'And in time it won't be a *persona* at all. It will simply be you.'

At that moment, the low drone of the village air-raid siren began to pierce the morning air. Erica looked up at the sky with irritation.

Laura said they weren't expecting any raids during daylight.

As if by rote, people started to leave shops and houses and hurry without running in the direction of the large communal shelter the WI had created in Frances Barden's cellar earlier in the year. Even those with their own small shelters preferred to go to the communal one if they could. Not only because the Barden shelter was deep underground and therefore harder to destroy from above. At a visceral level, people simply felt more reassured sitting through danger in the company of others.

'This way . . . ' Erica said, threading her arm through Dr Rosen's, and leading her away. 'This will be the perfect opportunity to get to know them . . . '

Chapter 26

With the support of the WI, Frances Barden had successfully campaigned to turn her cellar into a communal air-
raid shelter for the village after it became clear to everyone that
what appeared to be the most suitable venue, the village church,
was in fact the least suitable by far.

At the time, an intense rivalry had been raging between
Frances and Joyce Cameron for control of the WI. This played
out in several ways, but came to a head over the most suitable
position in the village for the communal shelter.

Frances had been concerned Joyce would undermine the
idea of a communal shelter at the Barden house just to retain an
edge in the race to become Chair. She set out to test Joyce's plan
by contacting the local RAF station at Tabley Wood for their
'official' judgement on a potential shelter in the church crypt.

To Frances's intense satisfaction, Tabley Wood reported back
that the church was in fact the very worst location. It seemed that
to German bombers flying over, the church's architecture pre-
sented the building as 'a bloody great cross to aim at, and therefore
the worst place imaginable for civilians to shelter en masse'. In one

blunt but devastating sentence the church and Joyce's credibility were dismissed.

Frances won both the day and the Chair of the WI.

Now, rather than the location of the Barden house being a handicap, it was recognised as a distinct advantage. Being on the very outskirts of Great Paxford meant it would fall on the periphery of any bomb sight a German bombardier might have placed over the village, should the order to release the bomb load come prior to hightailing it back to Germany. Consequently, if a bomb were to hit the Barden house it would likely be by mistake and not design, though they'd had one close call already.

During the first few air raids, villagers had huddled together in terrified silence in the Barden shelter. The shelter was fairly large and had been made comfortable with furnishings and lights. People could sit or lie down if necessary. Books and magazines were available for adults to pass the time, toys and games for children. A wireless stood in the corner for occupants to listen to news or music programmes on the Home Service. For an air-raid shelter it was surprisingly comfortable, if not cosy. Though no one forgot what it was, nor why they were there.

In time, since no bombs fell on the village, terror had gradually turned to fear, and then to irritation, and then to habit. The realisation set in that Great Paxford was not top of Goering's list of targets, and that German bombing raids had simply become yet another potentially life-threatening fact of life they must accommodate alongside road accidents, or illness. Even the two bombs that had managed to find Great Paxford hadn't inflicted human casualties – one had hit a small, vacant house that was due to be demolished anyway; the other had landed in the Bardens' garden without managing to explode. It had been disarmed by Czech officer Captain Marek Novotny and two of his men. No bombs had caused as much damage or injury as the Spitfire that had crashed into the Campbell house.

The jolt these two bombs caused to the villagers' insouciance dissipated relatively quickly, as the war became focused on the Battle of Britain in the south and east, which had begun in earnest that summer. Though it took place several hundred miles away over the Channel and southern England, the villagers of Great Paxford knew their own well-being was dependent on its outcome. They listened avidly to news reports on the wireless, and watched cinema newsreels of dogfights between German and British planes with hearts in mouths. The Germans' aim was to compel the British to sue for peace by imposing a blockade on goods and provisions coming by sea. The WI's Herculean efforts in preserving fruit the previous summer had been crucial to ensuring there were plenty of calories available to Great Paxford's population over the winter of 1939. If the German blockade failed, it was strongly rumoured that Hitler would seek to invade and occupy the United Kingdom with what everyone believed were superior forces. To many, it felt as if England had fallen between a rock and a hard place, with little chance of escaping intact.

With the fighting raging in the south, air raids over Great Paxford decreased for several months. Many villagers came to view the hours they were obliged to spend in the Bardens' shelter as an opportunity to catch up with folk they hadn't seen for a while. The atmosphere below ground was no longer framed with terror, but gossipy chatter and games and laughter and music.

And so it was when Teresa came down the staircase with her schoolchildren, settled them, and found a place on a bench next to Alison, who was looking intently at Frances, who was seated opposite, talking with her sister, Sarah.

With Teresa now moved out of Alison's cottage, Alison had many solitary hours in which to brood over her treatment by Frances since the closure of the factory. Alison had an analytical, unsentimental way of approaching life, and had come to the conclusion that Frances had treated her terribly unfairly. In her mind, Frances had wrongly laid all blame for her factory's closure at Alison's feet, without allowing Alison to defend herself against such a damning judgement.

After all, wasn't it Frances who in the immediate aftermath of Peter's sudden death had wanted to try to helm the factory to see if she had an aptitude for business, and keep its operation true to Peter's ambitions? Wasn't it Frances who enlisted Alison's help as a close and trusted friend and – as a bookkeeper – someone with a professional understanding of financial matters?

The reality was that both women had found themselves considerably out of their depth. That they each knew this, and viewed it as part of the challenge they were embarking on together, did not immunise the factory against potential exploitation and corruption. Within a few weeks of Frances taking the reins a pair of crooked Liverpudlians – the Lyons brothers – appeared as new suppliers of parachute silk. Even then, Frances might have escaped disaster but for a corrupt factory manager, and a police detective who wished to exploit the situation. Alison rued the day she had allowed herself to be talked into 'doing the right thing' for her country by assisting with the investigation. Sensing an opportunity to bring to book a pair of known criminals, the police persuaded Alison to convince Frances to bring the brothers in as the factory's new supplier. Alison was deeply reluctant to do it, but the police were insistent that she do as requested, offering her the reassurance – erroneous as it turned out – that the factory would not suffer in the long term.

In due course, the Lyons brothers began supplying substandard parachute silk, the cheaper, lower-grade silk had resulted in numerous injuries to trainee airmen around the country, which prompted an immediate investigation by the Ministry of War. The factory was rapidly identified as the guilty source, and shut down in short order. The factory manager and the Lyons brothers were arrested and charged. Frances was arrested but exonerated. In her fury and disappointment, she had blamed Alison for the whole debacle. Alison had tried to defend herself, but Frances had been in no mood to listen. Instead she had taken Alison's revelation about colluding with the police as further evidence that her one-time close friend and ally had been treacherously disloyal, and eventually blamed her for everything that had happened.

In her mind, Alison had only ever tried to help Frances, so to be cast as the 'villain' cut her to her core.

How long has Frances known me? How can she suddenly behave as if I've deliberately betrayed her? I've made mistakes. More than one. But she asked me to help at the factory because she couldn't trust anyone there, and I did my utmost to do that. What happened subsequently was entirely out of my hands—

'No Boris?' Teresa, who had managed to settle the children and sat beside her friend, halted Alison's train of thought.

Alison turned to Teresa and smiled thinly.

'There's as much chance of a bomb landing on him here as at home. Better he sleeps through raids in the comfort of his own basket than be needlessly dragged back and forth.'

'I suspect many here feel the same. I know I—'

With one eye still on Frances and Sarah, Alison cut Teresa off.

'Would you excuse me for a moment . . . ?'

Without waiting for Teresa's answer, Alison stood and started to cross the cellar towards Frances.

Sarah noticed Alison approaching before Frances, and alerted her sister with a nudge to her ribs. Frances turned and watched Alison make her way slowly towards them and braced herself, feeling every muscle tighten with anticipation. She decided to take control of a situation that could easily spiral out of hand in such an enclosed public space, before most of the village.

'I thought I'd made it very clear I had nothing left to say to you,' Frances warned in a low voice as Alison drew close. 'Then, now, and in the future.'

Alison looked at Frances with the expression of someone with little left to lose.

'You did. But I have something to say to *you*.'

'Alison—'

'Perhaps you ought to hear her out,' counselled Sarah, under her breath.

'Perhaps you shouldn't interfere,' replied Frances, under hers.

'I've decided to resign from the WI. Not merely my position as treasurer. I've decided to leave the branch completely.'

The news took both Frances and Sarah by surprise. Women like Alison were the bedrock of the Women's Institute. Alison had been a member of Great Paxford's WI long before Frances had moved into the village from London with Peter twenty years ago, or Sarah from Oxford with Adam eight years ago.

Sarah was the first to speak.

'Why would you give up something so central to your life?'

'Whatever you may think about what happened at the factory, I acted in good faith. That you won't see or accept that, and refuse to even try to understand the reasons behind my actions, pains me deeply given our friendship over the years. Now you have returned to chair the branch I realise I can no longer bear—'

'Alison . . . ' Sarah felt compelled to intervene.

'Please allow me to finish, Sarah.'

'Of course. Sorry.'

Sarah took a deep breath and sat back against the wall. She glanced at Frances, who was sitting bolt upright, her attention focused entirely on Alison's face.

This is all so unnecessary.

'I understand how hard you have been struck by Peter's death,' Alison continued, 'and by everything you've since learned about his life.'

Frances glanced round, not wanting anyone to overhear this. Alison continued.

'I have also lost a husband and well remember how bitter I felt towards the world and everyone in it for a long time afterwards. I can only assume that has informed your thinking towards me in some way in the aftermath of Peter's death – as if I had become yet another person conspiring against you in secret. All I can say is . . . I was not. And never would.'

Frances stared at Alison, feeling there was much she wanted to say. But Alison's startlingly blue eyes glistened with sorrow. A small lump of regret rose in Frances's throat.

'I have only ever wished you well . . . ' Alison concluded, 'and still do.'

With that, Alison turned and walked slowly back to her seat beside where Teresa would have been had she not been called away to intervene in a dispute between two seven-year-olds in her class.

Frances and Sarah looked across the cellar at Alison, who sat down and looked at the floor.

'Well?' Sarah asked her sister.

'Well what?' Frances replied.

'Oh . . . I think you can do better than that.'

Frances absolutely hated it when her younger sister chastised her, mainly because she knew that Sarah only dared to do so when she felt she was absolutely in the right.

'Whose side are you on?' Frances asked brusquely, wanting to get off the spot Sarah was trying to pin her to as quickly as possible.

'I've learned from Adam that taking sides in a dispute is the easiest thing one can do, and often the least helpful towards finding a resolution.'

Frances folded her arms tightly, and stated firmly, 'In this instance there is nothing to resolve. I've said my piece. And now Alison, after some deliberation, has come to a decision and said hers.'

'It took a great deal of courage to come over and speak to you like that, *here*.'

'If only she had demonstrated as much courage by standing up to the police when they asked her to allow the Lyons brothers to run amok with the factory.'

'Not "asked", Frances. They told her to invite the Lyons in. She had no choice and no idea what the outcome was likely to be. Even the police seemed to be in the dark as to what course of action the Ministry were likely to take.'

'She should never have got involved in any of it.'

'One might say the same about you taking on a business you didn't know how to run.'

'I would have learned, with time. She rendered that impossible.'

Sarah started to lose her temper with her sister.

'Do you really not understand how this came about? The poor woman had no choice! You followed her advice. You didn't have to. But you chose to.'

'Because I trusted her.'

'Why? She's a bookkeeper, not a business person. That was your mistake, so take some responsibility for it and stop blaming everyone else.'

'Always *such* a bleeding heart, Sarah. But it really won't do. Alison betrayed me in the most grotesque manner in which one friend can betray another.'

'The world isn't black-and-white, Frances. In between there is rather a lot of grey. It's mostly grey, in fact. I'd go further and advocate for a world of grey if it meant losing the extremes at either end of that particular spectrum.'

'You sound like one of Adam's sermons.'

Sarah leaned close to her sister, and hissed, 'If I sound like anyone I sound like a woman who's coming very close to losing her temper with you completely. Have you learned nothing from Peter's death? Has it taught you *nothing* about how complex life can be?'

'It taught me a great deal about *loyalty*. Because of her the factory is gone.'

'You still own the buildings and the land. You could reopen under a different name.'

'I had a name. She ruined it.'

Sarah sat back and looked at Frances. She had plenty more to say but suddenly realised Frances was being deliberately unreceptive to anything that was coming out of her mouth. Sarah knew it was eminently possible her sister had heard, understood and even agreed with her feelings regarding Alison. How could she *not* have seen how hurt and upset the woman had been? But Frances was wilfully blinding herself to it.

Sarah was tired of arguing with Frances. Since he had been captured at Dunkirk, most of her time had been consumed by trying to find out where Adam was being held in Germany, and under what conditions. The lack of information was emotionally draining, leaving little appetite for going toe-to-toe with Frances over her treatment of Alison. Nevertheless, she couldn't allow the conversation to end on this point. She had known Alison too long, and liked her too much.

'You may switch off your friendship with Alison if you choose, Frances. I will not.'

Frances looked at her sister out of the corner of her eye.

'It's a free country,' she said. 'For the moment.'

Frances turned away and glanced at Alison, who was still looking miserably at the floor. For the briefest of moments, Frances wished she had sold the factory as soon as she had inherited it.

Damned Luftwaffe. Get on with it and blow us all to kingdom come – or go home and let me out of this damned cellar, away from these people . . .

Chapter 27

Pat and Claire sat in the telephone exchange, each reading *The Times*, Pat with an old army helmet strapped to her head, and a gas mask in its box on the desk in front of them. The exchange needed to be operational during air raids to allow military personnel across the region to maintain contact. While the rest of the village sought shelter, Pat and her fellow telephone operators were to remain in their post. None of the female operators were compelled to stay during an air raid, but such was their determination to do whatever they could to assist the war effort, none opted out.

The helmet was heavy on Pat's head, and made her scalp itch with sweat, but she thought she had better keep it on just in case. Claire didn't like wearing hers, and kept it on the desk in front of her, ready to don if needed. Pat assumed Claire's reticence was the vanity of a young woman who didn't want her hair messed up unless it was a matter of life or death. Had she been ten years younger she might have felt the same.

It doesn't matter to me now. Bob doesn't care what I look like, and Marek is . . . Marek is somewhere else. But where? In

England somewhere, training for a mission? Or is he already on the Continent, working behind enemy lines? Is he well, or injured? Or dead? Stop thinking like this. There's no point to it. There are a million possibilities, but until you know for sure you must only think positively about his well-being. He's no hothead. He fought his way out of Czechoslovakia and across Europe to the west coast of France. He can look after himself. It's why he's so revered by his men. He's kept them safe, and he can't do that without keeping himself safe. I can't fall apart each time some tidbit about the war comes out. He can't be everywhere, can he? He's just one man.

To distract herself Pat looked at Claire, who was engrossed in the first serialised instalment of Bob's new novel. With little help from that direction, Pat started to read back over the article about the Mass Observation reports.

After a moment, Claire looked up from the newspaper and turned to Pat.

'Is this true?' she asked sternly.

'Is what true?' Pat murmured, reading.

'Everything Mr Simms writes about in his book.'

Pat knew there was a glib answer to Claire's question, in which she would state that yes, Bob had accurately captured what had happened to him at Dunkirk. But she knew Bob was both a lazy writer who considered fact-checking a bore, and an egotist who couldn't resist giving his main character extraordinary feats of bravery to execute regardless of whether they had actually happened, on the understanding that his reading public would assume his main character was a veiled portrait of himself.

Pat hadn't been thinking about Bob for the last hour and wanted to get off the subject as quickly as possible so she could return to the small article she had been reading.

'I assume it's all true, Claire, yes,' Pat lied. 'I think he made up some of the characters, but I think the events he describes all happened.'

Claire smiled with delight. It was exactly what she wanted to hear.

'He really captures the horror of war, doesn't he?' Claire said, trying to sound as if she was someone who could tell the difference between a writer who could *really* capture the horror of war and one who could only make a rough approximation of capturing it.

If you really want to know the 'horror of war' you should try living with him. It's a war of attrition. A daily battle to survive each moment without setting off an explosive display of temper, until nightfall, when you can lay your head on your pillow and fall asleep.

'Yes,' Pat said dryly, 'he's *very* talented.' She looked up sharply, but needn't have worried; Claire had failed to pick up her ironic tone, and was continuing to read Bob's serialisation.

Pat had to admit there *was* a certain degree of deviant talent involved in the control with which Bob administered her life. It was evident in the way he kept her on the edge of her nerves from morning to night as a matter of habit that he didn't have to give conscious thought to. Pat's tormentor was one aspect of who he was, inseparable from the others. Bob managed it whilst giving nothing away to Joyce about the true, parlous state of their marriage. In fact, in the month he and Pat had been living with Joyce, Bob and Joyce had formed quite an admiration society. It was the kind of admiration Bob liked – one-way, from her to him. Pat watched it from the shadows. It made her stomach turn to see Joyce fall for the charm Bob could switch on and off like a light bulb; illuminating a room one moment, plunging it into darkness the next. He would review Pat's behaviour over the course of each day every night, in bed. He scolded her for any perceived misstep she had made, though he might occasionally praise her for something she'd done that had pleased him – a good supper, a witty remark, a clever mend of his trousers. These were constant reflections on Pat's 'performance' as his happily married wife, for an audience of one: Joyce.

'Until we find somewhere else we've got a cushy number here,' he instructed Pat at least once a week. 'Don't mess it up.'

The exchange switchboard suddenly lit up and buzzed as it registered an incoming call, causing Claire to jump in her chair.

'I'll get it!'

Pat nodded and returned to the brief article she had been considering for the past forty-five minutes. She'd seen a similar article before, describing something called the 'Mass Observation organisation', which invited ordinary members of the public to write down a daily account of their 'ordinary' lives, and send it anonymously to an office in Manchester. It was a form of diary. No special instructions were given. The unknown diarists could write about whatever interested them, at whatever length, with the aim of recording everyday life in wartime Britain. The idea was intriguing. Here was a way to give voice to her most private thoughts and feelings about her life. And about Marek. She could perhaps write a letter to him one day, as a report. Instead of going round in endless circles of worry about his safety, and his intentions towards her, Pat could explore her fears on the page, in complete privacy, and then send them away to be read by someone she didn't know and who had no idea who she was, and then be filed – perhaps on a high shelf, never to be disturbed. Pat liked the idea of sending her innermost concerns away. It made her feel that she might escape from Bob one thought at a time.

That would be wonderful!

But as ever with Pat, the moment of positivity was swiftly undercut by self-doubt.

You'd have to be out of your mind to want to read an account of my life. And I'd have to be inordinately arrogant to assume other people might be remotely interested in it. It's a stupid idea.

Nevertheless, the secretive nature of writing Mass Observation reports appealed immensely. Pat had become adept at secrecy while conducting her affair with Marek. Or so she'd believed, until Bob had revealed he had discovered their illicit communications and had been monitoring their covert meetings for several weeks.

This would be different. I'd learn from past mistakes. Keep everything from Bob. He wouldn't have an inkling what I was doing. What I was writing.

The more time she gave the idea, the more it started to excite her.

I'd write about him. Not the man Claire and Joyce and all the others round here think he is. Who he really is. I could document how he is in great detail and send it off for them to read so that someone else would understand what he's truly like. Would know what it's like to live with a man like Bob, day in, day out, month after damned month.

Though it was only a question of putting pen to paper, the secrecy and anonymity of the exercise made Pat feel as though she would be committing daily acts of revenge for everything Bob had done to her – and would continue to do. Where Bob had reported from the war in France, Pat would report from the front line of her marriage in Great Paxford. If Bob put her down, or dismissed her, or shut her up, or struck her, Pat would record how this left her feeling, and could send that to be read and understood by others, elsewhere. Whoever read her account would have to accept it, unmediated by Bob's deceitful intervention. The entire process was anonymous, so what would she have to gain by lying? In effect, she would be bearing witness to her own life, and no one could gainsay her. She felt a thrill of excitement. She no longer needed to suffer in complete silence.

Someone else would know. There would be nothing they could do about what they read, but they would read what I was living through. My secret would be out. And I would write the reports with more truth and cogency than Bob writes his pulp drivel. I have no need to ginger up anything. Merely the truth, pure and simple as I see it. Not Bob. Me. Every word I set down will be an act of rebellion.

Pat would have to work out the best times to write so Bob wouldn't know. She would also need to find a hiding place for the pens and paper she would use so Bob would never find them (a typewriter was clearly out of the question because of the noise and bulk). She wouldn't tell anyone else in case Bob was inadvertently told. It would be a completely secret part of her life. It would make living with Bob easier knowing she would have another mental compartment into which she could climb, to think about which of her thoughts she wanted to write down. And to think and write about Marek – how she felt about being unable to see him ever again, and reflect about their brief time together. She could explore those feelings on the page, and it would help her come to some form of acceptance that what she'd once had was precious in and of itself.

Pat allowed the thrill of this new project to sit with her for a few moments. She looked across at Claire. The young woman's eyes were open wide in concert with her mouth, as she read yet more of Bob's disingenuously reimagined account of his time in France. Claire, sensing she was being watched, looked up and saw Pat smiling.

'What're you smiling at?' she asked.

'I was thinking about a fun competition we could stage at the next WI meeting, just something to help us all relax, to help take our minds off our missing loved ones.' Pat dissembled quite easily. She had learned the hard way.

Claire looked immediately excited.

'I love competitions!' she squealed. 'What is it?'

'How many objects can you fit in a matchbox?'

'Oh, gosh!' Claire's eyes widened at the thought of the task. 'How big do they have to be? The objects, not the matchbox.'

'There would have to be some rules, like no ants or grains of sand, or anything silly. And only one of each item.'

'Yes, that would do it!'

Claire considered it for a moment, nodding to herself as she thought of some of the objects she might include, before being drawn back to Bob's purple prose. Pat looked at the young woman for a moment before returning to her own thoughts about the Mass Observation project.

I will only write the truth, as it appears to me. Without embellishment. All my hatred of Bob. All my love for Marek. Every truthful sentence I put down will be an antidote to every specious one he types. This will be my voice. Unadulterated and unafraid.

Pat thought about the day Marek had been shipped out of the area, and she had stood drenched in rain and sweat as she stared at the devastation caused by the fallen Spitfire, steeped in her own loss.

Where are you, my love? Are you safe? Are you warm? Do you think of me at all as I think of you?

She adjusted the helmet on her head and decided to try a Mass Observation piece of writing. She smiled at the prospect and wondered if this was what it felt like to join a resistance movement, and operate behind enemy lines. She looked at her watch and then out of the window, wondering how long before the wardens would sound the all-clear.

Chapter 28

WILL HAD MARKEDLY deteriorated since Erica and Laura's previous visit. His breathing was becoming even more laboured as he slept, and when he did eventually emerge from sleep into drowsy consciousness he simply stared at those around him for several seconds, his brown eyes moving slowly between Erica and Laura as his mind grasped for recognition. It did come, eventually. Will's eyes widened and he blurted out, 'Erica!' as if he'd been holding his breath until her name returned to him. Laura gripped her father's hand tightly, fearing loosening her grip would cause him to be sucked into the pillow and down into the folds of the bed, and away from them for ever. He would then look around the clean, white ward, trying to remember why he was here. Erica had no problem prompting him.

'The Spitfire,' she said.

It was all it took, and Will nodded sagely. He lifted his hand and held it out, then let it fall onto the sheet covering his lap, illustrating the last moments of flight of the stricken fighter plane.

'And you were underneath.'

Will nodded and pointed at Erica, who nodded.

'But you bore the brunt.'

Laura lifted her father's hand and gently kissed the back of it. 'Protecting Mim's baby,' she said.

Will managed a small smile. Erica could tell he was tired already and glanced at Laura.

'So soon?' Laura asked, sotto voce.

'Concentrating on us is a strain at the moment,' Erica replied quietly. 'I don't want him to expend more energy or effort because we're here.'

Erica stood and leaned forward towards Will.

'We're going to leave you now, my darling.' His face looked a little pained. 'To rest, Will. You need – above all – to rest.'

Will seemed reluctant to accept this.

'I have . . . one . . . doctor. I do not . . . need . . . a . . . nother.'

'Whether you need one or not, you've got one. At least until you're out of the woods.'

Laura looked at him. 'Make that two more. Three, when Kate comes home to visit.' She leaned forward and kissed his cheek. 'Goodbye, Dad.'

Will nodded, and solemnly watched them walk out of the ward. When the door closed behind them he leant his head back on the pillow, shut his eyes, and let out a sigh that allowed the strain of paying attention to flow out of his body.

* * *

Laura's face appeared in the window of the door to the ward as she looked at her father. 'He's already asleep . . .', she whispered quietly as she turned to leave.

Dr Mitchell intercepted them on their way out of the hospital, and took them to one side. He removed his round, wire-framed glasses and slowly pushed a lock of grey hair off his forehead. He looked from Erica to Laura before saying what he needed to say.

'Will is fighting as hard as he can. That's his nature. He has a remarkable will to live. But the contaminants ingested during the crash have exacerbated his cancer, and his lung capacity is diminishing daily. I think he knows what I have suspected for some time,' he said calmly. 'This isn't a fight he can win.'

'None of us will,' said Laura, 'in the long run.' She refused to cry and make the ordeal any worse for Erica.

Dr Mitchell smiled softly and nodded.

'That is very true.'

Despite Laura's mature stoicism, Dr Mitchell's description nevertheless sounded like dominoes of hope falling inexorably onto one another until the last one collapsed, and her father would be dead.

Erica blinked back tears and tried to remain focused on what did remain of Will instead of what did not.

'When he woke up just before it seemed to take him a few moments to recognise us. Is that the sedatives?' As a pharmacist, Erica was well aware how well they could dull and confuse the senses. 'Because it seemed like something more profound than a drug-induced fug.'

Dr Mitchell cleaned his glasses on the hem of his white coat and put them back on, returning the owlish quality to his round, friendly face. He cleared his throat, choosing his next words very carefully.

'We believe the cancer has spread.'

He looked at Erica and Laura and waited for this information to sink in and prompt the inevitable question, which came within seconds.

'Where to?' Laura asked.

Before Dr Mitchell could reply, Erica spoke.

'His brain.' She looked at Dr Mitchell. 'It's in his brain now, isn't it?'

Dr Mitchell looked at Erica and Laura with practised yet sincere melancholy, and nodded.

'We think it's affecting his eyesight and—'

'His memory.' Erica already knew what was happening to Will. Why wouldn't she? She knew him better than anyone, and was attuned to the slightest changes in his capacities. She had worked out the cancer had spread to Will's brain during the hours and hours she sat with him, watching him struggle to remember who she was.

'Yes,' said Dr Mitchell. 'It's in his brain for the moment.'

'For the moment?' Laura was confused.

Erica wrapped her arm slowly around Laura's shoulders.

'You know his condition isn't going to improve.'

Laura nodded. 'Yes, but—'

'Neither is it going to plateau, Laura.'

Dr Mitchell's voice sounded more clinical now, driving through to the end of what he had come to report.

'What is now happening to Will is what we mean when we say a patient is entering their final days. His body has tried to fight this disease with everything it has – assisted by additional weaponry from medical science. But there was always a limit to how much he would be able to fight, and for how long. However strong he has been – and Will is one of the strongest patients I have ever treated – he was always going to eventually reach that limit. He knew that. Well . . . it would seem he's now reached it. The cancer is spreading too quickly to be held in check.'

Erica and Laura left the hospital in a fug of their own. Dr Mitchell had torn down any remaining threads of hope connecting them to the vaguest possibility that Will might make some form of recovery. They walked through the hospital doors and along the front driveway arm in arm, in silence. They had each anticipated this moment, but not how empty it would leave them feeling. Will would soon be absent from the world, and nothing they or anyone else could do would ever bring him back. It was a feeling beyond hopelessness.

Evening swallows zigzagged in the air around them, as if vying for their attention. Neither Erica nor Laura noticed them. The low winter sun sank slowly below the treeline, pulling the last of its rays down after it. Neither Erica nor Laura noticed darkness extend from daytime shadows, consuming all in its path. Despite their numbering between twenty and thirty, dressed in suits and ties, jackets and overalls, fresh from their work in Liverpool and Crewe, Erica and Laura barely noticed the city folk huddled in the surrounding fields around tents and small campfires, exhausted yet relieved to be out of the line of aerial bombardment for another night.

Deep in their own thoughts, Erica and Laura walked along the dark lanes towards their new home on the village outskirts, seeing nothing and no one but Will in his hospital bed, struggling for life.

After half an hour they arrived and went inside. Erica took off her hat and coat and hung them on the peg. Everything felt utterly unfamiliar in the gloom. Neither woman wanted to go any further into the house; the doors to other rooms seemed superfluous when they had no desire to make food in the kitchen, or turn on the wireless in the front room. Neither reached to turn on the light. Laura sat on the bottom tread of the stairs and stared straight ahead, allowing the tears to flow down her cheeks. Erica stood in the hall, looking at her.

For the first time in her life I don't know what to say to my daughter to ease her sadness. I have absolutely no idea.

Laura's sister, Kate, had lost her young husband in a training crash on the airfield at Tabley Wood. And though they had all mourned his death, they were quietly conscious they were mostly mourning the loss of a young man they had barely got to know.

Losing Jack was dreadful for Kate. But she had only known him months before he was taken. Losing Will is a different order of magnitude. Losing Will is vast. Losing Will is a catastrophe that is almost too big for the girls to grasp. But I have to grasp it for their sake. This is happening. We're losing Will. In a matter of days or weeks he will be gone. After twenty-four years of marriage together he will no longer exist in my life, except in my thoughts and memory. I must steer them through this.

The thought made Erica's legs suddenly buckle beneath her. She held on to the banister and waited for the moment to pass.

The only man I've ever wanted. The kindest, cleverest man I've ever known. The sweetest kisser by miles . . .

Erica smiled as this verdict from her younger self bubbled to the surface. She recalled the first time they'd met, at the 1916

Christmas lecture at the Royal Institute. She had been nineteen, he was twenty-three. The talk was entitled *The Human Machine Which All Must Work*. Erica and Will had separately taken younger siblings and cousins, and found themselves on the same row in the lecture hall. As the talk progressed they found themselves taking more interest in one another than in the subject matter. At the end of the afternoon, Will had slipped past Erica and asked how she'd found the talk. She had replied, 'Interesting.' He had then asked what she thought about the idea of going for a walk with him one afternoon in Regent's Park, without children in tow. Erica had looked at his young, handsome, clever face, smiled a little, and replied, 'More interesting.'

Laura wiped her face on the sleeve of her coat and looked at her mother standing in the dark.

'We'll have to tell Kate,' she said.

Erica sat beside Laura on the bottom tread, wrapped her youngest daughter tightly in her arms, and looked at the front door. A car passed the house outside and disappeared into silence.

'We'll have to tell everyone . . .'

Chapter 29

TERESA LAY BENEATH Nick as he made love to her on their bed and supper cooked slowly downstairs. She'd previously had sex with only two other men, and had enjoyed neither experience. One had been with a young, skinny youth, with sharp features, and thin, bony hands. The other had been with an older, flabby man, with a terrifying amount of body hair. She had found both men painfully grabby and over-eager to simply prise open her legs, like burglars breaking into a downstairs window. Fortunately, Nick was nothing like them. He was gentle and considerate. He kissed her all over and told Teresa how much he adored her, and how beautiful she was, and how lucky he was to have her as his wife, and she would respond that she was the lucky one, which she felt genuinely. Nick didn't rush things in bed, and took his lead from her, yet directed proceedings too without ever seeming controlling. He seemed to want Teresa to enjoy herself every bit as he was enjoying himself. And it was good. Unlike with the other two men she had been with, Nick's lovemaking wasn't painful or without pleasure. But . . . put simply . . . and it was hardly Nick's fault . . . if making love with women was the equivalent of fine dining for Teresa, making love with Nick was the equivalent of an enjoyable cottage pie, with nice veg; lovely in its own way, but not the haute cuisine she was used to. She so wanted cottage pie to be enough.

I love this man. I want him to be all I need to feel happy and loved and safe.

Annie—

The name of the ATA pilot flashed into her mind.

Oh God – thinking of her while making love with Nick is an appalling betrayal. So stop thinking about her. Just stop thinking about her in any – by which I mean every – way.

As much as she tried to move past any variant of thinking about Annie, and tried instead to focus entirely on what was taking place in that moment in her marital bed with Nick, the more Annie's face took shape in Teresa's mind's eye.

I need to overwhelm my senses with Nick . . .

Teresa opened her eyes wide and looked into Nick's eyes with an intensity that caused him to ask if she was all right. She nodded.

'Don't stop,' she pleaded, wanting him to overwhelm her, and stop her mind from thinking of anyone else but him.

Teresa gripped Nick's face in her hands and kissed him. Even after a day at the RAF station he still smelled fresh and wonderful.

'Just lie back and think of England,' Alison had once told her. 'It's what most women do most of the time. At least . . . in England they do.'

Teresa lay back and tried to think of England, and Nick, but only managed to think more about Annie.

It isn't fair – I'm not trying to be unfaithful and I don't want to be! Why have I gone to all this trouble to prevent people gossiping about my status if I fall at the very first hurdle? Am I really so feeble?

She tried again to think of something other than Annie's face, but it only left her thinking *more* about Annie's face, and then the rest of her. This left her more excited, which had the side effect of exciting Nick even more. Teresa was left feeling fraudulent and frustrated.

Lying in post-coital exhaustion in Nick's arms, his warm breath on her neck, Teresa struggled to contain her emotions. She had found a wonderful man. She so wanted their marriage to work, and make each of them happy.

How she would negotiate regular sex with Nick had preoccupied Teresa before they were married. She thought she had come to terms with it in principle. Sex with a man once in a blue moon was fine. She could tolerate that – more than tolerate it, if he knew his way around a woman, and was prepared to be guided in areas with which he was less familiar. But once or twice a week? Or more? Teresa wasn't sure her acting prowess could sustain that level of attention.

'Just fulfil your duty,' Alison had counselled, 'and everything will be fine. Nick is a very attractive man.'

'What if he wants me to fulfil it every day? I have friends who tell me their husbands expect them to fulfil their duty every day.'

'Then do that.'

'What if I don't want to?'

'Then find a happy medium.'

This sounded like a sensible answer, but it failed to take into consideration the true nature of Teresa's problem. For Teresa, the happy medium for having sex with a man would be to instead have sex with a woman. But that wasn't now possible.

It seemed to Teresa that the only solution was to stop resisting the situation and give in to it. In other words, have relations with Nick but fantasise – if she couldn't stop herself – about having them with Annie when those thoughts arose.

It isn't ideal, but would it be so awful? Neither Nick nor Annie would ever know. Fighting it only seems to aggravate the situation. The secret would be mine alone. And I'm good with secrets. I'm very good with them. As long as I never call out her *name when I'm in bed with* him *– and I've never been in the habit of calling out my lovers' names during the act. Not even when they've deserved some kind of vocal accolade. The truth is . . . I have strong feelings towards each of them. But I'm married, and to all intents and purposes that – and Nick – has to take precedence over everything – and everyone – else. Eventually, I'm sure I'll simply stop thinking about her altogether.*

'I love you so much,' Nick whispered, kissing her neck. She could feel him becoming hard again. Teresa smiled, and said, 'I love you too. With all my heart.'

Nick began to kiss her breasts. Teresa opened her eyes to give Nick her full attention, then lay back and thought of England, Scotland and Wales.

And for just a fleeting moment, Annie . . .

Chapter 30

Who am I? I am a middle-aged woman who lives in a small village in Cheshire. I live with my husband and — for the moment — with another woman who has taken us in after our house was recently destroyed. We have lived in this village for nearly fourteen years, since 1926. Before that we lived in Manchester. At first, it was difficult adjusting to rural life. The pace of everything is definitely slower than in a city, and it's strange at first to realise that you're seeing the same faces day after day, but you get used to that, and the smells, which were difficult to begin with but which soon became familiar and, in some way, reassuringly specific. A city has no distinct smell. It could be anywhere. But as soon as I approach my village I know where I am before having to see a single house.

From one day to the next I look after my husband, who I met at a literary event following the publication of his first novel. At that time, I was a secretary at a small publishing house, with ambitions to become a book editor, though that won't happen now. Some days I feel extremely sad about what I will never be. I adore literature and have quite good taste, if I say so myself. But there's nothing I can do about it. What's done is done.

My husband is very particular about noise in the house while he's working, which means I have to be very quiet so as not to disturb him. I can't put on the wireless, for example. He doesn't like music or voices in the house. So I am unable to have friends over for a cup of tea and a chat. I'm not to disturb him in any way, except when he calls for me to make him something to eat or drink.

If I'm perfectly honest, he eats like a pig. I'd never dare say it to his face but it disgusts me. He doesn't so much eat the food I've made for him as attack it, cutting and slashing it into pieces with his knife and fork and then putting as much of it into his mouth at a time as he can so it won't take long to finish. His expression never changes to surprise or even mild enjoyment when he eats, but he does make little grunting noises of appreciation.

I hate the sound his cutlery makes on his plate, metal on china. Sometimes, in his haste to be done with meals, he bashes and scrapes the plate so hard with his knife and fork I think he's going to crack it. It's not dissimilar to his approach to most aspects of his life and his work, which he bashes out on his typewriter with seemingly little care for the consequences. When he finishes his meals he pushes the plate away and gets up from the table and goes back into his room to continue his work. I eat in peace when he's gone from the kitchen.

Most of my day is taken up with washing and cleaning and cooking. A bit of shopping. It's not a very interesting life. I read when I have time. I love the contemporary fiction I find in the mobile library that comes to the village once a month. My husband doesn't like me to read 'literary' books about female characters who think too much about their lives. I think he believes they'll give me ideas, without realising I already have ideas that he's never asked me about. He recently told me he was going to find me 'better' books to read, ones with 'proper stories'. We had an argument over it. In the end I had to let him give me a list of books he was happy for me to take out. But I also took out three books of my own choosing, which I've hidden with my underwear. It's a little like living under siege, in that I have to keep the things I really treasure away from him, or suffer the consequences.

If I were to say I hate my life I think it would be difficult for someone else to understand. But I am quite sure that I do hate it. I am utterly trapped in a marriage to a man I have come to loathe, who seems to loathe me back in equal measure. He blames me for his lack of success since his first novel, but I realised quite early on that he was an author who more or less only had one book in him. I thought he might develop into a really very good writer. Instead, he has merely developed into a quick one, albeit hard-working. This second novel is one he's managed to squeeze out because he was fortuitously posted to Dunkirk at precisely the right time to give him a story to tell. It seemed opportunistic to me, with the war still raging, and people dying left, right and centre. In poor taste, though his publisher clearly doesn't think so.

My husband is a bully and I sometimes think I haven't stood up to him enough in the past. He sometimes hits me. I can see his anger rising and I know I'm going to cop it. There's nothing I can do. I can't even run because he's faster than I am, even with an injured leg. I try and placate him but it seldom works. The shocking thing is I've grown accustomed to it now. I didn't realise this until I met another man while my husband was away in France.

The 'other man' treated me with great kindness and respect, and we fell in love. I felt so enormously happy with him. He made me feel completely different about myself, which I suppose is what love is, isn't it? It transforms us into happy, better people. Anything less isn't love. It can't be, by definition. He was very caring and attentive and loving. We made love, and it was completely different to the mechanical relations I have with my husband.

We had started to talk of a future together, after the war. I said I would leave my husband for him and we could move away and live together as man and wife. But he was called away suddenly, and I don't know if I shall ever see him again. He could be anywhere now. I've read that Churchill ordered some British troops in North Africa to be sent to Greece. Is he in North Africa? If so, will he now be on his way to Greece? I've no idea. Like so many women, I find myself wondering each minute of each day if the man I love is safe.

I don't think I've ever hated another human being in my life before this point, but there are two I hate now with a fierce passion. My husband, and myself. Him for his constant control over my life – what we eat, where I go, who I can be friends with – his constant insults and use of violence. And me, for staying.

I don't think a day goes by that I don't wish my husband had been killed in France. Or one when I don't wish I was with the 'other man'.

If it wasn't for the WI I think I would go mad. It angers my husband no end that I spend time on WI business as it's time away from looking after him. He thinks the WI is stupid, largely because he thinks most women are stupid. He thinks the WI is full of silly women making up activities for themselves because they're bored. I have tried to explain that we do so much more than what he calls 'idiotic activities' but he doesn't listen or understand how important even these 'silly' activities are to us all. A dance or a cake or floral competition, or even a game of 'guess the ankle', helps us let our hair down and enjoy ourselves at the end of a long month – which we need to be able to do now more than ever.

But the reality is that the activities he thinks are frivolous and pointless are just one aspect of the WI. In fact, the organisation does a tremendous amount of serious work in the countryside for countrywomen, and for the country as a whole. It was one of the first organisations the Ministry of War contacted when the government realised war with Hitler was inevitable. All us 'silly women' were mobilised into preserving fruit to ensure the country had sufficient calories to see it through the Atlantic blockades the Germans would impose. We also raise money for ambulances in areas suffering from bombing, and make a wide range of warm clothing for our young men serving overseas in every branch of the armed forces. And more recently, when the war came to the village in a very shocking way and wiped out two houses, it was the WI that rehoused people and refurnished properties and found clothes and support for those involved who had lost everything. It was the WI that enabled our village surgery to get back on its feet within two weeks of being flattened. In my experience, men often like to sit around talking about doing great things, but it's the women who get on and do them. If I couldn't attend my WI meeting once a month I don't know what I might do.

As this is a completely anonymous account I can write that I once considered killing my husband. It was a very bad time. I was feeling exceedingly low. He had beaten me quite severely for something, I can't remember what, and I thought he was likely to kill me if he came at me again. No one in the village knew what happened behind our front door, just as I have no idea what happens behind theirs. A friend of mine is the wife of our local butcher, so one evening I asked how they killed various animals. She was a little taken aback by the question at first, but I am our WI's 'Talks Sec' and told her I was thinking about asking her to give a talk on butchery and wanted to hear more about it. I learned so much. I decided my best bet was to use a *hammer. I took my husband's and hid it under the mattress on my side of the bed. Then I waited until he fell asleep and slowly took the hammer out and got out of bed and tiptoed over to his side. I stood over him with the hammer in my hand—*

Pat stopped writing the instant she heard footsteps on the stairs outside the small spare bedroom Joyce had allocated to them. In a single movement, Pat buried the paper and pens she was using to write her first Mass Observation report under her side of the mattress. She then lay on top of the bed, and pretended to be asleep.

After a few seconds, she realised the footsteps had been Joyce's not Bob's, and opened her eyes, releasing an almost silent sigh of relief.

In future, respond just like that. Hide everything at the first sound of someone approaching – until you know it's safe. You can't take any chances. It's how he found out about Marek. We weren't vigilant enough.

Pat lay on the bed, thinking of her Czech lover, falling back into the warm habit of wondering where he might now be, and if he ever thought of her, as she did him. Until now, rerunning her memories of the Czech captain provided her only respite from Bob.

I was loved. You may have destroyed it, but you cannot take the fact of its existence from me.

But now, in place of unanswerable questions about Marek that were driving her slowly to distraction, Pat had secret Mass Observation reports into which she could discharge any thought or anxiety she wanted, without fear or censure.

If I wanted, I could write that I had killed Bob, and got away with his murder scot-free.

She was tempted to free herself from Bob in fiction as she was unable to in life.

But . . . this is meant to be an accurate account of things. If I make things up as and when I feel like it, how can my report stand as a truthful, historical record? What kind of witness would that make me? Tell the truth. Always. Just tell the truth. I didn't kill Bob. I'm not sure I'm capable of murder, not even if I consider it to be in self-defence. But until one finds oneself in that situation it's impossible to say what one is capable of. We both live to fight another day . . .

Chapter 31

WHEN FRANCES HAD challenged Joyce for the Chair of Great Paxford's WI a year earlier, she did so on a platform of wanting to keep the branch open during the war. Joyce had wanted to mothball it until hostilities came to an end, whenever that might be, arguing that the women of Great Paxford would have more urgent matters to attend to than 'WI business'. Frances couldn't have disagreed more. She remembered from the Great War how important it was for women to provide support and distraction for one another when their men went to fight.

Frances had won a huge mandate from a membership tired of being treated like sheep by Joyce. She immediately encouraged women who had been previously put off joining by Joyce to become new members, and they had joined in droves.

Looking at their faces now, Frances couldn't be more pleased with the new membership.

Steph Farrow would never have considered joining under Joyce. I've made Steph – and working women like her – feel welcome. And they've contributed so much. And gained so much. Look at Steph herself. When the WI turned the cricket pitch into an allotment to grow food, it was Steph who supplied most of the equipment, and drew up a plan for what and where to plant. All the while running the farm while her husband Stan's away fighting. You can see in Steph's face every time she walks through the door of the village hall – she feels equal to anyone. Everyone loves her clear thinking and antipathy towards waffle, and what her husband apparently likes to call 'utter bollocks'.

Consequently, when Steph approached Frances in town to discuss the influx of people into the area at nightfall from Liverpool and Crewe, Frances listened very carefully indeed.

Steph reported that incomers coming to shelter from nightly bombardment from the Luftwaffe were similar to the 'trekkers' in the south she'd heard described in wireless bulletins – thousands who literally trekked on foot from London every night into the surrounding countryside to avoid being caught in the Blitz. Since her first sighting of them on the tractor with her son, Little Stan, a few weeks ago, Steph had seen them grow in number at night in the countryside around Great Paxford. She had seen some camping in her own fields, the light from small campfires visible from her bedroom window.

'I'm not happy about it 'cause they're trespassing,' said Steph. 'But I don't know what to do 'cause I understand why they've come. A lot of the farmers feel the same. So far, they haven't given any trouble. But more come all the time. They don't know how things work round here. There's a lot of fires being lit on dry ground, for example. All it takes is a spark to jump to a barn and you could lose a farm without much problem. Lot

of unprotected livestock too. I've heard reports of farmers seeing children walking up to cows and sheep like they're tame.
Which they're not. We haven't seen animals taken for meat yet,
but a lot of us think it's only a matter of time. We don't have
the police we did 'cause so many have joined up, so who knows
what could happen—'

'And then there's the other thing!' interrupted Mrs Talbot,
a thin and angular woman, with small eyes, a large nose in the
shape of a small tomahawk, and a small head on a scrawny,
red neck, a woman perfectly at ease with interrupting someone
else's private conversation. In look and demeanour, she resem-
bled an affronted chicken, ready to peck or claw someone's
eyes out at the slightest provocation.

'Other thing?' asked Frances. 'What other thing?'

'Some of them are darkies.'

'So?'

'They have different ways to us, don't they?'

'Do they?' said Frances. 'I honestly wouldn't know.'

'They might see chickens in a field and think, "Thanks very
much, free food."'

Frances looked at Mrs Talbot for a moment.

'They might, I suppose, Mrs Talbot. But we hear no accounts
of them doing that in Liverpool, where they live perfectly peace-
fully alongside everyone else, so why should we fear it here?'

'They might think things're more relaxed out here.'

'I'm sure they are perfectly civilised people, Mrs Talbot. And
like civilised people everywhere, they are most likely to do what
everyone else is doing.'

'You say that but we don't know, do we?'

'Well, if we look at how they behave where they live, we arguably do know. And where they live they behave like everyone else.'

'People are scared – that's all I'm saying.'

'But of what, Mrs Talbot? Something real and tangible, based on actual evidence? Or are they simply scared because of their skin colour, and that alone?'

'They come from savages, Frances. We all know it.'

'You listen to the wireless a great deal, don't you, Mrs Talbot?'

'Yes.'

'You follow the war very closely.'

'I keep abreast of the news.'

'Do you honestly believe savagery is limited to the black races?'

Mrs Talbot looked at Frances, flummoxed by the philosophical turn of the conversation.

'Well . . . '

'As far as I know, no "darkie" has ever dropped bombs on a civilian population, as Hitler did at Guernica, and now across Europe.'

It was this conversation that had persuaded Frances to call a committee meeting at her house, to discuss any friction that might arise from the increasing numbers of these trekkers coming into the area around the village. That and, if she were completely honest, the opportunity to organise a distraction from her anxiety over Noah's progress at his new school – not helped by the fact that she hadn't heard from the boy since he left. She missed him terribly, and thought about Noah a very great deal. She might have agreed to curtail her daily telephone calls to the school to check how well he was fitting in, but this didn't mean her anxiety was any less. But the headmaster had promised to call if there were any causes for concern, and as yet there had been none. Realising she'd once again let her mind wander to Noah, Frances dragged her thoughts back to the matter at hand.

Strictly speaking, dealing with trekkers was within the purview of the parish council rather than the WI. However, the parish council was riddled with local pompous retired men who, for want of anything better to do, loved playing 'local politics' – two words that sent a shiver of horror trickling down Frances's spine. The parish council was notoriously slow to react with any coherence or very much at all, except issues surrounding 'fishing rights' on local rivers. By the time it ever managed to get to grips with the trekker situation things could already have begun to spiral out of control. Frances thought it prescient for the WI to be prepared with possible ideas for tackling trouble before it occurred.

Frances sat at the head of her own dining table and looked at the faces of her inner circle: Steph, Teresa, Sarah, Miriam, Erica and Pat. But not Alison, her absence causing Frances a small twinge of regret, eliciting a sigh and an instruction to herself not to dwell.

What's done is done. Move on.

'I called this meeting, ladies, to discuss what seems to be a developing situation. Clearly, if the Luftwaffe stopped bombing Liverpool and the north-west today the issue would literally disappear overnight. But that seems like extraordinarily wishful thinking. The Germans are hell-bent on razing the city to the ground in much the same way as they seem hell-bent on levelling London. Bombing the world into submission seems to be Hitler's favourite military strategy. That said, before we get too hot under the collar about the presence of city folk in our midst, we first need to establish whether this is a phenomenon that should cause us real concern.'

Miriam raised her hand to speak.

'I think it very much will cause us concern.'

'Very well. Why do you think that, Miriam?'

'One or two have started coming in the shop to buy meat with their ration books.'

Steph frowned. 'That's allowed, isn't it?'

'It is. Bryn asked why they don't buy closer to home and was told it's increasingly difficult when butcher's shops are getting hit by the Germans, alongside everything else.'

Teresa didn't quite see the problem. Being Liverpudlian her natural inclination was to spring to the defence of her people.

'That certainly chimes with what I've been hearing,' she said. 'But if they can't find meat to buy at home why shouldn't they buy meat here?'

Frances turned back to Miriam.

'Is there an issue with the trekkers buying meat from Brindsley's, Mim?'

'Not at the moment, because there haven't been many of them. But should the numbers increase we might have problems meeting demand.'

'In that case you'd prioritise regular customers,' said Steph, assuming the solution was quite straightforward. 'Isn't Brindsley's there to serve Great Paxfordians first?'

'We might want to,' said Miriam, 'but it might be impractical. Imagine you're one of these trekkers who can't get meat in Liverpool, and you're standing in line at ours, and David or Bryn says, "Sorry, love, I can't serve *you* but I *can* serve the person standing right behind you." You can imagine the reaction, given they know we're meant to serve anyone with a ration book. Puts us in a very tricky spot. Bryn can handle himself if things get out of hand, but not David, with the injuries he got when his ship went down. It's a growing worry, I can tell you.'

The other women round the table looked at one another. Until now, any fears they had harboured about the trekkers had been fairly abstract. Miriam's were not. Soon, unless the situation was brought under control, theirs might not be either.

Sarah generally hung back in discussions of this nature, often feeling that people rushed to judgement too early. She would have stayed silent longer had she not already given the issue some consideration after seeing a trekker family make camp around the back of the church three nights ago.

'I believe a similar issue might arise concerning the air-raid shelter,' she said.

The others looked at Sarah with interest. She was renowned for her calm common sense.

'The shelter here was created with the village in mind. *Specifically*, for the villagers. What happens during an air raid when these people are out in the open? Do we say, "Sorry, but there's no room for you here," and leave them to their fate? If Adam were here, he would have something very forceful to say about that.'

'We could put them in the crypt,' said Miriam. She didn't see there was much of an argument.

'The crypt was decreed unsuitable as a village shelter,' said Frances. 'Are we happy to say it's not good enough for Great Paxfordians but it's fine for anyone else?'

'We can only do what we can,' said Steph.

Sarah looked at the others, slightly irritated her point was being missed.

'I fully accept that. But what if the trekkers won't accept it. Turning away potential customers in your shop, Mim, because there's a limit to how much meat you can sell is not the same as turning away terrified people from our shelter with the sirens blaring. Don't forget, these people are already so frightened they routinely abandon their own homes every night to seek safety out here. Some or all may not be in a fit state to be reasoned with – if it's even possible to talk "reasonably" about denying others protection from aerial bombardment.'

'And we don't know them,' said Mim. 'We know everyone who comes into our shelter, but we don't know them. We know nothing about them. Nothing at all. I think we're asking for trouble to expect the village to sit cooped up with a bunch of strangers for hours on end.'

The other women looked at Miriam and nodded. Sarah sighed pointedly.

'What choice would we have?'

Frances looked at her sister with deep admiration. Whether it was to do with taking Noah in, or helping Frances come to terms with all the consequences resulting from Peter's death, Sarah had an innate ability to isolate the moral nub of an argument.

'Shouldn't we have more faith in our ability to accommodate these people safely, without getting carried away with phantom anxieties? We're at war, ladies. We pull together. We help one another. As a village. As a country. It's what *civilised people* do.'

'We could take *some* into the shelter, I suppose, if we had space,' Miriam conceded.

'How would we choose which ones?' said Sarah, continuing to interrogate the issue.

'Children first?' Pat suggested.

'What if we only had space for *some* children but not all?' Sarah persisted. 'Which children? The youngest? The most scared?'

'First come first served,' said Miriam, feeling this generally settled most questions of prioritisation in the shop.

Sarah nodded. 'That might work in the shop, but . . . turning people away from your shop is hardly a life-and-death situation, Mim.'

'It is if you're gasping for a bacon buttie,' said Teresa. The others laughed at the joke, glad of some light relief.

Frances turned to Erica, who hadn't spoken since the meeting opened.

'What do you think, Erica?'

Erica didn't answer. She'd barely heard the question. She had been too immersed in thinking about Will to register any of the discussion taking place around her.

'Erica?' repeated Frances softly.

Erica looked up.

'You've been very quiet, dear. What do you think?' Frances asked.

Erica looked round the table. The other women regarded her with growing consternation, sensing something might be wrong.

'I don't know. Sorry.'

Erica smiled unconvincingly and hoped Frances would move the discussion on to someone else. But she didn't. Frances was sitting closest of all the women to Erica, and could see that below the table, out of sight of the others, and despite holding them tightly together, Erica's hands were trembling fiercely.

'Erica. Is everything all right?'

Erica looked at Frances.

Why did you have to ask me that? Why didn't you continue to talk about whatever you were all talking about before? Because now I have to answer, and I'd sooner not because once I do . . . everything changes.

'Will . . . ' Erica said flatly.

'Will?' said Frances. 'What about him?'

Erica looked at Frances.

Say the words, Erica.

'He's dying.'

She heard someone gasp to her left. Probably Teresa.

'He's been unwell for some time. And then the crash—'

She couldn't continue. The women stared at her in shock.

'What do you mean, "he's dying"?' asked Miriam.

Erica put both hands to her face, covering her eyes, and sat there like that.

Help me, help me, help me . . .

Sarah was first to her feet, crossing to Erica to put her arms round her. Next came Steph, who rested her hands on Erica's shoulders and laid her head against hers. Then Pat and Miriam rose and crossed the room to Erica, adding to the embrace. Teresa was next, kneeling beside Erica and taking her hands. Held in their embrace, Erica began to sob.

Frances stood and looked at the women cocooning Erica, offering their strength and support while she wept. Peter had died suddenly, giving Frances no time to prepare. Everything about that event, and everything arising from it, had turned Frances's life on its head. She had only just started to find a clear path through it all. She needed more time before she was ready to absorb more tragedy. But war compresses time, and the human brain can barely keep up, clinging to certain constants we hope will see us through to when the fighting stops.

Will Campbell had been one of the solid constants of village life. If you were ailing, Doc Campbell got you through. He was regarded as one of the pillars of Great Paxford, holding the village together day after day, getting *everyone* through. The revelation about his imminent demise shocked every woman present.

Frances looked at the women holding on to Erica, as they had once held on to her at Peter's funeral, keeping her on her feet.

I can help you prepare.

Frances rested her hand on Erica's shoulder and lowered her face to the side of her head.

'You're not alone,' she said quietly. 'Never alone.'

Chapter 32

TERESA ARRIVED HOME from the committee meeting at Frances's house, only to be disappointed not to see Nick's car already outside. She was eager to tell him her first piece of significant news since they'd been married, and was interested in his thoughts about Erica's revelation concerning the declining state of Will's health. Teresa had been as deeply upset as any of the women in the room at the time, and hoped that discussing what had happened with Nick would give her a sense of perspective on the situation, not to mention the solace of a problem shared. After all, wasn't sharing views, thoughts and feelings how husbands and wives established common ground? She and Nick talked every day, but almost exclusively about things that happened at the RAF station or at school – though while Teresa was free to talk about anything that happened at work, Nick was often unable to reveal a great deal about what took place at the RAF station. That said, Erica's breakdown in front of her closest friends was far from work-related chit-chat, and Teresa was interested to hear what Nick thought about it. The news had been profoundly shocking. Teresa wanted to discuss it with her husband.

As a man in charge of men who face death many times, Nick constantly deals with extreme emotion. His insights might be very helpful.

At any given moment, Teresa liked knowing what was going to happen over the course of the next few hours. It meant she didn't have to worry about the unexpected. It was one of the reasons she enjoyed teaching. If you planned things properly, as she always did, there should be no unpleasant surprises. Consequently, Teresa planned to spend much of the evening discussing Will and Erica with Nick, and then mention what she had learned about the trekkers. She looked forward to having a long, serious conversation with Nick about weighty issues, and felt confident it was an aspect of marriage at which she would excel.

Teresa entered the house and called out Nick's name on the off-chance he had been dropped off by his driver, Tom. Nick didn't answer, and his coat and cap were not hanging on the peg by the front door. She hung up her own coat and hat and went through to the kitchen to put on the white apron with a wild-flower print on the front – a wedding gift from a relative. Teresa had never previously bothered with an apron when cooking, and didn't much like the pattern on this one. But she had never cooked in earnest before, and it had been useful to have an apron to defend her clothes against the range of splashes and spills that accompanied culinary experimentation. She didn't enjoy the sensation of tying herself into the apron, but gave herself over to it. Nick said he liked it, telling Teresa it made her look *maternal*. The word had sent a little shock wave through her. Their new home was comfortable, with modern furniture and colourful wallpapers. But there was nothing about it yet that suggested it was a home-in-waiting for children. Teresa had tried to laugh away Nick's 'maternal' comment by pretending to scold him for suggesting the apron made her look like 'his mother'. By the time Nick had explained that wasn't what he meant at all, his attempt to gently reintroduce a conversation about starting a family had been scuppered. Teresa had breathed a small sigh of relief, but she knew he would return to the topic at some point. She just hoped it wouldn't be soon.

But why wouldn't it begin to preoccupy him? Why else did people marry unless to have a family? The war hasn't turned everyone against bringing children into the world. A lot of people take it as a sign that life is short and unpredictable, so they'd better get on with it.

It wasn't that Teresa had ever consciously decided that she didn't want children of her own, more that she believed children were out of reach for women like her. She had carried that assumption into her marriage to Nick, until Alison raised it one day.

'You'll have children, of course.'

'Will I?'

'I expect Nick will want a family, don't you?'

'You and George didn't.'

'If he had survived the war I'm sure we would have. We often spoke of it. Nick will want a family with you, Teresa. I guarantee.'

When left alone to think about the possibility, it hadn't alarmed Teresa as much as she thought it might. She adored children, and had made their education her vocation. To her surprise, when she did give the possibility some thought, the prospect of having her own children excited her.

But only when I feel completely ready. Events must happen in the correct order. One thing naturally leading to another. I have to prove I can make a success of marriage. It wouldn't be fair to Nick, or to any child we might have.

Marriage had been a huge step for Teresa to take, and she needed to feel it would endure before she could justify becoming pregnant. It would mean giving up teaching, though she knew it was possible she would have to give it up simply for being married and taking up a position that could be given to men too old to fight. She had discussed all of this with Nick, stating that she didn't wish to fall pregnant while the war was ongoing when the possibility existed that something terrible could happen to him, leaving any children he left behind to grow up fatherless. Nick had joked that he could just as easily be hit by a bus in peacetime as a Messerschmitt in war, but understood Teresa's concerns, and agreed to follow the rhythm method for the time being.

Tonight, Teresa had decided to cook something simple. Not only because something simple offered her the best chance of cooking something edible, but because she didn't want a sudden breakthrough in her culinary skills to amaze Nick so much that it interfered with their conversations about Will Campbell, and the trekkers. She settled on soup.

You can't go wrong with soup. Nobody knows what's meant to be in it so it's nicely open to interpretation. As far as I can see, soup has few rules. It's very difficult for anyone to be disappointed that soup failed to meet their expectations because most people's expectation of soup is low. Because it's just all sorts, mixed together. And as it isn't a thing in its own right, as long as it has enough salt it's difficult to mess up. Easy. Even I can make soup. I have made soup, many times. No one died. People actually finished it. More or less.

Teresa was chopping the last carrot to go into the saucepan when she heard Nick's car pull up outside. Now she had in mind to tell Nick about Will and the trekkers over supper, she was slightly disappointed he'd arrived back before she was ready for him. Her schedule was based on Nick returning home *just* before supper, but not *too much* before, since that would leave them with too much time to fill with conversation before supper itself. She wanted them sitting down when she told him what had happened at Frances Barden's house. She wanted Nick to give the matter his serious consideration, *across the kitchen table*. Like a real married couple. She wondered if other women found married life so complicated.

Still chopping, she heard the front door open.

'Teresa?'

She smiled every time he called her name when he returned home. Each time he sounded excited. It was lovely to be anticipated without fail.

'Kitchen!' she chirruped back, already comfortable with the conversational short cuts used by married couples. Kitchen! Upstairs! Garden! Love you! You too!

She turned as he opened the door, and smiled at his very handsome face, beaming from under the peak of his RAF cap. She sometimes thought he looked like an American film star in his uniform. It fitted him so well, and vice versa.

'I've brought someone back,' he said.

Teresa must have frowned slightly, because Nick then asked, 'Is that a problem?'

Inasmuch as it disrupted her plans for the evening it *was* a problem, but Teresa swiftly calculated it needn't be an insurmountable one. If the guest was staying for supper, then she could tell them both about Will. If the guest *wasn't* staying for supper then Teresa could wait until they'd gone before talking to Nick as planned, over soup.

'Not at all. Who is it?' she said a little more loudly than necessary, hoping her cheery tone would travel into the hall and welcome their guest.

Nick had brought officer colleagues back for supper on a few occasions since they'd moved in. They were usually unmarried young men with their nerves on edge after too many sorties against Luftwaffe bombers and their fighter escorts. All of them benefited from a few hours away from the RAF. Teresa had been fond of them all, even the near-silent ones. She had a graphic sense of what combat was like from Nick, who would whisper answers to her careful questions in bed, while she held him. Teresa found herself awed in the company of these extraordinarily brave young men, some no more than teenagers. They had all undertaken and witnessed such unimaginably terrible things. Teresa's admiration for the young pilots Nick brought to their kitchen table was always fringed with sorrow, knowing the odds were stacked against seeing them again. When she thought about the dead pilot she had watched being carefully lifted from the Spitfire cockpit on her wedding day, Teresa tried to shut out the idea that one of her young guests from Tabley Wood might meet a similar fate. Or a much worse one. Each tried so hard to be cheerful and good company.

Nick stepped to one side, revealing Annie, in her ATA uniform.

'Annie flew a Hurricane up for us this afternoon. Invited her back for a drink and a bite.'

Teresa looked at Annie and felt sick. It was one thing to think of Annie in secret. It was another to have the object of her desire standing three feet from her husband in her own house. She felt herself turn red and hot with embarrassment, which embarrassed her further.

She knows why I'm embarrassed. This is wrong. Of all people, why has he brought her?

Annie looked at Teresa's expression and instantly realised coming back to the house with Nick had been a mistake. When Nick had mentioned coming over for supper Annie hadn't given it a great deal of thought. She was exhausted after flying a Hurricane up from Hertfordshire in rough weather, and accepted Nick's invitation without thinking. It was only in the car from Tabley Wood that it began to dawn on her that coming to supper might be a mistake. As they pulled into Great Paxford, Annie started to worry that Teresa would see her arrival, without prior warning, as an intrusion at best; predatory at worst. She wanted Teresa to think neither.

Annie smiled and tried to put Teresa at ease as best she could with whatever was to hand.

'I like your pinny,' she said.

Teresa looked at Annie and took the simple compliment the wrong way.

How dare you come into my house and snidely mock me?

'It was a wedding gift from a cousin,' Teresa said, trying to give the impression that under any other circumstance she wouldn't be seen dead in it.

It had been a long, gruelling day, and Nick wanted to get the evening under way. 'Who wants what to drink?'

When he disappeared with Teresa and Annie's drink requests, the two women shared an awkward pause.

'I hope you like what I'm making. It's . . . well . . . it's soup.'

'I didn't mean to put you on the spot,' Annie said, sidestepping Teresa's attempt at conviviality. 'I think I should leave.'

'You haven't put me on the spot,' Teresa said, maintaining her composure. 'Nick can bring home whomever he wants. You're very welcome.'

'That's very kind of you, but—'

'Besides, if you left now it would raise all sorts of questions.' Annie looked intensely at Teresa.

'Such as?'

Such as why you and I shouldn't be alone together with Nick in another room.

'Nick would think you were leaving because I'd said something to offend you.'

'He knows nothing offends me.'

Teresa scrambled for a different topic to disguise her awkwardness and the sense of dread that was beginning to overwhelm her.

'How was your hop up?' she asked, as if asking someone who had motored a few miles over from Chester or Crewe, and not from Hertfordshire in poor weather. 'Is it more difficult in poor weather?'

'I love flying in low cloud. Not quite knowing where one is. No bearings to speak of. Fully focused. More challenging, certainly, but I enjoy that. Keeps us ATAs on our toes. That, and not having a parachute to bail out with.'

'You don't have parachutes?' Teresa was shocked.

Annie smiled. It was a detail she had revealed on many occasions, always with the same reaction.

'We're non-combatants.'

'But what if something happened?'

'I think they rather want us to try and deliver the aircraft come what may. If something goes wrong, rather than saying "oh well, bad luck" and bailing, without a 'chute we have an incentive to try and get the crate on the floor somehow. Gliding, if necessary.'

Teresa was horrified by the potential dilemma, but deeply impressed by Annie's insouciant fortitude. She couldn't take her eyes off her. Annie's refinement wasn't only apparent in the way she conducted herself with such good cheer. It was built into her facial features, her bone structure, her eyes, nose, and lips – all in perfect proportion. It was in the graceful way she held herself.

Class. There's no other word for it.

'I'm shocked you're not given parachutes,' Teresa said.

'Don't be.'

'But what if—'

'Don't think about it. I don't. I'm an exceedingly good pilot. Touch wood, I shall continue to be an exceedingly good one.'

Annie looked at Teresa and smiled.

'I really do like that pinny.'

'Oh, be quiet!' Teresa smiled. 'It's hideous!'

'It really *isn't*. I like wildflowers.' Annie held Teresa's look for a few moments. 'The wilder the better.'

Teresa blushed.

They could hear Nick clinking glasses in the front room. Annie glanced towards the door, then back at Teresa, her cheerful demeanour suddenly dropping.

'You have nothing to fear from me, Teresa. I promise. Nothing at all,' she said quietly, with an intensity Teresa had not previously experienced.

Teresa was about to reply when Nick returned with their drinks and handed them out.

'One Scotch and water, one small sherry, and a large G and T for me! Cheers!'

Annie drank most of her Scotch in a single gulp while looking directly at Teresa, then turned to Nick, her customary ease returning to her expression.

'I really oughtn't have come, Nick. I don't know what I was thinking. I'm shattered. I'm in the air back south tomorrow. I really need to go back and get some shut-eye.'

Nick looked disappointed. Annie was generally a sure bet for an entertaining night.

'Are you sure?'

She nodded. 'It's only just starting to kick in. In five minutes, I'll be unconscious.'

'My food's bad, but not *that* bad,' Teresa said, smiling, relieved Annie might be going in short order. She wanted to appear as if she too would be disappointed if Annie couldn't stay. Teresa could have managed an evening with both Annie and Nick, but on her own terms, with planning and preparation.

'I'm sure it's lovely, whatever it is.'

'Like I said, it's just soup,' said Teresa, apologetically.

Please don't ask what kind because I don't really know.

'What kind?'

'That's a perfectly reasonable question,' Teresa offered, buying herself some time. 'Difficult to say.'

'A little of everything?'

'Yes.'

Annie looked at Teresa and smiled.

'Variety is the spice of life,' she said with an almost imperceptible glint in her eye that passed Nick by completely. But not Teresa, who felt a wave of anxiety pass over her that left her momentarily nauseous.

Please leave. This isn't fun or amusing in any way. I am a married woman. Behaving like this in front of my husband is completely inappropriate.

When Nick left to take Annie back to Tabley Wood, Teresa sat at the table and knocked back her sherry in a single shot. She reviewed the last twenty minutes, trying to calculate how much of a fool she had made of herself, and how much anger she felt towards Annie for behaving so recklessly in front of Nick.

Save it for the clouds, where no one else can get hurt.

Teresa concluded that she hadn't been *completely* ridiculous, despite the apron. Aside from her little game of innuendo, she grudgingly concluded Annie had behaved impeccably. Seeing Teresa had been wrong-footed and embarrassed by her arrival, Annie had offered a perfectly believable excuse and left without drama, leaving Nick none the wiser.

Just.

Teresa sat for a few moments, allowing the silence to restore her equilibrium. She then rose from the table and wandered into the front room and poured herself another sherry. She sat down in the armchair and looked around the room at the prints on the wall, and the photographs on the mantelpiece. Her eye was drawn to her wedding photo. She and Nick at their most beautiful and handsome. A dazzling couple by any standard.

Nick's wife is who I am now. Forget everything else.

She slowly sipped her drink, and told herself to stay away from Annie from this moment on.

Nick. This house. Our life together. Nothing is worth risking everything I have. Nothing. And no one.

Chapter 33

Erica walked slowly up the drive of the cottage hospital. A coal-black chorus of crows called earnestly to one another as they rode the thin branches of high treetops in the stiff, cold wind. Erica's pace didn't quicken when the hospital came into view. If anything, it slowed, as her dread began to rise at the almost certain prospect of listening to Dr Mitchell patiently describe further deterioration in Will's condition.

What will it be today? His speech? Sight? Hearing? Mental faculties? Will he recognise me at all? Because that will come, I'm sure. Or will he leave us before he completely loses control?

Having eventually secured the services of Dr Rosen for the next twelve months at least, Erica had tried to turn her thoughts to Will's remaining days, without much success. This failure was partly due to the unpredictable nature of Will's *decline* (a word she loathed but found difficult to replace with one more apt), and in part because she continued to struggle with the absolute certainty that her husband was going to die soon. Her breakdown at the WI committee meeting had been a sudden, explosive recognition of the finality of Will's journey, and had taken her completely by surprise. Everyone lives with the unspoken understanding of their own obsolescence, yet somehow manages to trick themselves into believing their loved ones will live for ever. The realisation that Will's days were now terrifyingly finite had rocked Erica in Frances Barden's dining room. She realised afterwards it had been triggered by the discussion about the possibility of leaving trekkers in the open to potentially perish under German bombardment.

Later that evening, Erica had told Laura she felt enormously relieved that news of Will's illness was finally out, at least among her closest friends.

'How did they react?' Laura asked. She was curious to know how different people would respond to the news.

'They were terribly upset.'

'What did they say?'

'Nothing.' Erica paused. She didn't want to get upset again. 'They . . . were very kind. So kind. We're very lucky to have such good friends at this time. Very, very lucky. You'll see for yourself.'

Erica wasn't yet prepared for the rest of the village to know that Dr Rosen wasn't merely the temporary replacement for Will – that Will would never return as their GP. Laura needed to prepare for the onslaught of sympathy that would come.

'Your father is greatly loved in the village. People will want to do something for him, even though there is nothing anyone can do. When they realise this they will want to do something for us, probably when we want to be left alone. At all times, Laura, remember – they only mean to help us.'

Erica pushed through the squat hospital's small entrance and walked along the corridor towards Will's ward. She had decided not to tell him that her friends now knew the real state of his health. She didn't want him thinking about anyone but himself, and how to ensure the last weeks and days of his life were the proper culmination of the forty-seven years that had gone before.

The hospital smell was a strangely reassuring mix of institutional stew and disinfectant. The sound of low voices, busy footsteps and doors opening and closing had become familiar to Erica, almost reassuring. As Great Paxford's pharmacist, Erica frequently came to the hospital, but never before as a patient, or as the daily visiting wife of one.

Entering the ward, Erica stopped dead, and the hairs on the back of her neck stood up in terror. Her palms were instantly clammy. She looked around the ward for some clue as to why Will's bed was empty, but no clue offered itself. There were no staff or other visitors she could ask. The other patients lay motionless, asleep and almost indistinguishable from the sheets and blankets they were buried under.

Without being conscious of making the decision to do so, Erica slowly started to walk towards Will's bed, as if her presence might trigger his reappearance between the sheets, or from beneath the bed, or from a cupboard nearby, in some elaborate revelation. Upon reaching Will's bed she could see it was not freshly made, indicating that, wherever he was, Will was not long gone. She laid her palm on the bottom sheet. It was still warm. Her head pounded.

Will is bathed in his bed. Fed in his bed. So why has he been removed from it?

Erica turned at the sound of the ward door swinging open, and saw Will being pushed through in a wheelchair by Jeremy, the stout, bearded, red-faced, friendly orderly from Chester to whom Erica had spoken on many occasions. Will's mouth and nose were covered by a face mask, and a small canister of what Erica assumed was oxygen lay on his lap. When Jeremy saw Erica, he smiled.

'Just been for a stroll. Hope we didn't shock you,' he said apologetically as he parked Will beside his bed.

Erica stared at Will as tears of relief filled her eyes, and she smiled like a happy idiot. She was preparing herself for Will to leave her, but wasn't yet ready.

Not yet. I need more time.

Some colour had come back to Will's face, and sitting upright in the wheelchair made him look much more like his old self than when he lay in bed. His skin hung better on his face in the same way a suit looks better on a hanger than draped across a chair. He even looked a little like 'Doc Campbell', sitting behind his desk in his surgery.

Will looked at her and slowly pulled the oxygen mask away.

'Thought you'd . . . seen the last . . . of me?'

'Your husband has a terrible sense of humour, Mrs Campbell,' said Jeremy. 'I don't mind the odd joke from patients about kicking the bucket. But his are continuous and *not very funny.*'

'They . . . keep me . . . amused,' said Will, smiling.

'Could you put the mask back on, please, and stop showing off.'

Jeremy winked at Erica.

'He thinks he can survive without oxygen. He can't.'

Erica smiled. Will hadn't looked this well since the day he had been pulled from the wreckage of their house. She'd thought she'd lost him then, and it had taken forty-eight hours before Dr Mitchell allowed her to have any hope he might live on for a while longer.

'I'll leave you to it,' Jeremy said discreetly.

Erica indicated she wanted a quiet word and followed him to the door of the ward.

'I don't understand,' she said, when Jeremy turned to face her. 'When I was here yesterday Will was barely conscious and lying slumped in bed. Now he's in the chair. His breathing seems so much better . . . '

Jeremy looked at Erica for a few moments, his cheerful expression transforming into one of empathetic seriousness.

'That's how it is with . . . *this*,' he said quietly. 'The side effects come and go, from one day to the next. Today's a good day. Tomorrow may not be so good. The day after, who knows. The oxygen helps a great deal. But what you're seeing . . . it's temporary, Mrs Campbell. Please don't forget that. I hope I haven't spoken out of turn.'

'No. Not at all. Thank you.'

Jeremy nodded at Erica then left the ward. Erica felt dizzy. When she'd seen Will's empty bed it was as if all the air had been suddenly sucked from the hospital, and her own lungs. When Will had returned with Jeremy, upright in the wheelchair, the air had rushed back in with him. She thought she might faint and decided to sit down. She picked up the chair reserved for visitors and took it around the bed so she could sit beside Will.

'You're looking a lot better,' she said.

'At death's . . . doorstep . . . if not . . . at his . . . actual door . . . ' Will replied. 'One hand . . . on the . . . knocker. This gas . . .

helps. You should . . . try . . . it. Everyone . . . should. In my . . . opinion . . . oxygen is . . . hugely under . . . rated.'

He placed the mask back over his mouth and nose and drew on the gas, letting it re-energise every corner of his exhausted body. Erica took his hand in hers.

'It's just so lovely to see you sitting up and alert.'

Will nodded. His skin-and-bone head sat on his thin neck like a lollipop on a stick. His pyjama collar and dressing gown grew looser by the day.

'I wish Laura had come with me today.'

Will nodded. 'Has he . . . told you?'

'Has who told me what?'

'Mitchell.'

'Has Dr Mitchell told me what?'

Erica was puzzled.

He's told me everything – at least, that's what I'd been led to believe. Is there something else? Some good news he's been waiting to spring on me when we next met?

Her heart started to thump harder in her chest.

'Told me what, Will?'

'How long . . . I have . . . left.'

Erica hadn't been aware that Dr Mitchell had discussed this with Will, owing to Will's condition. She had been labouring under an assumption that Will had no idea how far advanced his cancer was. Will looked at her over the face mask. He knew her so well. He knew what she was thinking, and nodded.

'I . . . asked him . . . of course.'

Will slowly wrapped her hand in both of his. She looked at his thin fingers and caressed the skin covering his thumbs, feeling how diaphanous it had become. Each muscle and sinew and vein of his hands was prominent beneath her fingertips. Each bone of his fingers and knuckles was perilously close to the surface. Will squeezed Erica's hands hard, forcing her to look at him. He took a deep gulp of gas and pulled the mask from his mouth.

'I want . . . to come home.'

Will stared at Erica with absolute determination, his eyes prominent in their sockets, burning with resolve. He swallowed hard, his Adam's apple slowly dropping in his throat before struggling back up to its resting position.

Erica blinked fast, clearing the moisture from her eyes before it could coalesce into tears. She felt an overwhelming urge to look away, but she continued to look back at Will. His love for her radiated across the space between them, giving her the strength to understand what he was saying, and agree to his request. For the past twenty-four years there hadn't been a significant decision either had made without consulting the other. *Partnership* was an insufficient description of their relationship. Their marriage had been a perfect symbiosis.

'I want . . . to come . . . home, Erica.' He took another slug of oxygen and lowered the mask. 'To die . . . with *you*.'

Erica became unaware of anything or anyone else on the ward. All she could see was Will's face. All she could think about were the last words he had spoken.

'Of course,' she said quietly. 'I wouldn't have it any other way.'

The tension holding Will's frame forward in the wheelchair lifted, and he relaxed back into the seat with relief. His head lolled back on his neck and he closed his eyes. For a moment Erica thought he was in distress, but she saw his chest rise and fall evenly as it sucked in oxygen. She looked at Will's face.

His eyes were closed, but beneath the oxygen mask Erica could see an almost imperceptible yet definite smile.

'Home,' he said in a whisper. 'Home.'

Chapter 34

FRANCES HAD DECIDED to grasp the metaphorical bull by its metaphorical horns and speak to Alison. It had been on her mind since their encounter in the air-raid shelter, after Sarah had upbraided her. Alison had come into Frances's mind again in the committee meeting when Erica had broken down. Like Frances, and as Erica would soon, Alison had also lost a husband. Her experience and wisdom would have helped Erica immeasurably in those moments. Frances had felt her absence.

With Noah away at boarding school, Frances had a lot of time to think about events at the factory, and whether Alison really had been as solely responsible for its demise as Frances had convinced herself. Was it possible she had rather shamefully laid so much blame at Alison's door to avoid taking any herself? She had to concede it was possible.

When Noah had left, Frances thought about him almost constantly. She punished herself with various scenarios, each more terrible than the last. To stop herself from pointless self-flagellation, Frances turned her mind to other matters:

the trekker issue, which had been left unresolved following the abrupt conclusion of the committee meeting; and to Alison.

Frances recalled Alison's words in the shelter, but focused mainly on her expression. After all, words were easy to assemble into almost any order to say almost anything, and yet give the faithful appearance of utmost sincerity and truth. Frances understood that facial expressions and mannerisms were not so easy to assemble into a convincing performance. She had known Alison over many years, in a range of circumstances. Alison's absolute honesty held true in all of them. Sarah had agreed one evening over supper.

'The woman is incapable of lying, you know that, Frances. Utterly incapable.'

Frances knew, but was reluctant to admit it, ashamed to concede she might have done Alison a great injustice.

'That may well be the case as far as the WI is concerned. But the business at the factory was an entirely different order of things,' she said. 'Consequently, what happened there may have forced Alison to behave *entirely out of character*. Under tremendous pressure very many perfectly decent people do some perfectly dreadful things. Look at Chamberlain and the Sudetenland.'

Sarah had put down her cutlery and looked at Frances despairingly.

'Please, I beg you, Frances. Do not equate Chamberlain's misjudgement of Hitler's ambitions with Alison's "misjudgement" of new suppliers of parachute silk. Even in *your* overactive imagination that would be a stretch too far. Besides, as she has explained to you, it wasn't a "misjudgement" on her part to bring the Lyons brothers in as new suppliers. She was pressured into it by the police.'

Frances had looked stonily at Sarah.

'I don't know whether or not to believe Alison was being directed by the police.'

'You've just acknowledged the woman can't lie to save her life!'

'No – I agreed she was *incapable* of lying. But only in the context of what we know of her. But beyond that context, I have no idea how she might behave if she were under tremendous pressure, or if her liberty was at stake.'

'Then why don't you check?'

'Check?'

'Contact the police officer who told her to do all these things to help bring the Lyons to justice, and see if he corroborates Alison's account.'

Frances looked at her sister and considered the idea.

'I might just do that.'

After thinking it over in private, Frances had decided she would write to the police officer, only to learn he had been transferred out of the area. She had initially thought this very convenient for Alison. But having asked for her letter to be forwarded to the detective at his new posting, Frances was surprised to receive a letter back within two weeks that corroborated everything Alison had told her. But the detective's letter went further, praising Alison as 'a woman of great integrity and courage, who risked more to help the fight against war profiteering than any civilian I've come across'.

Those words played over in her head now, as Frances found herself walking towards Alison's cottage a week after the committee meeting in which Erica had all but collapsed. She had decided to wear her most businesslike outfit. The one she had worn the night she had first been elected Chair of the WI, to the reading of Peter's will, at her first meeting with Noah's grandparents and on her first and last days at the factory. It was a dark tweed jacket and skirt, small pearl earrings and matching necklace. Minimal make-up. An understated yet necessary display of status that enabled Frances to feel she was wearing some form of 'armour' in the event that Alison wasn't interested in reconciliation.

I want to settle this if possible, but not at any cost. And I certainly don't wish to look too relaxed or 'overtly friendly'. If we are to become friends once more it will take time, and it must be from a position of strength, as the injured party. Alison is a bookkeeper. She understands the concept of making sure the right amounts of things are in the right places before a proper accounting can be made.

As she walked along the High Street, Frances rehearsed her greeting as she imagined Alison opening the door. Her arrival would take Alison by surprise, which was what Frances intended by turning up unannounced. It was a trick she had learned from Peter, to keep a negotiating partner on the back foot.

Advantage me.

It was reasonable to anticipate that Alison would be momentarily lost for words upon seeing Frances on her doorstep, which gave Frances a second advantage. In being the first to speak she would set the terms of the conversation that followed.

'Hello, Alison. I thought it was time we talked.'

Good. Informal yet in control.

'Hello, Alison. I've been thinking about what you said in the shelter, and thought it was time we talked.'

Far weaker. Very little is improved by over-elaboration. Possibly French cuisine. Moorish design. Perhaps jazz . . .

Her thoughts were interrupted by shouting from one of the shops ahead. It wasn't a shout of joy, but loud, aggressive, argumentative and female. It was coming from Brindsley's.

As she looked towards the butcher shop Frances saw a black man backing out into the street, facing an angry-looking group of Great Paxford women, who came after him, led by Mrs Talbot.

The woman was one of Frances's least favourite people, she found offence or slight in almost everything, living with a belief that the universe was configured to cheat her at every opportunity. At the WI, Mrs Talbot had been one of Joyce's key supporters. But when Joyce left the village with her husband at the outbreak of the war, Mrs Talbot stepped into the vacated space, becoming the reactionary figurehead behind which Joyce's rudderless cabal could recongregate.

As Frances drew closer to the butcher's shop she heard Mrs Talbot's voice above all the others.

'How would you like strangers turning up out of the blue where you live, snaffling up your rations?' Mrs Talbot shouted, her skinny face scrunched into a snarl. 'Go on! Get out of it!'

Bryn Brindsley followed close behind, trying to assume control of the situation.

'We haven't run out yet, Mrs Talbot!'

'Hardly a surprise *you* don't object, Bryn – all the extra coppers this lot're putting in your pocket!'

The black man faced the small angry crowd of shoppers.

'I'm only trying to feed my family,' he said.

'Do it in Liverpool! You're not welcome here!'

Bryn looked apologetically at the man.

'I'm sorry. Maybe come back later?'

'Don't bother,' said Mrs Talbot. 'There's nothing for you here. Go back where you came from.'

The group of ten women behind Mrs Talbot nodded in unison.

When Frances heard this remark she couldn't be sure if Mrs Talbot meant Liverpool or the Caribbean. Either way, she was shocked by the woman's vehement tone, and by the level of support she was clearly receiving from the women behind her.

What a revolting thing to say. It's one thing to object to strangers coming into the area unbidden, causing people anxiety. But to racialise the situation like this is repugnant. Beyond the pale and fundamentally dishonest.

The man hurried away from Brindsley's, towards Frances.

'Are you all right?' she asked as he approached.

He hurried past her without speaking, towards the village outskirts.

Mrs Talbot and her caucus stood in the road. They were still muttering about the receding figure as Frances approached.

'Was that entirely necessary?' Frances asked.

Mrs Talbot eyed Frances suspiciously. Like most bullies she made astute calculations about who to take on and who to leave alone. Known in Great Paxford for her stern intelligence and tart tongue when nettled, Frances fell into the latter category.

'These people are cowards, Mrs Barden. Cutting and running into the countryside isn't the British way.'

'Isn't it human nature to try and stay alive by whatever means necessary?'

'They've shelters in Liverpool.'

'They have *some*. Bursting at the seams by all accounts. And none that can survive a direct hit. Should they just stay put and get blown to pieces? Would *you*?'

Frances directed the question at Mrs Talbot but then looked at the ten women sheltering behind her. There was a moment of silence as they waited for Mrs Talbot to respond on their behalf, hopefully with a stinging retort.

'We're at war, Mrs Barden.'

Frances found this entirely predictable.

Ah, yes. The lazy excuse for appalling behaviour. I heard it all during the last war.

'I'm well aware of that, Mrs Talbot. But we're at war with the *Germans*, not with our own people.'

'He's not *our people*, though, is he?'

Frances felt a surge of anger, as she always did when faced with bigots and thugs, male or – as in this case – female. Mrs Talbot wasn't finished.

'He's not from the village, and we have a right to defend what's ours from anyone who tries to take it.'

The women behind Mrs Talbot felt she was gaining the upper hand and nodded approvingly. They hadn't the wit to take Frances on, but they admired any woman who would try.

'But he wasn't trying to *take* anything,' said Frances. 'From what I could see he was happy to pay for it, like any of you.'

'Give them an inch and they'll take a mile. Let *one* of them buy meat from Brindsley's and there'll be a stampede to buy up *everything*, before the people who live here get a look-in.'

'Not a very Christian attitude, Mrs Talbot.'

'On the contrary, Mrs Barden. As it says in the Bible – God helps those who help themselves. Well, we're helping ourselves by driving them out of our village before they gain a foothold. They've got their own butchers.'

'Their city is being bombed flat. I've no reason to believe butcher shops have been made exempt from German bombs. But perhaps you have information I'm not privy to?'

Mrs Talbot had no response to Frances's sarcasm, and fell back on a bald statement of fact masquerading as a definitive argument.

'Well, that's where they chose to live. I chose to live here.'

Mrs Talbot looked at Frances with manufactured contempt.

'Anyway. Whose side are you on, Mrs Barden?'

'Must there be sides, Mrs Talbot?'

'Don't be so naive. Not now. It's what gets people killed. Dog eat dog – that's what war is. That's what my husband says. Any who don't understand that are likely to get eaten by bigger dogs.'

Mrs Talbot gave Frances a farewell sneer and walked away, followed by her clucking friends, who looked over their shoulders at Frances disparagingly. Frances watched them, readying to blast them with her response.

Why do people like her always seem to know exactly the right buttons to push, without ever needing to justify their behaviour! It's a talent of sorts, I suppose. A rather repellent talent, but perhaps being rather repellent is a useful survival mechanism in times like these. Well, as long as there's breath in my body, she—

'Mrs Barden!'

Frances turned in the direction of the caller and saw Claire cycling towards her at full pelt from over three hundred yards away, her housemaid's uniform flapping around her legs. Claire's face was flushed red, and wet with sweat. She was panting hard, having raced all the way from the house. Frances was overcome with dread, her mind reaching back to the day of Peter's accident, and the voices shouting to keep her back from the wreckage where Peter and his lover of ten years lay dead – he, slumped at the steering wheel, she, face down in a cornfield, having been thrown through the windscreen.

Frances tried to control her fear as Claire braked hard and drew level.

'What on earth is it?'

From the moment she had hung up the receiver in the hall, Claire had been pedalling hard to tell Frances the news. But having cycled so far, so fast, the poor girl now hung over the handlebars of her bicycle, doubled over with a stitch.

'Claire, *please* . . . '

Claire took a huge breath, and sat upright to face Frances.

'Noah's school just telephoned . . . '

As soon as she heard the word 'school' Frances froze, Mrs Talbot completely forgotten. Claire fought hard to bring her breathing under enough control to voice the final two words of her message.

'Noah's disappeared . . .'

Chapter 35

For the first few weeks of their stay in her home, Joyce had been thrilled to host Bob and Pat. 'Great Paxford's very own man and wife of letters', as she called them both inside the house, and around the village. She had initially enjoyed the privilege of being allowed to sit in the same room as 'the great man' while he worked, and equally appreciated the help Pat was able to give her in lieu of a portion of their rent. While Joyce was additionally eager for the company they offered, she received much kudos around the village for taking the Simms into her own home when she herself was recovering from the same crash that had rendered the Simms's house uninhabitable. This helped dispel any lingering sense that the Joyce Cameron who had fled the village at the outbreak of war was the same Joyce Cameron who had returned a month later. 'Old' Joyce seemed to have been replaced by a new version who was more humble, charitable and generous. And this was true. Up to a point.

Joyce had imagined Bob to be a seasoned, thoroughbred writer from whose fingertips words flowed in a ceaseless, melodic rush. Before she heard it for the first time, she felt sure his typewriter would play a smooth tune as he assembled sentences and paragraphs and pages – its keys chattering out an ode to creativity that would pleasantly fill her house.

Instead, Joyce discovered that creativity doesn't come in smooth, seamlessly interlinked bars, but in jarring, percussive bursts, with recurrent interludes of dark silence punctured by blunt epithets from a man frustrated by his inability to translate thoughts to paper. What had started as fun and self-aggrandising for Joyce soon became disruptive and intrusive; and finally, quite painful. Joyce began to get bad headaches as the sound of Bob's furious typing drilled into her head, much as it had been drilling into Pat's for years.

'How on earth do you put up with it, Patricia?' she asked Pat on one particularly bad day, when Bob was having difficulty expressing himself.

'You get used to it,' Pat lied.

You never do. You shut it out any way possible. You talk to yourself. Read. Leave the house for stretches at a time. Sleep. I sleep a lot, haven't you noticed?

'You learn to ignore it.'

Joyce shook her head in disbelief.

'At least Mr Simms has the benefit of seeing his work appear on paper. At least he knows what all this noise *means*. For you and me it's just, well . . . '

'A dissonant, jarring racket?'

'Quite.'

Bob ensured that he kept his poor treatment of Pat away from Joyce, but he could hardly do the same with his work. For her part, Joyce recognised that Bob needed to work, but was also forced to admit that *she* didn't want – *couldn't have* – every waking hour inside *her* house shattered by the sound of Bob's hands incessantly thrashing his typewriter. She braced herself and asked him to limit his work to specific hours of the day. During those hours she would visit friends, or run errands, or work in the garden. Outside of those hours, Bob would have to stop.

'I'm sorry, Mr Simms, there really is no other way. Except to slip slowly into madness.'

This didn't sit well with Bob. He wasn't used to changing his working pattern for anyone. If Pat had asked the same he would have laughed in her face, and then scowled dismissively. But Joyce wasn't Pat. And this was Joyce's house, and Joyce was letting them stay at a reduced rent. Bob was nothing if not flexible if it might save him money. He fixed an ingratiating smile on his face and said, 'I'm sure we can come to some mutually agreeable arrangement.'

Bob agreed to limit his typing hours to two shifts. Between 7 and 11 a.m., and 3 to 6 p.m. He tried to compensate for this restriction by working twice as hard through each session. Gone were the intermittent tea and chocolate and cigarette breaks that gave him space and time to think about what he was going to write next. Instead, he thought about what he was going to write a great deal *before* sitting at the typewriter, and spent the first four hours of every day in a furious assault on the machine; repeating the offensive every afternoon between 3 and 6 p.m. All he asked of Pat was that she bring him a cup of tea on the hour every hour. The rest of the time he demanded to be left alone.

As the weather turned colder, he lit a fire in the hearth at the start of his morning shift, making sure there was sufficient coal to provide four hours of moderate warmth. He did the same in the afternoon. It wasn't that Joyce's house was so large it was difficult to heat. More that, like other cold-blooded creatures, Bob functioned more efficiently in the warm. It was a concession he'd won from Joyce that he be allowed to moderate the front room's temperature during his working hours. Indeed, Bob's precision about his working temperature only added to his artistic charisma as far as Joyce was concerned.

Unknown to Bob, his new writing hours suited Pat much better than his old. It meant she could get on with her Mass Observation reports in their bedroom upstairs secure in the knowledge that Bob would be glued to his chair for the duration, downstairs. Bob was a creature of deeply entrenched habit, especially where his work was concerned. If he discovered a work pattern that was productive, he clung to it like a zealot. And if, for some reason, the typing stopped, Pat would hear it immediately, and hide her own writing beneath the mattress and lie waiting for Bob to resume. All she had to do was remember to serve him his cup of tea on the hour – a routine that was easily maintained by the alarm clock on her bedside table. The remaining fifty-five minutes of each hour were hers, in which to write freely about her life, expressing herself in a way she had never been able to do before. Where once she loathed the sound of Bob's typewriter she now came to love its downstairs rattle. It meant her own writing time *upstairs* was secure.

Pat found writing Mass Observation reports addictive. The anonymity was liberating, as it was intended to be. She could write down her darkest thoughts and feelings without fear of censure or consequence. Often, she would be walking through the village and see something, or overhear someone talking, and make a mental note to write about it. To begin with she felt some guilt at writing down snippets of other people's conversations, but that swiftly disappeared.

'My husband has already made me a practised liar so why shouldn't I turn myself into an accomplished thief?' she wrote.

Pat wrote about Erica's emotional breakdown at the committee meeting. How moved she had felt when the other women had gathered round her in a silent show of support at her imminent loss of Will. She wrote that she felt compelled in the moment to join in.

Pat wrote about the trekkers appearing in ever greater numbers around the village at night, and how some had started venturing into the High Street to buy food, which was scarce in Liverpool. She wrote about telephone conversations between villagers she had overheard during shifts at the telephone exchange. Many expressed fear and concern about the trekkers, often in deeply unpleasant terms.

Anyone wandering into Great Paxford on any given day would be forgiven for assuming it was an idyllic refuge from the rest of the world. That its residents are smiling, open-hearted and kind. And they would be right, mostly. But some of the telephone conversations I've overhead in the last week or so have been shockingly unpleasant. I heard one person suggest that we should have armed nightly patrols to keep black and Chinese trekkers out of the village. Having written this, I have to admit that when I heard the suggestion I did not immediately disagree. I also have an urge to protect the village, and keep out strangers who might do us harm. But when I thought about it on my way home at the end of my shift yesterday, I had to ask what harm are these people doing? None that I know of. And yet I was agreeing with an idea to hold people at the end of a gun for the simple fact they are not like us. By which I mean, not white. Because people making accusations aren't making them about white folk, and the majority of the trekkers are white. It makes me ashamed that we can be at war with fascist Germany yet exhibit the same base impulse to discriminate against people who simply don't look like us.

The alarm clock by the side of the bed started to ring, signalling it was time for Pat to stow her report and make Bob his next cup of tea. She glanced at her fingers and saw that the tips of those that had held her pen were tinged blue. She went into the bathroom to wash her hands clear of any trace of ink that might give away what she had been doing upstairs. If Bob sensed anything unusual he would be on to it like a ferret.

The typing had stopped for a few moments. As she scrubbed her hands clean she heard the front door open.

Joyce back from the village. Perfect timing. Two women now revolving around Bob. Keeping out of his way. Accommodating him. How does he do it? Why do we allow it? Oh yes. Because he's a selfish bastard.

249

Pat dried her hands and walked onto the landing in time to see Joyce solicitously knock on the door to the front room. She was holding the newspaper and what looked like bills. She heard Bob say, 'Yes?' and Joyce went in. Pat continued downstairs. As she reached halfway she could hear Joyce and Bob talking through the door.

'Nothing of any great interest in the newspaper, I fear. Though I've only skimmed the front page,' Joyce said. 'And another of those letters for Patricia.'

Pat froze.

What did she just say?

'Thank you, Mrs Cameron,' Bob said, trying to suppress his irritation at being interrupted. 'Could you see if Pat is bringing my tea?'

Joyce came out of the room and quietly closed the door behind her, and found Pat reaching the bottom of the stairs. The thrum of Bob's typing had already restarted.

'The great man is ready for his tea, Patricia,' Joyce said, with no hint of sarcasm.

'Thank you. Would you mind putting the kettle on? I just need a quick word with him.'

Joyce smiled. 'Of course . . . '

Pat watched Joyce go into the kitchen. She approached the door to the front room and knocked. The typing stopped.

'Yes?' Bob's voice sounded irritated by yet another interruption, but as Pat was due to bring him his tea it was one he was expecting. He continued typing.

Pat opened the door and went inside, closing the door behind her.

'Just put it on the table . . . '

Pat hesitated, and then said, 'Your tea's being made.'

Bob stopped typing and turned to face her.

'I thought I made it clear the only interruption I wanted was a cup of tea *on the hour*. Nothing else. Yes?'

'It's coming,' Pat said, looking at him. Her eyes momentarily flicked across his desk, looking for—

'Then why are you here now? Why aren't you in the kitchen making it?'

'The kettle can boil itself, Bob.'

Pat hadn't meant to sound defiant but she felt past caring. Besides, what could he do with Joyce just one room away? Bob looked at her, his expression darkening.

'Then why are you in here, *disturbing me*, now?'

Pat felt the customary fear rising as it always did when he spoke to her like this.

'I heard Joyce tell you she picked up a letter for me from the post office.'

Bob looked up at her from his desk. 'You shouldn't eavesdrop, Pat. People who eavesdrop hear things they shouldn't.'

'I wasn't "eavesdropping", Bob. I was coming downstairs to make your tea and happened to overhear Joyce say that another letter—'

'Keep your voice down!' His eyes glanced towards the door.

'What did she mean by "another letter for Patricia"?' Pat wouldn't be deflected.

Bob didn't answer. She could tell he was choosing which way to handle this. Pat persisted.

'What *other* letters? From who?'

Bob looked at her, narrowing his eyes. He took a drag on his dying cigarette and then slowly released the smoke from between his lips.

'I told her they were begging letters from a cousin of yours, trying to screw money out of you on account of my book. I told her she was to bring them straight to me when they came, without troubling you. She did it as a favour to you. As am I by keeping them from you.'

'But I don't have any cousins,' Pat said. Her heart was pounding so fast in her chest it felt like it was trying to smash open her ribcage and escape.

'I know that. You know that. Joyce, happily, does not.'

'So who were they from?'

Bob leaned back in his chair and looked at his wife for several moments in silence, savouring her clear anxiety.

'You know who they're from.'

'Marek.'

The word came out before she could stop it. Bob simply looked at her, neither agreeing nor denying.

'Where are they?' Pat asked, her eyes scanning the room.

'I destroyed them.'

Pat felt giddy. Marek had been writing to her. The light in which she saw everything had suddenly brightened. Pat could barely control her emotions. She knew that to seem pleased would provoke Bob. She tried to keep her voice measured.

'What did the letters say?'

'You think I read them?' His tone was incredulous. 'Do you think I have the slightest interest in reading the slop another man would write to my wife?'

Pat took a deep breath and looked at Bob. She thought of the night she had stood over him with his own hammer in her hand, the way she was standing over him now.

I should have done it. Whatever the consequence.

'I did it for your own sake, Pat,' he said.

Pat curled her left hand into a ball, as if gripping that hammer's handle.

'Where's the letter that came today?'

Bob smirked.

'Where all the others went.'

He looked at the fire. It wasn't roaring now, but simmering. Digesting the last embers. Pat's mouth opened in shock.

'Nothing good could possibly come of it, you know that, yes? You're a married woman. Do you believe I would *ever* let you leave me for him? Embarrass me in front of these rural cretins? I'll see you dead first. And he's – what is he *really*? Nothing but a Slav philanderer, picking my pocket while I was in France. I expect he wrote asking for money. Once he knew he'd hooked a silly woman like you that would be the next logical step. I won't let him do that to me.'

Marek would never do that. You know nothing about him.

Pat looked into the fire, as if one or two of Marek's words to her might manifest themselves in the glowing ashes, or form within the last wisps of smoke.

Think now. Hold it back and think. Fear and hatred, yes. Write about this, yes. Bear witness to the bastard actions of my bastard husband, and report it. But what else?

'That kettle must be boiled by now,' said Bob, turning back to his typewriter and beginning to type again as if they had been discussing what sort of biscuit he might like with his tea.

Pat watched for a few moments, scarcely able to believe his nonchalant cruelty.

What was in the letters? Was Marek writing to confirm clo sure of the time we'd had together? Or the opposite – to ask me to wait for him? Surely . . . if he was writing to end our relationship why would he write more than once?

Pat left the room, closing the door behind her. She felt her chest rise and fall in a steady, controlled rhythm as she stood against the closed door, the typewriter keys hammering away.

She blinked back the tears welling in her eyes, lest Joyce or Bob see. But these were not tears of misery, as she had so often spilled since Marek had gone. Or of desolation, in moments Pat wondered where on earth Marek might be, believing she would never see him again. These were tears of unalloyed joy.

She smiled, and put her hand over her mouth to hide it. But beneath her hand her smile broadened as every particle of her vibrated with happiness. She wanted to say it out loud, but she knew she couldn't. She would write the words later in her next report:

Marek's out there, somewhere, and he's trying to find me . . .

PART THREE

Strangers Amongst Us

Chapter 36

Having called an emergency general meeting of the WI to discuss the impact of nightly trekkers on their community, on the given evening Frances wanted only to remain at home, within earshot of the telephone and possible news about Noah. Since he had run away a day and a half earlier from the boarding school, nothing had been seen or heard of the child.

As soon as Claire had run into the village and told Frances of Noah's disappearance, Frances had abandoned her plan to resurrect her friendship with Alison, and had run home to immediately telephone the school's headmaster.

'The first thing I want to say to you, Mrs Barden,' Dr Nelms intoned, in a manner designed to calm the fears of any mother anxious about their son in his care, 'is that there is no cause for alarm.'

'I really find it difficult to understand how you can say that, Dr Nelms,' Frances replied, astonished by his cavalier attitude in the face of what appeared to her to be a grave crisis.

'I can assure you, boys abscond quite regularly.'

'Odd how you didn't mention it when Noah and I came to look at your school prior to his enrolment.'

'Boys running away *is* a common occurrence in all boarding schools. While most absconders are new boys, it isn't unknown for more established boys to return to school after a particularly successful summer or Christmas break with parents, find school life difficult by comparison and try and make their way back home.'

'So you think Noah is on his way home.'

'It's quite likely. Though more likely that—'

Frances cut him off.

'May I remind you, Headmaster, we are talking about a child of eight years old. How on earth can you speak so blithely of an eight-year-old finding his way across country during war, with bombs falling nightly, and – if we are to believe even a tenth of the propaganda the government would have us believe – a landscape positively teeming with German spies?'

'I strongly believe you have no cause for alarm. I am reminded of a particularly ingenious boy who managed to run away from school on his second day, would you believe. He made his way to Switzerland, where he knew his parents had gone on holiday. The boy had no idea which part of Switzerland his parents were visiting, and was caught by a platform guard as he tried to sneak aboard a train at Zurich's central station.'

Frances was in no mood to be eased from her current state of extreme anxiety by supposedly reassuring stories that attempted to turn Noah's running away from a cause for concern into a common, almost whimsical occurrence she need not worry about.

'With the greatest respect, Dr Nelms, every minute you're wasting trying to reassure me that Noah's disappearance fits an established, harmless pattern is another minute in which we have no idea where he might be, or when he might come to light.'

'Mrs Barden, I can assure you—'

'No, Headmaster. I have little or no interest in your assurances. They count for nothing. You gave me every assurance he was fitting in very well. Assurances that now seem utterly baseless. A child who shouldn't be, is now *missing*. *All* I am seeking is *reassurance* that everything is being done to find him at the earliest opportunity.'

The headmaster of a respectable but middle-ranking boarding school stood little chance against Frances Barden in full flight. Few did.

'I expected you to take great care of my— of Noah. I entrusted him to you. And he is gone.'

Frances had nearly described Noah as her 'son' but corrected herself before the word left her mouth. She didn't want Dr Nelms to undermine her connection to Noah by correcting her description of him as her own child. Yet, to all intents and purposes, with both his parents deceased, Frances had started to consider herself to be Noah's de facto parent.

'Have you contacted the police?' Frances asked curtly.

'I really don't think that's necessary at this stage, Mrs Barden.'

'At what stage *might* you think it necessary? *After* Noah's been found? *Assuming* he is.'

Dr Nelms embarked on one final attempt to regain control of the situation.

'Mrs Barden, in our experience, when a boy absconds—'

'Would you please stop using that word – he's not a prisoner of war, he's a schoolboy, a small *child* in unfamiliar surroundings with unfamiliar people doing unfamiliar things. Contrary to what you told me, he has evidently found it all too much. Otherwise he would remain with you, rushing between classroom and playing field with the other boys.'

'In our experience, runaways are either found very quickly, or return to school of their own accord within hours, more often than not with their tails between their legs.'

'Do you mean to say you haven't even been looking for him? Noah hasn't returned within the *four* hours it's been since he was reported missing.'

'That's true, but— '

'Nor has he been found.'

'You're missing my point, Mrs Barden.'

'No, Dr Nelms. You're missing *mine*. I want the police involved. I want a manhunt. And I want it *immediately*.'

Dr Nelms reluctantly promised he would contact the police to see if Noah might have been picked up beyond the school grounds and handed into their care. He telephoned an hour later to report that the local police had received no stray children that day. Fortunately for Frances the police viewed Noah's disappearance rather more urgently than Dr Nelms. But, as Frances said to Sarah – who had rushed over as soon as

Frances telephoned her – 'The police don't have a reputation to shield, unlike that damned school!'

The Cheshire police assured Frances they would put all available resources into finding Noah quickly, starting with a painstaking search of the school and its grounds, and then spreading out from there. It was the only thing that kept Frances in Great Paxford.

They said there was nothing to be gained from travelling up to Warrington, where the school was based. It would only make Frances more anxious. It was far better that she remain at home in case Noah turned up, which was the most likely scenario. They told her to stay near the telephone and wait for news and not to worry. They didn't tell her not to feel terrible guilt for the whole affair. If they had it would have been futile.

If you hadn't sent him away—

She stopped that train of thought mid-sentence. There was nothing to be gained from returning to a track she had been round many, many times since Noah had left with Claire and Spencer. She had acted in what she believed was the best interests of the child, and in accord with Peter's wishes.

Frances had been tempted to pour herself a drink to settle her nerves, but a voice in her head told her not to venture down that particular path.

In your current state one drink will lead to another, and you cannot afford to be anything other than in complete control of your faculties.

Sarah asked if Frances wanted to postpone the WI meeting, or would like Sarah to lead it in her stead. Frances considered the option but decided against it.

'To postpone or send you instead would instantly make the entire meeting about me, when it shouldn't be. In the weeks and months following Peter's death I stayed away because I couldn't bear to see anyone, I just couldn't. And I think the women understood that.'

'They'd understand this,' said Sarah.

'Perhaps they would.'

'I'm certain of it.'

'Nevertheless, I don't want to send out the signal that the WI isn't somewhere they can go when they have serious events happening in their lives. On the contrary, it should be one of the very few places they can go to when they may be at their most troubled. Didn't Miriam receive tremendous support when David was missing? Haven't you, since Adam was taken prisoner? Erica and Will since they lost their home? Without the great kindness I received from the members, I don't know how I would have survived the terrible aftermath of Peter's death.'

'The support from the branch has been invaluable.'

'These trekkers fleeing into the countryside from nightly bombing challenge our sense of charity both individually and as a community. We need to take the situation in hand before it spirals out of control. Lord knows the parish council is all but useless, a collection of mediocre men locked in endless deliberation with no visible appetite for ever actually *doing* anything. No, Sarah. I need to be at the meeting. The members expect it, and will be unnerved to see me absent so soon after my return to the Chair. If I stay here I shall go mad pacing the floor. I've asked Claire to stay at the house in the event the police or Noah's headmaster should telephone. I'm only minutes away.'

Frances understood that one of the defining qualities of true leadership is the need to be visible and available, even when there are more pressing calls on one's time. Though she thought it might be best to be sitting beside the telephone alongside Claire, Frances had to be at the WI, leading what she expected would be a heated debate between those who wanted to assist the trekkers during their time of greatest need, and those who wanted to keep them out of Great Paxford with the aim of 'protecting the village'. Frances wanted to spend some of the evening examining the question: 'protection from what exactly?' As far as she could see, the trekkers were fellow countrymen who needed assistance at a particularly terrifying time. She already knew there was a faction within the membership, led largely by Mrs Talbot, who considered trekkers to be cowards fleeing in the face of enemy fire. Measured confrontation with this faction was, Frances believed, the best way to deal with the situation. Frances was determined to steer the branch towards its best, and not its basest, instincts.

'Somebody has to force all sides to be completely honest about what they fear from the trekkers. No use hiding behind mealy words. Let's get it all out in the open and move forward.'

Sarah looked sceptical. 'Are you sure that's wise? You don't want to start something you can't stop.'

'I have faith in the members.'

'All of them? Mrs Talbot? Surely not?'

'Women like her are frightened of any change. Anything new or unusual. We have to show her there's nothing to fear. That we are all trying to survive the same war as best we can.'

Sarah smiled at Frances. 'There are times I'm very pleased you're my sister.'

Frances looked a little put out. 'I'm pleased you're my sister *all the time*.' With that said Frances turned to call Claire into the sitting room.

'If either the police or the school telephone with news of Noah, however trivial it might be, you are to cycle to the meeting as quickly as you can.'

Claire nodded, and said, 'Of course, Mrs Barden.'

Claire wished her employer had taken more notice of her concerns about Noah being sent off to school. But taking Spencer's advice, she kept her own counsel.

'Whatever's happening in the meeting, interrupt if you must,' Frances instructed.

'I'll come straight down, and straight in.'

'Nothing is more important at this moment in time.'

Claire nodded, and replied, 'I agree.'

'Don't be more than twenty feet from the telephone while I'm out. If, for whatever reason, you have to be, make sure Spencer isn't.'

Frances wished Cookie and Thumbs, her housekeeper and groundsman, hadn't finally retired to Blackpool two months earlier, as they'd long threatened. They had planned to leave for the north-west coast nearly a year earlier, but had stayed on to see Frances through her bereavement. Frances always treasured the implacable calm and grounded wisdom with which they met any crisis.

Frances left Claire with pencil and paper to write down any information the police might leave, if and when they telephoned, and unenthusiastically stepped into the crisp evening air with her sister.

* * *

Frances and Sarah walked to the emergency general meeting knowing there wouldn't be a woman present without an opinion on the trekker issue. Since trekkers first began to trickle and then pour into the area from Liverpool and Crewe, everyone in Great Paxford had encountered them in one way or another. Their uninvited presence in the countryside around the village was broadly disconcerting for most. Despite the reason behind their sudden appearance being widely known, farmers simply didn't appreciate strangers suddenly camping on their land (city folk at that), lighting fires, erecting tents, potentially disturbing their livestock and trampling their carefully ploughed fields. Villagers found themselves unnerved by strange lights appearing at night in woods and forests that were meant to remain dark and undisturbed, except by nocturnal creatures. With so many policemen drawn out of the area to fight in the war, people felt suddenly vulnerable in the face of a low-level invasion that subtly disturbed the countryside's ancient equilibrium. Sarah understood that the trekkers' presence was causing disquiet, and had heard some in the village use the words 'being overrun' to describe how they were feeling.

The air had quickly cooled once the sun went down, and a wind had struck up from the west, blowing dead leaves up from the ground, and pulling the final remaining leaves from branches. Sarah turned up the collar of her coat and threaded her hand through the crook of her sister's elbow, as she had done since childhood. Arm in arm was how Frances and Sarah were usually seen walking around the village together.

'There'll be scarcely anyone who won't pass a trekker camp on their way to the hall,' Sarah said.

Frances nodded. Sarah knew Frances was silently agonising over Noah's whereabouts as they walked, and decided to distract her by getting her sister to focus on the matter in hand.

'How are you planning to approach tonight?' she asked.

'Square on. How else?'

'But do you have a position in mind with regard to the trekkers that you plan to lead the members towards?'

'To begin with, I'd like to do away with describing them as "trekkers". They are a group of *refugees* from German bombing.'

'So you'd prefer we called them "refugees" rather than "trekkers"?'

'It better reflects what they are, don't you think? They come here to take refuge from the bombing. Labelling them as "trekkers" detaches them from the very reason they walk such distances each night. I think that's made it easier for some in the village—'

'Mrs Talbot . . .'

'No names, but yes, Mrs Talbot and her friends. I believe just referring to them as "trekkers" makes it easier to demonise them. As if their ability to walk is their defining feature regardless of what they are walking away from. If it's just about them *trekking*, Mrs Talbot can ask why do they have to trek here? Why don't they walk somewhere else? But of course, their defining characteristic is their aversion to being blown to pieces at night.

And that's a characteristic we all share. So that's what I think we should reflect in how we refer to them.'

'Do you want the members to recognise that there but for the grace of God go they?'

'It would be a good place to start the discussion.'

Sarah nodded.

'But where would you want it to lead?'

Frances turned to Sarah and sighed.

'*Personally*, I'd like it to lead towards making these poor people feel welcome in some way. But *politically*, it has to lead to a place where all members of the branch are in complete accord. I don't want any splits or factions. That would be no good at all going forward. I would sooner accept a fall-back position that didn't satisfy me personally but retained branch unity than drive the majority to a position with which a minority won't agree.'

'Do you think that's possible?'

'All I know is that whatever any of us feel about these poor people, their plight is ultimately our concern. If the membership – the *entire* membership, Mrs Talbot included – is willing to find a way to help them that deals with all the mounting anxieties, well, excellent. If not, we shall have to accept there are some things we cannot do however much we may want to, and that's just how it is.'

Sarah smiled.

'I thought you enjoyed driving the branch to the edge of the abyss.'

'I did it *once*, Sarah, to break Joyce's stranglehold and keep the branch open during the war. I can't do it again. Besides, one can quite reasonably take the view that the trekkers—'

'Refugees.'

'Thank you. They didn't consult us about coming into our part of the world, so they can't reasonably have a deep expectation that we should embrace them. Though I certainly think we should *help* them as far as we can, because— '

'—there but for the grace of God go we.'

'Yes. But it won't happen if I try and force it on the members as an obligation. Times are taxing for us all, for some more than others. Our unity as a branch is what holds it together. I won't put that at risk. Only ask that we do what's easily possible.'

'You were spectacularly successful when you stood against Joyce.'

'I achieved my objective. But it was – as you say – a high-risk strategy. Constantly driving the branch to the brink of collapse and Chair re-election are not actions I wish to make a trademark. It will exhaust and depress everyone in equal measure. Not least, myself.'

'What if you could achieve both your personal and political objectives with regard to them? It could happen.'

'That would be a triumph you and I would celebrate over a drink. But it would have to happen without forcing it. I'm confident the branch will want to do a great deal to help.'

Sarah sighed heavily, causing Frances to turn to her.

'What?'

'Mrs Talbot,' Sarah said wistfully.

'Do you know how to neutralise a venomous snake?'

'I did watch Adam deal with a snake once, in India.'

'What did he do?'

'He dropped the collected works of Shakespeare on its head.'

'Did it work?'

Sarah smiled. 'Not only did it work, but the deadly volume fell open on Hamlet's soliloquy, "To be or not to be . . ."'

'To which the answer, from the snake's perspective, was sadly, "*not* to be".'

'Never has Shakespeare had such a profound effect on any living creature.'

Frances began to laugh almost uncontrollably. Sarah hadn't seen Frances laugh like this since before Peter's death, and was moved by the irrepressible sight and sound of it. It was infectious, and the two sisters strolled along, pulling one another this way and that as they struggled to regain their composure. As the village hall loomed into sight, Frances eventually drew a long breath to speak.

'Do you think we might get the same result from dropping the collected works on Mrs Talbot's head?'

'It might not be quite as successful as the effect on the snake, but it might knock some compassion into her.'

'The quality of mercy would be a good place to start.'

'Aside from assaulting the woman with literature, I think your best chance is to isolate her position by declaring it to be not in the WI spirit, and hope she'll realise she's fighting a lost cause. People like Gwen Talbot only have power if they think others can be bullied to their will. When they realise they can't, they often fold like a cheap suit.'

The two women hurried towards the village hall up ahead, the silhouette of its slanted roof recognisable in the blackout against the darkening skyline. The wind was now stronger and behind them, buffeting Sarah and Frances into the stream of women attending the EGM, all eager to get into the warmth of the hall and the heat of debate.

When Sarah and Frances reached the entrance, Frances turned to her sister. By the light inside, Sarah could see that despite the laughter of a moment ago, Frances was concerned.

'I do so hope I haven't misjudged them.'

'You're frighteningly persuasive when you want to be.'

Frances smiled, appreciating the encouragement. She looked into the hall at the rows of women from the village and surrounding farms, standing and greeting one another with smiles and laughter, their pre-meeting chatter already filling Frances with the encouragement needed to make her case. She then turned to look back outside, into the darkness that enveloped the village like a black glove. Her expression darkened to match the night outside. Sarah instinctively understood the thought that had muscled its way into the centre of her sister's consciousness, and gripped Frances's hand tightly.

'The police will find Noah. *I know it*,' she whispered.

Frances looked at Sarah, desperate to share her conviction.

'The reality is, Sarah, dear, none of us knows *anything*...'

Frances went inside. Sarah lingered at the open door for a moment, and realised Frances was preparing herself for the very worst.

* * *

There were two basic arguments about how to respond to what the women of the WI were happy to call – for the purposes of the meeting and until Frances could persuade them otherwise – 'the trekker question'. The first was to make the trekkers feel unwelcome, with the aim of driving them away to other villages. The second argument proposed engaging with them, and for Great Paxford to welcome them. It was the second argument that Frances supported.

'Ladies, thank you all for coming tonight. You are, I know, aware of why this meeting has been called. Each of us has encountered trekkers over recent weeks, and I think it imperative that we discuss how to handle the situation. Because one thing is clear: we cannot simply ignore these people. I perfectly understand the impulse to push them away. But I believe we must resist it. These poor people have fled their cities for their very lives, with no idea if everything they have will still exist when they return the next day. They walk miles at dusk to keep themselves and their families safe, in all weathers. And then walk back again at daybreak, to return to their jobs and schools. They do not come into the countryside to *stay* in the countryside. They don't want to do this. They are visiting only, being forced by the circumstances of war that decree their cities targets for the Luftwaffe. We haven't been forced to take such drastic action in the name of self-preservation. At least . . . *not yet.*

'Driving them away doesn't solve the root cause of their problem—'

'Perhaps not,' countered Mrs Talbot, wasting no time in presenting herself as the most vocal advocate of the faction for dissuading the trekkers from coming into the area and Great Paxford. 'But it solves the root cause of ours.'

Frances was aware of some heads nodding in agreement with Gwen Talbot, but ignored her comment, sidestepped her ever-present concern about Noah's safety, and continued.

'Driving them away, as Mrs Talbot suggests, merely displaces the problem for others to deal with. For me, that isn't good enough. Especially when we have it in our power to put ourselves in their shoes and make their daily trek less of an ordeal than it needs to be.'

Frances was not above a dash of sentimental rhetoric when she wanted to appeal to hearts over minds. The majority of hats in the crowded hall nodded in agreement. But there was a small minority for whom driving the trekkers anywhere else seemed a perfectly reasonable solution. If it meant the trekkers got pushed around the region so be it. Predictably, Mrs Talbot put it the most tartly.

'Keeping them moving sorts out the situation in three ways,' she said. 'Firstly, no single village has to put up with them for very long. Secondly, they still won't have to stay overnight in Liverpool. Thirdly,' she proposed, with a sarcastic curl of her upper lip, 'they get to make a twilight tour of Cheshire they'll talk about for years after the war.'

Miriam narrowed her eyes at Mrs Talbot, as if to better hone in on her bitter essence. She turned to Steph Farrow on her left.

'Is Gwen Talbot really that unpleasant,' she whispered, 'or really that stupid? Or both? Both.'

'Definitely both,' Steph whispered back. Miriam nodded.

'Even my little girl would recognise that as a stupid idea, and she can scarcely focus on my hand in front of her face.'

Steph stifled a laugh and raised her hand. Frances gave her the nod to speak.

'Yes, Mrs Farrow?'

'I'll admit, I was scared of them when they first appeared. First day I saw them I put the shotgun under the bed. Still there, just in case. You know.'

There was a small laugh of recognition from the women in the hall. Frances smiled.

Everyone listens when Steph speaks. She's a natural.

'Look,' Steph continued, 'we can argue the pros and cons of this all night.' She looked nervously at the listening faces around her, convinced they thought she was talking rubbish. 'But by my reckoning, whatever we decide has to be something that allows us to live with ourselves. Whether we drive them off or help them . . . I want a clean conscience.'

There were murmurs of approval that clearly alarmed the Talbot faction. Mrs Talbot sprang to her feet to beat back Steph's deceptively subtle appeal to decency.

'I'm perfectly happy to look myself in the mirror knowing a Liverpudlian face isn't going to suddenly appear behind it, having just broken into my house.'

The Talbot faction murmured 'hear, hear' and 'well said' and 'Great Paxford is for Great Paxfordians, not strangers'.

Teresa turned in her seat to look Mrs Talbot in the face and shouted, 'Utterly disgraceful! Take that back!' in her thickest Scouse accent.

But Mrs Talbot simply folded her arms and refused. Steph remained on her feet.

'In my book, this war's a test,' she said, raising her voice above the clamour until it quietened. 'Of all of us. Doesn't matter if you're English, German, French, Czech, Polish – we're all being tested. What sort of people are we? Well, I'll tell you what sort of person I want to tell my grandchildren I was – a woman who helped when she could, as I'd want to be helped if the shoe was on the other foot. What about you, Mrs Talbot? What would you want all of us to do if you were one of those coming out of Liverpool every night, dragging your terrified kids away from bombs and settling them in the middle of a wood in the cold and dark, and then getting them back in time for school and work next morning, fed and washed? Then doing it next day. And the next. And the next. 'Cause what's important isn't their blisters, or lack of sleep, but keeping them alive.'

Steph looked at Mrs Talbot, and then around at all the silent faces looking back at her. Every single one was gazing at her, riveted.

'What would you want us to do if you were one of those women? Push you off? Move you on?'

Sarah watched her with quiet awe.

Some people have an ability to strip away noise and nonsense and reduce things to what they actually are. Steph is one of them, and we are so, so lucky to have her in the branch.

Mrs Talbot looked at Steph with a triumphant sneer.

'I would never cut and run in the first place,' she said, spitting out the words.

'Easy for you to say, Mrs Talbot,' replied Steph. 'You're not getting bombed every night.'

Mrs Talbot looked hard at Steph, but couldn't match the farmer's intensity. Steph slowly sat down as Frances stood back up.

'These people are *refugees*, ladies. *Nightly refugees* in the true meaning of the word – fellow countrymen – coming into our part of the world *to seek refuge*. What are we afraid of? To paraphrase Steph Farrow just now – what kind of WI branch do *we* want Great Paxford to be?'

Isobel raised her hand.

'Yes, Miss Reilly,' Frances said, giving her the floor. Isobel stood.

'As some of you may know, I was sent here by my brother. When war broke out, he thought London was going to get bombed, and wanted me somewhere safe. It didn't happen immediately, but now's a different story, of course. As it is in Liverpool and Crewe, and all the other cities trying to keep the country going. I came to Great Paxford as an evacuee, or a refugee, or however you want to call it, and I was terrified at how I might be treated. All my life my blindness turned me into a burden in other people's eyes. I sat on the bus from Crewe dreading what I might find. And I found some of the most helpful, caring people I've ever met. This branch of the Women's Institute made the most difficult period of my life not just bearable, but astonishing. If you can do but a fraction of that for these trekkers for as long as they keep coming, wouldn't that be a wonderful thing to do?'

Frances looked at Isobel and could have kissed her. By the end of the night the branch had conclusively decided to offer the incomers a variety of initiatives to make their time away from home more comfortable. Some offered to put up families with small children so they didn't have to sleep outside. Steph and the other farmers' wives offered to make unused barn space habitable for people to sleep in, in dry and relative warmth. Others offered to donate bedding.

Frances was tasked with finding out if the village hall could be made over as a makeshift air-raid shelter after a certain hour each night, and offered to establish a basic soup kitchen at her house for any refugees who lacked for a warm, basic meal. She continued to use the term refugee throughout the evening, hoping it might begin to stick.

Pat immediately offered to help wherever she could, eager to seize upon another reason to spend less time with Bob under Joyce's roof. Having Joyce around curtailed some of Bob's worse behaviour, but Pat still lived in fear of further retribution over Marek.

A working party was set up to monitor the implementation of the agreed proposals, and another was established to go into the surrounding area to inform the refugees of what was being offered. Frances cautioned the branch not to overstretch itself.

'Ladies, as we know, and as is often said during war, the road to Hell is paved with good intentions. We do what we can do for these refugees, but no more. We can help people, but we cannot sort out, or interfere in, their lives. Do not offer more than you can give in both time and resources.'

As initiatives and offers came thick and fast in a flurry of proposals and shows of hands, Frances found herself looking more and more at the door. She willed Claire to burst in and blurt out the news of Noah's discovery, safe and well. But by the end of the meeting Claire still had not arrived. Having inspired the branch to help the refugees, a subdued Frances brought the meeting to a close. She thanked the ladies for their great, good hearts, and bade them goodnight.

Walking home alone, Frances glimpsed the scattered glow of several small campfires hidden among trees, away from the road. She imagined mothers and fathers and children huddled together around the warmth, keeping one another's spirits up, thankful that they were here, and not slowly coming into view under the Luftwaffe's nightly bombsights.

From these thoughts Frances made a swift connection to Noah, camped out somewhere, but with no fire or blankets to keep him warm, and no food, and almost certainly no sense of where he was.

What was he wearing when he fled the school? What had he eaten? What was the weather like? Has he gone back to Liverpool? Was he there now, beneath a bombing raid, screaming in terror?

It was too much to bear. To even begin to consider what Noah was experiencing at this moment created a tight knot in her stomach. He had escaped from the school, but to where?

Frances felt crushed. She could provide no answers to any of her questions. It left her feeling wretched that she could inspire and mobilise a packed hall of grown women to help possibly hundreds of strangers, yet could do not one thing for a single little boy, alone and miserable, whereabouts unknown.

Suddenly, a twig cracked to her right, causing Frances to turn sharply in its direction.

'Hello?' she said. And then before she could stop herself, 'Noah?'

It wasn't fear that gave her voice a cautious inflection, but the frantic hope he might step out of the shadows and reveal himself, having made his way back to Great Paxford for the express purpose of falling exhausted into Frances's grateful arms. Noah didn't appear. The vixen that had been the source of the sound darted out of the undergrowth, sprinted across the road and disappeared into the hedgerow. Frances could feel her heart pounding so hard in her chest it was almost painful.

How do mothers do this, day after day after day? How does any woman assume complete responsibility for the well-being of another human being year after year? Fathers too, of course, but not like this. Or perhaps it can be like this for some men. Not mine and Sarah's father, but for others. It's overwhelming. Almost unbearable.

After a few moments Frances took a deep breath and continued her journey home.

Please, Noah. Stay alive until you're found. Just do that and I promise I will never send you back.

Frances walked the remainder of the way in the dark, repeating those three sentences over and over to herself. It was all she could offer Noah at that moment. If he was discovered safe and sound she would offer him a great deal more, she was certain of that. More than she should, she expected. But she didn't care. *You can have whatever you want. Just come back to me.*

Before she went to sleep that night, Frances knelt beside her bed and prayed for Noah's safe-keeping to a God in whose existence she had always struggled to believe. She felt a twinge of disappointment in herself for succumbing to prayer in the moment, but it nevertheless gave her a small throb of comfort. Frances then climbed into bed, turned off the light, and slept for precisely forty-two minutes, before waking up with a gnawing sense of dread that kept her awake until sunrise.

Chapter 37

FOR ALMOST THE entire ride home, Will gazed out of the ambulance window at every sunlit field, tree, hedgerow, shrub, ditch, smallholding and house, knowing it would almost certainly be the final time he would see them. Erica watched him in silence. It was possible Will might have to go back to the hospital in the event of an unforeseen medical emergency, but they had left on the understanding that Will was leaving to spend his final days at home. Some of those would be better than others. For a spell, when his breathing eased and his speech became more fluent, it was like having the old Will back. Eventually, those days would become fewer, until every day was the same as the one before, only worse, and Will's body and faculties would begin their terminal decline.

Erica understood that this would likely be Will's final drive home from hospital. The realisation that everything Will now did might be for the final time was slow to dawn. There were times when she thought she understood and believed it. But then it slipped away. She forcibly spelled it out to herself.

His final meal. His final kiss. His final pipe. His final shave. His final haircut. His final sunset. His final sunrise. His final sleep. All now close on the horizon. And he knows it. I can tell.

A kestrel caught Will's eye, fluttering over a field as they drove past, flickering its wings to hold back gravity, and lock into position over unwitting prey beneath. Erica watched her husband slowly smile at the way the bird held its balance in the air, keeping high enough to cast no shadow of alarm, but not so high it would be unable to identify inviting movement among the field's furrows. Erica knew that, unlike many who feared it, her husband had always understood and appreciated the life cycle that was the engine of all of nature. His own included.

'It's a form of engine that connects you and I to every living thing on the planet,' he used to tell Kate and Laura when they were small. 'We live, we die. New life appears. It eventually dies too. And so on. That's how things are meant to be. And it's something to remember whenever you feel unfairly treated or bullied. Everything passes.'

Erica had always admired the way he had of explaining difficult concepts lightly, stripping them of their capacity to invoke misunderstanding or fear.

'Without the process of death,' he'd said, smiling, 'we can't have new life. Death ensures the world doesn't become too crowded with people, and plants and animals to the point where everything becomes old and clogged up and would stop working. Death is just a rather dull way of saying "it's someone or something else's turn now".'

Despite being six and four years old at the time, the girls had understood their father straight away, as his explanation perfectly fitted with what they had been taught about the virtue of sharing. For them, it seemed that death was a fair way to share out life. Every living creature got their share of being alive, and then died to allow others to have their share. And so on. It seemed quite reasonable to them, and because of that not remotely frightening. In this last respect, it helped that they were at the beginning of their own lives, with little awareness of their own time being finite too.

The ambulance bumped along country roads potholed by the constant gouging treads of thick military tyres passing over them at speed, day and night, in all weathers.

After Dr Mitchell had told her that Will's lifespan could now be measured only in days and weeks, Erica discovered that each moment in his company carried a certain charge she hadn't previously experienced. The imposition of a time limit suddenly heightened everything – colour, sound, movement and, of course, emotion. Erica had mentioned this observation to Will while he lay in the ward, an oxygen mask over his face to help him breathe. He had given a single nod, and slowly pulled the mask to one side to speak.

'Appre . . . cia . . . tion,' he'd said slowly.

Erica had smiled. Until now they had lived under the illusion that they could possibly, if they didn't play fast and loose with their health, live almost for ever. Logically impossible, of course, but human beings plot their course through life between the rational and the emotional, aided by the inability of the conscious mind to grasp the reality of its own extinction. The instant Dr Mitchell placed a fixed cap on Will's remaining time, Erica became alive to the passage of every minute and hour as one less she would be able to spend with her husband. The knowledge of it would catch her unawares at unpredictable moments, and she would suddenly start to cry. Will's future suddenly had an end attached. His tomorrows were dwindling in number. Soon, one of them would be his last.

As Erica observed Will watching the landscape speed past, he slowly turned away from the window and looked at her.

'It is . . . so . . . beau . . . tiful,' he said.

'Despite the war,' Erica agreed.

'Because of . . . war . . . it is . . . even more . . . beautiful. We . . . might . . . lose it.'

Our country. Our marriage. Our lives together. It is only at the point of loss that we absolutely value what we have. And then it's too late.

Erica knew this wasn't an original thought, yet its truth struck her more forcefully now than at any other time.

Will slowly held out a trembling hand and Erica leaned forward to take it. It felt colder than she'd anticipated. Less warm flesh than cold bones. The hand of an old man, yet Will was just forty-seven.

The ambulance drove through the southern outskirts of Great Paxford, towards its centre. During the thirteen months since the outbreak of war, villagers had grown used to all manner of vehicles hurtling through their village. Now, no one walking past batted an eye at the sight of the ambulance carrying their doctor and his wife. As the final survivor to be extracted from the ruin the Spitfire had made of their house, Will's endurance encouraged many to take his longevity for granted. They hadn't been told that Dr Myra Rosen had been offered the post for as long as she wanted it. Few yet knew that Will was never again going to be their doctor.

Will turned back and looked through the window as they drove along Great Paxford's familiar streets. Erica tried to see it as he now saw it – not merely as 'home', but as the community to which he had given so much of his life. She recalled the first time they had driven into the village, when they took over the surgery from a retiring German émigré, Dr Guggenheim. There was no tarmac on the roads, and barely a car. They brought with them four packing cases and a baby, Kate. Will stood outside their front door on a warm July evening, looked across at the stunning church opposite, glowing in summer sunlight, tightened his grip on Erica's waist with one hand, and around his daughter with the other, and said, 'Perfect.'

Since that day, there wasn't a soul under the age of twenty who Will hadn't delivered, nor an adult over that age who Will hadn't seen for some illness or other. Many of the older folk developed ailments as a pretext on which to pop into the surgery to see Doc Campbell for a bit of company and a chat. Will always had time for them, never rushed them, and never charged them a penny for popping by.

'I want them to feel that coming to see me is perfectly natural,' he had once explained, after Erica had become exasperated with a particular elderly 'patient' who clearly had nothing physically wrong with them but was just feeling lonely.

'Loneliness is debilitating too. But if they feel they can drop in when they're feeling well, when they fall genuinely sick they won't hesitate to seek my help.'

Erica passionately hoped Will considered his life in the village had been a worthwhile investment of his time on Earth.

I can't think of a better way to spend one's life.

The ambulance drove along the high street and came to the junction where the memorial to village men lost in the Great War stood, grey and austere. An army lorry was rolling through as the ambulance slowed at the junction, causing it to have to wait for a few seconds. Erica watched as Will stared at the memorial, his eyes blinking slowly as they reread the inscribed words: 'To the glory of God and in memory of the men of this village who gave their lives in the Great War 1914 – 1918'. She saw his eyes drop below, to the carved names of the dead.

His 'old chums', as he always called them, though he'd never been to Great Paxford before the war. I wonder if he's imagining his own name among them, joining them at last.

Will's survival had troubled him for several years after the end of the war. To offset the deep feelings of guilt he'd experienced, Will established his new practice with an uncompromising energy that impressed the locals but dismayed Erica. It left him exhausted at the end of most days, following long bicycle rides all over the district to make what turned out to be unnecessary house calls.

In those early days, Will would take the loss of a patient harder than was good for him. Erica became convinced he was punishing himself in peacetime for perceived failings during the war. For the sake of his health she had eventually forced Will to confront this. After long discussion, he conceded there had been no reason why he had survived over so many he considered better men than himself. For a man of science for whom every cause had an effect, the admission that the continuation or annulment of life during war was determined by pure chance almost broke his spirit. But for Erica's patient counselling, and for the love he received in an unbroken flow from his daughters, it possibly would have left Will profoundly depressed. Thankfully, Erica discovered her love of rambling, and used to drag Will out with her, kicking and screaming. A southern boy, raised and educated in Oxford, Will's idea of a walk was the journey required to get from whichever armchair he happened to be sitting in to the nearest pub. A Home Counties girl, Erica introduced Will to the treasure of the countryside – its sweep and its silences, its weather and its birdsong. What Will loved more than anything was the ability it offered him to walk for mile upon mile and never hear another human voice. If, according to the apostles, the poor are always with us, for Will it was the sick. Only walking with Erica in the countryside surrounding Great Paxford could he shake them off, if just for an hour or two a week.

The ambulance moved away from the war memorial and continued up a small hill towards the Campbells' new home, in a cul-de-sac enclosed by a broad copse of oak.

Erica noticed Will's eyes had now closed from exhaustion, though his hand continued to rest on the ambulance window, its fingers splayed, like a child's that had tried to reach out and touch all the interesting and exciting things he could see on the other side. His breathing was slow and laboured.

So little exertion seems to tire him completely. As soon as we get in I'll sit him in the armchair on oxygen for an hour.

Erica looked out of the window and saw they were approaching the new house. As they drew closer she could see Laura's face at the upstairs window, watching for their arrival. The moment she registered the approaching ambulance Laura's face disappeared from the window. Erica touched Will's hand and his eyes slowly opened and sought out hers.

'We're home, darling,' she said quietly.

Will looked out of the window, curious to see the new house. The smile that slowly spread across his face was not at the sight of the handsomely gabled roof, or at the young, recently planted wisteria growing up the left flank of the front door, or even at the neat front garden they'd never had before. It was at the sight of his elder daughter coming out of the front door. She looked more mature than when he'd last seen her. She wore her hair in a practical style, with fewer curls. She wore no lipstick, and her clothes were neat and functional, not designed to show off her young figure. Within a moment, Laura appeared behind her older sister, took her hand and pulled her along.

Inside the ambulance, Will turned gleefully to Erica.

'Kate!' he exclaimed with delight.

'She wanted to be here to welcome you home.'

Kate was studying to be a nurse in Manchester, and it hadn't occurred to Will that she might be here to greet him. His smile continued to broaden beyond the limit of the oxygen mask, as he watched his daughters run down the narrow, gravel garden path, towards the decelerating ambulance.

'My girls,' he said in an exultant whisper. 'My *Kate* . . .'

Erica looked at him and smiled. 'Do you imagine for one moment I could keep her away?'

I can't recall who once said 'children were the best medicine', but look at his face! They were absolutely right.

Chapter 38

Marek.

A few months ago, I had an affair with a man called Marek that lasted three months, and it was the most exciting, wonderful period of my life. I'm not writing his surname, or anything else. Not even the colour of his eyes. I understand that Mass Observation reports are anonymous, but given even the merest possibility either of us might be identifiable I shall write no details about him. This isn't a story, after all. This is my life.

Whoever reads this – assuming someone is reading this, possibly in some dusty office between the hours of nine and five, with a cooling cup of tea on the desk, and a packet of sandwiches for your lunch – you don't, dear reader, need to know anything about Marek except that I think he is the most wonderful man in the world, and that I had given up ever hearing from him again. He came into my life when I was least expecting it, while my husband was away, and transformed me completely. Looking back, I truly think I had begun to die inside, as a consequence of the way my husband treated me. I have written about that elsewhere, in other reports. If you have read those too, you may have noticed some parts of the paper were slightly wrinkled from where my tears fell, and then dried. Marek then went from my life. Was taken from my life. It doesn't matter now. None of it matters now. Nothing matters now except that he is back.

Not literally. Not physically in a form I can touch and hold and kiss. I don't know when that will be possible. Perhaps only when this war ends, assuming we both survive. There are no guarantees, and for now we must all live under the swastika's shadow. But Marek is alive and he is back in my life as surely as if he were standing at the foot of the bed on which I am writing. How do I know?

A letter.

Three days ago I received a letter from him. To be clear, I didn't take possession of the letter. It was intercepted by my landlady, who passed it on to my husband, who realised what it was and burned it on the small, mean fire he keeps alight near his feet as he works (other men returned from the Great War with terrible injuries and missing limbs — my husband returned with chilblains and poor circulation to his feet. If he were any other man I would be full of sympathy. But he is my daily tormentor).

See how readily I write about my husband, dear reader? My sick obsession. I can only hope these reports have not been assigned to the same individual. If they have been, if I have been assigned to you in perpetuity, whoever you are, I can only assume you must receive my reports with a sinking heart at the seemingly endless repetition of hatred and shame I send you. I can only apologise. Perhaps you have already learned to skim over parts relating to my husband. If so, many of my reports can't take you long to read as there is so little left. Apologies. I shall try and keep to today's news.

Three days ago, I received a letter from my lover. My husband destroyed the letter before I had a chance to read it, but no matter. Marek is alive. For that alone I can't express my relief. The not knowing was excruciating. But more than that, he is trying to reach me.

The fact that I now know he wrote to me is all I need to lift my eyes from the floor and smile (if only to myself – and to you, dear reader; if you were here I would be smiling at you at this moment).

I know what you're thinking, because I thought it myself. One letter does not a love-letter make. Correct. Because a single letter could be anything. That I have chosen to assume it is a love-letter from my still-lover is a desire on my part. But it could be the opposite – a letter explaining why, from his perspective, our relationship is dead. If I had received only a single letter I would be forced to accept that could be a distinct possibility. A letter delivering a full stop to any lingering hope on my part that our relationship was a living entity. It would have crushed me in a way I do not want to think about, let alone try and describe. But I don't have to.

Because this letter was not the only one Marek has sent me. According to my husband there have been others. He won't say how many, which implies that he doesn't want me to know or he's lost count.

My interpretation is this: if a man wishes to end an affair he will send a letter to his lover (imminently, ex-lover) to end it, and will move on with his life. Wouldn't you agree, dear reader? Isn't a man clinical in this regard in a way that a woman is probably less so? A woman might write such a letter of termination, but hope to keep open the possibility of friendship, if that were possible under the circumstances surrounding the end of the affair (assuming it concluded amicably enough). A form of friendship for a woman in that situation would be a compensation for the overall loss. We seek to salvage what we can, not cut our losses. Or is that only me? Is that why I have stayed with my husband and not fought harder to leave? Because I am trying to salvage some moments with him worth having? Here I am again talking about him!

If Marek had fallen out of love with me I believe he would have sent me one letter of termination and one only. What on earth would be the point of sending more, if he has said all he has to say? Dragging it out over several missives would be cruel. And he is the opposite of a cruel man. I know the difference, dear reader, believe me — it sleeps beside me every night of my life.

But in sending repeated letters I am convinced Marek is seeking my response to his same stated feelings, sent repeatedly until he gets a reply. And he is all too aware of my situation with my husband. He knows it might be difficult for me to receive his correspondence. But whatever he's writing to me, he won't give up until I answer. That much seems clear to me. I don't know this for certain. And I won't until I read his words. But I am convinced of it.

I know what you're thinking. I have convinced myself. Perhaps.

But, if so, so what? There is nothing to gainsay this conclusion except my husband's repugnant inter-pretation of Marek's letters (begging for money), so why can't I enjoy what I fervently believe until proved wrong? If proof comes, and I am shown for a fool, so be it. I'll deal with that then. Until that time, I remain convinced Marek is trying to reach me in order to establish contact, in order to ask why I failed to meet him on the last day he was stationed near my village. I would tell him – correction (because it has to happen) – I will tell him the moment I have the chance, I only failed to meet him because my husband stole the mes-sage instructing me when and where.

I believe Marek wants to know this because he wants to know if I effectively brought our relationship to an end by not appearing on his last day. That he writes over and over is evidence that he is yearning to hear I failed to appear for another reason (which is the case). Because I was always the fearful one. It was me who was in a constant state of fear that we might be seen around the village, even though we went to great pains to not be seen. Consequently, it is reasonable for him to assume I might have finally lost my nerve.

But I hadn't. And I haven't yet. On the contrary. I had finally decided to break from my husband, whatever the cost. For my own sanity, safety and well-being.

He will only stop writing when he has my reply. That's what I believe. And it brings me great solace, because even though I have no idea where he is, and so where to write, as long as he doesn't hear from me that it's over between us he will retain a spark of hope that it is not. I carry the same spark. Now I know he has been trying to write to me I shall imagine us waking each morning, and the first thing we will think of is one another.

I know what you're thinking, my dear bureaucrat, shut in your room until the end of your working day. You are thinking 'this woman is mad'. I agree! But, what is love but a form of madness? I am mad because I have been made that way by two men. Mad with loathing by one. Mad with love by the other. It can't continue. I'm an intelligent woman, I understand a life like this is not sustainable.

No matter what Bob says or does to me, I have never lost my grip on that, even if I've lost it on much else. Eventually, I will have to make a choice to settle for the impoverished life offered by my bastard husband (you've heard me call him that before, repeatedly, so you mustn't affect shock) or strike out on my own. With or without Marek. That day of reckoning must come.

And I can tell you as I can tell no one else, not even my closest female friends. I will not accept much more life on the bastard's terms. If I ultimately fail to strike out on my own I shall strike myself out. I've thought about it before. On more than one occasion. It would take moments to bring this misery to an end. I'd been contemplating the methodology when I learned of Marek's letter.

I don't have time to think of that now. As I write this to you, dear sir or madam, I imagine my Marek writing another letter to me, hoping that this will be the one I reply to. I must find a way to do so. What would you suggest? All correspondence addressed to either myself or my husband is handed to him by our landlady. Dare I risk bringing her into my secret in the hope she will deliver Marek's letters directly? Without informing? She is a strange old bird. I can't predict what she might do if I tried to take her into my confidence. The repercussions could be appalling, or wonderful.

The more I think about it, the more I believe she would harshly judge my adultery (it's what it is, I'm not ashamed to write it – I hope you're not scandalised to read it. I hope the Mass Observation project has chosen its readers carefully, people of experience, with strong stomachs). My landlady thinks the world of my husband because she only sees what he wants her to see. I fear she is completely under his spell.

I can't take the chance of speaking to her. But how else can I receive the next letter Marek sends without going to the post office every morning before she does, and alerting the bastard's suspicion?

I wish you were here, dear reader, sitting beside me. I could pick your brain. You must be intelligent or you would not have been chosen for the job of reading our reports, and no doubt writing reports of your own about them. I wonder if you are jotting down an idea or two in the margin about what I might do? What can I do? The letters from Marek are my letters, after all. Is it not illegal to interfere with another's mail?

I'm trapped, aren't I? It certainly feels that way. Trapped creatures often lash out to their own detriment. I mustn't give in to my impulse to do anything for the sake of doing something. I need to think clearly. I need help. I know Marek is out there trying to reach me. How do I reach back and connect? How can I receive his next letter, and not have it intercepted and destroyed by my husband?

Wait . . .

Perhaps there is someone.

It would be a great risk. But—

The bedside alarm clock halted the flow of Pat's pen across the page, signalling it was time to make Bob's tea. On the hour every hour while he worked. The alarm was Pat's idea to keep her prompt, but it had all too predictably become the cue by which Bob could harass her on the hour.

'Tea!' came Bob's peeved cry from downstairs. 'And a biscuit! *Two* biscuits, yes?'

'Coming!' she called down.

Pat carefully stowed her writing paraphernalia where Bob wouldn't find it, and hurried, smiling, from the room.

Chapter 39

NICK HAD TELEPHONED to tell Teresa he wouldn't be home until later that night. He couldn't divulge details, but used coded language to let his wife know the Luftwaffe was en route to bomb the north-west, which meant Crewe and Liverpool. Tabley Wood would be sending up its squadrons to try to disrupt the raid, and send the Luftwaffe pilots running for home before they could reach their destination. But whether dumped on their intended targets or prematurely over the English countryside, bombs would fall on Cheshire. Teresa put the telephone receiver down and offered a small prayer for the safety of her family in Birkenhead, and for the rest of the terrorised population of her beloved home city.

Having failed to smash the RAF and force a British surrender, Hitler's High Command was determined to crush British morale by pummelling its major cities from the air, and starving the United Kingdom into submission by destroying its ports and shipping. Facing the Atlantic with a port critical to shipping routes from the United States, Liverpool was a target second only to London. Hence its nightly bombing, and the nightly exodus of much of its population into the surrounding countryside. Grass and trees had no strategic value to the German air force, though camping out in the countryside was not entirely risk free. Stray bombs, or bombs released early, were a lethal hazard for exhausted trekkers.

After she had replaced the receiver on its hook, Teresa stood in silence for a few moments, wondering how she would spend the evening. She could have an early night and go to bed, but knew she wouldn't sleep until Nick climbed in warm and safe beside her. She could have supper and try to read, or listen to the wireless. But again, she knew she wouldn't properly concentrate on either while Nick was at the station, coordinating his flyers, waiting in silent agony for their safe return.

I need some company.

Teresa telephoned Alison to see if she might be free to come over for the evening with Boris, for a spot of supper and a natter. It would be like the old days, when they were lodger and landlady. Alison was just about to make her own supper, but accepted Teresa's invitation, and walked over with Boris within the hour.

Boris was almost beside himself to see Teresa, though his age made expressing delight increasingly limited. He could no longer jump up. His tail couldn't wag in the same sweeping arc, but vibrated stiffly from side to side. Yet the old dog's eyes shone with recognition and pleasure when he saw Teresa, even if she had once nearly killed him by allowing him to slip his lead and run into a road.

Alison watched Teresa prepare supper with a mixture of amusement and pride. She was clearly working hard to get to grips with the domestic duties of married life. She had made a

Woolton pie, and took it steaming out of the oven, humming the irritating ditty the Ministry of Food broadcast regularly to popularise the dish.

The inanity of the tune annoyed Alison almost as much as its capacity to stay in her head, no matter how hard she tried to expunge it from her memory. By way of protest she resolved to never make the pie herself, though she would, of course, eat Teresa's.

'You certainly seem to be taking to married life. You scarcely cooked at all with me. But here you are. Pinny. Oven mitts. Spatula. A changed woman.'

Teresa smiled appreciatively.

'It was either resisting it or rolling up my sleeves and getting stuck in,' Teresa explained. 'Especially with the cooking. I grew up with my father knocking my mother every teatime because she couldn't cook. I don't want Nick to dread meals.'

'Was your mother's food really as bad as your father made out?' Alison asked, as Teresa placed a plate of Woolton pie in front of her.

Teresa nodded. 'Terrible in every way. He used to say she was preparing him for life in prison.'

'Well, good for you for making the effort to learn to cook.'

'Oh, my mother could cook.'

'But you just said— '

'I said her food was *terrible*, which it was. But one day I came back from school and she'd cooked this amazing tea for us all. A very elaborate fish dish with beautiful vegetables, and a wonderful pudding that melted in your mouth. We were all amazed. My father was stunned into silence. She looked at us after we'd finished this wonderful banquet and said, "I just wanted you to know I can do it. When I want to. I just don't want to."'

Alison nearly fell off her chair with laughter. Even Boris lifted his grey head and seemed to raise his top lip to reveal a line of smiling, yellowing teeth.

'She never made that – or anything approaching it – again. Next day we went right back to the rubbish.'

'What did your father do?'

'Nothing.'

'He didn't try and cook himself?'

'You're joking, aren't you?'

After supper, they sat in the front room with cups of tea and Alison quizzed Teresa about how she was finding other aspects of married life. She was pleased to hear that Teresa wanted to be as good a wife to Nick as he was a husband to her. She hadn't found living with a man easy, but she knew from experience that Alison wanted to hear that everything was going swimmingly, so that's what she told her.

'What most worries me is having to give up my job,' Teresa said.

'Do you have to?'

'I'm expected to give way to a man now I have another "job". I'd never thought of being married in those terms.'

'But you can see why they think like that.'

'They don't ask men to do the same.'

'Men don't have the task of running the household.'

'No. But I don't understand why it can't be left to individual women if they want to maintain a career after marriage. Some will want to, some won't. But making it compulsory to retire when you get married seems terribly unfair. Not to mention a dreadful waste of talented, dedicated teachers. It's not a rule that's applied *completely* across the board. But it is here.'

'But you are still teaching.'

'Until they find someone suitable.' Teresa paused, clearly saddened by the inevitable prospect of having to give up her vocation. 'Someone with a penis.' She looked at Alison and smiled, not wanting the mood to drop.

'I'm hoping it will take them a while to find someone.'

'Nick hasn't asked you to give it up?'

'Not at all. He loves hearing about the children when he comes home from the station. At first, I thought it kept him connected to what they're all fighting for. Then I realised he just enjoys hearing all the barmy things they say and do. It takes his mind off everything for a few minutes.'

'How long do you realistically think you can stay in post?'

'It's entirely out of my hands. Of course, I'd have to leave if we start a family of our own.'

Alison raised a quizzical eyebrow.

'If?'

'I mean, *when*.'

Teresa chatted amiably about how much she was looking forward to having children in the house. Not only for Alison's benefit. Teresa did want children, though she was anxious about how much of her life might consequently change. She was gradually reconciling herself to everything that came with married life, and was sensibly taking things one step at a time.

'For the first few weeks I tried to be the greatest wife in the history of the institution of marriage. I nearly had a breakdown. And I think Nick became genuinely scared. Then he told me over supper one evening that he didn't know what he was doing either, so we both calmed down and agreed not to panic. Everything's been much better since. We've taken the time to get to know one another.'

'And is there more to the wing commander than initially met the eye?'

'So much more. Such a wonderful man, Alison. And properly funny. We laugh a lot. It's perfect.'

Nearly. But for . . . That, and the pressure to constantly maintain the façade in front of everyone. Everyone except for 'she who cannot be named', or so much as thought about, even casually. She who must be avoided at all costs, lest I slip up.

As the evening continued, their conversation ranged over many issues. But as the fire petered out in the grate, Teresa became determined to address one issue in particular.

'Please come back to the WI. You're greatly missed.'

Alison looked into the dying flames in the hearth and fell silent for a moment.

'It's difficult . . .'

Teresa knew Alison had fallen out with Frances, but was unaware of the details.

'Is it not possible to patch things up?'

Alison looked at Teresa, her blue eyes flashing with anger.

'The details are not mine to reveal, but I have been treated very badly. I don't think I'm one to harbour a grudge. But neither will I be walked over.'

'But you must miss it.'

'Of course. Every aspect. But just as how long you'll continue to teach is out of your hands, so is how long I'll keep my distance from Fr— from the WI.'

Teresa was running out of arguments. Without knowing exactly what had passed between Alison and Frances she didn't want to say the wrong thing. Alison's sensitivity about the matter was evident. Yet Teresa didn't want to give up without exploring every possibility.

'The branch is going to try and help the trekkers in some way. You'd be so brilliant at organising something. Surely, your sense of duty—'

Alison's eyes widened so quickly at Teresa's mention of the word that the younger woman immediately stopped talking.

'No one, not even you, who I value as one of my closest friends, need question my sense of *duty*, Teresa. Believe me, I'd be better off without one. *Far* better off.'

She glanced at her watch and stood up in a single, determined movement.

'I'd better get Boris back.'

Teresa leapt to her feet to try to placate her.

'Please don't go. If I said the wrong thing—'

'You didn't. You didn't . . . but the longer he lies in one position the more his back legs seize up . . .'

Teresa didn't believe for a moment that Alison was leaving for the sake of the dog, but was unwilling to challenge her.

How deep does it go between her and Frances? I had no idea. Let her go. Don't make things worse between us.

'If I've put my foot in it, I'm sorry.'

'You haven't. On one level, the situation is terribly simple. Frances and I have got ourselves in such a terrible mess that I don't know if we're able to get ourselves out.'

'Surely, in time . . . ?'

'Time, yes. The Great Balm. But some things cannot be forgiven. Some words are impossible to forget.'

Alison crouched to put the lead onto Boris's collar, then stood up and smiled with great fondness at the blossoming younger woman before her.

'I've had a lovely evening with you. I am so thrilled to see you doing so well with Nick, I cannot tell you. *So* thrilled.'

Teresa smiled, pleased with Alison's accolade.

If she thinks I'm carrying it off then I must be.

Teresa hugged Alison and immediately thought she had lost some weight since the wedding, when they had last hugged one another. Even through her coat, Teresa could feel the bones of Alison's spine and ribs. She knew Alison was sensitive, and took things terribly to heart. Isolation wasn't good for her, it allowed her too much time to turn inwards.

'Please just think about returning to the WI. I'll fight anyone you want on your behalf. Just point them out and I'll take them on. I'm your girl. You know that.'

Teresa felt Alison's hands squeeze her a little more tightly around her back.

'Thank you,' she whispered, and turned and led Boris out of the house, into the cold, dark, blacked-out night.

* * *

An hour after Alison's somewhat sudden, if not awkward, departure, Teresa was finishing washing up the pots and dishes from supper when she heard the familiar sound of Nick's car coming to rest outside the front door. Though she had worked hard at school all day, she nevertheless felt guilty if Nick came home in the evening to find her reading, or dozing in an armchair. She suspected it was because Nick's work dealt in life and death, though she knew it was nonsensical to compare educating children with fighting the Luftwaffe. She had tried to understand what it must be like for Nick and his men. Most people would never have to fight for their survival in the entire course of their lives. Nick and his team had to do it daily. Kill or be killed. The pressure seemed almost inhuman.

He's been working hard. I want him to find me working hard at making the house clean and tidy for when he returns. It's what a good wife does.

Nick didn't have to articulate how exhausted he was when he came into the kitchen. The moment Teresa turned round she could see it in his eyes. They were red and a little puffy, and his tie was loose in his collar. She suspected he may have stopped the car on the way home and wept, as he told her he did sometimes when he'd lost pilots in combat. He stopped before reaching home because he felt it unfair to bring his feelings of anger and despair back with him. It made no difference if he was flying with them or not. He would sit in the control tower during their sorties, and listen in to their communications with one another and Tabley Wood.

Teresa could tell immediately that he had lost some that night.

'How many?' she asked.

Nick looked at her, wondering how to turn statistics into meaningful words. Finally, he managed to speak.

'Two definite. But we think a third. We don't know for certain.'

During their short time together, Teresa had learned that only silence failed to make these moments worse. Her husband was a man who routinely sent ridiculously brave teenage boys to their deaths in machines they barely had time to master. He routinely listened over the radio as they were shot or burned to death. Teresa softly crossed the kitchen floor and held him.

'My love . . .' she whispered in his ear.

Nick wrapped his arms around her, and clung on tightly, as if Teresa was the physical embodiment of his own sanity. This was how he came back to her after a wretched night's work. She closed her eyes and waited for the final large sigh from deep within her new husband, signalling that decompression had taken place and he was finally back in Great Paxford, with her.

'How would you feel about a party?' he asked quietly.

The incongruity took her by surprise, as he had planned. It was Nick's way of forcing himself back into the blissful mundanity of ordinary life.

'What – *now*?' Teresa tried unsuccessfully to mask the panic in her voice. She wasn't sure what he was asking, and for a fleeting moment wondered if spontaneous dining with hitherto unknown (and uninvited) guests was a feature of married life that she hadn't been warned about. She felt Nick's body begin to shake within her embrace.

Is he crying or laughing? I daren't look.

Nick gently pulled away from Teresa's arms and looked at her with a broad grin on his face.

'Yes, I'd like you to whip up food for nine to be ready in about twenty-five minutes. I know it's rather short notice, but a woman of your culinary expertise—'

'One more word and I'll try and do it, and then I'll make you eat whatever I produce.'

She smiled and kissed his lips. He tried to respond but she could tell his heart wasn't in it, and didn't press him.

'Assuming not tonight, then when?'

'My new group captain is taking up his post in two weeks. I thought it might be politic and welcoming to invite him and his wife for lunch.'

'A group captain and his wife?'

'If you think you're up to it. If not, we can always ask them at a later date.'

'Of course I'm up to it. I think. What shall I cook?'

'Whatever you like. On second thought . . . why don't you ask some of your more experienced friends what *they* might cook?'

'Are you trying to be offensive?'

'Why go to all the effort of trying to make something up, when friends will no doubt have a range of dinners up their sleeves for any occasion.'

'I won't let you down, I promise.'

'You couldn't.'

'We both know that's not true.'

Nick took off his jacket and hung it across the back of one of the kitchen chairs. He stretched out his arms, rested his head back on the axis of his neck, and closed his eyes. Teresa recognised this was how he started to unwind at the end of particularly stressful days.

'I'm assuming you ate at the mess?'

'Uh-huh.' He opened his eyes and looked at her, yawned, and then said, 'I was thinking of also asking Annie . . .'

Teresa suddenly felt her body freeze from head to toe.

'Annie?'

She tried to sound nonchalant, as if Nick could have said any name and it would have held as little interest. But he hadn't said any other name. He'd said that one. The one she had avoided saying since Annie was last at the house.

'By all accounts the GC is something of a bore. Annie is a brilliant social lubricant when you're up against a really stuffed shirt.'

Teresa's mind started to race.

On no account can she come. I've gone out of my way to keep my distance from Tabley Wood, the Black Horse – anywhere our paths might cross.

'What do you think?'

I think NO.

'I think . . . isn't the form of these occasions that it's . . . well . . . *couples*?'

Nick looked at her wearily.

'Perhaps for a dinner, but we don't have to be so hidebound for a lunch, surely? Besides, I want you and Annie to get to know one another. I know you'd be great friends. She likes you enormously.'

'Does she?'

'She told me that of all her married male friends, you're her favourite "wife".'

Please stop this. Just tell him she can't come. You're the mistress of the house. Make a stand. For everyone's sake.

'I like her enormously too, but—'

'One more place around the table is hardly going to break you, darling. I have every confidence in you.'

He kissed her forehead as if to settle the matter.

'Have the same confidence in yourself.'

If I keep on, it will look suspicious.

'I need a drink,' Nick said. 'Perhaps two. Would you like one?'

'No. Thanks. Alison came over.'

He was already out of the room before she'd finished the sentence.

'Oh? How was that?' he called back, from the front room.

'Fine. She's— It's difficult to tell with her. She's such a closed book much of the time. Actually, that's not strictly accurate. She's like a book whose pages won't open easily.'

By the sound of clinking glass and lack of a response, Teresa could tell Nick was no longer listening. But neither was she interested in continuing to speak. She stood in middle of the kitchen in her apron, thinking about lunch with Nick's new group captain and his wife. And the one woman in the area to whom she was maddeningly attracted.

I'll leave her a note at the station telling her to decline the invitation. Too complicated. It could go awry and Nick might find out. Why does everything have to become difficult? Why can't we just live our lives? Why must something always muddy the water?

Nick reappeared in the doorway holding two glasses of Scotch, both his.

'Chicken!' he said, beaming. 'Make chicken. Everyone likes chicken. It's difficult to mess up chicken. Not even—' He stopped himself, but not in time.

Teresa smiled a thin, resigned smile, and thought of her mother. She wanted the entire event scrapped here and now, but knew she couldn't insist on it. The idea of having to produce a faultless, multi-course culinary display for Nick's new boss and the effortlessly perfect Annie filled her with utter horror. Yet her smile remained.

'If it's chicken you want, darling, it's chicken we shall have.'

Chapter 40

After making a more abrupt exit from her evening with Teresa than she would have liked, Alison was in no great hurry to return to her small, dark, empty cottage. Besides, it was around this time that she habitually took Boris out to undertake his ablutions before bed, so ambling around the village lanes at this hour was not unusual for either of them. Since Alison had exiled herself from her beloved WI, she relished any opportunity to be out of her house, even if the rest of the world was fast asleep. In fact, more so, as she still carried what she felt was an almost visible taint of shame from the factory fiasco, and preferred to avoid people as much as possible. It was this that prompted her to walk out of the village, into the surrounding countryside, even at this late hour. This, and a curiosity to see for herself the extent of the trekker issue around Great Paxford.

Alison had learned from experience not to rush Boris on their nightly sojourns. She enjoyed watching him root around the hedgerows, picking up scents that were beyond the detection – or interest – of any human.

This is his time as much as mine. He likes to sniff God knows what. I don't. He barely registers I'm with him, and that's how it should be. I'm only really here to make sure he gets home safely.

'Remember when there were hardly any cars on the roads, boy, and I used to let you out of the front door to go off by yourself for hours?'

It was Alison's habit to chat to her dog at home and as they walked round. It didn't feel odd to her in the slightest. Nor did it bother her in the least that Boris – a dog – didn't understand a word she said except 'walk' and 'food'. He *seemed* as if he understood her, and over time that's all she felt she needed by way of company. He was undeniably affectionate towards her when he wanted to be, without being cloying. Alison regarded Boris like an ideal relative who offered company without imposition, who didn't inflict his opinions on her, ate what he was given, did what he was told around the house, and went to bed on order. Furthermore, Boris would quite likely give his life to defend her if ever the need arose, and Alison couldn't say that about anyone else.

As they continued along the lane, the dark silhouettes of blacked-out houses gave way to dark silhouettes of trees, among which small pinpricks of light were visible. Alison chatted away as they walked. Away from the houses of Great Paxford, she felt no compulsion to moderate her volume. On a recent nocturnal outing around the village she had been barked at by an ARP warden to keep her voice down, which had amused her.

'Do you seriously imagine my voice can draw fire from a German bomber flying thousands of feet overhead? Do your job, man, by all means. And thank you very much. But there's really no need to be ridiculously officious about it.'

While keeping to the road, Alison's curiosity drew her towards the nearest of the flickering sources of light within the trees. Keeping her distance, she peered through the black trunks for a closer look. In the gloom, she could make out figures of men and women sitting and lying around a small fire, talking quietly and eating, the yellow flames flicking fragments of light onto their faces. Anxious not to be seen, or for Boris to suddenly get spooked and give her away, Alison moved on, passing more encampments that were revealed either by small fires, or low, unintelligible murmurs emerging from the darkness. Alison found it difficult to imagine making this walk every night, leaving behind homes and possessions, not knowing whether they would still exist upon their return. She could not help but be immensely sympathetic towards these men, women and children forced to abandon everything and flee into the countryside every night to escape the Luftwaffe. As she crept away, she wondered what might be done to help these poor unfortunates.

The lane that Alison had taken looped back into Great Paxford, and she and Boris soon found themselves padding along the High Street, past Brindsley's, from where they heard baby Vivian crying for attention. She no sooner started than stopped.

Miriam at the ready, no doubt. Day and night.

'That child will want for nothing in this world,' she whispered to Boris. 'Mark my words . . .'

Alison interpreted his silence as tacit agreement with anything she said.

They walked past the dark silhouettes of blacked-out houses on either side of the road, not a light beam emerging from any of them, their inhabitants most likely asleep. After a hundred yards, they turned left down a small side street that eventually opened on to the village green. The nettle patches on the left-hand side were the favourite toilet area for most of the dogs in the village, and Boris was no different. Once he had relieved himself they would make their way home.

As Boris sniffed around for the best place to go, Alison looked around the moonlit green, trying to maintain a sense of decorum and not to intrude on her dog's private business.

It had been a long day and Alison felt tired. Bookkeeping may not be the most complicated element of the accountancy process, but it required an almost superhuman diligence that put a strain on her eyes and brain. One missed or misplaced digit and Alison could lose a client, swiftly followed by her reputation. Her livelihood was entirely dependent on her powers of concentration, and they were harder to sustain the older she became. As Boris rustled around in the grass and nettles, Alison slowly looked towards the dark horizon, the point that most relaxed her eyes. It was then that she saw Frances. Or so she thought.

It can't be Frances. Why would Frances be out in the middle of the night? Why would she be sitting on a bench by herself out here? Why would anyone?

Alison's eyes were perfectly calibrated to the dark. The figure, sitting about a hundred yards away, had the shape of Frances, and sat as Frances customarily sat, with her back straight and her hands folded in her lap. She was also looking towards the horizon.

Alison was immediately caught in two minds: to yank Boris gently out of the nettles and return the way they had come, without drawing Frances's attention, or to approach her once good friend? Her sense of self-preservation propelled her towards the first option, but her curiosity pushed her towards the second. It was a position in which Alison found herself on many occasions, and self-preservation frequently won out. But not this time.

There must be something terribly wrong for her to be out here alone like this.

Alison gently pulled Boris from the nettles and quietly approached the still figure of Frances sitting on a park bench with her back to Alison.

Perhaps she came out for a walk and has fallen asleep? Surely too cold.

When she was within ten feet of Frances, Alison stopped and peered at the woman with whom she had once been so close. The face of her former friend was partially visible from the side, and Alison saw a glint of moonlight on her cheek, which she couldn't account for. Alison then realised it was moonlight refracted through a tear. All thought of retreat evaporated.

'Frances?'

Frances turned and saw the dim outlines of Alison and Boris standing just behind her. Their appearance was so unexpected and incongruous that for a moment Frances simply stared at them through the gloom.

'Is everything all right?'

In almost any other circumstance Frances would have swiftly wiped the tears from her face and bluffed her way through an awkwardly vulnerable moment. But sitting on a bench on the green facing Alison in the middle of the night, bluff was impossible. With Noah missing for a second day, and now a second night, Frances had no defences to raise against Alison's enquiry. Nor against Alison herself, a woman she had been on her way to visit when Claire had come running with news of Noah's disappearance.

'I'm afraid not,' Frances eventually managed.

Alison immediately recognised Frances was in trouble and – setting aside everything that had passed between them in recent weeks – sat on the bench beside her. Realising they weren't walking straight home as they usually would, Boris stretched out in the cool grass by Alison's feet, and closed his eyes.

The two women sat in silence for a few moments before Frances turned to look at Alison.

'Noah's gone missing.'

Alison had been feeling a little weary after all that walking, but was suddenly alert.

'What do you mean?'

'He ran away from the boarding school I sent him to. Two days ago. There's been no sighting of him since.'

Having fallen out of favour with Frances, Alison was ignorant of any of what Frances now told her.

'I had no idea you were sending him to a boarding school. I assumed—'

'It was Peter's wish.'

'Peter?'

Frances realised how little Alison knew about the scandal surrounding her husband's death. She knew Peter had died alongside his company accountant, Helen. But she knew nothing of their secret relationship spanning ten years, of which Noah had been the product.

'Noah is Peter's son by another woman, Alison. By Helen, in fact. The woman whose role you took over at the factory.'

Alison sat back on the bench, dumbfounded.

'I agreed to take him in after his grandfather pleaded with me to give him sanctuary from the bombing in Liverpool. I can't tell you how much I loathed the idea. Until I saw the child looking at me through the window of the taxi they had taken from Crewe station to Great Paxford. He looked as lost as I felt. I sensed an instant connection.'

'Through Peter.'

'Well . . . how Peter's sudden, terrible absence left each of us feeling.'

'No. I meant—'

'Yes, Alison. I know what you meant. Because he's Peter's flesh and blood. I cannot deny that is part of my fascination with the child. I cannot help but see many of Peter's features in him – both physical and psychological.' Frances paused, and hung her head, covering her eyes with her right hand.

Alison took her left hand in hers and held it. She felt Frances's fingers curl tightly around her own.

We live cheek by jowl with one another, yet how is it possible to know so little of each other's lives? What an extraordinary thing she has done in taking on this child. Would I – could I – have done the same?

Frances's hand felt freezing cold. Despite wearing her winter coat, she was shivering.

'How long have you been out here?' Alison asked.

'I left Sarah and Claire at the house in case of news. I had to get out to clear my head and think through any possibility I may have missed. It occurred to me early on that Noah might try and find his way back to his grandparents in Liverpool, but the police told me they had found letters in Noah's belongings at the school from his grandfather, informing him that they were moving up to Scotland, to live with his brother, out of harm's way. The police also interviewed other boys at the school and discovered Noah wasn't having as smooth an acclimatisation as the headmaster had led me to believe. Not by a long chalk.'

'The police contacted the grandfather's brother?'

Frances nodded.

'There's been no contact with the child. His grandparents are beside themselves. He is a much-loved little boy. But how—'

Frances stopped before she could complete the sentence. She swallowed back her deepest fear and continued.

'How can an eight-year-old survive outside for two days and two nights, without food or shelter?'

'Might he have returned to Liverpool?'

'That would be worse. The raids are almost nightly now. I cannot tell you the horrific scenarios my mind has been conjuring since I was told he had run away.'

'I can imagine.'

'What if he attempts to traverse countryside where exposure and terrain are more dangerous? What if he's slipped or fallen or injured himself in some way and is unable to attract help? What if he's tried to cross a stream or river and misjudged the depth and speed of the water, or loses his footing, or—'

'Frances, *stop.*'

Alison's voice was calmly insistent. It had the desired effect, and Frances stopped mid-sentence.

Alison couldn't answer any of these questions, and had no interest in offering glib reassurance. Frances would dismiss any attempt at mollification. A little boy had run away from school in a region of the country under heavy bombardment from the German air force. The situation couldn't be worse, and both knew it. If Alison couldn't answer her old friend's deepest concerns she could at least help her to control them. She put her arm around Frances's shoulders and held her tightly.

'You don't know what's happened. And until he's found, you won't. In the meantime, your mind will race to the worst possible outcomes, especially after what happened with Peter. You're preparing for the worst news, and that's to be expected. But, and I must stress this, that doesn't mean any of the scenarios you've described have occurred.'

'Then why have there been no sightings? Why hasn't he been handed in to the authorities? Surely, if he's unhurt and well someone would have come across him?'

'Again, I don't know, and neither do you.'

Frances looked searchingly into Alison's eyes. Alison had seen a similar expression on her face in the long, sad days following Peter's death. Similar, but not identical. With Peter, Frances had been stupefied by events in which she had no involvement. That wasn't the case now. With Noah, Alison could see that Frances was additionally being consumed by the guilt she felt at sending Noah away.

In that moment, what enmity had formed between Alison and Frances like a brick wall after the factory's collapse suddenly seemed to crumble and fall away. Sitting side by side they were two old friends once more – one desperately needing help, the other willing to offer as much as she could under the circumstances.

Before Alison could see them she felt the first tentative drops of a larger downpour start to fall on and around them. Boris opened his eyes with irritation. Alison stood up from the bench and looked down at Frances.

'Let's get you home,' she said, holding out her hand. 'Before you catch your death.'

Chapter 41

Before collecting Will from the hospital, Erica had prepared the house for the arrival of a man who found mobility difficult and was likely to spend his remaining days in bed. She had managed to find a wheelchair in the event Will wanted to be moved to another part of the house, or possibly into the small garden, but she wasn't optimistic it would be used much, if at all. Both Kate and Laura declared they would push their father wherever he wanted to go, which, Erica explained patiently, rather missed the point.

'It's unlikely he'll either want to go anywhere, or be in a fit state to.'

Both girls were bright, and Erica knew they understood that with cancer attacking his lungs and brain, their father was coming home to die. Nevertheless, she had begun to wonder if their determination to offer Will a range of distractions was more to distract themselves from the inevitable than to help Will. She had tried to emphasise the point in the front room on the morning she was due to collect him.

'To all intents and purposes, this room is the extent of your father's world now. Asleep or awake, this is the extent of his physical life. I need you to understand that.'

The girls nodded in silence. Erica pointed to the armchair.

'If he wants to come out of bed and sit down, he will sit there.'

She pointed to the camp bed they had set up alongside the single bed Will would lie in, which they had brought down from Laura's room. Laura would now be sleeping in her parents' bed upstairs.

'At night, I will sleep here so I can be on hand if he needs anything.'

'Why don't we take it in turns?' suggested Kate. 'It seems very gruelling for you to have your sleep disturbed night after night, which is probably what's going to happen.'

Erica recognised in Kate's offer just how brief her marriage to Jack had been. He had been killed training to be a fighter pilot. They'd had no chance for their nascent love to deepen and mature to the stage where sitting beside your suffering partner night after night was viewed not as a chore, but as an almost sacred act of devotion.

Kate and Jack had fallen in love extremely quickly. When they first declared their intention to marry, Erica and Will had gone along with it, while wondering in private if it was really *love* they were experiencing, or simply a heightened sense of romantic mania suffused with lust, brought on by the hostilities of war . . . Both Erica and Will had experienced something similar during the Great War. Suddenly, even the most average-looking chap was transformed into a fit, clean-cut, rather glamorous young man of action, blasé about what lay ahead, arrogantly proclaiming that whatever it was, he – regardless what he might have been before war had been declared – would be its match. Young women fell hook, line and sinker for the transformation, and marriage was the only respectable option. With some foreboding, Erica and Will had recognised the same dynamic this time round, in accelerated relationships striking up around them. As much as they recognised it in the way Kate had fallen for Jack, they knew there was little they could do to alter their chosen course. The young will have their own lives. And sometimes, tragically, their own deaths too.

'I won't find it gruelling if your father has cause to wake me in the night. I might even hope for it, as long as he isn't in pain or discomfort. It will give me more time with him.'

Erica knew it sounded selfish, and she half-expected the girls to ask her to share the experience. But despite their young age they seemed to understand that their parents' relationship existed at a depth they couldn't completely appreciate, and made no more of it.

Erica had everything planned out. After his long-anticipated arrival, she didn't want it to take long for the household to fall into a daily routine around Will's care. Medication and meals would be taken according to a strict timetable, while the rest of the day would be given over to keeping him comfortable. Will would sleep a great deal, and during daylight his daughters would take it in turns to sit in the armchair at his bedside, watch over him and simply sit with him for as long as he was there.

To reduce the physical stress that speaking seemed to cause him, Erica had decided that Will could communicate urgent needs by writing down single words on a pad. 'FOOD' if he was hungry. 'LOO' if he needed to use the toilet. 'READ' if he wanted one of the girls to read to him. And so on.

'It will upset you to see your father – the most intelligent, articulate man we've known – reduced to expressing himself in monosyllabic scrawl. But remember, it will allow him to communicate with us without exhausting him, and that's what's important. He will still be here.'

In hospital, Will loved Laura to read to him, and would peer serenely over his oxygen mask as she read his favourite works by the poet John Keats. Invariably, he seldom remained conscious for long. It made no difference to Laura; conscious or asleep, she was content to simply sit and watch her father breathe.

* * *

Within twenty-four hours of arriving at his new home it became clear that Will was going to be a less compliant patient than Erica had imagined. While he did sleep a great deal, when awake he demanded to be lifted into the wheelchair and pushed to wherever his family congregated, in either the kitchen or the dining room. When they sat and listened to the wireless, Will would sit with them. When they played cards at the dining table, Will would sit in the wheelchair and watch. He might quickly drop off to sleep, but that was beside the point. He wanted to spend as much time as possible with them, in their company, participating in life around the house – if only by being present. When the weather turned fine on his second day home, Will asked to be taken into the garden – not by writing 'GARDEN' on a pad as Erica had planned, but by expending the energy to say, 'I would . . . very much . . . like to . . . be taken into . . . the garden . . . please.'

There was a price to pay for such effort. It exhausted him. The brief fits he had begun to experience in hospital, as if he were epileptic, became more violent, and lasted longer than before, leaving him unconscious for up to half an hour – a consequence he called 'Sleeping . . . it . . . off', as if he'd had one too many drinks over lunch. Nevertheless, he adamantly refused to be contained in bed around the clock.

'I have no . . . desire . . . to be hori . . . zontal . . . any longer . . . than I . . . have to . . . be,' he told Erica on his first night home, after she had expressed her concern about his refusal to follow her regimen.

'Plenty . . . of time . . . for that . . . soon. Now . . . I want . . . to be *with* . . . you all. *With*. Not . . . next door.'

He promptly fell asleep again, but his point had been made. When he woke before supper, Erica explained herself.

'If we can conserve your energy you will stay stronger, longer.'

Will slowly shook his head and drew in a long breath to fuel his next sentence.

'Conserve . . . to what . . . end? Lying on . . . my back to . . . stare at . . . the . . . ceiling?' He drew another long breath and looked at his wife.

'No.'

He held out his hand for her to take, and she slipped her hand into his and held it, as she had done during every hospital visit.

'Quality,' he said. 'Not . . . quantity.'

Erica knew he was referring to the time they had left together. During his stay in the hospital she had become expert at interpreting Will's increasingly gnomic statements, which were a consequence of the sheer amount of energy it took for him to speak. She squeezed Will's hand to reassure him she understood, and nodded in agreement, and was rewarded with a small squeeze of his hand in reply.

There was a knock on the door. Kate entered, and informed her mother that Pat Simms was at the front door asking if she could have a quick word.

'What about?'

'She didn't say.'

'Sit with your father.'

Erica transferred Will's hand into Kate's and left the room, puzzled.

* * *

Pat waited nervously on the Campbells' doorstep, preparing herself for the task ahead. Erica had been a good friend to her in the past, but Pat had also been on the receiving end of her high-minded morality. Erica hadn't approved of Pat's extra-marital relationship with Marek. She felt guilty about taking Erica away from Will, if only for a minute or two. But there was no one else to whom she could now turn.

The front door opened and Pat faced Erica.

'Hello, Pat,' Erica said, smiling a social smile that also managed to communicate that she hoped that whatever it was that had brought Pat to her door wouldn't take long.

'I'm so sorry to disturb you, Erica. I really don't want to keep you. Kate told me Will is home. That must be . . . How is that?'

Pat's first impulse had been to suggest it must be wonderful to have Will back from the hospital, but she caught herself in time.

It might not be wonderful for her at all. It might be hellish to have to sit and watch the man you love slip away a second at a time. Could I bear to watch such a thing with Marek?

'It seems that the perfect patient in hospital has ideas to be significantly less perfect in his own home.' Erica paused for a moment, smiling bravely. 'Not that I'm complaining about having him back with us. It's wonderful.'

Pat smiled supportively.

'If there's anything I can do to help. I still consider us neighbours despite us being elsewhere in the village.'

'Thank you,' Erica said, keen to go back inside to Will.

'I'm sure you and the girls have everything covered here. But perhaps you might like me to let Will's condition be more widely known, so the village can let you get on without constant enquiries about the state of Will's health?'

'That would be very kind, Pat. Thank you.'

'Not at all.'

'What was it you wanted to see me about?'

Pat looked at Erica and tried to gain control of her nerves.

'I wouldn't have come unless I had to, Erica. And I really had to.'

'Whatever is it?'

Pat lowered her voice. 'You are the only person in Great Paxford who knows of my affair with Marek.'

The name of the Czech captain was most certainly not what Erica was expecting to hear. She could not approve of adultery on principle, and knowing Bob as she did, she felt Pat's relationship with Marek only placed her in greater jeopardy with her unpleasant husband. While Erica had actively tried to help Pat deal with Bob's behavioural excesses, she had also actively tried to dissuade her from continuing to see Marek.

'Marek? But . . . I thought Marek had gone. Shipped out on the day of Teresa's wedding. You told me yourself.'

Pat nodded.

'Yes.'

'Which has to be for the best, surely.'

'No, Erica. It is most definitely not for the best. More than anyone, you know how my life is with Bob.'

'Yes, but—'

'Since moving in with Joyce, he has been even more vile, taking great sport in treating me one way in front of her, and another behind her back. And at the moment he's limited in what he can do with Joyce as a witness, but eventually we'll have to leave . . .' Pat took a deep breath before continuing. 'That was difficult enough to live with, but by chance I recently discovered Bob has been intercepting and destroying letters Marek has been sending me.'

'What?'

Erica closed the front door behind her to prevent these details leaking into the house – a combination of wanting to protect Pat's privacy and wanting to prevent what Pat had come to say contaminating her own home.

'Are you sure?'

Pat nodded vigorously to underline her certainty, not wishing to leave Erica in the slightest doubt.

'He's admitted it. Whenever I think I have his measure he exceeds it. Joyce collects our post with hers every morning from the post office when she buys her newspaper. All letters – whether for Bob or me – are given to Bob. This is how his mind works, Erica. It never occurred to me he would do such a thing, or even think of it. But he operates on a level beyond the comprehension of most people. I'm sorry . . .' Pat sounded utterly drained. Erica could see the effort this was taking.

'You have far, far more important things to be thinking about at the moment. But literally, I have no one else—'

'I understand. But what is it you want from me?'

'I know you disapproved of my involvement with Marek—'

'Mainly because of the trouble you could get into with Bob. A fear that has been borne out, has it not?'

Pat ignored Erica's question.

'As I said . . . you know what life is like with Bob. You heard it daily, through our adjoining wall.'

Erica felt she was being drawn into something she had neither the time nor inclination to be drawn into. Yet she felt torn by the evident distress her friend was suffering.

'Pat, I'm sorry, I honestly don't know how I might help—'

'Let Spencer deliver any letters addressed to me here.' Pat rattled the words out before she lost courage, then took a breath. '*Please*.'

Erica looked at Pat for a moment, unsure she had correctly understood what Pat had just suggested.

'Are you suggesting—'

'I could tell Spencer the letters are from a relative asking for money in light of Bob's new novel being serialised in the national press. I'll tell him I don't want Bob troubled by the letters, and that delivering them here will allow me to deal with the matter without troubling my husband. It will only be one letter, in fact. If there are to be more after the first, I'll tell Marek to address them to you directly, so Spencer wouldn't know he's delivering *my* post. There will be nothing for you to do except notify me when they arrive.'

Pat knew she was asking Erica to get involved with something she might not be comfortable with, but was driven by her acute need to re-establish contact with Marek.

'Pat . . . under any other circumstances—'

'Erica, *please*. I am begging you to do this for me. *Please*.'

The tone of Pat's desperate plea made Erica feel increasingly uncomfortable.

'I cannot have every single aspect of my miserable life placed in the palm of Bob's hand. I simply cannot,' Pat continued.

Erica realised she may have underestimated the strength of Pat's feelings for Captain Novotny. She had assumed theirs had been a reckless, casual affair. But she could see it clearly meant a great deal more to Pat. Yet she couldn't help thinking it might be for the best if Pat were to let it go and get on with making her life better with Bob.

'It was only an affair, Pat,' Erica said, trying to sound as kind as possible. Pat started to shake her head, but Erica was committed to her thought.

'Wouldn't it be for the best to put it behind you?'

Pat stopped shaking her head and looked fiercely at Erica.

'If you had been married to someone who treated you as badly as you know Bob treats me, and then met Will, would you let *him* go?'

Erica was stunned by the question, followed swiftly by a wave of anger that Pat was comparing her decades-long marriage to Will to a relationship Pat had with a man she'd only known a few weeks.

'That is *entirely* different.'

'I won't ever have what you've had with Will. Bob didn't want a family so I won't have a family, as you've had. I will never watch children grow up as you've watched Kate and Laura. I threw my lot in with Bob and thought he would soften, but Bob doesn't soften. Year on year he just gets crueller. Marek came into my life and I suddenly caught a glimpse of what you experience on a daily basis. Love. Respect. Feeling cherished. Wanted. You have to understand, I believe Marek is to me what Will is to you. I thought I'd lost him but I suddenly have a chance, the slimmest opportunity, to make contact with him and find out if he feels the same way about me – as he once said he did. For that I need to be able to read and reply to his letters. That's all I'm asking you to do, Erica. Take them and keep them for me, so Bob can't destroy them.'

Erica experienced a powerful impulse to send Pat on her way and return inside to Will and the girls. But to do that she would have to ignore what she knew about Pat's life with Bob. How he verbally abused her. Controlled her. Taunted her. Shattered her self-respect, and occasionally beat her black and blue. Erica had heard each of these occur on more than one occasion through their dividing wall, and had despaired at her powerlessness to intervene – except once, and that had been a terrible blunder.

'The last time I became involved—'

'It went too far but I know it was well-intentioned. The "tonic" you gave me for Bob worked. But it was my fault for increasing the dosage. Had I kept to your instruction he would have never been in danger. I'm not asking you to become *involved* now, Erica. I'm only asking you to let me know when Spencer delivers a letter addressed to me "*by mistake*". There would be no danger to anyone, and no question of you getting drawn any further into the situation.'

'By mistake?'

Pat paused for a moment and looked at Erica, waiting for the penny to drop.

'What with the post office and the fire service and Claire, Spencer's rushed off his feet. I wouldn't be surprised if he didn't make mistakes with post all the time.'

Please, Erica. You are the only one who can help me reach him.

To Pat it seemed like an age before Erica released a small sigh of acceptance, and said, 'Very well. Tell Spencer to divert your letters here.'

Tears of gratitude began to pour down Pat's cheeks, and she stepped forward and kissed Erica.

'Bless you,' she said softly. 'I cannot begin to tell you how much this means to me.'

Erica stood on her doorstep and watched Pat disappear round the corner. The expression on Pat's face suggested Erica had done the right thing, but the feeling in her stomach left her doubting the conviction almost immediately. She wondered if she should discuss it with Will. His advice was always worth hearing, even if Erica didn't always follow it. She decided against.

He'll be gone soon. I have to learn to lie in beds of my own making.

Erica went back inside and closed the front door.

Chapter 42

STEPH FARROW'S KITCHEN was plain but intensely functional, reflecting the farm and its buildings outside the window; the kitchen of a family that spent most of its waking life working the land. For Steph, who shared the farm's work with her husband, Stan, and in his absence with their son, Little Stan, the kitchen was just another place of labour on the farm. Where the milking shed produced milk, the kitchen produced food. She had it finely tuned to her purpose.

Steph could find any utensil she needed for whatever she happened to be cooking, simply by reaching out and grasping it, without having to look – everything where it needed to be to produce meals quickly from jars and cupboards, without fuss or unnecessary elaboration, for Stan, Little Stan and their farmhand, Isobel. Plates and cups and blackened pots and pans were stacked within arm's reach on the dresser, or on simple, time-warped shelves, or hanging from hooks from solid beams running the length of the ceiling. There was a dark, dented stove and hob at its heart, and a thick, stone sink, chipped and lined by years of having crockery and hot pans dumped in it unceremoniously, prior to cleaning. The floor was covered in thick red clay tiles, scuffed and scratched from decades of boots tramping across them, and faded by hot liquids splashed across them, and bleaching summer sunlight burning the colour from them.

For all its lack of sheen and finish, the Farrow kitchen nevertheless had its own dignified simplicity, stripped of unnecessary flourish. This was a room where tired farmers came to fuel themselves for the day ahead, and where they sat in silence at sundown and fed themselves, their drained muscles craving armchairs beside the parlour fire, where they could doze, full-bellied, and forget tomorrow's work for an hour or two.

Steph looked around her wooden kitchen table at the five friendly faces of the 'Trekker Accommodation Subcommittee', and then at Gwen Talbot, who had insisted she be included to represent WI members who were unhappy about unduly helping trekkers, or *refugees*, as Frances called them. Mrs Talbot, and those she claimed to represent, believed assisting them would put pressure on local resources and encourage more and more people to come into the area, until the village became overrun. If she couldn't prevent Great Paxford's WI from helping them, she could at least do everything in her power to try to limit the damage she believed would be done by the majority's naive impulse to help those beyond help.

Steph had been clever in the composition of the subcommittee, choosing farming women, like her, who were her friends and shared her general outlook.

She had also asked Isobel, who was not only intensely loyal to Steph, but who had been sent away, out of a major city, at

336

the outbreak of war precisely because her blindness made her more vulnerable. Steph believed Isobel's experience gave her additional insight and compassion into the trekkers' experience of being displaced. She was also calm and thoughtful, and wouldn't agree to anything just because Steph had suggested it.

Steph had also asked Teresa to join the subcommittee, a woman she knew to be considerate and compassionate, and one who could offer a Liverpudlian perspective on any discussion they might have.

'You know better than anyone what they're going through. You can talk to them about our proposals, and they'll listen.'

'I'm sure they'd listen to you just as much.'

Steph shook her head. 'You're one of them. Makes all the difference.'

Teresa knew Steph was right. Their location on the west coast, and their city's distinct, maritime history, meant many Liverpudlians saw themselves as an almost separate ethnic group to other Britons. Hearing someone with their own accent explain the situation in Great Paxford, and what was on offer, would, Teresa agreed, reassure many that they were being treated fairly, with good intentions.

All the faces around her – bar one – smiled at Steph encouragingly, willing her to take charge and steer the meeting where it needed to go. Mrs Talbot, however, looked at Steph with thinly veiled disdain. She was predisposed to disappointment, and expected the worst.

From inside a folder Steph pulled out a sheet of paper on which she'd written a list and picked up her pencil, hoping it made her look 'businesslike'. Twelve months ago, such a simple action would have been impossible. Able to manage a farm as well as any man, before Frances became Chair, Steph would have never imagined herself joining the WI. The way Joyce had run it meant Great Paxford's branch wasn't for women like Steph. Working women. Women who could neither read nor write. Frances, and then Teresa, changed all that – the former by taking over the branch and throwing its doors open to *all* women of *all* social backgrounds; the latter by painstakingly teaching Steph to read and write. Now she was sitting at her own kitchen table, heading a WI subcommittee.

She was determined to look and sound the part. To help overcome her nerves she had decided to mimic Frances to some extent – sitting up very straight, and pitching her voice at a slightly louder level than anyone else.

'First off, thank you, ladies, for taking the time to be part of this subcommittee. I know you're all busy, so it's very good of you to come out and do extra to help us decide what we can do for the trekkers – or refugees – coming into our neck of the woods.'

'And indeed, our woods,' said Isobel, smiling.

The women around the table – bar one – nodded in gratitude at Steph's appreciation of them, and at Isobel's joke.

'Our conversation today is based on the assumption Liverpool and Crewe will carry on getting bombed for a while yet. The weather will only get worse with winter. The refugees will arrive colder, wetter and hungrier than they do now. They'll need *proper* shelter. Fields and woods won't be any use.'

Mrs Talbot let out a loud sigh of disdain, designed to reveal her exasperation at the entire conversation. Steph had anticipated she might be somewhat disruptive and refused to be knocked off her stride.

'My first suggestion is we use the village hall for families with children, other buildings – barns, unused sheds – for everyone else.'

'*All* children?' asked Mrs Talbot, sensing the first opportunity to quibble.

Steph was minded to consider any intervention from Mrs Talbot as potentially mischievous, but tried to resist the temptation to dismiss her out of hand at the outset.

Frances would be fair, until Mrs Talbot lost the right to be treated fairly.

'How do you mean "all children"?' Steph asked.

'Do we need to prioritise a *fifteen-year-old* child in the village hall in the same way as a *six-year-old*? They're both children, but one would fare well in a farm outhouse, while the other might not.'

To everyone's surprise, it was a reasonable point. Though Steph suspected Mrs Talbot was raising it more to sabotage the meeting by picking holes in every proposition than in a genuine attempt to resolve the issue, she felt obliged to take it seriously.

'What do you think?' she said, throwing Mrs Talbot's question to the others. The faces looking back frowned in contemplation. Teresa was the first to speak up.

'The problem with a cut-off age is that it could split up families, and no one would stand for that. I don't think we'd want to either.'

Mrs Talbot was quick to pounce.

'If they're coming into our area and expect to be looked after then they'll just have to accept what's on offer. The villagers are people trying to get through the war as much as they are. We are not hoteliers, and Great Paxford *is not a hotel*.'

Steph felt all eyes turn to her. She swallowed hard as words started to form in her head. In any other circumstance, she would wait until entire sentences had come together before voicing them. But here, she was expected to have answers, and quickly.

'No one's suggesting Great Paxford becomes a hotel. Teresa's saying there's no point having rules like "children of this age go there" and "children of that age go there" if the refugees—'

'Can we please stop calling them that? It sounds so silly.'

'They are people taking refuge,' said Isobel. 'It's accurate.'

'It's melodramatic, designed to extract more sympathy than they deserve.'

Teresa could feel her cheeks growing hot with anger.

If she was a man I'd punch him.

Steph felt the meeting was beginning to slip from her control.

'We can't split up families. There'd be riots,' she said, trying to sound firm. 'We'd be the same in their position.'

'In their position, I would stay put,' snapped back Mrs Talbot, 'and not force myself on the kindness of strangers.'

'That's funny, Mrs Talbot,' said Teresa. 'You don't sound very kind. *Ever*.'

Mrs Talbot turned to face Teresa with a face like that of a snake preparing to strike, open-mouthed, tongue tasting the air, fangs ready to deliver a venomous blow. But before the first acid words could leave her, she was suddenly distracted by something through the kitchen window, over Teresa's left shoulder. Something that managed to stop Gwen Talbot in her tracks was something worth seeing. Everyone but Isobel turned to see what she was looking at.

Through Steph's kitchen window they saw the same man Mrs Talbot and her cabal had hounded out of Brindsley's a week earlier, walking slowly along the lane towards the farmhouse, holding a child in his arms. Mrs Talbot stood up.

'This is what happens when you give them an inch at dusk,' she hissed. 'They take a mile in daylight.' She narrowed her eyes. 'Leave him to me.'

Steph was already standing and placed a restraining hand on Mrs Talbot's arm.

'This is *my* farm,' she said.

'You've a shotgun?'

'Who is it?' asked Isobel, trying to keep track of the conversation.

'A coloured, carrying a child,' said Mrs Talbot. 'Coming towards the house.'

Mrs Talbot consciously made what was happening outside appear threatening.

Teresa watched the man approach the farmhouse, her expression becoming increasingly confused.

'Not his child, though . . .' she said, almost to herself.

The other women looked at Teresa, whose gaze was fixed on the approaching man, and on the small child he was holding.

'It's white.'

Chapter 43

SARAH WAS TALKING on the telephone to Noah's headmaster in the hall, asking why none of his staff had noticed that Noah was clearly feeling distressed about his life at the school. So distressed that he had fled.

'Fled is such an emotive word,' said Dr Nelms.

Sarah well understood why he made Frances so angry.

'Children are emotional creatures, don't you think, Headmaster?'

Sarah was in no mood for semantics. Noah's disappearance was taking its toll on everyone in the household and this infernal man was refusing to shoulder any responsibility for not knowing the child's state of mind. Arguably, it should have been Frances speaking to him, but she had started to despise the sound of the man's voice, and no longer trusted herself to be civil.

Alison had brought Frances back very late the previous night and she hadn't made it to her bed. Instead, she'd had two glasses of brandy to warm her up, before swiftly falling asleep on the sofa. Sarah covered her sister with a blanket before retiring to the spare room. She had come down in the morning to find Frances still asleep, and decided to let her rest for as long as she needed.

She was the same when Peter died. Everything in her life had gone so smoothly until then. It's left her ill-equipped for serious shock. It overwhelms her completely. Was I any different when I learned of Adam's capture? I think so. I went into a state for a few days but I forced myself back into the world. I still struggle every day with the absolute silence on his whereabouts – on how he is. A vicar's wife learns to conceal her own anxieties. Lead by example. People expect you to smile serenely and keep paddling.

That morning, Sarah had found Claire keeping herself occupied in the kitchen by furiously polishing items of silverware that had no need of it. She had made herself a pot of tea, and then called the police in Warrington to see if they had received any news of Noah since they had last spoken. They hadn't. Alison then called round with Boris to see how Frances was faring, and whether there was any news about Noah. Upon hearing voices at the door, Frances had woken with a start, believing the caller might be connected with Noah's whereabouts, believing the worst. When she saw it was Alison at the door and not the police, Frances had almost wept with relief, and invited Alison and Boris inside. It was then she'd asked Sarah if she would telephone Dr Nelms for an update.

Sarah dragged her attention back to her conversation with Dr Nelms. It seemed he had nothing to add. He sounded increasingly beleaguered as he simply reiterated, 'While Noah's disappearance is a cause for concern, it isn't necessarily a cause for *alarm*.'

'Last night was his second night by himself. An eight-year-old child. And you have the temerity to suggest there is no cause for alarm?'

Dr Nelms had little more he could say that he hadn't already said over the last two days several times over. Boys are resilient. Boys are resourceful. Someone will almost certainly have taken him in. He's possibly lost but that won't last long. On and on in a chain of empty reassurance. Without further information the headmaster knew he had little option but to repeat everything he had already said.

It was while listening to the headmaster dispense more palliative platitudes that Sarah suddenly heard the approaching rumble of a large vehicle on the drive. As far as she was aware, Frances wasn't expecting delivery of anything requiring a lorry for its transportation. Perhaps it was a military vehicle taking a wrong turn? Dr Nelms was in full emollient flow when Claire appeared in the entrance to the passage to the kitchen, her own curiosity piqued by the noise outside.

'Mrs Collingborne . . . ?' she said in a loud whisper. Sarah turned to Claire. 'Can you hear that?'

Sarah nodded.

'Shall I go and see what it is?' Claire asked.

Sarah nodded again, and covered the telephone's mouthpiece.

'If you wouldn't mind. I'm talking to Noah's useless headmaster . . .'

Claire hurried along the hallway to the front door. What she saw when she opened it and looked out on to the drive almost caused her heart to stop, just for a moment.

Steph was coming up the drive on her green tractor. Sitting beside her was a coloured man, on whose lap sat . . . Noah, curled into the man's protective arms, asleep. Steph waved, smiling. Claire turned back into the house, and shouted at the very top of her lungs.

'Mrs Barden! Mrs Collingborne! Mrs Barden! Noah! *Noah*!'

Not waiting for a response, Claire found herself hurtling towards the tractor, her heart thumping. By the time she reached the slowing vehicle, Noah had opened his eyes. He saw Claire running towards him – and behind her, Frances and Sarah, followed by Alison with Boris, who sensed this was a moment to bark his throat hoarse. Noah slowly rubbed his eyes as Claire drew near, bringing her into focus. The clearer she became the wider his smile grew.

As the women reached the tractor, the stranger holding Noah carefully handed the weary boy down into a grateful net of outstretched arms, his hands and fingers touching and grasping theirs as anxiety melted into unalloyed relief on all sides. Frances eventually held him in her arms and peered into Noah's eyes, red from lack of sleep and exposure to the elements. She carefully brushed the matted hair from his forehead, and squeezed his little hand as if to prove to herself he was back in the flesh.

'Where on Earth have you been? I've been worried sick!' she said.

'We all have,' added Claire, wanting Noah to know how much she and Spencer had also worried over his absence.

'Are you hurt?' Frances enquired. 'Hungry? You must be hungry—'

Sarah could see the child was wilting under so much concern, and decided to step in and save him from drowning under a wave of questions.

'Why don't we let Noah tell us what happened and how he's feeling in his own time? Once we've got him back into the house.'

Noah slowly blinked at the women looking down at him then reached up and put his arms around Frances's neck, resting his hot little face against her shoulder. Frances looked up at Steph on the tractor.

'I can't thank you enough for bringing him home. How on Earth did you find him?'

'I didn't,' said Steph. 'This gentleman did.'

The women looked from Steph to the stranger sitting beside her.

'With God's help,' he said. 'I wouldn't have found him on my own. I was guided every step of the way.'

The women looked up at his smooth, dark face, and gentle eyes and smile. Alison was immediately taken by his refusal to accept credit for what amounted to rescuing the boy from wherever he found him, and bringing him home.

'Thank you, sir,' Frances said. 'You have made us all very, very happy and relieved.'

'Oh, you are more than welcome. More than welcome. It was my privilege.'

There was something familiar about the man's face, but Frances couldn't recall what. Sarah placed a soothing hand on Noah's back.

'Let's get him inside,' she said. 'He looks utterly exhausted.'

Frances nodded, feeling a lump of affection welling in her throat.

'Nothing more will be said, young man,' she whispered in his hot left ear, 'until you've had something to eat, a long bath and an even longer rest.'

* * *

Exhausted and starving, Noah was swiftly fed, bathed and put to bed, where he slept the sleep of the dead in his own bed, in his own room. Downstairs, John Smith, the fifty-two-year-old man who had brought Noah back to Great Paxford, sat before an emotional audience of four women, and explained how the previous night he had come upon Noah lying like a foetus among the roots of a large oak.

'I don't believe it was an accident, ladies. You're looking at a man who doesn't believe in much beyond what he can touch, see, smell and hear. But I believe *something* guided me to that oak tree. Call it what you will. God, or Fate. But do not use the word "coincidence". It was meant to be. Why else was I released from Walton three days early for no apparent reason.'

Frances, Sarah, Claire, Alison and Boris stared at John, agog.

'Walton?' said Sarah, trying not to sound nervous. 'As in Walton *Prison*?'

She knew the name because Adam used to occasionally visit if one of his parishioners had been unfortunate enough to find himself behind bars, and needed guidance or comfort.

John nodded.

'No cause for alarm, I give you my word. I was held for six months for teaching respect to two white lads I caught throwing stones and worse at an elderly woman from my community.'

'What's worse than stones?' asked Alison.

'Names.' He looked at her solemnly with his dark brown eyes. 'Certain names I won't repeat in respectable company. I hope you understand.'

Alison nodded, appalled yet intrigued. She admired his dignified refusal to deliver a cheap shock. She could guess the names to which he referred, and the fact that he had stood up against their use only raised her respect another degree.

'Of course,' said Frances.

'I was released on the sixteenth of September. Three days early. Administrative error. I didn't question it, just collected my belongings and walked out, hoping not to hear my name called between my cell and the front gate. It wasn't, and I ran home. Two days later my old wing was hit by a German bomb. Twenty-two souls, it took, in a heartbeat. Twenty-two hearts blown to kingdom come in their cells.' John leaned forward conspiratorially. The women leaned in to listen.

'Should have been twenty-three.'

Frances looked at him and shook her head.

'I am so glad it wasn't.'

'A week and a half later my street was flattened in a night raid. Every house and every soul in them, *up to my house.*'

'No . . .' said Claire, scarcely believing John's run of luck.

'It was then I decided to sleep outside the city for as long as the bombardment continued. A man only has so much luck. I'd used all of mine, and someone else's too.'

'Whose?' asked Claire.

'It's a turn of phrase, dear,' whispered Sarah, not wishing to interrupt John's story.

'Do continue, Mr Smith,' encouraged Alison. 'You joined the trekkers.'

John nodded.

'I walked out with them. You couldn't not, there were so many. But once we were in the countryside I split away to find my own place to sleep. Easier to find a small, perfect spot for one person than something similar for dozens. If there's one thing life's taught me, it's that it's hard enough taking care of *yourself*.'

'Where did you sleep?' asked Frances.

'A small copse away from the road. Good shelter. Little stream bubbling through, so I'd not want for water in the night. Used it for weeks and no one came within a mile. Literally a mile. Until yesterday.'

'Noah . . . !' said Claire, excited to be one step ahead.

John nodded.

'I came into the copse as per usual and found a little intruder in a school uniform, fast asleep, spark out between the roots of an oak I was using to bed down in myself. I woke him up, asked his name. He looked me dead in the eye, said, "Noah, sir." Polite child. We shared the food I'd brought out, and he told me he'd run away from school because other boys picked on him 'cause of how he spoke. 'Cause of the Scouse in his throat. He told me he tried to talk like them but they bullied him all the more, even locked him in a closet, poured salt in his food and hid his uniform. I told him, there are some things worth being bullied for – the things that make you who you are.'

'Children can be dreadful,' Frances muttered.

'He said one day he woke up and decided to go home. I asked where that was and he said, "Was Liverpool, but now it's a village called Great Paxford."'

Frances smiled, tears brimming in her eyes.

'Well, I knew the village.'

'How?' asked Alison.

'Chased from its butcher's trying to buy bacon for my aunt. Not for the first time told to go back where I came from.' He smiled. 'I'd just come from Liverpool so why would I want to go back until it was safe?'

'I think they must've meant—'

'Yes, Claire. We know what they meant,' said Sarah.

Frances now recognised John as the man who had hurried past her to escape the barracking he was being given by Mrs Talbot and her cronies.

'That was you . . .' she said, almost inaudibly.

'My family's been English nearly two hundred years. Came as sailors or slaves, one or the other. We don't know which. Anyway, I asked young Noah how he'd found my spot. He told me his father once read him a story about a man who escaped from prison and walked along a stream to stop dogs picking up his scent and dragging him back. So I asked if he'd walked along the stream after running away and he nodded. He told me his father had taught him how to navigate using the sun. So he tore out a map of England from a geography textbook, and headed south. I think he must have got lost, and decided to follow the stream. That's where I found him. He was shivering quite severely. His clothes were wet.'

'The poor boy . . .' said Sarah quietly.

'I served with the King's Regiment in 1914. I've seen strong men die of exposure. I had to raise the boy's temperature before we could do anything else. So I wrapped Noah in my coat to get warm and rest, then made a fire to dry his clothes.' He paused and looked from one face to another. The women were hanging on his every word.

'Watching him sleep I realised saving this child was the reason I'd been twice spared.'

John told them that as soon as Noah was warm and his clothes dry they set off to find Great Paxford. John had only chanced upon the village before. Now, with road signs taken down to make it more difficult for German invaders, it wasn't easy to find. Noah had managed to walk for an hour but soon flagged, so John had carried him. When John thought they might be in the right area for the village he had ventured onto a farm to ask for directions. That had been the Farrow farm, and Steph had recognised Noah immediately, and driven John and Noah straight over on the tractor.

When John finished his account, none of the women could speak for several moments. Alison was the first to break the silence.

'You saved his life, Mr Smith.'

John looked up, surprised at the accolade and touched by her kindness. 'Not sure about that. He doesn't look it, but he's a tough little fella. Must be, to've got all that way by himself.'

'Take credit where credit is due,' Alison said, meeting his gaze straight on.

'How on earth did Noah get so far without being spotted?' asked Sarah.

'He made sure he wasn't,' said Claire. 'He's ever so clever.'

'Words cannot express how grateful I am to you,' said Frances. 'Will you stay for some breakfast? You must be starving.'

John patted his knapsack.

'I still have an apple left.'

'An apple by itself is no way to start the day,' said Alison.

Frances turned to Claire.

'Take Mr Smith to the kitchen and give him the run of our larder. Whatever you want, Mr Smith. It's yours.'

'That's very kind,' he said.

'It's nothing of the sort.'

Claire stood up.

'Come along, Mr Smith. Mrs Barden doesn't take "no" for an answer.'

John smiled, got to his feet and looked at the women in front of him.

'Thank you for your kindness.'

He looked from Sarah to Frances to Alison. He glanced down at Boris, dozing by her feet.

'How old is he?'

'Coming up for fourteen.'

'He'd still give his life for you, no doubt.'

Alison smiled at John. 'Yes. But I'm hoping he won't have to.'

John laughed, taking his gaze from Alison, crouched over Boris, and slowly stroked his back. Boris didn't open his eyes, but stretched out all four limbs in response to John's touch.

'Consider yourself part of his inner circle. His Lordship would have most people's hand off for that,' Alison said, admiring John's gentleness.

John stood up, smiled at Alison, and followed Claire out of the room.

Frances also stood.

'I'd better inform the police of what's happened,' she said. 'And then the school.'

'I'm afraid I simply put the receiver down as soon as I heard Claire shouting Noah's name. At least Nelms had been right about Noah either going back or trying to find his way home,' said Sarah.

'Yes. Unfortunately, completely clueless about the cause of his departure.'

Sarah was thinking along similar lines.

'Will you ask why he was *so* completely in the dark about the bullying?'

Frances looked at her sister for several moments, considering her question.

'I don't think so,' she said. 'I think I'll just tell him that Noah won't be going back, and leave it at that.'

Chapter 44

As Nick had warned Teresa, his new commanding officer, Group Captain Michael Buey, was a crushing bore. Thirty years older than Nick, short, corpulent and bald, Group Captain Buey hadn't flown in anger for over twenty years. He had none of Nick's charm or wit, and talked to everyone at the table with his head tilted upwards so he seldom made eye contact with anyone while he spoke. Teresa had seen this trait in many poor teachers with little interest in whether their pedagogy held any interest for their class. They simply enjoyed holding forth. Buey seemed no different.

'Of course, what you have to understand is that Liverpool, Bootle and the Wallasey Pool complex are strategically very important locations to us. It's such a large port, you see. Blighty's main link with North America, and absolutely vital in the Battle of the Atlantic. In addition to providing anchorage for naval ships from many nations, its eleven miles of quays will handle over ninety per cent of all war material brought in from abroad. In a very real sense, without Liverpool, Britain could not prosecute this war. Not by a long chalk.'

Teresa wasn't sure who the group captain thought he was educating with this information since everyone around the table almost certainly knew it already. She did, and she wasn't even in the RAF. Nor was she clear about who he thought would be interested in discussing it. That said, she was quite happy for the man to chunter on if it ate up the time until everyone would leave.

For the past hour, she had barely dared look at Annie, in case she gave away something incriminating in her expression that Nick might pick up on. Reason told her that Nick could only detect something awry if he had been primed to look; and Teresa knew he hadn't been. Nevertheless, the effort of ensuring the status quo was palpable. She sat at the table with her blouse glued to her back with sweat. If she had dared to glance across at Annie she would have seen Annie looking at her almost constantly.

Sensing an opportunity to break into the group captain's monologue and force the hostess to look at her, Annie dropped her spoon loudly into her now empty soup bowl and shattered his hold on the room.

'Terrific soup, Teresa. You must let me have the recipe.'

Teresa was now forced to look at Annie.

'It isn't my own.'

The group captain's wife, Lucinda, leaned over and placed her pudgy hand on Teresa's forearm. Her sharp fingernails bit into Teresa's flesh like the talons of a predatory bird.

'A word to a newlywed – a wife should never admit that any of her ideas come from elsewhere, my dear. Take sole credit for everything as if you have created it *sui generis*. Accept every accolade that comes your way while you can – from guest or husband.' She glanced faux-conspiratorially at her own husband for a second. 'They soon dry up.'

Annie smiled mischievously at Teresa. It was obvious she was openly flirting with her.

Don't you dare . . .

'So . . . accept my compliment.'

Teresa paused for a moment, and then said, in the flattest way she could, 'Thank you, Annie. Very kind of you.'

Nick smiled amiably. The lunch was proceeding like a well-planned mission, all targets met. Boss happy. Wife and Annie getting to know one another. Food more than edible. Teresa looked beautiful, as always, and though a little quieter than he'd anticipated, she was effortlessly clever and funny at key moments. Teresa was even getting silly little marital tips from the silly little boss's silly little wife, and taking it all admirably on the chin. She simply never put a foot wrong. It couldn't be going better. With each passing minute, he loved her a fraction more. He caught Teresa's eye and subtly charged his glass in her direction by way of congratulating her for the lunch party. Teresa smiled, accepting his compliment.

'If it's true that Hitler has shelved plans to invade, we can only assume it's for the time being.'

Group Captain Buey had found a new point on the wall opposite to engage in conversation.

'Winston must understand that we need to use this hiatus to build more planes and train more pilots for when he tries again. I know Beaverbrook is—'

Teresa turned to the group captain, trying to maintain her composure.

'I'd hardly call pounding Liverpool into dust a "hiatus", Michael.'

The group captain was unused to being interrupted and turned towards Teresa with a patrician air, suggesting in body language alone that she clearly hadn't grasped the profound point he was making.

'In relative terms, I mean. What, after all, is the demolition of one city – albeit a strategically important one – against the capture of the entire kingdom?'

'If it's your home city, as Liverpool is Teresa's, that comparison might sound a little, dare I say it, Group Captain, *glib*.'

Teresa glanced at Annie. Her expression was serious. She was taking the man on. Defending her. Teresa couldn't deny the warm glow of appreciation in the pit of her stomach. Nick decided to step in before things became too personal.

'I don't think it is glib, Annie. Michael is taking a broad strategic overview of the situation. Hitler's decision to bomb instead of invade us means we have an opportunity to build newer, better aircraft before re-engaging.'

'Yes, of course I understand that,' Annie said. 'Nevertheless—'

'Think how exciting that will be for you, my dear,' Lucinda interrupted. 'All those new machines to fly around. What fun!'

Annie looked at Lucinda and fixed a smile on her face.

'What *fun* indeed. I can hardly contain my anticipation.'

Teresa felt a pang of alarm shoot through her, certain that the group captain's wife would pick up on Annie's sarcastic tone.

You think you're impressing me but you're not. I don't need you to come to my defence. I can handle myself. However stupid and offensive they may be, I won't have you mocking my husband's guests at my table.

But Annie's sarcasm sailed clean over Lucinda's head.

'What are you transporting at the moment, my dear – Spits?' Lucinda asked.

Annie smiled indulgently.

'The factories in and around Southampton were all but destroyed over the summer, so there are fewer Spitfires to relocate than there should be. But there are plenty of other aircraft to move around while production gets relocated.'

'That can't leave much time for chaps,' Lucinda said.

Teresa glanced at Annie with trepidation.

Just smile. Say nothing. And move on.

'Chaps?' Annie said, as if she was unfamiliar with the word.

'Boyfriends?' Lucinda said.

Just smile. Say nothing. And move on.

Annie considered smiling demurely and batting Lucinda away gently with consummate ease. But Lucinda and her dull-as-ditchwater husband had been boring her all afternoon, and she had had enough.

'I don't have boyfriends, Mrs Buey.'

Each word was like a small grenade going off in Teresa's head.

Please shut up. Please . . .

Nick leaned in to Teresa and whispered, 'I told you she was good value . . .'

Lucinda looked at Annie, puzzled.

'No boyfriends, my dear. Pretty girl like you?'

Annie leaned forward and placed her elbows on the table and looked Lucinda squarely in the eye.

'I stopped being a girl when I was eighteen, Mrs Buey.'

Teresa tried to interrupt.

'Annie?'

'As for being "pretty", I really don't like the description. It's a word men use to keep women in their place. I don't like it. I don't recognise it. I am a pilot, Mrs Buey. As good as any on the station—'

Nick was intensely entertained by this exchange and charged his glass to Annie's self-assessment.

'In fact, better than most,' he said.

'The only thing better than flying crates around the country for the chaps to fly against the Luftwaffe would be to fly *with* them.'

Group Captain Buey looked appalled.

'But that would mean you would have to kill.'

Annie swivelled her head to face Nick's new boss, like a gun turret taking aim at a new target.

'Do you think women aren't up to fighting to save the realm? This is our country too.'

Teresa felt herself growing increasingly angry. This was to have been a gentle social event for Nick to get to know his new group captain, not a platform for a suffragist diatribe. She sensed that Lucinda Buey was unaware of what she was getting into, and was making the mistake that Annie's rank would make her somehow subordinate. Annie's rank in the ATA was one thing.

But her social ranking put her far higher than Lucinda Buey, and it was from this position that Teresa recognised Annie was now speaking.

'Despite everything you say, my dear,' Lucinda continued, visibly irked, 'it is impossible to argue that while one or two of you may do what you do, a woman's place is, and always will be, in the home.'

Annie looked at Lucinda Buey coldly.

'Not every woman is destined to be a wife or mother.' She turned to Teresa. 'No offence.'

'I'm currently only one of those, and I'm also a teacher, so none taken.'

Teresa seized the opportunity to steer the conversation towards less choppy waters.

'But why don't we stop talking about the war for a bit—'

It was too late. Lucinda had clamped down hard on the bait, fixing Annie with a dark glower.

'There is *nothing* wrong with being a wife and mother, young lady.'

Her voice sounded manifestly aggressive.

'I didn't say there was,' Annie replied, looking Lucinda directly in the eye.

Lucinda may not have been the brightest of women, but she knew when she was being patronised.

'Kindly adjust your tone,' she said calmly.

'Do I have a tone, Mrs Buey?' Annie replied.

'I know the sort of woman *you* are, my dear. All too well.'

Teresa could stand it no longer.

'May I borrow you for a moment in the kitchen, Annie. I need a little help with the next course.'

Nick smiled at the group captain and his wife.

'Chicken. A French recipe. *Poulet!*'

* * *

Teresa followed Annie into the kitchen and closed the door behind her.

'Now listen to me. You can either be civil to that woman or you can make your excuses and leave. It's your choice.'

Annie was riding high on gin and adrenaline, and in no mood for compromise with Lucinda Buey, or anyone.

'*I know the sort of woman* you *are.*' She aped Lucinda's tone perfectly. 'Condescending bitch.'

'This lunch is for Nick to get to know his new group captain,' Teresa said, keeping her voice low and firm. 'Not for you to get stroppy and pick a fight with his bloody wife!'

'Are you going to be like this all your life, Teresa?'

'Like what?'

'A coward.'

Teresa felt a strong urge to slap Annie across her face, but resisted for Nick's sake.

'Whatever I've made of my life I've made it by my own efforts. Without support or financial backing. Whatever I've struggled with, and continue to struggle with, I do so to the best of my ability. What I don't require is some over-privileged fly-girl sitting at my table putting everything I value at risk. So, what's it to be?'

I've half a mind to just tell you to leave. But that would raise more questions than I want to answer. I'm tired of this. I don't want it. I simply want to get on with my life with Nick. Whatever that must involve, it won't include constant fear. He doesn't make me feel this way. He's calm and considerate. He would never do to me what you've just done.

Annie had never seen Teresa like this. She stared at Teresa for a few moments then stepped forward and kissed her on her mouth, enveloping Teresa in her arms.

The shock of Annie's embrace momentarily stunned Teresa. She felt the pilot's soft lips on hers, and her slender hands pull her close. For a few seconds Teresa simply wanted to lose herself in this feeling, and allowed herself to be kissed and held. Suddenly, Teresa's mind cleared, and she remembered that her husband was entertaining their guests just a few feet away. Teresa pulled herself free of Annie's arms and took a step back.

'What in God's name do you think you're doing?!'

'I'm sorry,' said Annie.

Annie had never looked more beautiful to Teresa than she did at this moment, or more dangerous – her hair up, her eyes perfectly accentuated with discreet flecks of mascara, and her cheeks flushed with passion. Teresa had never felt more scared in her life.

So much to gain. So much to lose.

'This cannot happen. Do you understand?'

'Teresa—'

'You've clearly had far too much to drink.'

'I'm not drunk, Teresa. And neither are you.'

'Go back in while I prepare the next course,' Teresa instructed. 'Now.'

'I'm sorry,' Annie repeated, sobering up from the rush of adrenaline that had momentarily overtaken her. 'I thought—'

'Clearly you did nothing of the sort,' said Teresa. She had to regain control of the afternoon before everything was destroyed.

'You feel the same as I do,' said Annie. 'I felt it.'

'If you have the slightest regard for my husband you will go back, sit down, and *behave.*'

Annie looked at Teresa for a few moments, and nodded her acquiescence.

'If that's what you want,' she said.

'It is,' said Teresa firmly.

Annie looked at Teresa for a few moments, examining her eyes for what was anger and what was fear, and then exited the kitchen.

Teresa stood in the middle of the room and became aware that her heart was racing. She took long, slow breaths to calm herself as she always instructed the children to calm themselves after a fight or a scare, and listened as Annie made a gracious apology to Lucinda Buey, the Group Captain and to Nick. Teresa breathed a sigh of relief.

Disaster averted. For now.

The kitchen door opened and Nick popped his head round.

'Everything all right?' he whispered.

'Why wouldn't it be?'

'How's the chicken?'

'Dead.'

He smiled.

'Well, that's a start.'

'And cooked to perfection.'

'Perfect. All going swimmingly so far. Isn't Annie a wonderful tonic?'

Nick smiled at Teresa, and disappeared back to their guests. Teresa stood looking at the door.

'Yes,' she said miserably. 'Wonderful.'

She slowly licked her lips and the thrill of Annie's kiss flooded back. Teresa closed her eyes to savour it all over again.

If only Nick could make me feel like this. But he can't. And never will . . .

Chapter 45

Erica stood outside the new surgery, trying to listen to the conversation on the other side of the door. At the old house this would have been an unthinkable breach of the doctor–patient confidentiality Will had always been fiercely protective of – even where Erica was concerned. Will's failing health turned everything on its head. Rules and etiquette and all the mores that make society function only have force if the normal conditions of civilised life apply. Yet if someone has no expectation of significant future life due to terminal illness, consequences over time become meaningless. It is a cruel price to pay to become liberated from the daily civilities of ordinary life, but it is a liberation nevertheless. Will felt it keenly, and he wanted Erica and the girls to feel it too. Kate and Laura seemed to have little trouble falling in with the philosophy Will brought back from hospital. Perhaps it was the spirit of wartime, or merely their youth, but both wholeheartedly agreed with Will that his remaining time should not be stretched out thinly for as long as possible by keeping him preserved in a cocoon of bedsheets and blankets, to be visited and sat with for prescribed minutes each day as if he had already become his own headstone. Erica had more difficulty with the idea that Will should be as active as his health allowed; not as inactive as possible to string out his withering health for its own sake.

Standing at his surgery door Erica wondered if it was because she and Will had spent so much time together, while he and the girls had spent so much less.

For me, sitting in silence together is sufficient. But they want him to be their father to the last. Perhaps they're right. Perhaps they're braver than I am. They want to make the most of the time he has. I want it to go on indefinitely, and it can't. I know it yet I refuse to acknowledge it. They have lives separate from Will. When he dies their lives will continue to unfold. But my life is his life. In his absence what am I?

Under ordinary circumstances she knew Will wouldn't suggest, let alone insist on, sitting in on Dr Rosen's first surgeries, but normal rules no longer applied. Erica had told Will that Myra was a terrific diagnostician, and a fierce defender of scientific principle, but lacked the finesse Will's patients had come to expect. She would not have blamed him if he'd responded with a shrug of his frail shoulders and said, 'She will . . . have to . . . learn.'

Instead, Will slowly explained to Dr Rosen that his patients were his legacy to his family – if looked after properly their patronage would maintain them in a comfortable standard of living for as long as Erica wished to run a surgery in Great Paxford. Myra too. He would show Myra how to look after his patients *properly*, ensuring a seamless transfer of care from him to her. Erica wasn't sure it was a viable proposition.

'You'll have your work cut out. She's the new breed. She's all about the pathology not the person. She told me herself, if it hadn't been for the war she would be holed up in a research lab, counting bacteria under a microscope.'

Will had smiled.

'She is . . . here now.'

When Erica had told Myra about Will's determination to sit in on her first week of surgeries and guide her through the foothills of general practice, the young doctor had been categorically opposed. It took an hour for her to understand why Will wanted to do it, and another hour to agree that it might be a worthwhile idea. If nothing else, it would show Will's patients that he had faith in his young protégée, and therefore they should too.

Despite the agreement of both parties, there was no guarantee the arrangement would work. Which is why Erica was standing outside the surgery with her ear to the door, hoping against hope that neither Will nor Myra would lose their temper in front of a patient and send them scuttling away to advise the village to take their ailments elsewhere. Ideally, she would have preferred the door to be just a little bit ajar. Hearing what was being said on the other side of a closed door was proving more difficult than she'd imagined. She knew that holding a glass to the door and her ear to the glass might be a more effective way of listening in, but it was also more shameful if caught. Her ear was hot against the door, as she managed to catch odd words and phrases. Will's speech was harder to detect because his condition forced him to speak more quietly and less frequently and in shorter bursts. Also, Will was there in a more observatory capacity.

I suppose I'm only really checking there are no outbursts of temper. I can't afford to allow her to rub Will up the wrong way.

Suddenly, a peal of laughter erupted from inside the surgery. Not only from the patient, Mr Quigley, but from Myra too. For the moment, everyone seemed to be getting on like a house on fire.

Erica pressed her ear hard against the door to try to obtain a more accurate sense of what they were discussing. Indeed, she was concentrating so hard on what was being said on the other side that she failed to notice Spencer slip four letters through the letterbox, where they dropped silently onto the mat.

If she had she would have seen that two were bills, and one an invitation for Will to attend an alumni dinner at his old college, which his condition would render impossible, even if he survived until then. And the fourth letter . . . the fourth had been delivered by mistake. It wasn't addressed to either Erica or Will or Kate or Laura.

Rather, the clear, masculine hand on the front of the envelope had simply addressed the letter to: *Patricia Simms, c/o Great Paxford, Cheshire.*

Chapter 46

CLAIRE AND SPENCER stood silently holding hands at the French windows of the dining room, and looked down towards the bottom of the extensive garden, where Frances was sitting next to a revived and refreshed Noah, on the bench Peter had installed some years ago overlooking the pond.

The sun sat low in the sky, sending dark fingers of shadow across the lawn.

Both Claire and Spencer had felt the same when Noah had been sent to boarding school. Both had felt the same when he'd run away, and the same when he had been brought home by John Smith. Emotionally, it had been an exhausting few days for everyone. Claire had overheard Frances tell Mrs Collingborne that she was going to telephone the school's headmaster to inform him that Noah was safe, and wouldn't be returning. Yet she hadn't overheard the call itself, and doubt had started to creep into her mind as to whether Dr Nelms had persuaded Frances to change her mind.

* * *

Down by the pond, Noah sat close to Frances on the bench, wrapped in a thick coat, cap and mittens.

'Are you feeling better now?' she asked.

Noah nodded.

'You must have been scared when you were out there all by yourself.'

'Sometimes,' he said matter-of-factly.

'How did you cope with that?'

'I just wanted to come back.'

Frances felt a surge of affection rise in her chest.

'Your father would have been very proud of you for getting all that way. And your mother, I'm sure,' she added.

Noah continued to look down into the water of the large pond.

'Do you want to go back to the school, Noah? I've spoken to Dr Nelms and he would be delighted to see you return, and continue under his direct care. The boys who made fun of you have been punished, so that simply would not happen again.'

Noah stayed silent.

Is he scared to say what he wants for fear of upsetting me? His face is so small under that cap.

'What do you want to do, Noah?'

Noah looked into the large pond, his eyes following a large water boatman skidding across the surface, careful not to break the delicate tension beneath its feet.

He's thinking. He's trying to think what would be the right thing to say to me. Don't rush him. Let him think it through. If he decides he wants to return to the school, so be it. It's his choice.

Noah slowly turned to Frances and looked up into her face.

'What do you want?' he asked.

Frances looked down at him, completely taken by surprise.

What do I want?

'What do I want?' she asked.

Noah nodded, waiting for her to answer.

Tell him the truth. Always tell children the truth, isn't that what they say?

'I want you to stay,' she said. 'I want you to go to school in the village so you can be with me and Claire and Spencer every day. Because I want . . .' She faltered, wanting to frame her next words carefully so that Noah was in no doubt; but not wanting to bully him with her own feelings.

'I thought about this a great deal while you were away. You need a mother, Noah. And if you would like that then I would very much like to be your mother. And for you to be, well, my son.'

Noah continued to look into her face, scrutinising every pore and wrinkle.

'That's what I want too,' he said, as matter-of-factly as before.

He leaned his head into her arm, which she lifted to wrap around his small frame, pulling him into her.

Frances sat in silence, so happy she couldn't speak.

* * *

Claire and Spencer stood at the French windows in silence. Tears streamed down their faces, over their cheeks and into their broad smiles. The telephone started to ring in the hall. Claire kissed Spencer and slipped out of the room to answer it.

Spencer continued to watch the distant figures of Frances and Noah on the bench. Not moving. Content in each other's company. It made him yearn for a child of his own. Preferably a son, though he wouldn't object to a daughter.

'It's Noah's grandfather . . .' The alarm in Claire's voice made Spencer turn sharply.

'He wants to speak to Mrs Barden *immediately*. He said it just like that. *Immediately*.'

'What about?'

'He asked if I was the maid, and when I said I was he said to have Noah packed and ready to leave by nightfall.'

'He said what?' Spencer could hardly believe his ears.

'He's coming to take Noah back, Spencer!'

Spencer opened the French window and held it open.

'Go and get Mrs Barden.'

Claire ran through the door and over the patio, across the lawn and down to the pond. Spencer watched his young wife take Frances away from Noah and repeat what she had just told him.

Frances turned and looked towards the house, then started to stride up the lawn looking every inch a woman about to go on the warpath.

Frances swept past Spencer, glancing at the young man. 'Packed and ready to leave by nightfall? We shall see about that . . .'

Chapter 47

PAT SAT ALONE in the telephone exchange towards the end of a long shift by herself, reading over her latest Mass Observation report, in which she described two recent developments with Bob.

The first was that his literary agent in London had wired to say that his new novel about the evacuation at Dunkirk was selling very well indeed following its serialisation in *The Times*, and he would soon be receiving a handsome royalty cheque. Money always made Bob easier to be around. It took the edge off his self-loathing and it gave him the opportunity to play the big 'I am' to a wider audience than simply Pat and Joyce Cameron. Though recently it had seemed Joyce should be audience enough; her having become his number one fan now that Bob was getting some more recognition.

On the back of the news, Bob had ventured into the pub on several occasions to bask in the veneration in which some in the village held a man who made a living out of doing nothing all day but type and stare out of a window.

If they actually read his work, and saw for themselves how poor his writing is, they wouldn't fall over themselves to buy him drinks.

If they actually read how weak he is at characterisation, resort-
ing time and time again to cliché and stereotype. The plucky Brits!
The cowardly French! The sadistic Nazis! The intrepid small boats
'plucking' our boys from the jaws of death! All hail the great literary
lion of Great Paxford!

Pat thought it underhand of Bob not to tell Joyce about the
forthcoming royalty cheque, in case she decided to increase the
rent they currently paid to lodge in her house.

It's not as if we're paying the going rate as things stand.
She shouldn't be subsidising us simply because she's cock-
a-hoop about having a published author under her roof.
I don't like this feeling that we're cheating an old woman. But
what can I do? Bob holds the purse strings.

The second recent development had occurred in bed a
few nights ago. Pat had been lying still, trying to get to sleep
as quickly as possible, when Bob came in from the bathroom,
closed the door, and told her that he had read one of Marek's
letters before destroying it.

'I thought I had his number, and I did,' he'd said.
'I wasn't joking when I told you he was *probably* writing to ask
for money. That's exactly why he wrote.'

'I don't believe you,' Pat had said, rolling onto her side, turning her back on him.

'Think about it . . .'

She felt the mattress distort under his weight as he got into
bed.

'Look at *you* and look at *him*. I mean . . . *physically*. He's a
strapping bloke. Approaching middle age, yes, but handsome.
Seasoned. And a soldier. Women fall over themselves for that.
I've seen it. A man like that could have almost any unmarried

woman he wants, so why would he settle for a short, plain, married woman like you?'

Pat lay in the semi-darkness trying to ignore Bob's words. But she couldn't. Bob's unique gift was to know exactly how to provoke Pat. After many years at it, he was the world's expert.

'Perhaps he didn't see it as "settling",' Pat said, mounting a defence. 'Perhaps – and I know you'll find this difficult to believe – but perhaps, in his eyes, I was precisely the sort of woman he's attracted to.'

Bob's snort of derision served as his answer.

'I read the letter. You didn't. He hooked you, and then he came for what you had. Personally, while stationed at the castle. And then, now he's out of the area, *financially*. Clever.'

'How is that clever when I have no money to give him?'

'Compared to what he has, he must think you have something to come after. Clever.'

'You keep saying "clever" as if it means something. What's so clever?'

'That he targets someone like you. Someone flattered by his attentions. Pathetically flattered, and pathetically grateful. You assume I'm saying this to rub your nose in a mess of your own making but that's not the case. You're my wife, Patricia, yes? Always have been, always will be. It pains me to see you in thrall to a man like that.'

* * *

Pat sat in the exchange and turned Bob's words over and over in her mind. She didn't believe he had read any of Marek's letters. She was convinced he'd made it up after he'd seen how hurt she looked when he'd suggested Marek was probably only writing to ask for cash.

Typical Bob consolation. First stick in the knife. Second, twist it. Third . . . enjoy the result.

Pat didn't believe it. And yet . . . what if it was true? Could it be possible that Bob *had* read one of Marek's letters? It hardly seemed likely.

Bob is feeling good in himself at the moment. Like this he sometimes reverts to how he used to be with me, if only for a brief period.

There was a sudden tap at the window that caused Pat to look up and almost jump back in her chair. Erica Campbell was looking at her, holding something up in her hand.

An envelope.

Pat blinked, scarcely believing what she was looking at.

She took the headphones from her head and all but threw them onto the desk, crossed to the door of the exchange and flung it open as Erica came round.

'I was on my way to Brindsley's and on the off-chance thought you might be on duty. I thought I'd look in through the window as I didn't want to disturb you, if you were busy. I hope I didn't frighten you?'

Pat shook her head.

'I was just surprised.' She looked at the envelope in Erica's hand. 'Is that what I hope it is?'

Pat was trying to keep her excitement in check but it was almost impossible. Erica offered the envelope to her former neighbour. Pat looked at it for a moment with a sense of wonderment.

'It came mid-morning.'

How can a few pieces of paper have such an effect on me? Far, far more than anything Bob has written.

'Take it, Pat. I have to get back.'

Pat struggled to resist her urge to snatch the letter and tear it open. She calmly reached out and took it.

'Thank you so much, Erica. You have no idea what this means to me.'

Erica looked at Pat doubtfully, and said, 'I only hope it gives you what you want.'

Pat closed and locked the door, returned to her desk and sat down. She had waited months to receive word from Marek. Now it was here.

Finally! Finally!

The letter didn't feel particularly thick in her hand.

Perhaps he didn't have much time to write. The important thing is he wrote. He kept writing.

Pat held the envelope up to the light to see if it revealed some hint of what was inside, but it didn't. She took a deep breath to control her nerves.

What if it isn't what I want it to be? What if . . . he doesn't write what I want him to write?

'Just open it and find out,' she whispered.

What if Bob was telling the truth and he's asking for money? I don't believe that, but then . . . I never believed a man like Marek could love a woman like me.

'Just open it.' Her voice was more insistent.

What if everything I've pinned my hopes on is a sham? What if I'm the complete fool Bob takes me for? What if Marek saw that too? Oh God . . .

Pat felt suddenly hot as the inside of the exchange started to swim before her eyes. Hearing from Marek had meant everything to her in the weeks since his departure. In her mind, it had meant confirmation of their love, and the hope of eventual release from servitude to Bob.

But what if it amounts to nothing? What if marriage to Bob is all a woman like me can either expect . . . or deserve?

Pat looked at the letter on the wooden desk. Her name in Marek's hand. But what else inside? It could be everything, or nothing at all.

Absence doesn't only make the heart grow fonder. It can also make the mind grow less and less certain about things we think are true. I think . . . I thought I knew him. What if I was completely mistaken?

As Pat looked at the letter she became aware that her hands were sweating.

'Just open it,' she whispered. 'Just *open* it . . .'

She slowly reached forward and picked the letter off the desk. She then carefully slipped her thumbnail under the left-hand corner of the envelope's sealing flap, and slowly prised it open. . . .

My dearest Patricia . . .

PART FOUR

A Soldier Returns . . .

PART FOUR

Chapter 48

*I*F LAKIN THINKS HE *can threaten me, he's got another think coming. If he wants a fight he's going to have one – on the telephone or face to face. The last thing Noah needs is more upheaval. I made a mistake by not trusting my own instincts and digging in my heels about not sending him away to boarding school. I shall not do so again.*

When preparing for confrontation it was Frances's habit to rehearse her core arguments to herself as she approached the arena of conflict, whether that was the village hall and a WI meeting, or the hallway of her own house and a telephone conversation with Noah's grandfather, Morris Lakin. This frequently saw her striding through the village or – as on this occasion – across her own lawn, muttering animatedly to herself, like a boxer geeing himself up between the dressing room and the ring. Though she would often try to second-guess what the opposition might throw at her, Frances found it wasn't essential, so convinced was she by her own conviction and prowess.

The child doesn't need any more pushing from pillar to post. What he needs above all else is stability – of location, and of the people around him. Enough is enough.

By the time Frances picked up the receiver she had pumped herself into an uncompromising mood. She knew the police had informed the Lakins of Noah's return earlier in the day, and saw little point in beating around the bush.

'Mr Lakin,' she said, 'I was planning to telephone you this evening to discuss matters. Once I'd seen to Noah's needs.'

'Your maid told me Noah is already up and about, Mrs Barden.'

'Such a relief to have him home safe and sound.' She placed some emphasis on the word 'home' to make it clear to Lakin where she believed Noah's home now was. 'He slept like a log for nearly seven hours and, rather remarkably, seems none the worse for wear. Though I dare say he won't completely recover from his odyssey for a few days yet.'

'I'm mightily relieved, Mrs Barden. Any other outcome doesn't bear thinking about. I've had to keep the entire business from Mrs Lakin for fear of triggering a relapse of her emphysema. Not an easy matter, I can tell you.'

'It was a tremendous shock to everyone's system, Mr Lakin. When I think of what— No. The time for terrible speculation is – as you imply – thankfully over.'

'Is it, Mrs Barden? I'm not so sure.'

What are you suggesting, old man? I didn't believe Claire had it right, but it does sound very much as if you are threatening something.

'Forgive me if I'm mistaken, Mr Lakin, but I'm picking up a tone of misgiving in your voice. Is that the case?'

'I'm afraid it is, Mrs Barden. I'm disappointed. Tremendously disappointed. I did wonder if something like this might occur. But not so soon as this.'

Frances had met with Helen's father several times to discuss his grandson's future, and on each occasion had found him reserved but respectful. This version of the man seemed openly confrontational.

But about what? It wasn't my desire to send Noah away to school. I was merely acting on Peter and Helen's wishes. If you have any kind of problem with what's happened over the past few days it is surely with them and not with me.

'Would you mind explaining yourself, Mr Lakin, when you say you "did wonder if something like this might occur"?'

If I'm not mistaken, Lakin has spoken as a man who has already arrived at his conclusion. Stay calm. Don't antagonise. He's no doubt still upset by what's just happened. This is undissipated anxiety. Let him talk it out if he must.

'You were asked to take Noah in to keep him out of Liverpool during the bombing campaign, and to see that Peter and Helen's wishes for his education were met.'

'Have I not done exactly what you've described?'

'You did. Yes, you *did*.'

'Am I wrong to pick up that you are placing a definite emphasis on the past tense, Mr Lakin?'

'You are not, Mrs Barden. I have just spoken with Dr Nelms at the school—'

'You have my sympathies. I find the man impenetrably dense.'

'He said you've decided Noah won't be returning.'

'It's what Noah wants. And if I may be frank, it's what I have come to realise I want too.'

'I *see* . . .'

Lakin's voice trailed off ominously.

'You see *what* exactly?'

Frances took a deep breath and prepared herself for his attack.

'Did it not occur to you, Mrs Barden, that your decision to remove Noah from the boarding school is not yours alone to make? Where will he be educated if not there?'

'Great Paxford has a fine village school, Mr Lakin. Noah will fit in splendidly.'

'That's as may be. But it is neither what your husband wanted for the boy, nor *my daughter*.'

In his delivery of those two words Frances suddenly understood the reason for his hostility.

'I can assure you, Mr Lakin, I am only thinking of what's in *Noah's* best interests.'

'Noah *has* a mother, Mrs Barden,' he said pointedly. 'You are not her.'

Tears immediately pricked Frances's eyes.

Have I ever said I was? Have I ever pretended to be her?

While she would never contest Lakin's statement, she could nevertheless qualify it.

'Noah *had* a mother, Mr Lakin. And a father. Their tragic loss will remain with each of us until our dying day. Were Helen and Peter alive you and I would not be having this conversation. Were they alive, I dare say you and I would never have cause to speak, or know of one another – as we did not when they were alive. I didn't know Noah then. By which I mean I wasn't merely *unacquainted* with him – I mean he was kept *completely* secret from me. As you know.'

'Nevertheless—'

'I should like to finish my point if I may?'

Frances was counting on Lakin being unused to becoming entangled in debate with women as forthright as she.

'Very well,' he said, with an audible sigh.

'When Helen died, her status as Noah's mother did not die with her. But her *role* as his mother did. In her absence, someone has to take up that role—'

'That wasn't the basis upon which we asked you to take him in,' said Lakin, his voice hardening. 'It was simply to provide refuge from the assault on—'

'Liverpool, yes. I agree, providing a maternal influence was not the basis upon which I took Noah into my home. That said, at the time I agreed to have him I could not foresee the effect he might have on me, and vice versa. Neither do I believe you foresaw it, or else you would have warned me against it. I took him in and in spending time with the child I could feel myself naturally bonding with him. And he with me. Here was a vulnerable child under my care. Vulnerable not only to German bombs, but to finding himself in the world without a mother or father. He needs more than a safe roof over his head, and I realised I could give him more. What was I to do, Mr Lakin? Deny my growing feelings of affection? Curtail his?'

There was silence at the other end of the line.

'We have lost our daughter, Mrs Barden.'

'I can assure you I am not trying to replace Helen. As painful as her involvement in my life has been, I would never seek to supplant her in Noah's heart. I talk about her and Peter all the time. But they are no longer here to act on his life. I – *we* – are.'

'Helen's wishes must be respected alongside Peter's. They decided Noah should go to boarding school.'

'I understand that. But ask yourself this, Mr Lakin: if Helen and Peter hadn't perished, and had sent Noah off to school, as I did, according to their wishes, and Noah had run away as he did, do you believe Helen would have sent him back?'

There was another silence at the other end of the line.

'Mr Lakin?'

Lakin eventually spoke, his voice calm but cold.

'We need to meet, Mrs Barden. Of course, Noah has opportunities living with you that we can't begin to match. But that doesn't mean we don't think of him day and night. I won't have you riding roughshod over ours, or Helen's, wishes.'

Frances suddenly felt intensely frustrated. During Noah's flight from boarding school she had become increasingly confident in her conviction that sending him away had been a terrible mistake. With his safe return she had become even more convinced that was the case, and that everything he could need as a growing boy could be found here in Great Paxford.

'I can assure you I have no interest in trying to ride roughshod over your feelings, Mr Lakin. Nor ignore Helen's – and Peter's – wishes for the child. I believe if you could see me in person you would believe I am sincere in this regard. However,

Noah's feelings must also come into consideration now he has experienced life at boarding school. In a very clear way, he has voted with his feet, has he not?'

'He is a boy of eight, Mrs Barden. Who can say what was going through his mind when he chose to bolt?'

'Noah can. And has. You underestimate the boy's intelligence if you believe he has been incapable of explaining his actions, Mr Lakin.'

Frances could feel herself growing impatient and tried to calm herself before saying something she might regret.

'Noah told me he ran away because he was mocked by other boys for the way he spoke, that they played terrible tricks on him. And, yes, he told me he missed being here. And would tell you the same if you were to ask him.'

'Very convenient to your purpose to suggest that one of the reasons Noah ran away was to return to *you*.'

Frances could feel her face growing hot with anger.

'I deliberately didn't specify "me", Mr Lakin. I said "here". By which I meant Great Paxford. The house. The grounds. My maid and her husband, who happily fuss over and play with Noah each and every day.'

There was another silence on the other end of the line that Frances found difficult to interpret. She felt a strong urge to jump in and keep Lakin on the back foot, but didn't want to antagonise him further.

'We need to discuss the matter,' Lakin finally said.

Frances closed her eyes at the prospect of a protracted negotiation over a matter she believed required no negotiation whatsoever. However, she had no wish to provoke further intransigence.

'Very well, Mr Lakin. May I invite you to come to Great Paxford at my expense, and see what we can offer Noah? We can show you the village, and the school I'm proposing he attend. I would be delighted to host you at the house. But if you'd prefer, I would be more than happy to book you into the Black Horse overnight. Again, at my expense.'

It took a moment for Lakin to consider her offer, but he eventually spoke.

'I think that may be in the best interests of the boy,' he said. 'Thank you for your kind offer but I will travel and lodge at my own expense.'

Frances was sure she detected a hint of suspicion in his voice about her proposal to foot the bill, as if it might compromise Lakin's judgement.

He's not altogether wrong. There was an element of that in my invitation. Good for him for resisting. I would have done the same.

After the arrangements were made, Frances put down the receiver and heard Noah laughing in the garden. She walked into the sitting room and looked out through the French window. Spencer had finished work for the day and Noah was helping him set up stumps for a game of cricket. Once the stumps were in place, Spencer tossed Noah the small, red cricket ball, and took up the batsman's position in front of the wicket.

He needs to be nurtured. And this is where he wants to be, so why not let him be here? Life with us is hardly a consolation prize. He is a special boy. It's visible in the effect he has on everyone he meets. Everyone seems to respond to him the same way. Except in that damned school, where it seems everyone must behave the same, like little English gentlemen. Future governors of the Empire. I wonder how much will be left to govern on the other side of this war?

Noah strode down the imagined 'crease' to the start of his run-up, then turned and looked at Spencer with an expression of intense seriousness. Spencer half-crouched, anticipating the ball, tapping the bottom edge of the bat gently on the turf.

Claire appeared at Frances's side, and watched Noah stare intently at Spencer, before starting his run-up.

'According to Spencer,' said Claire, 'he's surprisingly good for his age.'

Frances smiled, and watched Noah approach the bowler's wicket in the same manner she had seen full-sized cricketers on the village green approach the bowler's wicket. When Noah reached it he should have taken one, two, three little hops and hurled the ball overarm towards Spencer with all his strength. He didn't. Instead, Noah continued to run towards Spencer without releasing the ball, and when he reached him, he threw his arms around Spencer's waist, and stayed like that, hugging the young man.

Spencer looked down at the child and then up at the house, where Frances and Claire were watching.

'This is where he wants to be, Mrs Barden,' she said, wiping her eye. 'With us.'

Claire glanced at Frances, hoping she hadn't spoken out of turn.

'I know,' said Frances quietly.

Spencer laid down the bat, knelt in front of Noah, wrapped his arms around the child, and hugged him back.

'Can his grandparents take him away?' asked Claire, her voice faltering with trepidation.

'They can,' said Frances softly, recognising the realities of the task ahead. She then turned to Claire and looked her directly in the eye.

'But I shall do everything in my power to ensure they won't.'

Chapter 49

WALKING ALONG THE High Street at the end of her shift, Pat pushed her left hand deep into her coat pocket, wrapping her fingers tightly around Marek's letter as she would wrap them around a lifebelt in a rough sea. The wind and rain buffeted her, but she barely noticed.

He still loves me . . .

Pat moved her fingertips over the flat surface of the envelope, and slipped them inside, finding the paper on which Marek's letter was written, tracing the soft indentations of his handwriting on the densely packed page.

Dearest Patricia,

    Once again I am finding myself writing to you, in hope that this will be the letter that will cause you to reply to me. I remain in England but cannot speak where. I can only give the enclosed address to send your reply to, and your letter will be sent on to me. If you choose to reply. Soon I am to go to the north for more training. I think of you every day. I cannot help myself.

Always the same question returns. Why did you not come to meet me on my last day? Did you not find my message? Could you not endure to say goodbye? Some days I wish I was able to stop thinking of you so I can forget and move on. But I cannot.

Pat was careful not to smile, or skip along the road as she felt compelled to do. She contained the urge to run through the village calling out, 'He still loves me!' at everyone she passed.

Yet she knew she dare not make a single misstep or look in any way out of the ordinary. Any incongruity, no matter how slight, would be noticed by someone somewhere in Great Paxford, and anything could get reported back to Bob by one of his cronies from the pub, or their wives.

'Saw your missus the other day, Mr Simms. Well chuffed about something, she looked.'

That's all it would take to arouse Bob's suspicions, and the nagging and incessant probing would begin. He wouldn't rest until he knew the cause of Pat's good humour, so he could winkle it out of her and crush it. She would hold out, of course, but until he knew what was making her happy he would make her life unbearable.

Wherever Pat now looked, everything seemed different. It wasn't that the rain and scudding clouds brought more contrast to the colours and shadows of the world around her. It was her own sensibility, altered in the wake of Marek's letter, that changed how she perceived the world.

. . . If you are hoping perhaps that I shall stop writing to you I will repeat what I have written in previous letters.

I will not stop until you write back and demand I stop. These letters shall continue, Patricia, until I hear that you do not want them. You are all I have in the world to love. If I fight to stay alive it is to see you again . . .

It was as if a screen of mist had lifted, and the world had been revealed as a place that once again allowed her to feel happy. In the days since Marek's departure, Pat had occasionally walked to the edge of the village and stood by the small hole in the earth where the GREAT PAXFORD sign used to stand, before it was removed to disorient invading German forces. Pat would look along the road leading out of the village, and feel its pull, tempting her to start walking and see where it took her.

Away from Bob. As far as possible.

As much as she yearned to start walking and submit to the temptation of life without Bob, her feet would remain frozen to the spot, as if her legs became paralysed at the very thought of escape.

He would come after me. Find me. Punish me. Make my life three times more difficult.

Like a prisoner convinced there was no viable life beyond the prison wall, Pat would sigh and return to Joyce Cameron's house . . .

My cell.

. . . and Bob.

My jailer.

But that was yesterday, and the day before. Today, happiness had flooded back into Pat's life via Marek's letter like a long-forgotten tide, and with it, hope. She wanted to take Marek's letter out of her pocket and reread it one more time before she joined Bob and Joyce for supper, but she was afraid the rain would dissolve Marek's expressions of love and longing into incoherent inky puddles on the page. No matter. Pat was a quick reader. In the six times she had read the letter since opening it at the exchange, Marek's most impassioned sentiments had etched themselves in her mind.

'*I think of the life we might have together when war ends.*'

'*I need to be with you, Patricia. I need to know if you feel the same.*'

Odd how Marek uses my full name to express love, but Bob only ever uses it as an admonishment.

'*Do you think of me at all?*'

'*I must know.*'

'*I must hear in your own words that you no longer have the feelings for me that I have for you.*'

'*I must . . . I must . . .*'

His need to know her state of mind was overpowering and intoxicating. In many ways, Marek's questions were reflections of her own unanswered questions to him that she would utter in Bob's absence under her breath – her way of 'conversing' with Marek, asking him questions and then responding with answers he might conceivably offer. Sometimes, she forgot Joyce was in the room with her, and the older woman would overhear this almost inaudible catechism and ask, 'What was that, my dear?'

There was now no longer any need to imagine Marek's responses to her questions. His letter had answered everything, and any new ones she could put to him in writing.

As Pat stepped onto the front path of Joyce's house, she was met by the rattle of Bob's typing emanating from the sitting-room window. She could see Bob's thin, dark silhouette swaying from side to side at his typewriter, as he did when the work was flowing. The sound of the keys slamming repetitiously onto the typewriter carriage usually made her instantly anxious. Today she gave it little heed. Or Bob, for that matter. Marek's letter had reduced her fear of her husband, just as Marek's presence in the village had once reduced it. Knowing he was back in her life made her life – and Bob – more bearable, and she breathed more easily.

Squinting to focus in the low evening light, Pat could just about make out the shape of Joyce in the armchair, watching Bob's hands on the keys, as if he were a piano virtuoso giving her a private performance.

Pat entered the house and closed the front door behind her. The typing stopped. As she hung up her coat and hat the door to the front room opened behind her.

'You're late,' said Bob accusingly, closing the door behind him. 'I'm hungry.'

Pat turned to look at her husband, and couldn't help superimposing an image of Marek from her mind's eye over Bob's frame. She smiled amiably.

'So sorry, Bob. The shift after mine got irrevocably waylaid.'

'This keeps happening. Don't you ever say anything?'

'It wasn't wanton tardiness, Bob, I can assure you. She's usually extremely punctual.'

'You're too trusting. That's why people take advantage of you.'

'Why would she lie?'

'To spend less time at the exchange and more time doing whatever she'd rather be doing.'

'That isn't how operators behave. We are an extremely diligent group.'

Bob shook his head in mock pity.

'Honest to God, they must see you coming.'

Between the exchange and Joyce's house, Pat had trans-ferred Marek's letter from her coat to her dress pocket. She held it now in her hand, as Bob looked at her, out of view.

If you only knew what I have in my hand . . .

'I need something to eat,' Bob said. 'I'm in the flow. I need to keep my energy up.'

Pat was the only person who understood the mechanics that underpinned Bob's work. The constant need of fuel in varying forms: food, coffee, chocolate, tea, silence, solitude, appreciation.

'Didn't Joyce make you something?'

'She fell asleep in the armchair. Besides, she cooks like a woman who's hired cooks all her life.'

Pat smiled slightly.

'Careful, Bob. You almost complimented me.'

Bob turned up the corner of his mouth in a half-smile.

'Don't flatter yourself. Her food's dreadful. Yours is passable by comparison.'

Pat shook her head wearily. On another day she might have said something back to defend herself. But today she found his performance contrived and ineffectual.

'I'm a very good cook, Bob,' she said patiently, not rising to his bait. 'We both know it, so why pretend otherwise?'

He looked at her in silence for a moment, sensing a difference in his wife. He couldn't put his finger on it but there was some-thing. A form of defiance in the way she was now talking to him, more like a slightly exasperated mother, and less like a dutiful wife.

'What's got into you?'

'What do you mean?'

A flash of fear shot through her.

What has he seen? Rein it back, Pat. Don't be an idiot.

'Giving me cheek.'

Pat felt a sudden charge of dread ripple outwards from her stomach.

You're barely a minute indoors and you're already giving the game away. Just be the Pat he expects. Nothing more.

'I'm sorry, Bob,' she said meekly. 'I didn't mean to answer back.'

'"*I'm sorry, Bob, I didn't mean to answer back,*"' he said, mimicking her voice. 'Christ, you're pathetic sometimes.'

Yes, yes. The bully's oldest, most villainous trick of blaming the victim for bringing it on herself.

'Sorry, Bob,' she said quietly.

'Like a blob of jelly wobbling this way and that, however the wind blows. Where's your bloody backbone?'

You tore it out when I first tried standing up to you, remember? You wouldn't have that, so you snapped it.

'No wonder the Czech bastard took you for a ride. Easy pickings.'

Bob had taken to calling Captain Marek Novotny 'the Czech bastard' with a triumphant sneer. Yesterday, the possibility that there might have been a fragment of truth in Bob's snide remark about Marek might have weighed on Pat's mind. But not today. Not a syllable of Marek's letter suggested anything but the devotion he had shown Pat during their time together.

'I'll make your supper,' Pat said flatly, refusing again to rise to Bob's bait.

'You do that.'

Pat turned and walked away from Bob, along the narrow hallway towards the kitchen, slipping her hand back into her pocket. She knew Bob would be watching her, but she didn't care. The letter she'd been waiting weeks to receive had finally come, and now was nestled in her pocket between her fingers.

I'll write this up in a new Mass Obs report in the morning. They want to know what we're going through. I'll tell them. The bad and the good.

The farther from Bob she walked the more she risked smiling to herself. She knew he was still watching her from the end of the hall but her back was to him, so he couldn't see her expression. After a moment, she heard the door to the front room close as Bob returned to work. Pat stopped and looked back up the hall.

'Marek still loves me,' she said under her breath. 'Say what you like, Bob. But "the Czech bastard" still loves me . . .'

She then turned into the kitchen to prepare Bob's supper.

Chapter 50

Over the course of their career, a teacher will teach many hundreds of children. A succession of faces that will inevitably turn into an indistinct blur over time. Yet each child will be taught by just a few teachers, and each will leave a deep and lasting impression on their pupils for the length of their lives.

When Teresa Lucas (née Fenchurch) walked into a classroom her pupils immediately stopped talking, sat upright, and waited with breath bated. For boys and girls alike, Mrs Lucas was their teacher, their leader, taking them to the foothills of Knowledge, and beyond. They looked up to and idolised her. Teresa rewarded their loyalty with kindness, fairness and patience. She was never cross without reason, and was never, ever unjust. Her overriding philosophy in the classroom was to lead by example.

Though she never played up to it or took it for granted, Teresa implicitly understood her importance in the lives of her pupils. Which is why she set aside time every year to write each child in her class a personal message in a Christmas card, congratulating her or him for their achievements, and gently encouraging him or her to achieve more the following year. For those who were not academically able, Teresa would find a personal attribute or quality to highlight and praise – a talent for friendship, perhaps, generosity towards other children, good humour, or some kind of sporting prowess. No child went unheralded.

With over thirty cards to write, Teresa usually began to put pen to paper in mid-November to ensure she would be finished in time for the end of the Christmas term. Before she could write each card she had to *make* each card, and it was this she was starting to do one evening at the kitchen table, when she heard a polite knock on the front door.

Teresa wasn't expecting anyone to call. She glanced at her watch. It was five past eight, surely beyond the time for a spontaneous social call. Since Annie had kissed her unexpectedly in the kitchen, Teresa had tried – with variable degrees of success – to put the ATA pilot out of her mind. It was in neither of their interests to continue to play the game they had been playing since their first meeting. Flirting was enjoyable when harmless. When it threatened to jeopardise Teresa's marriage it had to stop. She had said as much to Annie as she walked her to Nick's car when the lunch party came to an end.

'I didn't mean to embarrass you in any way,' Annie had said. 'I thought you felt similarly.'

'Marriage to Nick isn't a game, Annie. I thought I made that clear some time ago.'

'But one's true feelings are one's true feelings. They must be expressed.'

'Or superseded by *other* feelings.'

'One's *true nature*, Teresa—'

'Yours is to embrace risk. Mine is to avoid it. You have a fearlessness that I admire greatly, Annie. It's apparent in your flying, and in the way you live your life. I don't have that. I wish I did, but I don't.'

'And would you say your caution has worked out for you? Driving you into married life.'

'Married life offers more than just sexual fulfilment, Annie. It also offers companionship, the possibility of a family—'

'But couldn't you have both? Wouldn't it be better with both?'

'Attraction is all very well—'

'You say it as if that's all there is between us, but it isn't. We have a shared history of growing up differently to other girls. We share the same sense of humour. Intelligence. The same independent spirit. The same dream to one day find someone— '

'I don't have that dream anymore, Annie. I've found someone.'

'Nick?'

'Of *course* Nick.'

'That's not what I meant, and you know it.'

'Perhaps not—'

'You and I have more in common than you will ever have with Nick – even if you live to be one hundred together. Think about that, *Mrs* Lucas—'

Their conversation had been brought to a close at that point, as Nick ran out of the house to take Annie back to Tabley Wood. It was the last time they had spoken.

Teresa couldn't think why Annie would be knocking at this hour, but she couldn't preclude the possibility. Nor could she ignore the upswell of excitement she felt at the prospect.

The knock on the front door was repeated. Teresa stood up, put the scissors on the small stack of card waiting to be cut out, and walked out of the kitchen. As she crossed the hall she hesitated as a word flashed into her mind: refugees.

The talk about the refugees had left most inhabitants of Great Paxford on edge. Not because the refugees had done anything except venture into their community; but the fact they were strangers who came at night seemed enough to generate a degree of anxiety in most people. As much as she considered herself above such a knee-jerk response to outsiders in their midst, Teresa was unable to deny that their presence made her slightly more, not less, anxious; if only for the conflict they threatened to spawn. Her irrationality angered her, especially as a fellow Liverpudlian, and member of the WI Trekker Accommodation Subcommittee, but there was little she could do about it. There was also a rational side to the general fear of strangers at this time. Though the immediate threat of a German invasion had dissipated over the summer, the fear of spies being parachuted onto British soil in the dead of night was stoked by the government and the newspapers in a bid to keep the population vigilant. Where better for German spies to hide and gather information than among crowds of refugees roaming the English countryside?

'Who is it?' Teresa called out.

'Teresa, it's Sarah Collingborne and Joyce Cameron,' came the reply.

Teresa sighed with relief and opened the front door. Sarah and Joyce's faces were illuminated by the light from inside, and they each looked at Teresa warmly, like two saleswomen who wanted to convey sincerity and a certain amount of seriousness of purpose.

'Well, this is a nice surprise,' Teresa said, smiling. She meant it. Married life had removed the constant companionship Teresa had grown used to living with Alison, and with Nick staying late at Tabley Wood most nights, she spent many evenings by herself.

Joyce exchanged a glance with Sarah and looked back at Teresa.

'May we come in, dear?'

Teresa was suddenly overwhelmed with dread that something must have happened to Nick. Such was its instant grip, she was unable to reason that if that was the case then it wouldn't be Sarah and Joyce dispatched to break the news, but a senior officer from Tabley Wood.

'Is something the matter, ladies?' she asked.

Sarah and Joyce looked at Teresa for a moment, neither wanting to begin the conversation that would end in what they suspected would be a crushing disappointment for their very good friend.

In that pause Teresa's intuition supplied one answer, followed swiftly by another, and finally the reason for the visit. For though Teresa had seen Joyce and Sarah many times at the WI and elsewhere, in the company of many other women, she remembered that there had been only one other occasion when she had seen them side by side like this: when she had come to Great Paxford to be interviewed for the position at the village school. As school governors, Sarah and Joyce had interviewed Teresa for the job, alongside the male teacher she was replacing, who was leaving to join the army. Teresa suddenly felt sick, as if the ground had shifted beneath her feet, leaving her disoriented and nauseous.

I'm about to lose my job and there's not a damn thing I can do about it.

'May we come in?' repeated Joyce.

Teresa took a deep breath, smiled and opened the door wide for Sarah and Joyce.

Neither was able to look Teresa in the eye as they passed, thereby confirming her deduction about the visit.

'Of course. Come in. Go through to the front room.'

She closed the front door, followed them in and offered them tea, which each declined, and something to eat, which they also declined.

As she sat before them, Teresa was again reminded of the original interview for the position at the school. Only now it was Sarah and Joyce who were nervous, and Teresa who seemed calm and composed.

'I've lost my job, haven't I?' she said, with a matter-of-factness that took both Sarah and Joyce by surprise. They each looked at her and saw Teresa smile bravely.

It's not their fault. There's no need to make this worse for them than I can see it already is. The education authority will have forced this upon them.

'The local education authority has now instructed all schools to enforce the marriage bar.'

'They have a teacher to take my place?'

Joyce nodded.

'A man, or a single woman?'

'A single woman,' said Sarah solemnly, the sadness all too apparent in her voice.

'Had you remained single yourself—' Joyce began.

'Yes,' said Teresa. 'But I was told our LEA had relaxed the bar – or at the very least, was not zealous in enforcing it.'

404

'I'm afraid a more conservative element has become influential. They strongly believe married women should give way to those who need the income.'

Teresa looked at Sarah and Joyce and sighed.

'I didn't marry Nick so he could support me. But it's more than just money. While I am appreciative of my salary, I teach because that is my vocation, and I am very, very good at it.'

Joyce and Sarah looked miserable, offering no resistance to Teresa's argument.

'Teachers are driven by their sense of vocation,' Teresa continued. 'At least, every good one I've met is. They love children. They love the skill and talent involved in teaching children *well*. Every teacher knows this.'

'Of course,' said Sarah. 'You'll find no quarrel here.'

'So excluding married women from the profession is nonsensical since it removes a great many experienced teachers from the classroom.'

Joyce and Sarah could only sit in dejected silence. A year ago, Joyce would have argued against Teresa. At her interview for the job at the village school she had indeed argued against Teresa's appointment because she favoured the other candidate, almost exclusively because he was male. But Joyce had changed a great deal in a year. Though she remained socially conservative, her recent experience of separating from her own husband meant that she regarded the edict now being imposed on Teresa as fundamentally unfair.

'I would be a hypocrite if I was to say that I haven't always believed a woman's place is in the home, Teresa,' said Joyce. 'But I don't believe that should be imposed by law. As you say, it deprives the professions of qualified, experienced personnel, and drives many women into enforced domesticity.'

'Clearly, "happy women" is not a government priority,' said Sarah.

'What a tremendous shock that is.'

Teresa was unable to mask the bitterness in her voice.

'I'm sorry, ladies—'

She broke off. Since marrying Nick, Teresa had been aware this day might come, but had convinced herself that Great Paxford's isolated location and small size would inoculate it against a severe application of the marriage bar.

If I knew I would definitely lose my career as a consequence of marrying Nick, would I have gone through with it? Marriage protects me on the one hand yet now exposes me on the other.

'It's a heavy price to pay for marrying the man you love, Teresa,' said Sarah, 'but you mustn't let this come between you and Nick.'

Sarah felt at pains to safeguard her old friend.

'This isn't Nick's fault.'

'Of course not,' said Teresa. 'But ...' she started, then stopped herself.

Joyce leaned closer.

'But what, dear?'

But if I could be who I am without fear or discrimination none of this would be happening. None of it.

'I appreciate you coming here like this, and telling me in person. It can't have been easy.'

Teresa had hoped that marrying Nick put her in a foxhole that offered protection from the rumour and gossip that were customarily aimed at unmarried women of a certain age. And indeed, marriage seemed to have had that desired effect. But the sudden loss of her job and independent livelihood now caused the foxhole to suddenly give way under her feet. Teresa couldn't help but feel that marriage was no longer protecting her; it was beginning to swallow her whole.

'You are to see out the term,' said Joyce, as kindly as she could manage.

'For the sake of the children,' said Sarah. 'It will give you time to prepare them for the transition.'

Teresa's mind momentarily returned to the unmade Christmas cards for her class on the kitchen table, waiting to be made and written in. She had intended to conclude her cards by telling each child how much she was looking forward to exploring the new year with them at school. She had no idea what to write now. How would she explain her sudden, enforced absence in a way that wouldn't dishearten the girls who had quietly declared to her that they wanted to be teachers, just like she was?

Teresa looked at Sarah and Joyce and thought of everything she had done to fit in to their world.

I've always had one rule with my children. Whatever they ask, tell the truth. And what is the truth now? Be whatever you want, girls. But pray to God you don't end up like me.

Chapter 51

Teresa's wasn't the only household to receive callers that night. Erica and Laura were clearing away after supper, while Kate and Dr Myra Rosen made Will comfortable in his makeshift room in the front parlour. Will's desire to be in the bosom of his family had come at a price for them all during the two weeks since his return home. As Will became exhausted he became more prone to fitting. Kate had seen similar tendencies during her nurse's training in Manchester, but for Laura it was new and terrifying.

As strong as Laura was in almost every other area of her life, the sight of her beloved father temporarily reduced to a convulsing body unable to control itself scared her tremendously. She had tried to remain in the room when it happened, but couldn't. She had tried to explain her response to her mother, but was aware it sounded unconvincing.

She needn't have worried. Erica understood how difficult it must be for a daughter to see her once-strong and impregnable father so diminished and afflicted by illness. As mature as Laura had become over the past year, there was still a part of her that was Will's little girl, and that part was terrified to her core of losing him. Each seizure re-emphasised that inevitability. Erica had told Laura not to be too down on herself for her reaction to Will's condition.

'We would all like to be as strong as we think we should be. But this is likely to affect each of us in different ways. No one is judging you, darling. We each have to find our own way of coping.'

While Laura knew that no one was judging her, she couldn't help judging herself, and found herself wanting.

During supper that evening Will had suddenly slumped in his chair, his head lolling to one side, as his muscles began to spasm. Kate and Myra rose immediately from their chairs and laid Will carefully on the dining-room floor, placing a rolled-up napkin between his teeth to prevent him from biting his own tongue. Erica fetched a pillow for his head. Laura had stood to one side for a minute or two, unable to help, and then quietly left the room until Kate came to tell her that the firestorm in Will's brain had subsided. When Will finally became still, all four women carefully lifted him back into his wheelchair and took him to his room to recover – a process that would include a deep sleep that might last for hours.

'I won't ever get used to seeing it,' Laura confessed quietly to her mother later that evening in the kitchen.

'None of us are getting used to it, darling,' Erica replied. 'We just have to accept it's part of who your father is now, for—' She stopped herself, hoping Laura hadn't noticed that she had started a sentence she didn't wish to finish.

'For as long as he's here,' Laura said.

Erica nodded and took Laura by the hands. She looked into her daughter's eyes, and knew that she understood Will wouldn't survive a great deal longer.

'I know it's hard on all of us, but each time he recovers, I can't help but marvel at your father's immense bravery in returning to spend a few more precious moments with us all.'

'How do you know that's what he's thinking when he comes back to us?' asked Laura.

'Because he *always* smiles when he sees us again. Every single time.'

Like any loving wife, Erica loathed watching her husband suffer. But for Will, the suffering seemed endurable as long as theirs were the first faces he'd see on regaining consciousness.

'He likes Myra, doesn't he?' said Laura, drying the dishes from supper.

Erica, realising Laura needed to change the subject, nodded. 'He appreciates her willingness to listen to his advice about how to handle his patients. He thinks she's beginning to understand that we're not just asking her to take over the practice, but everything Will represented to the village.'

As they began to stack the cleaned plates there was a knock on the front door, sharp and businesslike. Erica looked at Laura, almost hoping it'd be someone come to take her daughter out to give her a moment of normality in all this madness. Perhaps Laura's friend Tom, a young private Laura had recently befriended. Catching herself wool-gathering, she turned to Laura and asked, 'Are you seeing Tom tonight?'

'He's hardly getting any time away from the station at the moment. Besides, Tom doesn't knock. He beeps. Shall I see who it is?'

Erica shook her head.

'If it's not for you it will be for me.'

Erica wiped her hands dry and walked out of the kitchen. On the way to the front door she paused and looked into the front room to watch as Kate and Myra tucked Will into bed. He had the oxygen mask strapped onto his face, and was drawing hard to get the gas into his damaged lungs.

How much longer can you do this, my darling? I wish I could release you . . .

Erica didn't know who to expect when she opened the front door, but the very last person she would have nominated was Gwen Talbot, a woman with whom she frequently found herself at odds, most recently over the refugee debate. The woman seemed to embody every atavistic and reactionary impulse that lurked in Great Paxford's darker corners. Erica had no idea why the woman was calling, and had little inclination to spend much time finding out. But here she was in the chilly night air, in coat and hat, holding a pie dish covered with a cloth. Erica was so surprised she was unable to conceal it.

'Mrs Talbot?' she said, in four brisk, questioning syllables that simultaneously confirmed the woman's name and suggested the question, 'What in God's name are you doing on my doorstep at this hour?'

'Good evening, Mrs Campbell. I hope I'm not disturbing you?'

By her tone, Erica surmised this was not a social call. Though in her experience, Mrs Talbot used the same sharp tone for everything she said, so it might well have been. Erica glanced over Mrs Talbot's shoulder, half expecting to see at least a few of the women who seemed to accompany her wherever she went, like a shoal of pilot fish in permanent attendance on their protective shark. Mrs Talbot caught the glance, and its inference.

'I came alone, Mrs Campbell,' she said, with a brief smile. 'I wanted to bring this for Dr Campbell.' She held out the pie dish. 'It's an apple pie.'

Erica was momentarily lost for words.

'When my Alan was ill, Dr Campbell came every day, all weathers. Never made us feel he was in a hurry to leave. Always made Alan feel like he was the doctor's only patient. Alan never forgot it. He was there at the end, as well. Stayed. Not just for Alan. For me and the children too.'

'Yes,' said Erica. 'I remember.'

'Oftentimes, he'd sit with us over a piece of apple pie and just talk. You know, the way he has of just talking and making everything seem . . . bearable. Never said no to a piece.'

Erica knew exactly what she meant.

'There's a rumour going round Dr Campbell's in a bad way. So I brought him a pie.'

Mrs Talbot proffered the pie again, compelling Erica to take it.

'Thank you,' she said, reaching out and taking the dish.

'If you don't mind me asking, Mrs Campbell, how is he?'

Erica looked at Mrs Talbot, a woman she loathed. But not at this moment. It was as if another, softer, more kind-spirited Gwen Talbot had usurped the original. Her eyes looked into Erica's, and for the first time Erica noticed deep lines from a difficult life scored into her face around them.

'He's dying,' Erica said, the second word almost failing to make it out of her mouth.

Mrs Talbot nodded slowly.

'Some who've been to see him with the new doctor thought as much. Was it the crash?'

'He was already quite ill before the crash,' Erica said. 'But the crash made things considerably worse. His lungs, you see . . .'

Mrs Talbot absorbed the information solemnly, guided by her own experience of grief.

'If there's anything I can do . . .'

Mrs Talbot left the offer suspended in the space between them.

'Thank you, Mrs Talbot. That's very kind of you.'

'Not if you knew how highly we regard your husband in my house. I've always believed he gave us an extra few weeks with Alan. Just by popping in every day. Checking. Adjusting. Taking care of him. Time we wouldn't have had.'

'I'm sure he'll be most grateful for your gift.'

'You can have some as well of course.' Mrs Talbot smiled. 'And your girls. I don't expect Dr Campbell to be able to eat it all before it goes stale.'

Erica smiled.

'Thank you. We shall.'

The two women looked at one another. At the WI they generally found themselves on opposite sides of most debates and discussions. But none of that was of any relevance as they stood facing one another – a woman who had lost her husband facing one who was about to lose hers.

'Well then. Goodnight, Mrs Campbell.'

'Goodnight, Mrs Talbot.'

Mrs Talbot nodded once, turned, walked back down the garden path and disappeared into darkness.

Erica stood on the doorstep looking out into the black night, listening to Mrs Talbot's footsteps diminish and disappear. An owl hooted a mile away, trying to locate its young on the ground. Erica had never had a good word to say about Gwen Talbot, and all the bad ones suddenly seemed petty and misjudged.

Who would imagine Gwen Talbot had the capacity to make such a graceful gesture? And was the first to do so.

'Who was it?'

Erica turned to see Laura standing at her side.

'Gwen Talbot.'

Laura instinctively wrinkled her nose up at the sound of the name.

'What did *she* want? To put you right about something, no doubt.'

Erica smiled patiently.

'She brought an apple pie for Dad.'

'Made with crab apples, no doubt.'

Erica couldn't blame Laura for being so determinedly negative about Mrs Talbot. The woman had been unutterably cruel to her when the scandal of her affair with Wing Commander Bowers was made public. Erica was hardly proud of Laura for becoming embroiled with a married man, who should have known better, but she felt the cruel gossip women such as Mrs Talbot had aimed at a naive young girl was despicable. Until three minutes ago Erica would have readily dismissed the woman in words similar to those used by Laura. Now here she stood, having to amend her opinion of someone she had only hitherto loathed.

We form an opinion about someone based on what we see. But what they reveal of themselves is merely a fragment. The rest is out of view, below the surface.

'Dad wants to see you,' said Laura. 'Before he goes to sleep. You can show him Mrs Talbot's almost certainly bitter-tasting pie. Give him something to smile about.'

Erica turned to tell Laura that she believed Will would accept the gift in the spirit with which it was given, and that she might do well to follow his example and remain open to seeing different sides of people, but Laura had already gone back inside to sit with her father. She was seldom long from his side.

I'm going to have to watch her like a hawk when he's gone. She's going to be devastated in a way she's never experienced. We all are. But it's going to hit Laura terribly.

Chapter 52

FRANCES HAD HOPED Noah's grandmother might accompany his grandfather to Great Paxford. But when he made the trip a week later, she was still too ill to travel. Frances had hoped the woman might act as an ameliorating influence on a once-reasonable man who had become brittle and inflexible where Noah was concerned – as if he felt the need to constantly defend his deceased daughter's interests against people determined to undermine her – or so it seemed to Frances on the morning of Morris Lakin's arrival. Her sister, Sarah, was less convinced.

'You can't deny he has a significant and valid interest in what happens to Noah,' Sarah had said, watching Frances pace the sitting room.

'Of course not,' replied Frances. 'But it is crystal clear that Noah's best interests are served by staying in Great Paxford, and not being sent away to a school he has no desire to attend.'

'Crystal clear to you, Frances.'

'To everyone, surely.'

'To everyone who thinks like *you.*'

Sarah understood the subtleties of her sister's mind. Frances didn't assume that everyone thought as she did about any given subject. But when she became convinced of the right solution to a problem she did become frustrated that everyone else didn't recognise the solution as plainly as she did.

Frances had arranged for Claire and Spencer to take Noah out for the day so that she and Sarah could show Morris Lakin the best points about village life, unencumbered by Noah, who would spend time with his grandfather later in the afternoon. The 'grand tour', as Frances described it, would culminate in a visit to the village school. Frances had requested that Sarah, in her capacity as one of the school governors, ask Teresa to show Lakin round the school, and explain how the staff were every inch as ambitious for their children to achieve academic excellence as staff at any school of any stripe, anywhere.

'Might Teresa also be persuaded to say that should Noah choose to run away from the village school for some unspecified reason, he would have significantly less distance to travel before arriving home?'

Sarah gave her sister a reproachful stare.

'Perhaps not.'

As the taxi from Crewe station came to a stop outside the Barden house, Noah's grandfather was pleased to see Sarah waiting with Frances to greet him. When the pair had first visited his home in Liverpool to discuss the repercussions of Peter's relationship with Helen, it had been Sarah to whom he had most warmed. She had a natural empathy that seemed to cut across the rights and wrongs of accepted morality, even when extended to Noah, who many people would have written off as 'illegitimate' and consequently beyond the pale. While he had understood why Frances's conversational tone had been one of scarcely veiled hostility, he had been gratified to see that her sister had come in the spirit of understanding and mediation. It hadn't surprised him to learn later that Sarah was the wife of a vicar. As he stepped out of the taxi onto the wide gravel drive of the Barden house, he hoped for more of the same approach from her.

Frances was the first to step forward to shake his hand.

'Good morning, Mr Lakin. I trust you had a pleasant journey?'

'Pleasant enough,' said Lakin stiffly, offering no embellishment whatsoever to his answer. Sarah steeled herself for a tricky visit and stepped forward as Frances reintroduced her.

'Good morning, Mr Lakin,' she said, offering her hand. His hitherto expressionless face broke into a thin smile when he turned to her.

'Good morning, Mrs Collingborne. A pleasure to remake your acquaintance.'

Frances glanced at Sarah archly. Lakin was clearly delineating between the two sisters.

Very well. No matter. Sarah and I are of the same mind so it's immaterial which of us he feels more positively disposed towards. The same argument will come from each of us. And she is no more a pushover than I am.

Greetings over, Frances and Sarah offered Lakin a cup of tea to revive himself after his journey, and then proceeded to escort him around the village. They showed him Great Paxford's thriving High Street, with its post office and telephone exchange, as well as its few beauty spots, and areas where children could play. They passed several villagers who wished Frances and Sarah 'good day'.

After they'd walked around the village, Frances and Sarah took Lakin down to the canal to meet Noah. Claire and Spencer had spent the morning with him on a rowing expedition. They arrived to see Noah noisily playing football with Spencer as Claire laid lunch out on a soft tartan blanket on the canal's grassy bank. When he saw his grandfather, the boy stopped in his tracks for a moment, as if his eyes might be deceiving him, and then delightedly cried, 'Grandad!' and broke into a sprint towards Lakin. When Noah reached his grandfather he ran straight into Lakin's outstretched arms, buried his face in his chest and hugged him tightly.

'Careful, lad,' said Lakin fondly, kissing the top of Noah's head. 'You'll squeeze the puff out of me!'

'I missed you!' said Noah.

Lakin glanced at Frances and Sarah, his eyes moist from the strength of the reunion. He placed his hand lightly on top of Noah's head and gently ruffled his hair.

'Having fun?'

Noah lifted his head and looked up at Lakin.

'Playing football.'

'I can see.'

'Spencer thinks I could play for England one day.'

'Does he now.'

'At either football or cricket.'

'Which would you prefer?'

'Both.'

'Of course. No point setting your sights low.'

'Before the outbreak of war, Great Paxford had a very good cricket team,' said Frances, seizing another opportunity to sell the village to Lakin. 'Something Noah could aspire to as he gets older.'

Lakin looked at her coldly. He didn't take kindly to anyone pushing him to think anything he didn't want to think when he wasn't ready to think it.

'Lots of cricket teams all over,' he said. 'If the same happens to this generation of young men as happened after the last shout, I can't think he'll want for a place in a team, wherever he is.' He looked up and down the canal. 'Is it safe down here?' he asked. 'With the Luftwaffe targeting canals.'

'They seem more focused on our industrial and port cities,' said Frances.

'They've been dropping incendiaries and high explosives on Chester a fair amount,' chipped in Spencer, who had followed Noah over. 'Probably mistake it for Liverpool.'

'Spencer is a member of the local auxiliary fire service,' said Frances, keen to show off the upstanding citizenry Noah would be growing up amongst.

Lakin held on to Noah, turned to Spencer and gave him a nod of respect. Spencer smiled back.

'Claire is his wife,' Frances continued. 'They live in private quarters in the house.'

Throughout lunch, Lakin watched his grandson with Frances and her staff, noting the great affection – perhaps even love – that passed between them. The boy was clearly at ease with these people, and they, equally clearly, revelled in his sparky confidence and familiarity. Nevertheless, neither Frances nor Sarah believed that Lakin's reservations would be swept away over high spirits and a few sandwiches in the sunshine.

As Claire packed away the picnic things, Frances and Sarah took Lakin to their final destination of their tour of the village – the school. Teresa had been happy to open her classroom on a Saturday morning, and had been briefed by Sarah to present the school's very best face. If Teresa felt any irony at being asked to be the school's greatest advocate barely a week after being told it no longer required her services, she was far too professional to show it. She knew how well an inquisitive, bright boy like Noah would thrive within its classrooms and ethos, and, knowing something of his recent 'adventure', emphasised how much pastoral care took place there.

'This is a small community, Mr Lakin. Every child is known to us before they arrive. We know their parents. I'll almost certainly know their mothers from the WI as a friend. Nurturing the children sits at the heart of what we do.'

Lakin bridled.

'I'm afraid you won't have an opportunity to know Noah's mother. She's dead.'

Teresa looked momentarily aghast, but quickly regained her footing.

'I'm so sorry to hear that, Mr Lakin. Knowing that, we would keep an extra eye on Noah to ensure he fits in with the other children, and doesn't feel left out in any way.'

Frances nodded at Teresa appreciatively. Lakin nodded too and moved on, giving little away. If he had been impressed by what he had seen of the school, and by Teresa, he didn't reveal it.

They walked back to the house in silence, Frances and Sarah letting Lakin take in the bucolic rural atmosphere that settled on the village and surrounding countryside in the late afternoon. Neither of the sisters had been native to Great Paxford, but each had experienced its recalibrating, restorative effects following lives in London and Oxford respectively.

'It's very peaceful,' said Lakin, as he watched a small group of wood pigeons striding around a field in search of dropped berries and seeds.

'It's deceptive,' said Frances. 'It is peaceful when you want it to be. But when you need activity and company they're very easy to locate.'

'As true for children as much as adults,' chipped in Sarah. 'If Noah were to come and live in Great Paxford he would never want for company his own age, nor peace and quiet should he want time alone to think. And the countryside is the most wonderful playground.'

Lakin looked at them and kept his counsel. When they arrived at the house they sat down to a tea of scones and a Victoria sponge cake in the dining room. Over tea, Frances had told her sister, was where the nitty-gritty of Noah's future would be decided. To end Lakin's visit on as high a note as possible, Frances had instructed Claire to be as generous with their cream and jam as they could be. She wanted to give the impression of simplicity yet plenitude, subtly suggesting that Noah wouldn't have his head turned by fancy things if he remained at the house, but neither would he want for anything. She was pleased to observe that Lakin enjoyed both a healthy appetite and an appreciation of good cake.

As Lakin worked his way through two scones and a slice of sponge cake, Frances glanced across at Sarah and nodded, signalling that it was time for the negotiations to begin.

'You've seen the house, the village and the school, Mr Lakin. What are your thoughts?' Sarah began.

Lakin looked up at the two women regarding him intently, and finished chewing his current mouthful. Eventually he swallowed and took a sip from his teacup.

'I think it's very nice,' he said, offering no more than the basic truth.

'I meant, as an environment for Noah to grow up and be schooled in?'

'I'm aware of what you meant, Mrs Collingborne. I *think* . . . it's very nice.'

After a long day of taking Lakin around the village and subtly buttering him up to the idea of Noah remaining in Great Paxford, Frances was eager to put her cards on the table. 'When you say the village and the school are "very nice", Mr Lakin, does that mean you give your approval to Noah both living and being schooled here?'

He looked at Frances as he chewed another piece of scone.

'I didn't say that,' he said.

'That is the purpose of today, is it not?' said Sarah. 'To resolve once and for all where Noah lives and goes to school?'

Lakin swallowed the scone and looked at Sarah.

'I dare say that's what you'd both like. But . . . I dare say it's not as straightforward as you would like to think.'

'Because of Helen and Peter's wishes?'

'Exactly so, Mrs Collingborne.'

'We went through this on the telephone, Mr Lakin. Both Helen's and Peter's desires for Noah's education may well have changed had they seen the effect boarding school had on him.'

'Likewise . . . they may well have *not*.'

'Yes, of course. But with all due respect, we will never know what they would have wanted. They are not here but we are. We have seen the effect. We have lived through three days of torment. And I can honestly say that I vehemently—' Frances caught Sarah's eye. Her expression said 'too much'. 'I *strongly* believe,' Frances corrected herself, 'that Noah's best interests will be served by my proposal.'

Lakin set his plate on the small table at his side and looked solemnly at Frances.

'Brass tacks?' he asked.

Frances nodded.

'Brass tacks, absolutely.'

'All this,' he said, looking around the beautifully appointed dining room, and then through the window at the garden. 'It's very nice . . .'

'You keep saying that, Mr Lakin—'

'But Mrs Lakin and I can't help thinking Noah is just a temporary replacement for you.'

Both Frances and Sarah failed to understand what Lakin was driving at.

'A temporary replacement for what?' asked Frances.

Lakin paused for effect, before continuing.

'Noah is your little piece of Peter, isn't he? We understand that. He's our little piece of Helen. And while he's small and unspoiled you want to have him around, as would we if we could. He brightens up the place, I can hear it in your voice. Brightens up your life, Mrs Barden. Fills a space.'

'Is that such a terrible thing?' asked Sarah, stepping in to advocate on her sister's behalf. 'Doesn't it suggest the deep connection my sister feels to the child?'

'Possibly,' said Lakin. 'But what happens as he grows older?' He fixed his gaze on Frances.

'Small children become big children, Mrs Barden. What was winsome and winning one year can become obstreperous and recalcitrant the next. What then, when you can no longer see your Peter in him? Cast him out of a life he's got used to, job done for you?'

Both Frances and Sarah looked at Lakin with considerable trepidation. Evidently, he and his wife had come at this from a completely different perspective to the one propelling Frances. It momentarily threw Sarah. But not Frances.

'I have wondered the same, Mr Lakin,' said Frances, her tone soft and thoughtful, devoid of any of her earlier dismissive impatience.

Sarah snapped round to look at her sister, clearly taken by surprise by her placatory words.

'I have questioned whether my desire to have Noah at Great Paxford is a consequence of a desire to keep Peter's flesh and blood in my life. I have asked myself the same questions you have just asked. What might I think of Noah once I am able to continue my life in full? Would he continue to be part of it? Might he have served his purpose? How might I regard him once he has changed from the delightful little child he is now into an independent-minded adolescent, and young man?'

'And your answer, Mrs Barden? In all honesty? Brass tacks.'

'Brass tacks, Mr Lakin. My answer is that I believe I have grown to love the boy in his own right, for himself, and not for the resemblance to Peter I see in him. And I shall continue to love him as he grows up. And, I believe, for as long as I live. It only truly became clear to me when he ran away from school, and I had to engage with the unutterable terror that I might never see him again. The thought was unbearable.'

Her voice cracked with a resurgence of the fear she had experienced during those dark days of Noah's disappearance. Nevertheless, Frances looked at Lakin with a steadfast gaze, unblinking, despite the film of tears that glossed her eyes. It was a gaze of utmost sincerity with which Sarah was all too familiar. She had never heard Frances speak like this about Noah, nor reveal quite such a depth of feeling for him. Until now, Frances had only spoken of what would be in Noah's best interests, not in her own. Noah's grandfather also seemed taken aback by the intense declaration Frances had just made. He opened his mouth to speak, but Frances hadn't quite finished.

'Which is why I propose I formally adopt him.'

Lakin's face seemed to freeze with surprise.

'Adopt?'

'With all the will in the world, Mr Lakin, you and Mrs Lakin won't be here for ever. By my formally adopting Noah he would have additional security when you eventually pass. In the meantime, it would formalise my relationship with him, his with me, and mine with you and your good wife. Any major decisions concerning Noah would be taken with your agreement. I'm not proposing adoption to whisk him away from you. But to properly connect us all, once and for all – and give Noah the firmest platform on which to move forward. In the absence of his true parents, adoption seems to me to be the best solution all round. Don't you?'

Frances fixed her gaze on Lakin once more, and waited for his answer. Lakin looked back at Frances, clearly blindsided by her proposition.

'Frances,' Sarah said quietly, 'why don't we step outside and give Mr Lakin some time to consider your proposal?'

Frances turned to Sarah, a flicker of irritation passing across her face, a saleswoman interrupted at the point of closing arguably the most important deal of her life.

'I really don't think that's necessary, do you, Mr Lakin?'

Lakin looked from Frances to Sarah, his mind turning over Frances's words.

'Actually, I think that might be a good idea, Mrs Barden. You've given me a great deal to think about. A very great deal indeed.'

* * *

When she and Sarah left the room, Frances turned to her sister.

'Why did you say that? I had clearly wrong-footed him with my proposition.'

'Wrong-footed us both,' said Sarah.

'I was about to press the advantage.'

'But there's no need.'

'What do you mean?'

'Didn't you see how he was? You've already won him round. It was in his face the moment you mentioned adopting Noah.'

'I didn't see anything.'

'His instant reaction was surprise, not antagonism. He'll agree. I'm sure of it.'

'He really should. It's the best solution all round.'

'You didn't think to discuss it with me?' Sarah chided, gently. 'You might have tried to change my mind.'

'Of course I wouldn't, you stupid woman! I think it's an utterly brilliant idea.'

'Oh,' said Frances. 'Good.'

Sarah turned and looked at the closed door to the sitting room, behind which Morris Lakin was weighing up Noah's future.

'Do you think Noah would ever call me "Aunt Sarah"?' Sarah asked nervously, glancing at Frances.

'Would you like him to?'

Sarah nodded. 'Very much.'

'Then I'll absolutely insist on it.'

Sarah's face broke into the broadest smile.

'And "Uncle Adam", when Adam gets home,' Frances said.

'If he ever does . . .' Sarah replied. 'I have so little news. I've called and written to every government department I can think of. Other than the reassurance I've received from the Soldiers, Sailors, Airmen and Families Association about the treatment of prisoners at Dunkirk, I've had no news. Sometimes—'

'He *will* come home, Sarah. I'm certain of it. You must be too. Adam is simply too sensible to allow anything to prevent him from returning to you.'

Sarah looked at Frances, momentarily unable to speak, trying to absorb some of her sister's certainty by a form of spiritual osmosis.

Frances gently brushed an errant strand of hair from her younger sister's face.

'I can see Noah and his new uncle Adam getting on like an absolute house on fire.'

Chapter 53

Laura Campbell sat in the observation post on the southern outskirts of Great Paxford, and scoured the sky through a pair of large, regulation binoculars. She was searching for enemy aircraft, all of which she could now identify as accurately as any aviation-obsessed schoolboy. Laura wasn't aviation-obsessed in the slightest, but had volunteered for the Observation Corps to fulfil a desire to do her wartime duty – a desire that had previously been met by joining the RAF. For a time, the RAF had more than met Laura's ambition to serve her country. But after finding herself ruthlessly scapegoated then cashiered by an RAF tribunal for her part in a brief affair with a philandering wing commander, Laura had eventually sought another way she might play her part. With Tom's gentle nudging, she had eventually found it in the form of the Observation Corp. Not only was the work important, the observation post offered Laura shelter from the prurient public gaze that followed her citation in the local paper as a co-respondent in the wing commander's divorce. Laura's name had been unceremoniously dragged through the mud. She had been unable to walk through the village without feeling a dozen pairs of narrowed eyes upon her.

The observation post had also given Laura an opportunity to think carefully about her part in the affair. Over several weeks, she had been able to isolate moments of wilful blindness on her part, as well as many more moments of manipulation on the wing commander's. He would come into her office while she was working and simply watch her, for minutes on end. He always made the first move in terms of physical contact. He never invited her to call him by his first name, so it was very clear who held the balance of power in the relationship. He always spoke of his sadness in relation to his marriage, without ever talking of ending it. Perhaps worst of all, he repeatedly told Laura that the time he spent with her helped alleviate the stress of sending young men to their deaths on a daily basis. Laura was willing to admit she had enjoyed the attention Bowers had given her, and the sex they'd had. She enjoyed finally feeling she had graduated to 'womanhood' and the feeling of being an important confidante to someone so obviously *dashing* as a wing commander. She believed she had lost her virginity in a swirl of romantic love; in hindsight she had been forced to admit to herself that she had given it up rather cheaply to a pretty powerful scoundrel. When Laura discovered she had merely been one of many conquests Wing Commander Bowers had made of young women over the course of his in fact *very happy* married life, Laura was shocked by her own naivety. This was compounded when she expected Bowers to also be punished by the RAF for inappropriate behaviour, only to discover he was going to be allowed to retain his position and rank, but would be moved to a neighbouring RAF station to allow the gossip at Tabley Wood to wind down.

Laura's short-lived, unhappy affair with Wing Commander Bowers would have been a scouring experience for a mature woman; for a girl of seventeen it had been emotionally devastating, and the seclusion of the Observation Corps position allowed Laura time and space to regroup and gain some perspective on what had been a cruel baptism of fire into adulthood. Some of the best advice about men had come from her sister, Kate.

'They will try it on, Laura, all the time, under almost any circumstance. Just weeks after I lost Jack, men who knew I was recently widowed tried to get me into bed. It's shocking, I know. I think they thought my resolve might be weakened. Or that I'd be desperate for company, or consolation. Some men are plain desperate. Some are complete pigs. A lot think we're stupid. But many more are genuine and lovely. Your task is to rebuff the swine – with a stick if you have to! – and save yourself for someone who deserves you. Look at Mother. Look at me. Campbell women do *not* throw themselves away on rubbish.'

Being someone of value was a concept that appealed to Laura. It allowed her to put her old self, and the mistakes made by her, in the past, and re-enter the community anew. She decided she wouldn't be scarred by her experience with Bowers, but educated by it. She wouldn't be cowed by the judgement of others, but her actions would show that the tainted girl they whispered about behind her back was long gone. What with her affair with Bowers and her father's illness, Laura was taken aback by the speed with which events had both challenged then changed her over the last eight months.

Coming to terms with everything had been helped by the quiet friendship of Air Crewman Tom Halliwell, who had never wavered in his loyalty to Laura as her friend, and then as her boyfriend.

Laura smiled as she thought of Tom. She loved his unaffected honesty, delivered with kindness. His company made her feel she was with someone who was protective but never indulgent. She wished she had spent more time with Tom before the business with Bowers. Every now and then she gave in to the idea that she was 'spoiled goods', and that if she and Tom ever grew too close someone would whisper in his ear that he was too good for her.

Laura put the binoculars to her eyes once more and looked around the empty sky. Following clouds and birds that floated across her field of vision helped clear her head. As soon as German bombers crossed the east coast, a wave of warnings would be triggered westwards, and Laura would be ready to spot them. Now was the time to acclimatise her vision to the dwindling afternoon light. She let her thoughts drift back to her father. While her mother and sister created, and then inhabited, the pretence that Will's existence in the house was entirely normal, Laura was struggling to go along with it. She did try, but sometimes she simply had to remove herself from the room, or the house, for a few moments to gather her thoughts.

The bell of the observation post's telephone suddenly brought Laura back to the moment. She set down the binoculars and put the telephone's receiver to her ear. The message was coded and clear: the Luftwaffe was on its way. Thirty bombers. Estimated time of arrival overhead, twenty minutes.

The sky was quickly darkening as Laura replaced the receiver and the slow drawl of the local air-raid siren started to drift out across the region. Laura gathered her notebook and pencil and took up her position beside the aeroplane recognition chart, next to a mechanical sighting Post Instrument plotter. She set the instrument with the aircraft's approximate height, aligned the sighting bar with the aircraft and used the vertical pointer to determine the approximate position of the aircraft on the map grid. Once she had everything in place Laura could then report the map coordinates, height, time, sector clock code and number of aircraft for each sighting to the control centre, which would monitor the progress of enemy aircraft into UK airspace and divert RAF fighters to intercept them. Laura was a small but essential cog in the elaborate mechanism that protected England from the Luftwaffe.

As she worked she imagined villagers hurrying from their homes to the shelter, and thought of her mother, Kate and her father. Will had insisted they leave him in the house during raids, and hurry to the shelter without him to slow them down. Laura imagined her father lying quietly in his bed as people rushed past the window. She wondered if he was scared in those moments.

Laura took a deep breath, sent up a brief prayer for the safe-keeping of her loved ones – as she always did prior to a raid – and cleared her mind. She lifted the binoculars to her eyes once more and focused them on the eastern horizon. By controlling her breathing she could keep the binoculars steady, as she had been trained to do. Her heart raced with excitement. Within minutes of reporting her observations, fighters would be scrambled from Tabley Wood, and Laura would watch them speed off to attack the approaching German bombers and their escorts. It was life and death in action. She felt the weight of responsibility settle on her shoulders once more. She may have been just one link in a long chain of command, but it only took one link to break through a lapse in concentration to render the entire chain ineffective. Laura was determined to keep up her end. All thoughts about Wing Commander Bowers, his wife, the village gossips, her parents, sister, Tom and her father disappeared.

For the next thirty minutes, nothing else mattered on planet Earth for Laura, except what would take place directly overhead.

Chapter 54

GREAT PAXFORD WAS deserted for two hours while the air raid came and went, its population keeping itself distracted in shelters while training one ear on what was happening above them. German aircraft soared overhead, as RAF fighters raced to intercept.

When the all-clear finally sounded, the women from the WI were the first out of the shelter, hurrying to resume preparations for the nightly arrival of refugees into the village, which had been taking place since they had started making food and accommodation available two weeks earlier. While some less experienced women in the WI wanted to try every initiative that had been suggested, wiser heads counselled that overreaching could lead to the collapse of *all* of them. As a consequence, the original idea of distributing exhausted refugees to homes around the village had proved too controversial, and was quickly dropped. Limiting the WI's operation to providing food in one location and shelter in another kept everything clean and simple. If a refugee wanted to eat they went to the church; if they wanted to sleep, they went to the village hall, which also doubled as an air-raid shelter for the refugees. If they wanted to do both, they could, but in that order.

The village hall could accommodate many people, and being at the centre of Great Paxford meant it was easy to locate, even in the blackout. The hall opened at 6 p.m. each night, and provided a place to bed down in the warm and dry for any who needed it. In the fortnight since the scheme began, the hall had been well occupied but had yet to reach capacity. Mrs Talbot had voiced a manufactured concern to the effect that the hall offered little protection from stray German bombs, but Steph had swiftly shot it down.

'First, *no* shelter can survive a direct hit. Second, Great Paxford's not a target for German bombers. The two bombs we've had were strays. The chance of another falling on the village is small. The chance of one falling on the village hall even smaller. We offer what we can under the circumstances.'

The WI would offer refugees only basic food and shelter. Following some discussion about the suitability of a private home for use as a soup kitchen, it was decided that hot vegetable soup and bread would be better distributed from the church than the Barden house. The soup would be cooked on-site on gas in the vestry, while the bread would be baked in people's homes, and brought in. Evoking Jesus feeding the multitudes after his sermon on the mount, Sarah encountered little difficulty in persuading Adam's acting stand-in, Reverend James, to allow the church to become a nightly soup kitchen – though she was quick to make clear that no theological succour would be added to the victuals by members of the strictly secular WI. Again, and somewhat predictably, Mrs Talbot raised an argument against, now claiming the church would become dishevelled and spoiled by trekkers pouring in every night, tramping up and down the aisles with muddy feet. Joyce effortlessly wrestled the concern to the ground.

'The church does not belong to *us*, Mrs Talbot. It is *God's* house. And Jesus is the son of God.'

'I know who Jesus is, Mrs Cameron.'

'Good. Then you won't have any difficulty imagining what Jesus might do if faced with tired and hungry people knocking on his front door. Would he turn them away because they had a little mud on their sandals? Or would he welcome them in for a lovely bowl of vegetable soup and fresh bread?'

'What about the dirt and the mess?'

'I don't believe it will be beyond our abilities to *mop up* a bit of mud, do you?'

Joyce had been among the first to volunteer to help. It took her out of the house, and provided her with an opportunity to be a significant force within the WI once again. She couldn't turn down the chance to help organise a major initiative.

Pat was less free to leave the house to help. If Bob was writing, Pat would need to be on hand with refreshing cups of tea on the hour, whatever the hour. There was little she could do about it without provoking Bob's anger. Though he kept his grinding animosity towards Pat well hidden while Joyce was present, when she left he could be unsparingly harsh towards his wife.

On this night, however, Bob wasn't working but going through a list of prospective properties he was considering purchasing with income from the success of his new novel. The thought of moving somewhere where Bob's behaviour towards her could go unchecked by the presence of someone else in the house filled Pat with dread. She had asked if he wanted to go through the list with her in order to ensure they didn't move far away from her friends and neighbours.

'I need to find somewhere conducive to work.'

'I understand that, Bob. But wherever you choose, I'll have to live there too.'

'I've always liked the idea of peace and quiet that some-where remote would bring. I think it would greatly enhance my productivity. Don't worry. You'll have a decent enough kitchen to work in.'

'Don't you think I should have a say *beyond* the kitchen?'

'Why? You won't be paying for it.'

He looked round Joyce's front room with disdain.

'Anywhere that doesn't include the ghastly Joyce will be bet-ter than this.'

Though she hadn't been a natural ally of Joyce's for many years, Pat nevertheless bridled at Bob's ingratitude towards the woman who had immediately offered them a roof over their heads when their house had been irreparably damaged by the Spitfire.

'I don't think that's very generous. Joyce can be a little over-bearing at times. But she's been extremely kind to us.'

'On the contrary. She's thoroughly enjoyed being able to live vicariously through my success. "Kind" is what she's had to pretend to be in order to do that. Though she does have her uses,' Bob uttered with an ugly smirk.

439

His comment left Pat with a great sense of unease. Between the decimation of their house, the move to Joyce's and the success of Bob's novel, Pat worried she'd been lulled into a false sense of security, believing Bob had been too busy to be plotting more behind her back. However, she also knew there was no getting anything out of Bob in this mood.

'If you're not working, and you have no interest in my view about where we might live next, do you have any objections to my helping with the WI tonight?'

Bob was engrossed in paperwork from the estate agent and barely heard Pat's request. He caught the words 'the WI', which Pat knew he would, and looked up suspiciously.

'It's not a Thursday.'

'It's not a branch night, Bob,' she said patiently. 'We're assisting people fleeing nightly bombardment.'

'More pointless do-gooding.'

'If you say so,' she said wearily.

Bob looked at her for a moment before deciding that nothing of what Pat had just said was of interest to him, then dismissed her with a wave of his hand.

'Don't be late back.'

Though the WI operation to help the refugees had been up and running for two weeks, this was the first night Pat had been able to leave the house and assist.

She struck out for the village hall, where she found nearly seventy people being settled for the night. Alison, Teresa and a team of WI volunteers clearly had the situation in hand. They were assisted by John Smith, the man who had found Noah and brought him back to Frances. After returning Noah and eating a large breakfast, Frances had told John about the WI initiative to help the refugees, and asked if he would help spread the word among those who came regularly into the area from Liverpool.

'I'd be happy to,' he had said. He was greatly impressed by the women's initiative and kindness.

'You would be a terrific intermediary between us and your fellows,' Alison had suggested. 'I think your support for the initiative could only encourage people to take advantage of it.'

'That's very kind of you, Mrs . . . ?'

'Scotlock,' said Alison.

John had walked into Great Paxford on the first night they opened with over thirty refugees from his home city.

* * *

Pat looked round the hall and thought about writing what she saw in her next Mass Observation report.

Low light by oil lamps. The women of the WI moving among them, checking they have everything they need for a good night's sleep. Blankets. Pillows. Most households offered at least one of each. People of all ages. Families with children. Some very young. A few coloureds. A Chinese family.

Pat wasn't needed so she made her excuses and slipped out. She contemplated returning to Joyce's house, but didn't think Bob would be in bed quite yet. She pulled the collar of her coat up against the cold night air and set off in the opposite direction, towards the church, where she might be able to help those giving out soup and bread.

Each time Pat now approached the church, day or night, images from the day Marek was shipped out flashed through her mind. The incessant rain. The trees bending in the wind. Teresa's wedding. Bob's smirking face. Running along a drenched road in her best shoes. The Spitfire sticking out of the Campbells' house, like a dagger plunged into its heart.

In the six weeks since, Pat had almost given up hope of ever seeing Marek again. His letter not only made immediate daily existence alongside Bob bearable, it had changed Pat's outlook on everything. In two tightly written pages of military-issue foolscap, Marek reignited her hope that they might one day be together, and lifted the enervating grey veneer that seemed to have settled on everything around Pat. Though he had offered scant detail about his military duties, he had reiterated his hope that they might be reunited after the war.

If I survive, Patricia, it will be because I will be driven to return one day, and to once again hold you in my arms. If such a thing could ever happen I would never leave you again.

Bob's sudden determination to leave Joyce's and find their own place to live unnerved Pat, but changed nothing in her mind. Knowing Marek was alive, and that he felt towards her as she continued to feel towards him, was as sustaining for Pat as food and drink. In her reply, Pat had restated her love for Marek, and begged him to take care of himself.

As long as I'm able to receive Marek's letters it doesn't matter where I am. Hearing his voice in my head as I read his words will be enough for me to hold on until he returns. And then . . . ?

Pat dared not imagine the answer to the question. Too many obstacles stood in the way of a future life together. Marek's survival. Her own. Bob. The war. Each obstacle might be overcome, one after the other, but taken together a future life with Marek seemed almost impossible. *Almost.* She allowed herself to create a perfect image of them walking slowly through the fields surrounding Great Paxford a few years from now, hand in hand, and returned to it as and when she needed to calm herself, or endure a difficult encounter with Bob.

Pat approached the church and saw silhouettes entering and leaving through the front entrance. A delicate skeleton of scaffolding had been erected on the left-hand side of the edifice to facilitate repairs to the damage caused by the Spitfire as it fell to earth.

Passing through the church door, Pat saw a line of refugees waiting patiently for food in the dimly lit interior. Knowing they would receive supper in Great Paxford meant they no longer had to carry food and pots and crockery and cutlery out of the city, lightening their loads considerably. They seemed genuinely grateful for what they were given, and took their bowls to the pews, where they sat and quietly ate. The branch had held a competition to devise the most appetising recipes from the non-rationed food at their disposal, which meant the variety of vegetable soups from one day to the next all tasted good. What conversation there was emerged as an ecumenical murmur. Pat smiled to herself at the effect on everyone present of the imposing figure of the crucified Christ carved in dark wood, looking down from above the altar.

If Jesus hadn't been the son of God he would have made an excellent librarian. No need to shush anyone. A single look from those eyes and any chatterbox would fall silent immediately.

Pat smiled a second time as she remembered Marek's hand finding hers as they had stood wordlessly side by side here, alone before the altar at the end of a service to commemorate the silencing of the bells. His first touch had sent a delicious shock shooting from her fingertips, along her arm, through her shoulder, and into her heart.

'Pat.'

Pat turned and saw Erica looking at her from behind the soup- and bread-laden trestle table, working with several women from the WI to keep the food moving from cauldrons and baskets into bowls and plates. Pat walked over to her.

'How's Will?' she asked.

'Kate and Laura are at home with him and Dr Rosen. They all but pushed me out of the house for a couple of hours' respite while he sleeps.' Erica smiled thinly. Even by the candlelight inside the church Pat could see she looked utterly exhausted.

'You look shattered, Erica. Why don't you go home? I can take over,' Pat suggested.

'His cancer is remorselessly advancing,' said Erica, as if she hadn't heard Pat's proposal. 'We've been told to expect periods of not much change and then sudden deterioration. Would you mind cutting more bread? There are more loaves in the baskets under the table.'

Pat took the hint, and asked no more questions about Will.

She has to live it every waking hour. I can understand why Erica wouldn't want to talk about it too.

As Pat began to slice the loaves into thick slices, Erica asked, 'How's Bob?'

'The same,' said Pat.

'And . . . Marek?' Erica's voice dropped in volume at her mention of his name. 'Was his letter what you hoped it would be?'

Pat looked at Erica and nodded.

'Do you think it's wise, Pat? To reignite this? I'm not talking about Bob, but for yourself. Captain Novotny is a soldier. War is escalating across Europe. Anything may happen to him. If it does, you will be left utterly devastated.'

'If that does happen I will have had *something*, Erica, where I had *nothing*.'

'Bob is becoming quite successful now. His new book serialised in a national paper . . .'

'Yes.'

'Kate saw an article by him about Cheshire life under the bombing run into Liverpool.'

'Yes.'

'Mightn't he change?'

Pat was puzzled.

'I gave up all hope of that years ago.'

'But with success, I mean. He hasn't had that before. What reason would he have to continue to behave the way he has, when he now has *every* reason to be happy? And treat you better as a result?'

'You're right to say that when Bob is happier he does treat me better.'

'Well then—'

'Treating me *better* still isn't the same as treating me *well*, Erica.'

Erica frowned, struggling to see the world from Pat's perspective. Pat could see it in Erica's face and decided there was little to be gained by further explanation. She simply needed Erica's support.

'I replied to Marek straight away. Please look out for another letter from him soon. It will be addressed directly to you this time. I told him to put his initials on the flap, so you'll know it's from him.'

Erica looked at Pat for a moment, considering whether to say what was on her mind. Looking after Will in recent weeks had conditioned her to be more assertive about voicing questions and concerns she might previously have kept to herself. Certainly, time to talk about important matters with Will was running out. But it was a fact of life that time was *always* running out, so why not speak one's mind?

'People change, Pat. When their circumstances change, people do too. Even Bob must have that capacity. After all, didn't he change from the man you married to the man he is today? If so, isn't it possible for him to change back?'

'You don't understand, Erica. He's *always* been the man he is today. He was able to control it better when he was younger, that's all. I can't thank you enough for passing on Marek's letter, but—'

'Could I have another piece of bread?'

Pat and Erica looked round and saw a tired-looking young woman standing before them on the other side of the trestle table.

'My daughter's ravenous.'

'Yes, of course,' said Pat. 'Take what you need.'

'Thank you. Thank you so much for what you're doing.'

The young woman took one then a second piece of bread and hurried back to the pew where she had been sitting with her husband and small daughter.

Mrs Talbot was standing in the door to the vestry, keeping a close eye on each of the trekkers, as Steph Farrow and Little Stan approached with more collected vegetables to add to the store.

'The greed of it,' Mrs Talbot said when Steph was in earshot.

'The greed of what?' Steph asked as she and Little Stan edged past with the heavy load of swede.

'Not one of them has offered to pay a penny for the food they're getting. Not *one*, on any of the days we've been doing this.'

'They haven't been asked to,' said Steph from inside the vestry. 'It's a soup kitchen, Mrs Talbot. Not a restaurant.'

'Missing my point, Mrs Farrow. They should at least offer. Instead they just take and take. Someday they'll take too much!'

Steph came out of the vestry, wiping her hands on an old piece of cloth.

'Why can't you look at what's being done, and how much they appreciate it, and feel proud you're part of it?'

'Because I don't like to see the village being taken advantage of, that's why.'

'How is it *being taken advantage of* if they're accepting what we've offered?'

'Of course, you're a staunch ally of Frances Barden so I'd hardly expect you to see things in anything but the most simplistic manner, to not see the threat they pose.'

'Since when was being nice to strangers "simplistic", Mrs Talbot? It's basic human decency. Come on, Stanley.'

Mrs Talbot watched Steph and Little Stan make their way to the main door and leave.

447

'We're at war,' she muttered under her breath. 'It's no time to be *nice*. Mark my words, this won't end well.'

Pat let out a breath as she saw Steph and Little Stan walking away from Mrs Talbot. For a moment, she'd feared an ugly outburst. Relieved that all was well, she turned back to Erica, and saw she was taking off her apron.

'Are you sure you're all right to take over from me?' Erica asked.

'Of course I am.'

'Thank you.'

'No, Erica. Thank *you*. I mean it. Knowing I can receive Marek's letters without having them intercepted makes living with Bob endurable and gives me hope. Believe me, I have given Bob so many opportunities to change. Too many to count. I've been forced to conclude the capacity to change simply isn't in him. And never will be.'

'I sincerely hope you're wrong.'

Pat nodded.

'You could never hope it as much as I have over the years. Goodbye, Erica. And thank you again.'

Erica smiled wanly, put on her coat and hat, and walked towards the church door, where a few tired stragglers were still coming in. As she reached it, Erica turned and looked back at her old neighbour with a look of profound pity.

I wish you could feel a fraction from Bob what I feel from Will. Even now, at his weakest, though he can barely speak, I feel nothing but love from him. What you have with Marek isn't the same. The heat and pressure of a moment. One that will inevitably pass. How can it not, when the world is so rapidly turning itself inside out? How could anyone hope to hold on to something so flimsy in all this?

As Erica watched her, Pat looked over from serving refugees and raised her hand to her. Erica raised her hand back, and hurried from the church, eager to return home and to Will.

Chapter 55

A<small>S THE LAST MEMBER</small> of the WI remaining at the end of the evening, Alison quietly moved through the village hall, making one last check that all the visitors had what they needed for the night, before collecting her hat and coat and leading Boris out, closing the door behind her. She had rejoined the WI shortly after her encounter with Frances on the village green when Noah was missing, and it felt good to be back at the heart of the community.

Coming out into the cold and windy night, Alison glanced into the cloudy, moonless sky, trying to assess whether or not it was likely to rain before she reached home. The wind was certainly up, and Alison could see thick cloud rolling over the village. That it wasn't yet raining meant nothing. If she could coax Boris into a brisk walk they might be home before it started.

As they came down the path connecting the hall to the high street, Alison saw the pinprick glow of a cigarette, and then the silhouette of the man holding it, sitting on the wall opposite, looking up at the sky. As her eyes adjusted to the darkness she realised it was John Smith. He heard her footsteps on the path and turned his head towards her.

'The rest of your colleagues left a while ago, Mrs Scotlock.'

'I offered to stay until everyone had what they needed, and settled,' Alison replied. 'You should get your head down, Mr Smith. Long walk back in the morning.'

'It takes me a while to get in the right frame of mind for sleep,' he said. 'Too many thoughts tumbling around. Most nights I have to make myself dog-tired before I can put my head down.'

'I know the feeling,' Alison said. She recalled how often she had lain awake in bed over the past twelve months, unable to ignore the plethora of worries that seemed to boil and churn on the ceiling overhead.

John shuffled forward and dropped off the wall, landing lightly on his feet.

'I find that difficult to believe. You don't look to me like a woman who's missed a minute of beauty sleep.'

Alison was glad it was so dark that he wouldn't be able to see her blush.

'Beauty sleep and I parted company many moons ago, Mr Smith. Believe me.'

He smiled.

'Nonsense,' he said sincerely.

Alison hadn't received a compliment about her appearance in nearly twenty years, and quickly changed the subject.

'On behalf of the WI, I would like to thank you for all your help since we started this initiative. Not only have you spread the word wonderfully, you've been as busy as any of us helping people feel reassured and welcome.'

'What you're doing deserves to be brought to their attention. People's nerves have been shredded by the constant raids. They badly need to rest. And while I don't mind sleeping outdoors if I have to, it hardly suits everyone. Especially those with kids.'

'And what – if you don't mind me asking – makes you so robust, Mr Smith?'

'I've travelled a great deal, Mrs Scotlock. Worked in many great shipyards. Sailed in many great ships. When you've slept through a mid-Atlantic storm, the English countryside seems like a giant mattress.'

At that moment Boris let out a loud yawn.

'My apologies, Mrs Scotlock. I'm keeping your dog from his bed.'

'I don't know why he should be remotely tired. He sleeps for ninety per cent of the time these days.'

'Have you far to go?' asked John.

'Not at all.'

'Will . . . Mr Scotlock be waiting up when you get home?'

'I sincerely hope not, Mr Smith. He's been deceased for twenty-two years.'

Alison could see John's mouth open in horror at the faux pas he'd just unwittingly made, and smiled.

'I'm so sorry,' he said.

'Don't be silly. How on earth were you to know? Do you have family, Mr Smith? You seem like the type who would, and yet you appear to travel alone.'

'Perhaps I seem like the type who would like to have had a family? My luck didn't fall in that direction. Came close several times, but the knot refused to be tied.'

'Tell me, Mr Smith: did you really go to prison for beating two men who were attacking a woman? I know you said as much at Mrs Barden's house, but it occurred to me later that you might have doctored your story a little, under the circumstances.'

'Why would I do that?'

'If it was for something worse, you might not have wished us to know.'

'I had no need to tell you at all. But it was part of how I came to find the boy. I was spared, Mrs Scotlock. I have no doubt. Spared to save *him*.'

Alison looked at John for a moment.

'God bless you, Mr Smith.'

'And you, Mrs Scotlock.'

John graciously doffed his hat and looked intently at Alison. She was no longer blushing. She smiled and gently tugged on Boris's lead to prompt him to start moving.

'Come along, boy,' she said. 'I'll see you tomorrow, Mr Smith.'

'I dare say,' he said, smiling. 'By the way, Mrs Scotlock, friends call me *John*.'

'Do you consider me a friend, Mr Smith?'

'I would like to, Mrs Scotlock.'

'Very well, *John*. My friends call me Alison. And this,' she said, gesturing towards Boris, 'is Boris.'

'Unusual name for a dog.'

'Named after my favourite actor.'

'You're a fan of Boris Karloff?'

'Very much.'

'Me too!'

'Really?'

'You like his films?'

'Very much. There's nothing like a scary picture to get the pulse racing.'

'I couldn't agree more. I've seen all his pictures – *Frankenstein, Bride of Frankenstein, Son of Frankenstein.*'

'Did you see him in *The Mummy*?'

'As Imhotep, yes, I did.'

'Did you know he was born in Middlesex?'

'Middlesex? I assumed he was Hungarian or from somewhere like that.'

Alison shook her head and smiled.

'His actual name is William Henry Pratt.'

John smiled back.

'Well I never. Were you tempted to call your dog William?'

'I liked the name Boris before I knew he was really a William. So Boris it was.'

Alison and John looked at one another for a moment.

'Well, good night, John. It was very nice talking to you.'

'And to you, Alison. Perhaps we might continue our mutual admiration another time.'

'Mutual admiration?'

'Of the work of Boris Karloff.'

Alison smiled.

'I'd like that. Good night.'

Alison led Boris away. As they walked, Boris glanced up at her.

'What an agreeable man,' she whispered to the dog. 'Don't you think?'

Boris turned away and focused on the road ahead.

'Of course, you don't think anything except walk, bowl and sleep,' she chided matter-of-factly. 'But I'm telling you. Very agreeable indeed . . .'

Chapter 56

After helping refugees settle for the night, Teresa made her way back to an empty house. Following every air raid, Nick stayed at Tabley Wood until the last of his pilots finally touched back down, remaining to help them depressurise. So it was with some surprise that Teresa walked through the door to be immediately embraced by her husband.

'I heard you coming up the front path,' he said as he kissed her. 'Surprise!'

The odour of cologne, tobacco and beer that rose from his uniform was comforting. After the momentary surprise subsided, Teresa relaxed into Nick's arms and kissed him back.

'Don't ever do that again or I won't be responsible for my actions.'

Nick apologised and kissed her again, more passionately. He tried to draw her towards the staircase and the bedroom, but Teresa subtly dug in her heels.

'I'm exhausted,' she said apologetically. 'Perhaps after a nightcap?'

Teresa watched as Nick prepared them each a drink. Every movement he made was effortlessly fluid, each flowing into the next in a way that reminded her of Annie, who shared the same natural grace that good breeding imbues.

'Why are you home so soon?' she asked, relaxing into the armchair.

'We had a spectacularly good night for a change. Forced back a squadron of Heinkels and brought one down. All over very quickly.'

'Where did it come down?'

'Within ten miles of Great Paxford. We have search teams out.'

'Did the pilots manage to get out?'

It was the question Teresa always asked when Nick reported a kill on either side. From him, she had learned a respect for all pilots, overcoming her natural antipathy to understand that the Germans too were drawn from ranks of young men driven to serve their country.

'We think two parachutes were sighted. But it was dark and overcast, low, dense cloud, so . . .'

'Two? But that's good, isn't it?'

Nick hesitated.

'Heinkels have three pilots.'

He said this without emotion, then sipped his Scotch. Teresa sometimes struggled to remember that as kind and loving as Nick was, he was a soldier, with the instincts and emotional landscape that came with that. He could tell from her expression what she was thinking.

'The loss of that one life will almost certainly have spared many more in Liverpool tonight.'

Teresa nodded.

'I know . . .'

He crossed over to her and crouched before her, taking her hands in his and looking deep into her eyes.

'Don't think about it.'

'I'm not.'

'Ever since you saw the pilot being lifted from the Spitfire you think about what happens to them, and there's no point to it except to hope that it was over quickly. Beyond that you'll simply drive yourself mad trying to mourn every pilot, soldier, sailor, man, woman and child killed by war, because the whole thing is an act of collective insanity.'

For as long as she had known him, Teresa had always marvelled at how clearly Nick viewed war, without a shred of jingoism, without losing a drop of determination to do whatever was needed to protect his country.

'Periodically the most intelligent species on the planet goes crazy and does truly depraved and appalling things to its own kind, with the most sophisticated tools at its disposal. Eventually, the madness clears and we all go back to walking the dog on a Sunday morning, wondering what on earth came over us. It's like a terrible storm that sweeps across the planet until it exhausts itself. There's nothing you can do but step back and let it pass.'

'You don't.'

'I have no choice. I'm in the RAF. I'm of fighting age. I suppose I could become a conchie but I'm simply not configured that way. Never have been. Never will be.'

'Annie doesn't step back and let it pass.'

'Annie's different.'

'If I'm no longer to be allowed to teach, why don't I learn to fly, like her?'

'Because she knew how to fly before she joined the ATA.'

'You could teach me.'

'If you think I want you up there under any circumstances in the current climate you are mad.'

Teresa hadn't been serious about learning to fly. She had suddenly felt a sense of dread about her final day as a schoolteacher, after which she would have all the time in the world to reflect on the terrible accounts Nick brought home from work, unmediated by the daily distraction of classroom drama.

'How would you feel about starting a family when I leave my job?'

Nick looked at Teresa, caught unawares by his wife's question. Then smiled.

'What brought this on?'

'I have to do *something* with my time. And since I'm no longer allowed to be with children *professionally* and you won't let me fly—'

'Isn't it preferable to start a family because you really want children, than as a substitute for a job you'll no longer have? I'd like nothing more than to start a family. But on balance, I'd rather it was because you really wanted to have my sprogs than because you want to produce your own class to teach.'

Having encountered many parents of children in her classes, Teresa felt few behaved as if they had actively chosen to have them. Most seemed to have been drawn along by an ill-defined impulse over which they had little or no control.

'Does it matter, as long as we love them?' she said, smiling.

Nick took a long sip of Scotch and thought about it for a few moments.

'I suppose not.'

At that moment, the telephone began to ring in the hall. Both knew it would be for Nick at this hour. Teresa raised her eyebrows at him, as if to say, 'Now what?'

Nick sighed, set down his glass and hauled himself out of the comfortable armchair in which he'd hoped to see out the evening before bed. He gently kissed the top of Teresa's head on his way out of the room.

Teresa thought about the children she might like. Boys or girls? Little boys were more straightforward, more obedient, but little girls were often more emotionally sophisticated and interesting. However, on balance she thought a boy might be preferable.

Then I can't pass on to a girl the way I am. I would hate a daughter of mine to have to endure this. To have to force herself not to think of . . . certain people . . . because it could destroy her life. Or to give up a profession she loved and was wonderful at because she got married.

The door opened and Nick returned, sombre-faced.

'They've found the plane.'

'The plane?'

'The Heinkel. We had a decent fix on its location from the Observation bods.'

'And?'

'One pilot was still strapped into his seat. Another was dead on his parachute, hanging from a tree a hundred feet from the wreckage – sounds like the poor bugger left it too late to bail out.'

Nick let out a deep, mournful sigh, knowing he could be talking like this about German pilots tonight and in exactly the same terms about his own boys tomorrow. Boys against boys.

'And the third?' Teresa asked.

'Not found.'

'What does that mean, "not found"?'

Nick collapsed back into the armchair and let the air leave his lungs. He picked up his glass and swirled the Scotch around. He peered into the amber liquid, as if trying to divine the fate of the third pilot within its mini-whirlpool.

'Poor bugger's probably lying face down in the middle of a field somewhere,' he said wearily, 'waiting to be discovered by some equally poor bugger in the morning.'

Nick poured the remainder of the whisky into his mouth and swallowed it. He looked over at Teresa.

'Please don't think about it, darling,' he said.

'I won't,' she replied, though she already was.

We have to think about these boys. Even for a moment. If I was – when I am – a mother, I would want someone to think of my son on the night his plane went down.

'By all means let's start a family when you finish teaching. But let's have girls,' Nick said, laying his head back on the chair's headrest and closing his eyes.

'Lots of lovely girls . . . who don't fly planes, or carry guns.'

Teresa looked at Nick and didn't think she had ever seen him so tired.

'Some girls fly planes.'

'Not in anger they don't.'

'I've heard Annie say she would if she was allowed.'

Nick kept his eyes closed.

'Annie says a lot of things for effect. You shouldn't believe the half of it.'

Nick calmly folded his hands across his stomach, and sat there, with his legs stretched out, like an old man practising the most comfortable position in which to be laid to rest. Teresa looked at him for a few moments.

'Which half should I believe?' she asked, knowing he was already asleep.

Chapter 57

THE THIRD GERMAN pilot wasn't found face down in a field the following morning, or anywhere else. Nor the morning after that. By the third morning of the pilot's body failing to come to light the authorities flooded the area with personnel and sniffer dogs, and placed the local population on alert.

People were told to keep to population centres wherever possible, and not journey across country alone.

Those who worked the land were told to work in groups, and to keep a shotgun nearby.

Any sighting of any unknown person behaving in a suspect manner, or who looked as if they were carrying an injury, was to be immediately reported to the police. On no account were they to be approached.

Any theft of clothing from washing lines, or discovery of an abandoned parachute, was also to be immediately reported to the police. Similarly, any fresh damage or break-ins to outbuildings.

The authorities initially had no idea if the pilot was alive or dead, but they couldn't take any chances. To try to prevent incidents of mistaken identity and a potential lynching if the pilot should be found, they banned unauthorised, armed search parties roaming the countryside, and emphasised that the pilot was more use to them alive than dead.

The village school was closed until further notice.

On the afternoon of the third day a reconnaissance plane swept low over the area for any clues to the German pilot's whereabouts.

In Great Paxford, women queuing in Brindsley's for meat rations spoke nervously of their fears about the missing pilot; while their husbands propped up the bar in the Black Horse and outdid one another with gruesome accounts of what they'd do to 'Fritz' if they caught him.

Parents tried to avoid their sons and daughters being scared witless, but in the minds of most children in the village 'a Nazi pilot on the loose' was perhaps the most exciting thing to have ever happened in the history of the world. Most assumed he would look and sound like Hitler. They did a splendid job of scaring one another silly, though all their games ended in the pilot's capture and bloody execution.

Theories abounded about the pilot's whereabouts. One suggested he had landed injured, then hidden himself in woodland according to his 'Nazi training' to give his body time enough to recover before escaping – living off nuts and berries and anything he could shoot with a service revolver. Another suggested he had perished while parachuting down, but had landed in thick undergrowth, or in a ravine, his body invisible either from above or on the ground. Another thought his parachute might have caught a heavy gust during its descent and taken the pilot out of the area. Another proposed the pilot had landed perfectly safely, and left the region on foot long before the authorities discovered the downed aircraft and realised he was missing.

In reality, no one knew anything. Yet it took very little to make people nervous, and generate endless speculation and rumour. The population had been primed for it since the outbreak of the war, and the pilot embodied everyone's worst fears. In no time, he became characterised as a cold-blooded killer Nazi who would stop at nothing to slaughter as many English people as he could, children included. Suddenly, all strangers were looked upon with intense suspicion.

The hunt for the missing airman even affected the Barden household. With Noah returned and revived, and his grandfather responding favourably to Frances's offer to formally adopt the boy, Frances became extremely protective. When he played in the garden with Spencer and Claire, Frances stood guard at the French windows, looking this way and that for any unexpected movement in the shrubs, or around the large pond at the bottom of the garden. Sarah watched her sister from the comfort of the sofa.

'I don't know what you're expecting to see, Frances. I very much doubt this pilot is planning to launch a surprise attack on the house from your bulrushes.'

'Who knows what state of desperation he might be in?' replied Frances. 'He might be starving, driven to stop at nothing to find food. Or he might decide Noah could be used as a bargaining chip to secure his return to Germany.'

'Oh really,' said Sarah, despairing at her sister's tendency to opt for the most lurid possible outcome.

'My point is, none of us can afford to let our guard down until the man is captured.'

Sarah considered her sister's words for a few moments.

'In the interest of fairness, if not rationality, shouldn't you consider the possibility that outside of his cockpit he might not be the demon everyone assumes?'

Frances wasn't having it.

'You do speak such rot sometimes. The man is a Nazi. He wasn't dropping liver sausage and volumes of Goethe.'

'You're mistaking a man with his job. Out of his cockpit he's no longer a pilot, but a young man lost in enemy territory.'

'You sound remarkably charitable towards someone who has almost certainly been responsible for the deaths of many of your fellow countrymen and women.'

'Young men have been co-opted to kill on both sides.'

'We don't do to them what they're doing to us. This pilot could emerge from hiding and simply run amok, indiscriminately killing men, women or children. By all accounts, it's the Nazi way. So please do not scold me for being overcautious where Noah is concerned.'

Sarah sighed, realising Frances was not open to any form of reason on the issue.

'Adam would feel tremendously sad to see Great Paxfordians reacting like this. Talking as they are. Whipping one another into a frenzy. Terror spreads by association, passed on by word of mouth. We shouldn't be a part of it.'

Frances baulked at the implied insult.

'Being vigilant is not the same as being "in a frenzy", Sarah. You know, I really do object to the way you choose to characterise yourself as the only calm, sensible person in most given situations. It's the vicar's wife in you, and occasionally it really grates.'

'As Adam was at pains to point out in several of his sermons before joining up, while all Nazis are German, not all Germans are Nazis.'

'Then why doesn't he give himself up?'

'Because he's probably dead!'

Frances turned back to look out of the window.

'All the same, I think I'll have Claire and Spencer bring Noah inside.'

'Why don't you do that. And then you can wrap him from head to toe in cotton wool and stack him in the cellar on the one remaining wine rack.'

Frances turned again and looked at Sarah.

'We are at war, Sarah,' she said, her voice adopting the tone and timbre of the Chair of Great Paxford's WI.

'I know, "Madame Chair",' mocked Sarah. 'The empty space in my bed each night is a constant reminder.'

Frances was not put off.

'In life as in war,' she said, 'we should prepare for the worst and hope for the best. *Not* the other way round.'

* * *

By the early evening of the third day of the pilot remaining undiscovered, the village was starting to be consumed by mushrooming anxiety. People left their houses only if they had to. Though a few households had locked their doors and windows at night in response to the influx of refugees into the area, now every single front door and window was bolted shut as nightfall and rain swept slowly over the landscape. Men and boys looked out of windows and watched the ranging torch beams of official search parties in the distance, wondering how long the manhunt would continue.

Whether it actually was or not, it felt to many Great Paxfordians that a malevolent force was among them, poised to do them harm.

For the moment, it seemed as if their little Cheshire village had found itself on the front line of the war.

Chapter 58

IT WAS STILL RAINING at 1.43 in the morning when the telephone started ringing in the Lucas household. Giving her all to teaching was the only way Teresa knew how, or wanted, to do the job, but it was exhausting, and she customarily slept extremely well. She was fast asleep now, and remained that way as the telephone rang in the hall downstairs. But if Nick's wife slept like a log as a result of her job, then his own, placing him on constant standby, meant Nick slept like a twig, and he woke almost the instant the telephone started to ring. He hurried downstairs, knowing it wouldn't be ringing at this hour without reason. By the time he ran back up, Teresa had been roused enough to register Nick's absence from their bed, and heard him changing from his pyjamas into his uniform as quietly as possible.

'Don't tell me,' she mumbled, her face buried in a pillow. 'You've had word that Goering's sending over paratroops to rescue the missing pilot . . .'

'There's been an accident at the station,' he said, his voice low and clipped.

'There are always accidents at the station. What kind of accident at the station?' she said, trying to sound more interested in what may have happened at Tabley Wood than in going back to sleep. 'Someone slipped on some oil kind of accident? Fell off a wing accident? Isn't that the thing about accidents?' she burbled softly, her brain urging her back towards unconsciousness. 'They're accidental. Let someone else deal with it . . .'

She patted the still-warm empty space where Nick should be to emphasise her point. Nick was too focused on getting ready as swiftly as possible to react to Teresa's inchoate train of thought.

'Slightly more serious than someone slipping over. Two replacement Hurricanes were being delivered tonight. One landed badly in atrocious conditions.'

Teresa slowly rolled onto her back and reluctantly opened her eyes one at a time, and tried to bring Nick into focus in the dark. He was almost dressed, putting on his shoes. She could now hear the sound of the rain being driven against the bedroom window.

'How badly is badly?'

'Pretty badly.'

'The Hurricane or the pilot?'

'Both. I have to go.' His voice was professional. Orders given with ease. 'Go back to sleep.'

Teresa managed to sit herself up, resting on her elbows.

'I don't understand why you need to go. You can't single-handedly win the war, Nick. You also need to sleep. You've been informed. You've no doubt issued some orders. What can you actually do in that situation? Even a wing commander needs to rest if he's to wing-command effectively.'

Nick did up the buttons of his tunic and looked down at Teresa lying on the bed.

'The injured pilot is Annie.'

Teresa was instantaneously a hundred per cent awake. She had been rather successful at forcing the ATA pilot from her mind over recent weeks, but all her memories rushed back in the moment Nick said her name, and she suddenly felt sick with fear.

'Annie?' she asked.

'By all accounts, she came out of low cloud too fast. Perhaps her altimeter wasn't properly calibrated. Made a very hard landing. The undercarriage buckled and she skidded off the runway.' Nick tried to sound factual, but Teresa could hear the emotion in his voice.

'Is she hurt?'

Teresa tried to control her breathing so that she could get the words out without looking more concerned than Nick would have expected. As she did so she could hear her pulse pump in her ears.

'I've only been told that she was taken directly from the cockpit to the hospital. I'm going over to find out how she is.'

Teresa's heart was thumping so loudly she thought Nick must hear it.

'I'll come with you,' she said, swinging her legs over the side of her bed.

'Little point us both being exhausted.'

Teresa stood up and gathered her clothes.

'Annie's a good friend of yours. She's been a guest in my house. On the few occasions I've met her I have seen why you like her so much. If her family can't be with her at this time then we should be.'

Nick looked at Teresa with immense fondness.

471

'And that is precisely why I've never doubted for a moment why I married you.'

While Nick drove as fast as he dared along the dark country lane in heavy wind and rain, Teresa stared out of the car window.

Tears began to gather in her eyes. In daylight she would have brushed them quickly away so that Nick wouldn't see. But the only light came from the car's headlights, and Nick was focused on the road.

If Annie were to die tonight . . . ?

Teresa couldn't bring herself to finish the question, let alone begin to frame an answer. The very thought of Annie dying sent her mind reeling.

The car suddenly slowed, distracting Teresa from the dread that was spreading from the pit of her stomach. She turned and looked through the windscreen to see what had prompted the change in speed, and saw the cottage hospital emerge from the darkness.

Inside the hospital, they were told Annie was in the operating theatre. She had suffered multiple fractures and significant internal bleeding that the surgeon was trying to stop. The nursing sister didn't sugar the pill.

'Her injuries are life-threatening.' While she waited for Nick and Teresa to absorb this information, she continued, 'May I ask what blood groups you are? We're somewhat short of Miss Carter's type, and she is likely to need transfusions both during and after surgery.'

'I'm AB,' said Nick.

'Thank you, but no use, I'm afraid. Annie is type A.'

Much more usefully, Teresa was blood group O, which brought a momentary smile to the sister's face. The sister asked if Teresa would mind giving some.

'Of course not. Take as much as you need.'

'We can't take too much or you'll need some of it back,' said the sister gently.

'Of course. I meant—'

'I know what you meant,' said the sister with a smile. 'Please follow me and we'll take it right away.'

Nick took Teresa by the arm.

'Will you be all right to stay here? Only I have to get back to Tabley Wood and assess the damage to the Hurricane. If it's beyond repair I'll need to request an immediate replacement.'

'Of course. I'm only too glad to be able to do something useful, even if it's just having a needle stuck in my arm.'

'Don't minimise it. What you give could turn out to be the difference between life and death. I've seen it. A single pint can make the difference.'

The sister nodded in agreement.

'Absolutely.'

Nick kissed Teresa and hurried away. Teresa heard the screech of his tyres on the tarmac outside, and was then taken through to a side room and prepped to give blood.

As her arm was cleaned, and strapped up to raise a vein, Teresa imagined Annie lying unconscious, her life hanging in the balance. A lump of emotion formed in her throat, prompting tears to well in her eyes. She blinked them back and forced herself to watch the thin, red stream of blood pass out of her arm and into the blood bag.

What if, even with my contribution, they still don't have enough to save Annie? She took several deep breaths, closed her eyes, composed her thoughts for several moments, and addressed God.

You haven't heard much from me since Connie died. I won't apologise. I'm sure the number of times you hear from my mother makes up for my relative silence. But I'm speaking to you now. Not on my behalf, but for a friend. I won't waste your time. Just save Annie. Everyone's doing what they can here, but you might have more sway. Just save her. Not for my benefit. Because you should.

'Amen.'

Teresa hadn't meant to say the word out loud, but old Catholic habits die hard. She glanced up at the nurse taking her blood, and saw she wore a silver crucifix around her neck on a thin chain. The nurse smiled at Teresa knowingly, and rechecked the blood flow. Teresa felt suddenly self-conscious, as if the nurse could have divined the exact nature and context of her prayer. She rested her head back and closed her eyes once more.

Why take her now? What purpose would it serve? Don't do this. Not this. Anything but this.

Chapter 59

Erica, Kate and Laura had been sitting with Will for several hours. They had read to him for a time, and then helped him get comfortable for sleep, and watched him drift off. They then sat and quietly shared memories about him until he was prompted from unconsciousness and watched them, smiling, before eventually rolling back into sleep for another brief period. Such was the cycle as Will's life approached its end. He'd been home from the hospital for two weeks but now seemed to be slipping quickly away.

Will had been asleep when they heard a loud bang nearby, causing the women to turn towards the window.

'Did the noise wake you?' asked Erica.

Will blinked slowly at her.

'A car backfired outside, darling.'

Will looked at them for a brief moment and slowly closed his eyes once more.

'Do you think he understood what you said?' asked Laura quietly. 'I no longer know what he understands and what he doesn't. Do you think he even understands what a car backfiring means anymore?'

'I'm not sure,' said Erica. 'I assume he does.'

'I assume he understands everything we say,' said Kate. 'But it's difficult. He says so little now. And it's not always connected to what we may have said to him, so I don't know if he thinks he's having a conversation, or just saying whatever's in his mind.'

They watched Will as he drew heavily on the oxygen pouring into his airway through his face mask. Almost as if he sensed his wife and daughters looking at him, Will opened his eyes. They took a moment to focus on the space around him, a moment for him to recognise where he was, and who these three faces looking at him belonged to. Finally, his lips slowly curled into the rough shape of his once-dazzling smile.

'Hello, darling,' said Erica warmly. 'Welcome back.'

Will blinked slowly, and with some effort extended his arm so that his hand touched Erica's. She instantly placed her hand in his and waited for him to slowly wrap his fingers around it. But this time he did not. Erica looked down and watched as his fingers flexed feebly without managing to encapsulate Erica's hand. After a few moments, Will's muscles gave up and Erica's hand lay on Will's open palm. She gripped his hand instead, and looked at his face, sensing the fight to remain alive was draining from him. His eyes looked intently at her, the dark brown irises devoid of their customary gloss. After a moment, his mouth started to open and then close. Kate sensed he wanted to speak and reached forward and carefully pulled the oxygen mask to one side. Will followed her movements with his eyes and took a long, deep breath. He looked at Laura, then Kate, and finally Erica. She moved closer, putting her ear to his mouth.

'I think . . . it's time to . . . let someone . . . else have a go . . .' he croaked, almost inaudibly, in the hoarse whisper that had replaced his voice. All of them heard his words, and immediately understood what he meant.

Laura felt her throat tighten. Erica clasped Will's hand tight. Kate's vision became cloudy with tears.

'My three beautiful . . . girls . . .' he whispered as he exhaled.

Will looked at them and tried to smile once more. Kate reached forward to replace the oxygen mask across his face. He rested the back of his head against his pillow and closed his eyes. His chest took an age to rise again, and another age to fall.

'Mum . . . ?' Laura's voice was low and fearful.

Erica turned to her youngest daughter and looked at her with a steadfast gaze. She could feel that the corners of her mouth were involuntarily turned downwards with sadness, but fought the overwhelming urge to fall apart.

'We have to let him leave, darling. We can't insist that he stay on like this. Because he will try, you know that. He will try his utmost for us, as he always has. And it isn't fair.'

Erica managed to make her voice sound soft yet firm and in control. It reminded her daughters of how she used to speak to them when they were small children.

Kate placed her hand gently on Laura's shoulder and gave her a reassuring squeeze. Erica leaned forward so that her mouth was against Will's right ear.

'Go, my darling,' she whispered. 'I have never loved you more, and I shall never stop loving you. But you can go free now. You don't have to stay for us. We'll be fine. Because of you.'

Erica rested her head on his shoulder and calmly stroked Will's head with her right hand. A single tear slipped out of her eye and slid slowly down her cheek as she closed her eyes and listened to his chest slowly fill with air like a ruptured bellows, before slowly emptying once again. She stayed in that position for what felt like hours, soothed by the sound of his chest slowly reinflating after each exhale, according to its lifelong rhythm. Until, suddenly, it did not.

He's gone.

Erica lifted her head and looked at Will's face. His eyes were closed and his mouth slightly ajar. But his breathing had ceased. She could feel the last of his warmth through her fingertips. Everything in the room became suddenly still. Specks of dust gliding lazily across beams of late afternoon sunlight seemed to momentarily halt in their passage through the air.

Laura looked at her father's face. It seemed more relaxed than she had seen it since the Spitfire crash. She thought she had prepared herself for this, yet realised she wasn't remotely prepared for it. She heard her sister begin to sob beside her and took Kate in her arms, holding on to her tightly.

Erica lay against her husband as Laura gently rocked Kate back and forth, none of them resisting the tears that started to freely flow. Eventually, Erica forced herself to sit up. She gathered her daughters to her, and held them close.

They remained this way long into the night.

Chapter 60

Pat was standing behind the trestle table in St Mark's, ladling soup into a refugee's bowl, when she heard what sounded like a door being loudly slammed near by. Everyone looked round. Pat wondered if the wind had slammed the church door closed, but when she looked she saw it was still open, and people were still wandering in out of the rain.

Her thoughts swiftly returned to Marek's letter, and to how he might respond to her own. Though the arrival of Marek's first letter two weeks earlier had been an immense moment of happiness, Pat was eager to establish a reliable line of communication so as to deepen their relationship and seriously discuss the future. She had hoped Marek might reply to her own letter by return of post, but when it failed to materialise she hoped a new letter from him would be no more than a week away. It was now almost two, and nothing had come. She understood he would be busy with the new training he'd alluded to, but the longer Pat had to wait before hearing from him, the more difficult it was to keep doubts, old and new, from creeping into her mind.

She tried to persuade herself she was being over-anxious. Yet the line of contact now connecting her to Marek felt so fragile and vulnerable that she was unable to feel confident that it would be sustained. She had written as much to Marek.

I have no wish to write this, but you could be consumed by the war and I would never learn why or where. If there is a list of loved ones you can ask to be informed in the event of your death, please, please include me. I have lived in hope of hearing from you since your departure from Great Paxford, and almost gave up. Not knowing where you were, or how you felt, was the most desolate feeling in the world. It all but shattered my nerves. I have grown used to living with unhappiness living with Bob. But uncertainty eats away at a person from the inside out. Write back quickly, my love . . .

But he hadn't.

Perhaps his letter's been waylaid. If the Germans are targeting the railways it could be stuck in a sack in a siding. Will he write again if he doesn't hear from me soon? Should I write again in lieu of hearing back from him? Has he decided not to write again? Did I write something, some line, that pushed him away somehow?

Pat kept checking the door to see if Erica might walk through, hopefully with a letter for her. But she didn't.

I hope everything is all right with Will.

She noticed more refugees in St Mark's on this night than on the previous nights she had been here.

The weather's enough to drive a fox indoors.

News of Great Paxford WI's initiative had clearly spread, and more and more people were being drawn to the church by the seasonally inclement weather and dropping temperature.

The queue for food snaked around several pews. Pat served as fast as she could to meet demand. She found it helped distract her from negative thoughts about Marek's failure to reply. She barely looked up as she ladled soup from cauldron to bowl, cauldron to bowl, as the refugees nodded their thanks before walking on, keeping the queue moving at a brisk pace. On previous nights, Pat had heard one of Mrs Talbot's friends complain that the trekkers seldom voiced their thanks for the food and shelter, calling them 'ungrateful'. Pat felt their sincere nods of appreciation communicated thanks enough.

Basic decency doesn't require a slap on the back. It should be the norm.

As soup was dispensed from the cauldron more was added to it from the stove in the vestry. Pat continued to fill bowls with soup until the queue eventually began to dwindle. With her attention focused on the remaining refugees, she failed to notice a stocky-looking man wearing a cap low over his brow saunter into the church alone, look briefly around, then join the end of the soup queue. Had the church been full of paranoid local villagers and not folk from out of the area, someone might have nudged the person next to them to whisper, 'Is that him? The Nazi pilot? What do you think? Don't look! Out of the corner of your eye. Well? Go and find a policeman!'

The man took a bowl from the stack, shuffled forward, and patiently held out his bowl when it was his turn. He watched as Pat expertly poured the soup from the ladle into the bowl. When she had finished he said in a soft voice, 'Thank you, Patricia.'

For the briefest of moments Pat failed to question how the refugee standing before her knew her name. She looked at him, puzzled. Had they spoken on a previous night? There was something familiar about him. His height, and breadth across the shoulders. His hands. It was then that he lifted his head and Pat saw Marek smiling at her from under his cap, his pale blue eyes fixed on her. Pat's eyes widened in shock, the ladle slipping out of her fingers and clattering against the side of the cauldron before disappearing into the soup.

'Marek . . . !' she said so quietly that she barely heard it herself.

'Hello, my love,' he whispered back. 'I had to come . . .'

Chapter 61

Teresa had been dozing at Annie's bedside for a couple of hours when she was woken by a loud noise that sounded like a car door being banged shut on the drive outside. She had been determined to be present when Annie woke from the anaesthetic, but the consequences of having her night's sleep interrupted sixteen hours earlier had gradually snuck up on her as morning passed into afternoon and then into early evening. She had grabbed a bite to eat along the way, and Nick had popped back from Tabley Wood around three o'clock to check on Annie's progress. The surgery to repair a torn artery in her leg and reset several broken bones had been extensive. He would have liked to have stayed at Annie's bedside with Teresa, but couldn't afford the time.

'I wish I didn't have to, but I do have to get back,' he said.

'She'll perfectly understand,' said Teresa. 'I'll stay.'

'She wouldn't expect you to,' said Nick.

'Everyone should wake up from a serious operation to a friendly face. Have you contacted her family?'

Nick nodded.

'They all live in Africa. I've sent telegrams advising them of the situation, and promising further information as it arises. I've written too many telegrams of that ilk since taking over from Bowers. Never imagined for a moment I'd be writing one about Annie.'

'Is there a boyfriend in England you could contact?' Teresa asked, concluding the expected line of query, though she knew the answer.

'Boyfriend?'

Nick looked at Teresa for a moment, weighing up how to respond. He took a deep breath. Evidently, there were certain areas where Teresa was not as worldly as he believed. After a moment he said, 'Annie doesn't have boyfriends, darling. There's something you may as well know about Annie. Should she pull through, it may allay future misunderstanding.'

Nick had adopted a conspiratorial tone.

'What do you mean?' asked Teresa. 'Misunderstanding about what?'

'You're not to mention this to anyone . . .'

'Mention what?'

'What I'm about to tell you.'

Nick glanced up and down the ward then moved his head closer to Teresa.

'Annie doesn't have boyfriends because she prefers . . . female companionship.'

Teresa looked at Nick and blinked a few times, struggling to digest that Nick knew about Annie, had known all along.

'Female companionship?' she said.

'She prefers the company of other women,' said Nick, very much hoping this would be as explicit as he needed to be. He placed his forefinger over his mouth. '*Mum* is very much the word.'

Teresa saw an opportunity to glean more information about Annie.

'How do you know this?' she asked.

'Annie always has a lot of chaps buzzing around her in the mess. I noticed she never went farther than drinks with any of them. And never mentioned a chap she was seeing. On one occasion, one of the boys with too much beer inside him tried his luck and Annie politely declined his offer. He persisted and Annie told him in no uncertain terms she wasn't interested. He accused her of being a lesbian – or a word to that effect – and Annie threw her drink in his face and walked out. But . . . I hadn't been drinking that night, and I could see he'd struck a chord.'

'So, she has never actually told you what you've just told me? It's just supposition on your part?'

'*Informed* supposition.'

'I see,' said Teresa as flatly as she could manage.

'I suspect that's why I've always thought of her more in terms of being a pal than anything else. We got on famously from the off, but not in a boy–girl way.'

'No?'

'I've never had that feeling with Annie, ever. If you add it all up it makes sense.'

Teresa nodded sagely, trying to look as if she were weighing Nick's words carefully. Inside, a worry had started to nag at her.

If Nick can spot Annie, how long will it be before he'll spot me? No, stop. Think. He's spent far more time with me than with her.

485

If I was giving him anything to notice he would have noticed by now. Calm down. Don't panic. Unless . . . he thinks he's noticed something but isn't certain.

Teresa struggled to stop her imagination from running away with itself.

It may be easier to detect in the mess. Boys and girls together. Heightened emotions. Everyone copping off with one another in the heat of the moment. Why wouldn't I be good at pretending to be a normal wife? At a certain level, teaching a class full of children is a performance of sorts. You have to stand in front of a room full of children every day and persuade them your word is law, regardless of how you might be feeling.

Teresa gathered herself together, at least long enough to see Nick off. He needed to return to Tabley Wood for a briefing about the ongoing search for the missing German pilot. The local forces were coming under pressure from London to find the aviator dead or alive, and bring the matter to a close. The longer something like this went on, the more it chopped away at the population's faith in authority, which was bad for morale.

* * *

Disturbed from her own slumber, Teresa rubbed her eyes and turned to look at Annie. The sight of the young pilot covered in plaster and bandages raised a lump in her throat. Every other time she had seen Annie she had seemed invulnerable. The sight of her now, her life brought to the precipice, reversed that. In a single moment of miscalculation Annie had become the most vulnerable person Teresa had ever known.

She could yet die. The doctors may have missed something. Or made a mistake.

Teresa reached out, gently took Annie's warm hand in hers and held it tightly, hoping to communicate some sense of solidarity, companionship, support through her touch. Teresa looked closely at Annie's swollen, bandaged face to see if she was conscious, but there was no sign. Just a great deal of swelling and bruising.

Teresa looked round the rest of the ward. Mostly men. All asleep. She looked back at Annie and shuffled her chair closer.

'You need to be careful. Nick knows about you,' she said softly. 'Or thinks he does. But then, short of telling people, you've never really hidden it, have you? Not like me. It's what I admired about you from the moment I first saw you. Unashamed. You have to pull through, Annie. You simply must.'

Even now, smashed and discoloured as she was, Annie's refinement somehow managed to shine through. Teresa suddenly felt compelled to kiss the unconscious young woman. She looked round the ward, and then towards the door. No one was looking.

What if someone sees?

Teresa sighed and sat back in the chair. Annie's fingers started to tighten around her own. Teresa looked down at her hand and then at Annie's face. Her eyes were closed. She looked round the ward a second time, then leaned forward, closed her eyes and pressed her lips against Annie's, feeling their warmth and softness. As she lifted her face to take a breath Teresa was shocked to see that Annie's eyes were open, looking at her.

'Well done,' Annie mumbled. 'Don't stop . . .'

Chapter 62

STEPH FARROW WAS in the farmhouse preparing supper for herself, Little Stan and Isobel. Bryn always gave her a little 'extra' meat on top of her ration in exchange for a few extra eggs every week, and she was cutting it into strips for a stew. It was usually while preparing supper that Steph felt closest to her husband, Stan. She wondered where his regiment was, and what plans were being made for him by High Command. She wondered how he was faring with the physical side of being back in the army. Stan was extremely strong, but his muscles had been developed and fine-tuned for farm work, not for racing across open land, or crawling through ditches, avoiding shells and bullets. He was thickset and brawny.

An easy target.

She knew Stan would be taking the younger men – especially the conscripts – under his wing, building their confidence, allaying their fears. He had told her once that most soldiers lost their nerve before going into action, and the younger ones saw it as a cause of shame. He told them it was proof they'd put themselves on the line. When Little Stan was a boy and afraid to jump into the dark waters of Deer Park Mere, Stan told him, 'Bravery isn't having no fear. It's overcoming it'. It worked, and Little Stan learned to swim that day.

So proud of him, we were. Stan carried him all the way home on his shoulders.

Steph looked out of the kitchen window and could just about make out the figure of her son in Bottom Field. Farmers had been advised not to work alone while the German pilot was at large, but the authorities had checked all the buildings of Farrow farm, with no sign of disturbance or anything out of place.

Most of the farmers round here think he's long gone.

Though Steph had double-checked the henhouse before sending Isobel in to collect any eggs the chickens had laid during the day.

*   *   *

Little Stan was repairing the wall in Bottom Field, following the dry-stone method his father had taught him, filling any holes carefully, judging how to knit small stones with large to make a structure strong enough to withstand any weather, or livestock trying to rub away an itch. The light was beginning to wane and he reckoned on remaining out for no longer than five or ten more minutes. The ground was soft and wet underfoot. The previous day's deluge had left the ground sodden, before being blown east.

Little Stan looked forward to supper and then an evening stretched out in front of the parlour fire. His mind drifted to his father's whereabouts. He revisited images of military campaigns from newsreels he'd watched in the village hall, implanting his father into various acts of derring-do. He longed to join up himself, but Steph had forbidden it.

'I'm not planning on losing one man from this family,' she'd told him, 'let alone two.'

By the time Little Stan started to pack away his tools he was standing in the penumbral gloom between the still-light field and the darkness of the wood. He had picked up the tool bag and turned for home when he heard a small click behind him. If it had been the low snap of a twig under the foot of a fox or badger Little Stan would barely have registered the noise. But this was more subtle, mechanical, like a lever of some sort being carefully moved into position. He had started to turn back towards the wood when he heard two words in a foreign language.

'*Hände hoch.*'

The voice was low and firm and German.

Little Stan recognised the instruction from comics he'd read, and films he'd seen about the first war.

Hands up.

A tingle went from the very top of his head to the soles of his feet, as his body suddenly flushed with adrenaline.

'*Hände hoch,*' came the command a second time. '*Jetzt.*'

Little Stan dropped the tool bag, slowly raised his arms and turned to find himself facing a young German man, no more than a year or two older than himself, pointing a pistol at him. He was about the same height as Little Stan, with similar sandy-coloured hair. The German's hands were filthy, and the hand pointing the gun trembled with cold. A field dressing was wound around his head to staunch the flow of blood from an injury he'd suffered on landing.

'*Lebensmittel*,' the pilot said exhaustedly.

Little Stan frowned with incomprehension and the German repeated the word with added force, '*Lebensmittel!*'

He followed this up with a brief mime of eating.

'*Hungrig.*'

The pilot gestured with his gun that Little Stan should start walking towards the farmhouse.

'*Bleib ruhig. Ich werde dich nicht verletzen.*'

Little Stan's attempt to fathom what the German was saying to him suddenly gave way to the primal impulse to save himself by whatever means necessary. He gave out a loud yell to distract the pilot, and broke into a sprint across the field towards the farmhouse three hundred yards away. He could hear the German screaming incomprehensibly behind him. Little Stan looked desperately over his shoulder and saw the German gaining on him, holding his gun out in front of him. Little Stan was gripped by a mortal terror and began to scream for his mother as he ran.

'Ma!' he cried out at the very top of his lungs. 'Ma! The Nazi! He's here! Help me! Ma!'

For every syllable yelled by Little Stan for his mother to come and save him the German shouted four more to entreat him to shut his mouth.

But nothing and no one could have stopped Little Stan running for his life in that moment. The sight of the pilot over his shoulder, still gaining on him, condensed his screamed words into an incoherent shriek of desperation.

When he was within reach, the German pilot launched himself at Little Stan, bringing him crashing to the ground, covering them both in wet grass and mud. Little Stan was convinced he was about to be shot, and flailed his arms around to try to wrestle free of the pilot's tight grip. The two young men tumbled across the pasture, each trying to gain supremacy over the other, each screaming words in a language the other didn't understand. One moment, the pilot was on top of Little Stan, pinning him to the ground. The next, Little Stan threw him off and scrambled to his feet, only for the German to grab him by his legs, and pull him back down to the ground. Suddenly, the pilot was on top of Little Stan once more, pressing one hand over the Englishman's mouth to prevent him from shouting out and giving away his location, and pointing his service revolver at his face with the other, all the while hissing at him in German to stop screaming.

The next moment brought a deafening gunshot.

With the report still ringing in her ears, Steph watched the pilot slump forward on top of her son. Almost immediately, her hands began to tremble, but she was unable to lower the shotgun. The muscles holding it had completely locked up. Momentarily shocked by the noise, Little Stan slowly turned his head and saw his mother standing ten feet from him, still aiming the shotgun at the motionless pilot.

'St-St-Stanley?' she said, unable to stop her teeth chattering from the adrenaline racing around her body.

'Ma?' he replied, sounding five years old again.

'Are you hurt?'

'I . . . don't think so.'

'Come away, then.'

Little Stan took a deep breath, pushed the German off and ran to his mother. He looked at her, still holding the shotgun aloft, as if ready to shoot someone else.

'He's dead, Ma. Put the gun down. You killed him.'

'*Killed . . . ?*'

Steph stayed in position for a few moments longer, then slowly forced her arms to lower the shotgun.

I killed him . . .

Mother and son stood and looked down at the dead German, now lying on his back, staring up at the first stars of the night. The pilot didn't look dead at all, but relaxed. His arms were outstretched and his legs splayed. Unseen, underneath, his blood silently drained out of his body, and soaked into the soft English earth.

Little Stan stared at the pilot with awe.

'Bloody Hell, Ma . . .' he whispered, as if speaking louder might reawaken his assailant. 'You've only gone and killed the bugger!'

Steph hadn't moved from the spot since pulling the trigger. Her only thought had been 'save Stanley'.

I have. Stanley's alive, thank God.

Isobel had left the henhouse in response to the shotgun blast, and started calling for Steph from the farmyard. Little Stan turned towards her.

'She's killed him, Isobel!' he shouted. 'Ma killed the Kraut pilot! One bloody shot! Straight through his back! He was going to kill me, but Ma killed him first!'

He turned back to his mother, who was still staring at the pilot, and gazed at her with admiration.

'Bloody hell.'

What have I done? Go back! Go back! Please, let me just go back sixty seconds!

But there was no going back.

The trigger had been pulled.

The blast had resounded across the field into the village, where some had mistaken the sound for something far more benign.

Steph had killed a human being, and everything had changed.

Go back!

As intensely as she wished it were possible, there was no way back from this moment. Only forward, into an increasingly uncertain future of truths and consequences.

Welcome to the world of
Keep the Home Fires Burning!

Keep reading for a Q&A with the author, to discover a recipe
that features in this novel and to find out more about
what is coming next . . .

We'd also like to introduce you to MEMORY LANE, our special
community for the very best of saga writing from authors you
know and love and new ones we simply can't wait for you to
meet. Read on and join our club!

www.MemoryLane.club

Dear Reader,

When *Home Fires* was cancelled on television after two successful series, I felt it inconceivable that I would ever return to Great Paxford and the characters who inhabited the small Cheshire village. At the time, I felt a form of grief over the sudden loss of contact with that place, and those women and men; and a deep sense of frustration that I wouldn't be able to see their stories through to the end of the war – which had been the expectation of both myself and the television audience. Consequently, I can't describe how wonderful it is to be writing this letter eighteen months later, having resurrected *Home Fires* here, as the first in a series of at least three *Keep the Home Fires Burning* novels.

When I sat down to start writing the book my ambition was for you to read the book and see the drama unfolding in your mind's eye. I did wonder if I would have the same access to the characters as I had when writing the television series. Yes, I could call them all by the same names, but I was concerned I wouldn't be able to bring them to life in the same way on the page as I had on screen; nor achieve the same tone that had so coloured the series. I thought it would be difficult, if not impossible. But after some trial and error, I began to hear their familiar voices once more, and felt their stories starting to flow from the moment they were left staring open-mouthed at the Spitfire sticking out of the Campbell house (at the end of series two).

Throughout the writing process, I have been extremely fortunate. Without the patience, support, and encouragement of the publisher I doubt I would be writing this letter to you. I have also been immeasurably helped by the fact that I have been able to acutely picture the characters in the book as they had been so magnificently been brought to life on screen, by what I considered at the time – and still do – the best cast on television. It also helped enormously to know there were so many *Home Fires* fans encouraging me to replicate in print what I managed on screen, and successfully take the saga forward (I'll leave it to you to decide if I have); while the challenge of introducing readers new to the world of Great Paxford was one I deeply relished.

Now, all I can now add is that I hope you enjoy reading this book as much as I've enjoyed writing it. No. I hope you enjoy it much, much more.

Best wishes,

Simon Block

Eggless Victoria Sponge

A wartime alternative to the British Classic, enjoy with a cup of tea!

You will need:

For the cake:

- Two 7 inch sandwich tins
- 170g self-raising flour
- 1 teaspoon of baking powder
- 60g of sugar
- 60g of margarine or softened butter
- 1 tablespoon of golden syrup
- 280ml of milk *or* milk and water.

For the filling:

- Raspberry jam (preferably homemade)

Method

- Pre-heat the oven to gas mark 5 / 190°C or 170°C, if you have a fan oven. Grease the two 7 inch sandwich tins.

- In a large bowl sift together the flour and baking powder.
- Cream together the margarine and sugar until light and fluffy. Then a mix in the golden syrup.

- Add to this mixture a little bit of the flour and then a little bit of the milk and water, continue alternating between the two until a smooth mixture is formed.

- Divide the mixture between your two sandwich tins. Bake for approximately 20 minutes or until your cake is firm to the touch.

- Once they're done, take them out of the tins, let the cakes cool and sandwich with jam. You might want to try other fillings and toppings such as fresh berries, lemon curd or whipped cream.

Enjoy!

In conversation with the author

Did you find it difficult switching from writing a script to a novel?

Yes, because I've been writing scripts for nearly 30 years for theatre and television, but had never written a novel before. I'm very used to telling stories through action and dialogue in scripts. In a novel, readers can't literally see setting, characters, and action in front of them, so it's necessary to help them visualise it. That was probably the greatest challenge.

What were the main differences you found?

In a script it's unusual for scenes to run for more than three pages. Often, they are considerably shorter. Scripts are usually driven by the imperative to keep the action moving forward. Pace is very important. While pace is also important in a novel, I found that it's a different pace to that of most of the scripts I've written. With the novel, I was able to write longer scenes, with greater emotional depth, which, in turn, allowed me to reveal what characters were thinking. I think this helps the reader get to know characters on a deeper level than they often do in a script.

The other main difference, or should I say, *challenge*, was to write prose that didn't feel clichéd. With experience, you gain the ability to spot it yourself. Nevertheless, bad writing has a habit of sneaking in when you're not looking. Thankfully, I've had extremely good editors to help highlight and excise 'troubling passages'.

Where do you find your inspiration for characters?

To be honest, I'm not entirely sure. Probably from people I've encountered during my life. Often people I've met or know have been the starting point for a character, who then develops away from that real person. With the main characters here, the starting points were many women I met during my time with the Samaritans. I think what I took from them was that they were all universally admirable for doing samaritan work, without being at all 'saintly' in their outlook. They each had complex lives outside of their volunteer work, and that's what I wanted to reflect with the women of the WI of Great Paxford. Interesting women, not martyrs or saints.

And what about for plotlines?

Once the characters had established themselves and taken on three-dimensional identities, plots going forward started to suggest themselves. Also, the war helped because it means everything is in a continuous state of change, and that has an impact on the characters – e.g. their men get drawn away, meaning that they have to take over responsibilities; or things happen in the course of the war that test their inner resolve and fortitude.

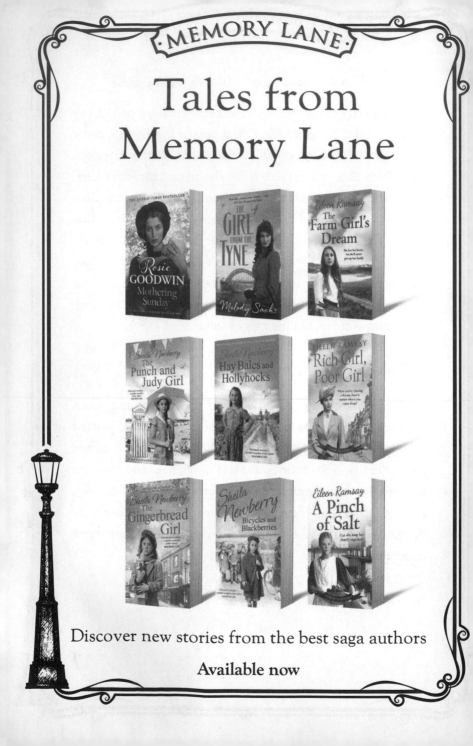